Magnolia

JAMES S. KELLY

Magnolia

A NOVEL

JAMES S. KELLY

Copyright © 2024 by James S. Kelly

All rights reserved. No parts of this book may be used or reproduced by any means, graphic, electronic, and mechanical, including photocopying, recording, taping, or by any information storage retrieval system, without the written permission of the publisher except in the case of brief quotations embodied in critical articles and reviews.

ISBN: 978-1-963565-52-2 (Paperback)
ISBN: 978-1-963565-53-9 (Ebook)

Library of Congress Control Number:
2024926455

Printed in the United States of America

Published by:

info@thequippyquill.com
(302)-295-2278

Contents

OTHER WORKS 1

ACKNOWLEDGEMENTS 3

PREFACE 5

CHAPTER ONE.. 9

CHAPTER TWO 21

CHAPTER THREE 25

CHAPTER FOUR 33

CHAPTER FIVE 45

CHAPTER SIX 57

CHAPTER SEVEN 69

CHAPTER EIGHT 75

CHAPTER NINE 83

CHAPTER ELEVEN 91

CHAPTER TWELVE 95

CHAPTER THIRTEEN 101

CHAPTER FOURTEEN 105

CHAPTER FOURTEEN 111

CHAPTER FIFTEEN 117

CHAPTER SIXTEEN 121

CHAPTER SEVENTEEN 135

CHAPTER EIGHTEEN 150

CHAPTER TWENTY 159

CHAPTER TWENTY-ONE 173

CHAPTER TWENTY-TWO 183

CHAPTER TWENTY-THREE 197

CHAPTER TWENTY-FOUR 211

CHAPTER TWENTY-FIVE 225

CHAPTER TWENTY-SIX 231

CHAPTER TWENTY-SEVEN 247

CHAPTER TWENTY-EIGHT 255

CHAPTER TWENTY-NINE 259

CHAPTER THIRTY 269

CHAPTER THIRTY-ONE 279

CHAPTER THIRTY-TWO 295

CHAPTER THIRTY-THREE 309

CHAPTER THIRTY-FOUR 319

CHAPTER THIRTY-FIVE 329

CHAPTER THIRTY-SIX 337

CHAPTER THIRTY-SEVEN 345

CHAPTER THIRTY-EIGHT 353

CHAPTER THIRTY-NINE 361

CHAPTER FORTY 381

OTHER WORKS

by

JAMES S. KELLY

❦

Mysteries
I Didn't Forget
Interned
Not in My Backyard

Westerns
A Man of Breeding
A Breed Apart
The Wounded Breed

Autobiography
Muddling Through

ACKNOWLEDGEMENTS

My wife, Patricia

Children

James S. Kelly Jr.
Mark Raymond Kelly
Nancy Jean Leachman
Michelle Patrice Leachman

Friends

John and Nancy Orchard
Robert and Marilyn Lang
Don and Noreen Pate
Lyndon Beauchene

Relatives

Jim and Ethel Lancaster
Thomas Kelly
Maryann Kelly

PREFACE

As soon as the seven southern states seceded from the Union, their sons and relatives in the Union Army and Navy resigned their commissions and became the elite officers of the Confederacy. They were euphoric; they threw parties and prided themselves on their great fortune. And they didn't stop there; they became aggressive. The state of South Carolina, one of the first to secede, claimed that Forts Moultrie and Sumter in Charleston Harbor belonged to the Confederacy; therefore, the Union soldiers in the fort must vacate. General P.G.T. Beauregard, the former Superintendent of Cadets at West Point, who immediately switched sides, was in charge of that state's militia, but was taking his orders from Jefferson Davis in Montgomery, the interim capital of the Confederacy. Whether Jefferson Davis' request to Lincoln to turn over the forts was rejected because it lacked merit or Lincoln took too long to respond, is moot in the long run.

The firing on Fort Sumter on April 12, 1861, began a war that had no reason to happen. It was as though a disagreement between father and son had escalated far beyond what either wanted. At some point, each realized that they had gone beyond the normal barrier of good behavior and tried to step back and assess their actions. The father made every effort to try to explain to his son why his actions were unacceptable, but a sense of freedom to do as he wished made that view almost impossible for the son to accept. He and his friends were caught up in a wave of excitement, which escalated into a cause. The normal civility between father and son was met with obstinacy and imprudence. Consequently, neither could see how to rectify a situation that continued to fester and finally got out of control. There seemed to be no common ground, no mediation and no chance for reconciliation. Just like a family, a nation was splitting apart.

So, too, did the distance widen between two childhood friends from Charleston, South Carolina—even though, in the early stages, they tried to maintain a sense of decorum and respect, ignoring all outside influences. But it was not to be. The tension had grown from anxiety to acceptance on both sides; their views were incompatible.

On that fateful day, James Stephen Harris and his wife Claire were sitting at the dining room table in their rented Georgetown residence in Washington, D.C. The lights on the black wrought-iron lamps on their porch illuminated their entrance steps and their beautiful white slumpstone exterior. They were hosting four of their closest friends to celebrate Claire's thirtieth birthday. Her mother and stepfather had planned to attend, but the situation was such that they wanted to see what would happen next before they crossed the Atlantic to be with the one they raised.

James had spent the busiest two weeks of his life getting acclimated to his new position as Special Advisor to the newly elected President of the United States, Abraham Lincoln. All six friends looked solemn; the neighborhood outside was quiet; it was as though an honored member of their family had died. No one spoke of the situation; no one wanted to. They talked of trivial things until ten that evening, and then the guests left.

Several hundred miles to the south, in their home outside Charleston, South Carolina, John William Beauregard, with his wife Louisa and their two children, were celebrating the same occasion with champagne at Magnolia, their magnificent plantation. He'd resigned from the U.S. Senate as soon as the State of South Carolina seceded from the Union. Interim President of the Confederate States of
America, Jefferson Davis, with an endorsement from John's cousin, General P.G.T. Beauregard, asked him to lead the Confederate Signal Corps. He was that new nation's chief spy.

They were embarking on an adventure, and everyone was excited. John looked over at his wife and said, "We won't be told what to do or how to run our lives any more by some Union bureaucrat in Washington."

"Be careful what you wish for, John," she responded.

"I just don't understand the provocation," said James Beauregard, their son, who was scheduled to attend West Point in the fall. "Why start something that can't be reversed? The forts weren't being supplied, so why not wait? The defenders would eventually have no recourse but to leave. Firing on the forts seemed to force the issue."

"I wouldn't have done it that way, but the die is cast," his father responded. "I believe that many in our new administration wanted to make the break as sharp and as quick as possible, so there'd be no recourse."

Over the next four years, the two childhood friends, James Harris and John Beauregard, would be antagonistic rivals, and would use every conscious moment during that period to assist their side in this ridiculous loss of life, property and dignity.

CHAPTER ONE

The Bureau of Indian Affairs, under the U.S. Department of the Interior, had its main office in the nation's capital. Cameron Harris had worked as an agent for them over the past ten years. Prior to obtaining this position, he had served as an Army Scout for ten years in the far West, leaving the service with a military rank of Lt. Colonel. There were twelve agents in the entire directorate who were responsible for all the Indian reservations in the United States, including about two hundred and fifty million acres of land. Cameron's territory was the mid-Atlantic States, including the Carolinas, Virginia, Maryland, Delaware, Pennsylvania and New Jersey; he was responsible for twenty-five reservations.

This week he was in South Carolina to witness the treaty signing between that state and the Catawba Nation—or what was left of it. The Catawba had lived in the South Carolina region for over five thousand years and at one time had been a great Indian nation. But the incursion of immigrants continually squeezed the nation into smaller and more confined areas. There were continuous claims made by the Catawba with very little resolution. Eventually, the federal government awarded the Catawba about fifteen square miles of land in York and Lancaster Districts to resolve their claims. As late as the American Revolutionary War, there were between four and five thousand Catawba; by 1820 their number had dwindled to less than one hundred.

There were many reasons for their decline, including the numerous viruses brought by the Europeans. But the primary one was that they fought on the side of the colonists during the war for independence, and the English retaliated. For siding with the Americans, the British destroyed their major villages, which had a huge economic impact on their future. It was the British vindictiveness that devastated their nation. It forced them to turn to the plantation owners for their livelihood. They were now dependent on cotton and tobacco for work and subsistence.

But the signing of this treaty wasn't the only reason that Cameron Harris left his office in the nation's capital to be in South Carolina today. He was going home to Charleston to be with his wife, who was expecting their first child. They already had the name picked out: he was to be named after his great-grandfather, James Stephen Harris—that is, if it was a boy.

The old chief of the Catawba nation, Running Deer, had known Cameron for ten years, and wanted to celebrate the treaty signing with his friend on this auspicious day. Members of the tribe had dressed in their finest, and several state officials remained behind after the ceremony to give support to the Catawba. There weren't supposed to be any spirits at the ceremony, but it didn't take long for a bottle to be passed around.

"I've got to go, chief," Cameron protested. "My wife is going to have a baby."

"Women have baby all the time. Don't need help. We drink to treaty."

"You're not supposed to drink in the courthouse," Cameron pleaded.

"No one care; you have drink."

Cameron smiled. "I'll come back next week and we can have a party. I'll bring a deer, but I'm leaving now. I can be home in three hours."

"You our friend. You have one drink and dance with my people, then you go."

After four drinks and a five-minute dance with Running Deer and five other members of the tribe, Cameron shook hands with several state officials, staggered to his horse, and started on his way home. His wife was living in Charleston with her parents until the baby came. It started to rain as he set out on his three-hour ride to be with her.

He'd come to Charleston two years ago to meet with South Carolina officials to discuss how to supply food to the reservation in their area when there was an emergency, which happened far too frequently. After the meeting, his contact within the State's Indian Section, Charles Morgan, asked him to join him and another state official downtown at the Beef and Rye Restaurant. Since he was by himself, he readily accepted. By 1800's standards, the restaurant was average, but the food and service were excellent. Cameron had had a busy day and was tired; besides, he needed to return to Washington the next morning, and he wanted to turn in early. But Morgan insisted he meet a friend of his, an expert on Indian affairs. Rather than be difficult, he allowed Morgan to walk him over to another table in the restaurant and be introduced to Frederick Hendricks, a professor of American History at the University of South Carolina.

It seemed that Hendricks wasn't the only one at the table. Cameron met Hendricks' wife Hilda and his daughter Amy, an attractive and perky daughter of twenty-one. After the introductions, Cameron went back to his table with Morgan, but he kept looking back at the Hendricks' table. His two companions became engaged in a spirited argument dealing with slavery, but he didn't hear a word they were saying. He had his eyes glued on Amy Hendricks. When their eyes met, she smiled. As soon as he got up enough courage, he went back to the Hendricks' table and apologized for the interruption. "Sir, I wonder if I could have a word with your daughter?"

The father nodded and Cameron turned to the young woman. "I hope that I'm not too presumptuous, but would you care to have lunch with me tomorrow at the inn in the town center?"

Amy answered immediately. "I'll expect that you'll call at my home tomorrow at noon. If that's acceptable, here's my address." She handed him a small piece of paper with her address printed on it.

He stammered a yes and went back to join Morgan; Hendricks and his wife smiled at each other.

Theirs was a white two-story, two-bedroom home with blue trim around the windows sitting in the middle of the block on First Street. Cameron arrived thirty minutes early and talked to her father while Amy was getting ready. The two men found that they had a lot in common and were engrossed in a discussion when Amy came down the stairs. Cameron got up and complimented her on the light green dress she wore with a matching shawl.

He shook hands with her father and promised that they wouldn't be gone long. As they walked to the inn, he was astonished at how small she was. Barely five feet tall with a slender frame, she walked with the grace of a dancer. Cameron was no giant. He stood five feet, ten inches tall on a 165-pound frame. His black hair and brown eyes were in stark contrast to her red hair and blue eyes.

This was the start of a one-year courtship from Washington to Charleston. Initially his visits were once a month, but gradually they increased to twice a month. His main transportation from the nation's capital was by a boat that resupplied Forts Sumter and Moultrie, lying on an island in the Charleston harbor. He made this commute for a year before he asked her father for Amy's hand in marriage.

When her father gave his permission, he stammered a proposal. The only thing she said before he kissed her was, "What took you so long? A girl could get tired of waiting!"

· · ·

The ride to see Amy took longer than the three hours he had estimated, primarily because of the heavy downpour that drenched him to the skin. His father-in-law met him at the door with a glass of wine and a wide smile on his face. "It won't be long now. She's in labor, and the midwife and my wife are with her. I think you can go up, but they'll throw you out when it's time. I suggest you change into something dry first. Use the kitchen; no one's there. I'll put your horse in the paddock out back and give it some oats."

Cameron only had time to kiss his Amy before her mother said he'd have to leave. Ten minutes later, he and Hendricks heard the cry of a newborn. Soon her mother yelled down the stairs, "It's a boy!"

•   •   •

At about the same time, on a plantation ten miles outside the city's limits, François Beauregard, a West Point graduate, was waiting with his father, Ambrose, for the birth of his first child. Similar to Cameron, he hoped and prayed for a boy to carry on his tradition. He wasn't to be disappointed.

The Beauregard family had lived in the Charleston area since the late seventeen-hundreds, when they'd left Haiti in the midst of a revolution and arrived at Charleston Harbor with forty of their slaves. Ambrose bought six hundred acres and planted cotton; they named their plantation Rosebud. Subsequently, their operation grew so large that they had to employ three white overseers to manage seventy-five slaves, who planted and picked cotton; tobacco was a secondary product. Ambrose was a firm but tolerant master, and his overseers took his lead in dealing with the blacks. What made his operation run so smoothly was the fact that he worked in the fields alongside the slaves. He personally operated the cotton gin and baled the product. To date, there'd been none of the runaways that plagued other plantations in the area. He felt grateful for his good fortune in coming to this country and tried to make life on the plantation as tolerable as possible for everyone, including the slaves.

•   •   •

Cameron owned a modest three-bedroom home on the Potomac, a few miles from the Capitol, where he had planned to move his young family as soon as his wife was able to travel. But he hadn't counted on his wife's depression that persisted after the baby was born. His mother-in-law told him that it was normal for a woman to feel tired and emotional after giving birth.

"You must have patience," she explained. "It may take a little longer than normal, but she'll come around. She's a tiny woman, and it may be weeks before she can build up her strength. I'm going to have Doctor Watson keep an eye on her. Maybe he can recommend a tonic that'll help."

"I've stayed longer than I anticipated," Cameron protested. "I must get back to my office, or I won't have a job! Do you think I can leave Amy and the child here for a couple more weeks? Then I'll come back and take them with me."

"Cameron, my husband and I want to do as much as we can to help you and our daughter. The boy will be fine with Frederick and me until you come back."

With a heavy heart, he took the ship back to Washington. His boss, the Under Secretary for Indian Affairs, wasn't happy with all the time he'd been taking to handle his personal business. "Look, Harris, you either get your personal life squared away or get yourself another job. I'm sorry to be so tough on you, but that's the way it is." With that he dismissed Cameron.

When he returned to Charleston two weeks later, Amy's symptoms were the same and the prognosis unsure, but this time there was a different doctor attending to her. When Cameron went into her bedroom, he kissed her on the forehead, but she barely acknowledged his presence. He stayed by her bed for over thirty minutes, holding her hand, and finally stepped out of the room. He walked down the stairs and joined Doctor Allen, who'd recently taken over Amy's care and was talking to both parents at the kitchen table.

"She doesn't look any better than when I was here the last time," Cameron interrupted.

Allen turned around to talk to Cameron. "I gave her a sedative to help her relax. She hasn't been attending to the baby, and she's not sleeping. I think I've done all I can at this time. Perhaps a psychiatrist might be better suited to treat her symptoms."

"You mean she's crazy?" Cameron blurted out as he sat down.

"No, I didn't say that—but she's troubled. I've tried everything I know, but it's not working."

"Doctor, I don't know what to do. My supervisor has threatened to fire me if I don't spend more time at my office. I'm just a simple man—what can I do? She seemed to be so full of life during her pregnancy. Tell me that this will go away!"

"I'm not sure. This is the worst case of post-pregnancy depression that I've ever seen. I'm out of my element. There is nothing physically wrong with Amy, but she's depressed. I'll contact a colleague of mine who's a psychologist; he may have better results with her than I. Since you were coming down this weekend, I took the liberty of asking him to come by and meet with you. His name is Doctor Herman Rosen."

When Doctor Allen left, Cameron and Amy's parents sat without saying anything for a few moments.

I don't know what to do," Cameron said finally. "I can't take Amy and the child with me. I'm gone three out of five weeks to Indian reservations and some military installations. She seems to need constant care. I don't know what the cost will be for that."

"She can stay with us as long as it's needed," Mrs. Hendricks reassured him. "We're her parents and we love her very much. We also think you're a fine man and we're glad that you're our son-in-law."

"But the child needs attention. You heard the doctor say that she's not taking care of young Jimmy. This seems like too much of a burden for you, since your husband is in Columbia during the week."

"If it gets too much for me, I'll let you know."

Cameron stayed long enough to meet Doctor Rosen. As they shook hands, Rosen said, "It will take me at least two to three weeks to evaluate your wife, and then a week to determine if there is a cure for her depression. Your in-laws told me of your predicament. How often can you visit?"

"I can be back in three weeks."

"Make it four, and I'll be able to give you a professional analysis."

Although sad at the turn of events, he went about his duties as before. But all the joy he had had in his marriage and the birth of his son was lost; he was lonely and he didn't know what to do. He travelled extensively before returning four weeks later. He was anxious to hear Doctor Rosen's evaluation. They talked for over an hour, and although Dr. Rosen was encouraging, Amy hadn't responded to any of his methods or medicine.

"To be honest with you, Mr. Harris, I've exhausted everything I know," Rosen said. "I don't seem to be able to help her, and I don't know who can. It may be just a matter of time—and then again, she may never recover. I'm sorry."

During the same period of time, her father retired from teaching at University of South Carolina and devoted himself full time to the care of Amy and young Jimmy. With the Hendrickses in one of the bedrooms and Amy and Jimmy in the second, Cameron would sleep on the couch in the living room when he visited. In spite of the trauma with his wife, he and her father had become close friends and often discussed the mood of secession that was gripping the South—especially in South Carolina.

"How can the South survive?" Cameron asked his father-in-law. "They seem to be so dependent on cotton and tobacco. What if they have a poor crop one or two years after they secede? Where will the money come from to allow them to survive?"

"They're optimistic that France and England will buy their produce, because those European countries are heavily dependent upon cotton. In addition, there are many who think both nations will interfere on the southern side if there is an armed conflict. Great Britain has cities that are so dependent upon cotton that there may be massive unemployment if the flow is stopped."

"I don't know what the southern states will do, but if they do secede, then a naval blockade would seem to be one strategy that could be used to bring then back into the Union. What do you think about the slavery question?" Cameron asked.

"I believe it's morally wrong, but those who own the plantations are also the drivers behind the secession movement. They don't think they can survive without the slaves; therefore, they're not going to give them up. The power of the plantation owners is immense. Although they represent only four percent of the population, they control the majority of the wealth, and therefore the legislature. You may not realize this, but the majority of the people in the Charleston area are black. With the law prohibiting the importation of slaves since 1808, they become an even more valuable commodity; those that control them become richer, and thereby they increase their power."

•   •   •

Weeks turned into months and then years. Cameron would visit every two weeks for the first year, but with no change in Amy's condition, his trips gradually became less frequent. All during this time, Amy would sit in her room and stare into space; she hardly recognized Cameron when he visited. The Hendrickses were acting as Jimmy's parents, though at no time did they intentionally ignore Cameron's rights to his child. He couldn't have asked for a more cooperative and sensitive in-laws.

After five years, Cameron came to an accommodation with Amy's parents. The boy and his mother would live with his in-laws in Charleston, and Cameron would reside at his home in the nation's capital. He'd be able to visit his son any time during the school year and would take Jim with him when school was out. In the summer, Jimmy would live in Washington with his father or accompany him on his many trips to the Indian reservations and military installations.

Meanwhile, even though the grandparents said it wasn't necessary, Cameron sent money each month to help defray Amy's doctor bills. When he returned Jimmy at the start of the school year, he'd hold Amy in his arms and kiss her on the cheek, but she didn't appear to know who he was.

•   •   •

Young Jimmy Harris' first exposure to any Indian was at the Catawba reservation, lying along the Catawba River in the

Western Carolinas. The Indians had cleared space for over two hundred tents, but only seventy were visible. James could see about thirty people in the village doing various chores as they rode up. It was Chief Running Bear who greeted them and took young Jim under his wing almost immediately. The young man idolized the chief and followed him around like a lost puppy. Jim delighted in dressing as an Indian brave and wearing the old man's headdress. It was large, filled with yellow and red feathers, and it dragged on the ground as he walked behind the chief. One of the braves taught Jimmy how to use a bow and arrow and throw a spear. Each summer he'd stay at the village for at least a month: this was the highlight of the young man's year. On one of his first trips with Cameron, they visited the Creek and Cherokee villages in South Carolina. Jimmy was exposed for the first time to the plight of the reservation Indian. He didn't understand it yet, but he knew what he didn't like and asked his father why the people in the village didn't have any energy.

"They've been squeezed into smaller and smaller plots of land that can barely sustain life. They're suffering from malnutrition and now lack hope; they seem to accept their station in life."

Most of Cameron's duties centered around ensuring that food supplies were being delivered on a timely basis, and occasionally mediating a dispute between tribal nations. On most trips to his list of reservations, he had to find out why the food supplies seemed to be late or not delivered at all; this wasn't lost on a six-year-old. Jimmy couldn't put his feelings into words; he just knew something was wrong.

Before the first summer was over, Cameron and his son went fishing on the Pee Dee River, making their way through the cotton plantations which were so important to the South until after the Civil War, when the dependency on slaves was lost. It was a three-day trip to introduce his son to outdoor camping. They stopped at one of the landings along the river and fished from the bank. They didn't save the young man's first catch, because Cameron cooked it over a fire and they ate it. Jimmy would have plenty to tell his maternal grandparents when they returned to Charleston.

It was September when Cameron brought Jim back to Charleston. His wife, Amy, was sitting in the parlor and welcomed her son; she seemed to have regained some color in her cheeks. The meeting between husband and wife was cordial and even friendly, but not warm. Cameron had resolved that his wife would never be the same, and he started seeing other women in the D.C. area. He spent most of his time with Abigail Stanton, the widow of Miles Stanton, a British diplomat who had been assigned to the consulate in Washington. Left with a small fortune, Abigail felt more comfortable in Washington society where she had lived for eight years prior to her husband's death, rather than return to her home in England. Cameron didn't feel guilty about his affair; he felt it was the way it was.

As the years passed, the visits to Charleston during the school years were becoming less frequent. When he came to pick up the boy in the summertime in the seventh year of their marriage, Amy seemed to have improved, but not enough for Cameron to spend any time with her. He didn't blame her for the affliction; he just lost interest. The love they had had when she was twentyone wasn't what they had now. The parents were getting older, and one day her father confessed to Cameron that he wasn't sure what would happen to his daughter after he was gone. Her mother was becoming impatient with her and devoted very little time to her well-being. Sooner than later, a decision had to be made about Amy. Cameron didn't know what to do.

Eleven years had passed when he received a telegram from Frederick Hendricks to come home immediately. It took him two days, but he was too late; his wife had passed away. He tried to remember how it had been during their first year of marriage, but too much had happened since then; all he could remember was how she seemed so distant for the remainder of her life. James Stephen was a fine young man, and although he spent some time helping his mother, it was his grandparents whom he was closest to. They filled the role of parents. The question now was, what would be best for the boy? With the grandparents, he had a home and love; with his father, he had love and adventure.

The grandmother seemed to be her happy old self again. The burden of the daughter had been lifted from her shoulders; she wanted Jimmy to live with them. "I know this is your decision, Cameron, but I believe my husband and I can handle his raising; he's such a wonderful child and he keeps us young. Frederick thinks the world of the boy. He doesn't want to replace you as a father; he just wants to be part of James' life."

"Why don't we leave it the way it's been and see how that goes? I want your word that when the time comes for him to be entirely with me, you won't stand in my way. You'll work with me and do what's best for my son. It's a couple of months until the end of the school term. I'll take him with me for the summer and then bring him back for the school year." Both grandparents agreed.

CHAPTER TWO

At Rosebud, François Beauregard and his wife Susanna welcomed their son John William Beauregard into the world. He was named after his maternal grandfather. His future was already planned. He would grow up on the plantation, go to the Citadel and then to West Point, as did his father. But the plantation was more in François' blood than a military career. After three years, he resigned his commission and came home.

At five years of age, young John William, as his mother called him, already had his own horse and a wooden play sword. He'd ride his horse around a closed arena and thrust and slash his saber as though he were in battle. He tried to mirror his father's every trait, from the way he spoke to the way he walked. If there was ever a son who loved his father, John William was that young man. When asked by anyone what he wanted to be, John William would say, "I'm going to West Point, just like my father."

At seven years of age, John William was entered into the Citadel. So began his military career, and so began the plan his father had initiated the day he was born. He and Susanna had three other children, two daughters and a son; it was left to Susanna to raise the girls while François concentrated on his two sons, who were five years apart. The mother loved her firstborn and tried to keep up with him, but he was such an energetic young man, he was more than she could handle.

At eight, he was riding a spirited horse named Vesper; he and the horse formed a bond that went beyond the normal pet/owner relationship. Susanna was frightened every time he got on the horse; the two seemed to do everything that was dangerous. She begged her husband to make him ride a gentler horse, but the father was like the son: the more dangerous it was, the better he liked it. A broken arm, a strained shoulder and a broken hand were only an inconvenience to John William. The young man would be back in the saddle as soon as he healed. Susanna prayed that the military academy at the Citadel would curtail young John's enthusiasm and his love of adventure.

It wasn't that John William was difficult to control. He just had so much confidence in his ability to see what the right course of action should be that he couldn't be deterred. He was also extremely competitive and didn't like to lose. If he did lose, he got over it immediately and moved on to the next competition. He wanted to be the best, and when he won, he wanted you to know it. His walk and stance bespoke a young man with a great deal of confidence, apparent to males and females alike. Women found that trait in John to be attractive and sensual.

As he grew older and went off to the Citadel, he showed an ability to size up a situation and immediately take charge; he expected to be the leader. His daring at school gave his instructors pause, but he saw this as a way of life and not threatening. He never showed weakness in front of others; with his friends he was less rigid, but even with them, he didn't let down his guard very often. He was an ideal military officer, calm in battle-like situations and decisive. When he faced a situation that didn't give him the result he wished, he worked until he was successful. He didn't have to

make everyone happy and was not afraid to say no when the issue warranted. Some of those he encountered were always shocked at how strong he came on, if he wanted to make a point. He never gave up; he always tried to succeed.

But John William wasn't the only Beauregard with military ambitions. François' older brother, Armand, had a son four years older than John William. His name was Pierre Gustave Toussaint Beauregard; his parents nicknamed him P.G.T. He would go on to a distinguished military career. Being four years older, P.G.T. took John William under his wing and taught him all the things he thought were important. If Susanna had been worried before about her son's daring deeds, she'd have a nervous breakdown if she knew what the two Beauregards were up to!

François tended to give John William a good deal of latitude. When his son and cousin informed him that they

were going on a bear hunt, the father only paused
momentarily before he gave his permission.

The bear hunt was almost as adventurous as killing the
bear. They took a canoe down the south river and got
caught in the rapids. They barely reached shore before their
canoe swamped and everything fell into the water. They
were able to salvage their ammunition and rifles, but most
of their food was lost. It was a good thing that P.G.T. knew
how to light a fire without matches, or they might have slept
all night in wet clothes. Dinner was a fare of soggy biscuits.

Luckily for them, they came upon the bear early the next
morning. Both boys were good shots, but Pierre was the
quicker to fire, though both boys claimed the trophy.

When the two came home with the bear skin, Susanna
fainted, and François rushed to attend to her and administer
smelling salts. As she became lucid, she yelled at François,
"You can't just relinquish your parental responsibility! He's
a teenager—you can't say yes to everything he wants to do!
I don't want to lose my oldest just because you think what
he does is so masculine!"

François wanted to keep peace in the family. "I'll try to
direct him toward less risky endeavors." He tried to keep a
straight face as he was beaming at his young son.

Susanna knew that her husband was just trying to placate
her, but deep down, she was extremely proud of her son.
When other families visited Rosebud, she couldn't stop
boasting about her young lad and the bear he and his cousin
had killed.

Pierre went off to West Point when John was fourteen,
leaving a void in his life. He wrote each week to his cousin,
asking about the life of a cadet. Hoping that John William
would take over the plantation when he retired, François
started him picking cotton and then working the gin mill
before helping transport the bales to market. Try as hard as
he could to give his son a feeling for the plantation business,

François knew he was losing the battle. Everything about his young son told him he wanted to follow P.G.T. to the Military Academy

CHAPTER THREE

Cameron and Jimmy went with Frederick and his wife to the annual Rosebud Race Days, hosted by Ambrose Beauregard at his plantation. Eight sprinters from around the South were entered, and the rumor was that the grand prize would be one thousand dollars. There was a wagering tent set up for those with sporting blood, and Cameron and Frederick wagered two dollars each on the favorite, My Lady. Young John William Beauregard and his horse Vesper were entered; the odds on that entry were thirty-five to one.

Two years earlier, Cameron had been sent by his supervisor to mediate a dispute between Ambrose and several members of the Catawba tribe. The Indians felt they had been cheated out of the proceeds from a sale of wooden crates made on the reservation and sold to Rosebud. The landowner's contention was that the correct number of crates had been delivered to the plantation, but only half had been serviceable. The Indians said that all of them were in good shape when delivered. It was Cameron's task to see that the issue was resolved. The owner was sympathetic, but from what he was told by one of his overseers, half of the crates were defective. What Ambrose wasn't told was that the overseer stored half the crates in a shed that overturned in a storm and destroyed everything inside. When presented with this new information, Ambrose readily agreed to pay the Indians; he subsequently fired the overseer.

Rather than having a nasty result, Ambrose was pleased with the way it had been resolved by Cameron. This was the beginning of a friendship between Rosebud's owner and Cameron Harris; hence the invitation to the annual clambake. They arrived at about eleven in the morning, and after entering Mrs. Hendrick's apple pie and grape jam in the bakery goods contests, they watched the race. The winner was My Lady, but the surprise of the race was young John William Beauregard, who finished third but was closing strong at the finish.

"Whom did you bet on?" Ambrose asked Cameron.

"Why, the winner, of course!"

"Next year, you may want to bet on my grandson and his horse."

"He certainly pushed the winner," Cameron responded. "I thought he'd close the distance at the end, but he didn't. Perhaps another few years and there will be someone from Rosebud in the winner's circle."

The riders had dismounted and were walking off their horses. Ambrose called his grandson over to meet Cameron and his son. The two boys were similar in height and weight, and they both seemed to have the same determination in their eyes. They shook hands and began a friendship that would have many good days and then some bad ones.

"After Vesper cools down, my cousin and I are going for a swim," John William offered. "You're welcome to join us."

Jimmy looked at his father, who nodded his approval. Jim turned to his new friend. "I'll help you walk the colt off."

"Do you know anything about horses?" John William asked.

"I've only ridden bareback on Indian ponies."

"Have you now!" There was a bit of admiration in John William's quip.

When they reached the paddock, John's cousin Pierre and another boy were waiting. "This is Jimmy Harris," John William told them. "His father and my grandfather are friends. I invited him to go swimming with us. Did you bring the beer?"

"Jerome is bringing it."

"Jimmy, this is François Renard. His family has the neighboring plantation, and he swims like a fish! The other guy is my cousin Pierre, who's leaving for West Point at the end of the summer."

Just then a gangly black teenager came up to the four young men, carrying beer on a tray. "Jim, this Jerome— he's my slave." It was the first time Jimmy had been in a gathering where one of the males was a slave. He was confused.

There was a pond on the plantation which was stocked with fish, but all the kids used it as a swimming hole. It had a small dock stretching out twenty feet into the water; two rowboats were tied to the dock. The four boys dropped their clothes on a rock. John grabbed the pitcher from Jerome and filled his glass, took a big swallow, ran down the dock and jumped into the pond. Pierre and Renard did the same thing. Jimmy wasn't going to be left out, so he did as the other three. The water was refreshing, and so was the beer. Somebody had brought along a weighted ball, and they took turns throwing it out into the pond and then diving down to retrieve it

They were in the water for about thirty minutes when they decided to get out and have another drink. Jimmy almost jumped when he heard a high-pitched voice on the bank. "I knew you boys would be down here. You have such skinny little butts and little things in front!"

The four boys ran down the dock and jumped into the water. "Do you have to follow us *everywhere?*" John asked.

She was standing on the dock with a big smile on her face, looking down at the four. Jerome was by her side and he couldn't stop laughing. She was wearing riding attire and carried a crop in her hand. "What makes you think I'd spend my time trailing after a couple of rude young men with skinny little butts?"

"Jimmy, this is Louisa Harrison, who thinks she's a Southern belle," explained John William. "She follows me and Pierre around all the time. I think she's in love with me."

"Well, of all the conceited and arrogant boys, you are the worst!" Louisa retorted.

"Want to come in for a swim? We won't watch you take off your clothes!"

"John William, you'll never get to see what you'd like to see." Louisa Harrison picked up the pitcher of beer, took a big gulp, and then poured the rest into the water. With that, she walked back to the party as the boys splashed water at her.

"Wow! Who was that?" Jimmy asked.

"That's the girl I'm going to marry someday." John smiled and then laughed out loud.

After dinner, the younger male revelers wandered over to a pavilion where there was a Negro group playing music; some of the whites were dancing. John, Renard and Pierre were standing on the periphery of the dance floor, watching some of the young girls dance.

"Aren't you going to dance?" Jimmy asked the three as he walked up.

"Why, sir, they can't dance a lick!" He heard that high-pitched voice again and turned around. It was the girl who had thrown the beer into the pond. But this time, she had changed into a beautiful flowered dress that seemed to flow as she walked. Instead of a riding helmet, she wore a wide-brimmed white straw hat. Her dark brown ponytail ran down her back; she was carrying a parasol. To Jimmy Harris she was positively beautiful. He stammered hello—or at least he *thought* that's what he said.

"Young man, what is your name?"

"James Stephen Harris at your service, miss." He'd regained his composure, and now he bowed while sweeping his hand low, just above the ground.

"My goodness, there's a gentleman here among children! Would you like to escort me to the dessert table?"

"Yes, I would!"

She placed her hand on his arm and they walked away.

"Hey, John, he's leaving with your girl," Pierre said.

"She's just trying to make me jealous. I'll take care of my new friend later."

Jimmy was introduced to Louisa's parents, Robert and Jessica Harrison, and her aunt Harriet. The father was a cotton broker in Charleston, and the family owned six hundred acres of planted cotton, about two miles from Rosebud. Their plantation was named Magnolia.

It was early evening now, and Louisa's parents were ready to leave. They thanked Jimmy for escorting their daughter and hoped they would see him again sometime soon. He graciously acknowledged their comments and Louisa smiled.

As he walked back to where he had last seen his father, John, Renard and Pierre ran up to him.

"Hey, Harris!" John yelled menacingly. "What are you doing with my girl?"

"I didn't know that you had proprietary rights. She told me that you were only a friend."

"I'm going to kick your butt and teach you some respect!"

"Well, you can try, but that's all you can do."

"I don't want anyone to come by and save you, Harris, so let's go down by the pond."

"Lead the way—but you're not going to like the outcome!"

As soon as they had reached the pond, John William took off his jacket and charged at Jimmy. But young Harris had wrestled with the Indians on the reservation, and he easily sidestepped the bull rush, stuck out his foot, and John went tumbling to the ground. He was up quickly and rushed at Jimmy again; this time he got his arms around Jim's waist and the two went to the ground, each trying to gain an advantage.

The outcome was never in doubt. John was more aggressive, but Jimmy was the more skilled wrestler, and since neither could gain an outright advantage, James offered to call it a draw, and John William was smart enough to accept. "All right, so I'm not going to kick your butt. Let's go have a beer and a swim—what do you say?"

Almost immediately, Jerome appeared with a tray, on which a pitcher of beer and four glasses were balanced. Pierre, who had kept out of the fray other than shouting encouragement to his cousin, grabbed a glass, and Jerome, the black man, filled it.

"It's a good thing you didn't tangle with Jerome here," John William laughed. "He really could kick your butt!"

As before, the four young men drank a glass of beer and then jumped into the pond. Jerome sat on the deck with the tray of refreshments close by. Jimmy thought he had seen Louisa hiding behind one of the trees as he and John were wrestling, but he knew she'd gone home with her parents— or had she?

"What about Jerome?" Jimmy asked the other three. "Maybe he'd like to come in for a swim with us."

"Jerome knows his place," John said quietly. "We grew up together and had a lot of good times, but that was in the past. Those days are over. You grew up here, Harris, so why the question?"

"I recognize that he's a slave on your plantation, but it's a warm evening and no one's around, so why not be gracious and allow him to swim with us?" It was obvious to Jimmy that Jerome could hear every word between the two boys, but he stayed on the dock and didn't make a sound.

"That's the way it is and that's the way it will always be," John said with finality.

*   *   *

Like the Beauregards, Robert and Jessica Harrison moved to the Charleston area with their slaves and bought six hundred acres about two miles from Rosebud. The

Beauregards came from Haiti and the Harrisons from the New Orleans area; Louisa was their only child. They had planned to name her after Robert's brother Louis, but nature took its course. She was spirited, unafraid, and a positively beautiful child in every way.

They met the Beauregards at a social function and found they had much in common. Their oldest boy John was a lot like Louisa, and the two children became friends.

Their only concern about Louisa as she was growing into a young woman was that she seemed to push all the boundaries. Some girls might see a ceiling, and they'd stop; Louisa wanted to see what was above the ceiling.

She was one of the few girls in her circle of friends who was given an education. It was her father, Robert, who brought tutors to Rosebud. He saw early on that Louisa had an insatiable thirst for knowledge. Since there weren't any young girls of her age or social position nearby, her playmates were the offspring of the slaves on Magnolia. One day she witnessed a slave being beaten, and she yelled at the overseer, Mr. Cook, to stop or she'd tell her father.

"Go ahead, missy," Cook replied. "You'll find out soon enough who's in charge of the slaves."

When she confronted her father about what she had seen, he said that it was the job of the overseer to discipline the slaves.

"How did they become slaves?" she asked.

"Well, it's a long story."

"Do you want to tell me?"

"I bought our slaves at an auction. They were from Africa; I think their chief sold them to a captain who transported them to America."

"So it wasn't their decision to become slaves?"

"I guess not."

"Can someone sell *me* to a captain and *I* would become a slave?"

"No, that's not possible."

"Well, it happened to *them*—why not to *us?*"

"I think we've talked about this subject enough. Don't you have something else to do?"

"Can you do something for me, father?"

"I'll try."

"Don't let Mr. Cook whip them again."

CHAPTER FOUR

When the two boys reached eighteen years of age, they decided to go on a hunting trip the last two months of the summer. John William was to enter the U.S. Military Academy in the fall, while James Stephen had been accepted at The University of South Carolina, majoring in History. Over the past four years they had been inseparable. Jimmy had spent one summer working at Rosebud, learning about planting and harvesting cotton. Another summer he, Pierre, Cameron and John visited military installations along the Atlantic Coast as far south as New Orleans. John William was also treated to a summer trip with James and his father at ten of the Indian reservations. Each boy was accepted by the other's family. In fact, they were treated by everyone as brothers.

Occasionally, Jimmy would visit Louisa at her family's place. He really liked the fiery young beauty, but he realized she wasn't for him. He knew that her family liked him, but she was encouraged to wed someone with compatible views, preferably someone within her social structure—specifically, John William.

Jimmy had adopted his grandfather's and father's view of the South. Its dependency on slaves and demand for states' rights seemed to permeate everything; it was their Achilles' heel. His grandfather had instilled in him the need to maintain the Union, and the belief that slavery was morally wrong, while his father passed on to him a love of country and its people.

Both young men sensed that their relationship would soon change when they went their separate ways at the end of the summer. They wanted this trip to be the last hurrah, the adventure of a lifetime; it would also serve as a rite of passage. Cameron took a few weeks before giving his permission, but once he did, he was on board with what the two young men wanted to accomplish. François was in bed with the idea from its inception, and even though John's mother, Susanna, voiced strong reservations, hers was not the final decision in their household.

But it was Cameron's counsel they sought concerning where to go, the logistics of setting up the expedition, and what pitfalls to be aware of. They decided on a trip to the Blue Ridge Mountains in western North Carolina, followed by a return trip by canoe down the Catawba River. James' father wasn't concerned about the trip home, but the initial leg concerned him. He suggested they travel to the Catawba village, hire a guide, rent a few pack animals and travel to the town of Asheville, North Carolina. The guide would take the pack animals back and meet them at the terminus of the Catawba on their way back. They planned to purchase supplies and pick up a two-man canoe at Ashville.

The boys were excited and wanted to get started immediately, but Cameron delayed their start by two days while he had them review the route until they could recite it verbatim. He'd travel with them as far as the Indian village to be sure that the guide they selected wouldn't lead them astray. Parents and grandparents gathered at Rosebud so see them off. The big surprise was the presence of the Hamiltons and their daughter Louisa, who had blossomed into a beautiful Southern belle. She was wearing a light pink summer dress accentuated with a blue hat, and carried a parasol, which she kept twirling. Jimmy couldn't keep his eyes off her. She kissed both boys on the cheek and was flustered slightly when she saw her mother glaring at her.

The Catawba village was small; there were only seventy inhabitants remaining of an Indian nation that had once boasted a population of five thousand. To maintain an economic standard above poverty, many members of the tribe worked alongside the slaves in the cotton and tobacco fields of local plantations. Cameron and the boys reached the Indian village in four days, their first leg of the trip. What struck Jimmy most about the small enclave of fifty tents was how neat and clean they were.

The next morning, Cameron negotiated with his old acquaintance, Chief Running Deer, for two pack animals and a guide. "I'm sending my son, Aaron, with your boys.

He's about their age and knows the route," the chief assured him. "He's very dependable and will make sure they have the right supplies and pick a good canoe to come back down the Catawba. There are a few pitfalls along the river. Aaron has a good map and he'll point them out to your boys before he leaves them."

Cameron was a concerned parent, but knew that Jimmy was level-headed and John William smart and courageous. He almost wished he could go with them, but this was their adventure. He had to let them do it by themselves; they were nearly men.

The three left the next morning, each on horseback, trailing one pack animal behind John and James. The two boys each carried a Springfield 1803 model rifle, which weighed nine pounds and had a thirty-three-inch barrel. Although it didn't have the accuracy of an earlier model, due to a shorter barrel, it was much easier to maneuver. It had a flintlock mechanism and used 54 caliber bullets. John and Jimmy had fired the weapons at least thirty times; both were competent marksmen.

Both boys were accustomed to the outdoors. What they weren't accustomed to was the constant rains in the foothills of the Blue Ridge Mountains that plagued their journey. It was an effort to keep their gear and supplies dry, but eventually they figured it out and made their way. A week later they arrived in Asheville, North Carolina, a town of nearly one thousand inhabitants resting on a series of rolling green hills. The weather was balmy but clear; they'd experienced five days of rain en route to the town. Their plan was to stay two days, rest up, and buy supplies for the four-week trek. It was assumed that they would provide much of their own food through their skills as hunters and fishermen.

In Asheville they took one room with two beds; Aaron would sleep on the floor. After they unloaded their gear in the room, they moved the three horses and the mule to the livery at the end of the street. "The first thing I want to do is get a beer and have a big meal," John William declared. "After that I'm going to get a good night's sleep."

"Well, there's only one restaurant in town, so whatever they serve, it's going to be okay with me," Aaron responded.

The three walked down the street and into Goldie's Kitchen, which served as eatery, bar, and community gathering place. There were about twenty tables in the one-room timber building, with a small bar in one corner and room to dance in the middle.

The Scotch-Irish folk who had settled in this area were slowly moving south to make a living. The glut of cotton in the European markets as a result of the opening of the Suez Canal, and the maturing of Egypt's cotton, had been an economic disaster to the citizens of Appalachia. Couple that with an undue amount of strife over Federal taxes and slaves taking jobs away from earlier emigrants, and you had a powder keg that was ready to erupt.

The three travelers ordered the dinner of stew, warm bread and a pitcher of beer. Toward nine o'clock that evening, the room was becoming boisterous, and a couple of fights broke out over who would pay for the beer, or whose girl Mary was. One fight ended at their table—at least, that's where one of the combatants lay after he was punched in the chin. Jimmy tried to help the young man up, but two of his kin picked him up and shoved Jim out of the way.

The Scotch-Irish had brought their music with them from the old country, and all the songs were accompanied by the fiddle. After they cleared away the damage and righted the tables after the fight, a group of men and young women started to dance in the middle of the large room. That's when a couple of the girls grabbed Jimmy and John, pulled them up and had them join in the dancing. Although his father was French, John's mother was of Scandinavian descent; he had inherited her blonde hair, blue eyes and fair complexion. Jimmy was dark-haired and bore a strong resemblance to Cameron in size and mannerisms. They stood out from the bearded, shaggy haired young men of this area.

The girls took a fancy to the two young men, and that didn't sit well with the more ragged looking locals. The boys had had two or three beers, the girls were flirting with them, and when one little red-headed girl kissed John, words with the locals were exchanged and knives drawn against the three outsiders. One of the locals slashed at Jim and his sleeve was cut. He instinctively lashed out with his fist and knocked the man down. Two burly bartenders grabbed the two boys and threw them through the front door; Aaron stayed out of the fray. He picked up the boys' hats and carried them out the door.

"I guess they don't want us here," John observed, as he rolled over on his back and looked up at Aaron.

They decided that they'd had enough fun for the night, so they went back to their room at the inn. "Did you see that knife the big guy had?" John inquired. "It had to be six inches long! Those guys were serious."

The next morning, they decided to leave Asheville rather than stay the two nights they had planned. Jimmy gave Aaron enough money to settle the hotel bill and buy supplies and a canoe. The boys were nervous; they had never experienced the kind of hostility they had seen the previous evening. Aaron was getting everything they needed as quickly as he could; he wanted to put some distance between them and anyone who meant them harm.

Aaron found a used canoe that was serviceable and purchased two fishing rods and six days of food for the two boys and three days for him. He planned to travel with them to the origin of the river and then take the horses and pack animal back with him; they would meet four weeks hence at the end of the Catawba River.

Aaron showed them how to fashion a travois over the mule's back to carry the canoe; they made the ten-mile trip to the Catawba in a day. Aaron was twenty-four years old. He'd attended a white school in Charleston, and after graduation had secured a position as receivables manager on the docks in the same town. He tried it for two years but didn't like it; he preferred the tribal life. After he returned to the Catawba village, he married an Indian woman and had two children. Most of his income came from working as a guide.

"I'll be gone at first light. I have a suggestion for you two. This is a very poor area, and many travelers are robbed, some are beaten and a few are killed. Until you get further down the Catawba and out of the Blue Ridge Mountains, I would have one of you stay awake while the other sleeps and then alternate. I may be overly cautious, but I'd hate to tell your parents that you were hurt while I was your guide."

They camped at the river the first night and the next morning said goodbye to their guide; they were on their own and couldn't wait to get started. They were traveling light, but even so, their gear filled the canoe, leaving very little room for them, but off they went.

They weren't satisfied with how they had loaded the canoe and how it handled in the water. They decided to use a day to try out the canoe while changing the loading of their gear. They finally felt comfortable at the end of the next day after many launches and many mistrials. That night they turned in early, and Jimmy took the first watch from eight in the evening until one in the morning. He sat by the fire thinking of the adventure that he and John had begun. He thought of his parents and how sad he was over his mother's plight. She had never enjoyed her husband, her son, or her adult life—what a waste! In a way, he felt guilty because she had become depressed after giving birth to him.

He stoked the fire a couple of times and then sat back against a tree trunk and waited out his watch. Around midnight, he placed his Springfield against a rock and threw two more logs on the fire. Just then, a solid rock was thrown into the camp and hit James in the back. He turned to grab his rifle, but he was hit in the left shoulder by the barrel of a rifle, falling to his knees. The next thing he knew, he was being kicked in the stomach, and he fell on his face.

"Stay right there, or I'll kill you!"

John was up by then, reaching for his rifle, but like Jim, he was hit in the back with the barrel of a rifle and he too fell to his knees. Their guns were taken and the two intruders pressed the ends of their guns into the boys' backs. "We want all your money, and if you're quiet, we won't kill you."

The only thing Jimmy could think about was the advice Aaron had given them; he had failed to take it seriously. Now here they were at the mercy of two ragged young men who might kill them—and it was all his fault!

The two intruders were becoming impatient. They told the boys to stand up and empty their pockets. John made a move to grab the shorter intruder's wrist, but the robber was too quick. He slammed the butt of his rifle into John's stomach, and the young lad fell to his knees once more. They were completely at the mercy of the mountain men.

"Where's the Indian?" the taller man demanded.

Before John could answer, one of the robbers suddenly pitched forward onto his face. An arrow was sticking out of his neck! He dropped his rifle and grabbed his neck with both hands to stop the bleeding, but to no avail; he slumped over and died on the ground. The other robber started to run, but he was hit in the chest with an axe thrown from the bushes. The two boys didn't hesitate. They scrambled to their feet and recovered their rifles from the two dead scoundrels lying on the ground. Jimmy and John looked in the direction the axe had come from and stood ready. But they weren't ready for the newcomer to be Aaron, who smiled at both of them as he stepped into their camp.

"I just wanted to be sure that you were following my advice," he told them. "I almost left a couple of hours ago, but I decided to stay through the night to be sure you'd be okay. I saw those two enter your camp, so I waited for a chance to help. Now, I don't want to be a nag, but I hope you learned something here tonight. You can have fun, but you must be alert that there might be something or somebody out there that means you harm."

"I'm sorry, John—I let you down," Jimmy admitted. "It was my responsibility to safeguard the camp while you slept."

Before John could respond, Aaron interrupted. "You weren't at fault other than maybe being a little naïve. What happened to you could have happened to anyone. You just got careless for a few seconds while you put the logs on the fire. I'll bet that'll never happen to you again."

John put out his hand to Jimmy. "I believe Aaron. This was a good lesson. I for one didn't take Aaron's advice too seriously; now I do."

"Roll them over. Let's take a look at them." Aaron was talking to John.

"These are the two from last night. Believe me, they would've killed you and never thought any more about it. I'm going to scout around to be sure there's no else waiting to pounce on us. I suggest you keep the fire up and stay awake, just in case." Aaron retrieved his axe, grabbed his bow and arrows, and slipped into the woods.

The two boys looked at each other. Even though there was limited light in their camp, it was clear that both were pale and that the killings had made an enormous impact on both. "This is the first time I've seen someone killed, and I'm unhappy about it," James said. "I know Aaron had to do it; still I didn't like it."

"I didn't like it, but I know that if Aaron hadn't acted as he did, we'd both be dead instead of these two," John responded soberly. "If it's my choice, I want *them* dead instead of *us*."

The Indian guide returned in forty-five minutes. "We're safe tonight, but their kin will probably come looking for them first thing in the morning; we need to leave at first light. Let's bury them in the woods and start cleaning up the camp. I don't think either of you can sleep right now. We should be ready to shove off as soon as the sun breaks."

Running Bear's son left the next morning after giving the two teenagers a valuable lesson on life and survival in the mountains. It started to rain lightly as soon as they got into the canoe, and by two in the afternoon it had turned into a downpour, so they decided to stop. They tied up along the bank and hastily set up their two-man tent. It took about thirty minutes to remove all their gear from the canoe and put it inside the tent. They waited out the rain, eating only some dry bread and nuts they had brought; the rain stopped about six that evening. Just to be sure, neither slept that night.

Since John was the better shot and Jimmy the better fisherman, Jimmy cast out a couple of lines from the bank while John stood guard in case they had any unwelcome visitors. "It took about two hours, but I have three nice flatheads," Jim said. "I suggest that we keep them for tomorrow. We're not far enough away from our last camp to start a fire to suit me."

"I vote that we get a good night's sleep here and then move on tomorrow," John replied. "Aaron thinks we have about a two day's head start. What do you say?"

"I'll go along with that. Let's turn in early and leave at first light again. We can troll the fish behind the canoe. I'll take the first watch."

According to their map, they made between ten and fifteen miles along the river the next day. Around six that evening, they tied their canoe to a tree along the bank, lit a fire and cooked the three flatheads that Jimmy had caught the day before.

"This is more like it," Jimmy grinned. "I was hungry and couldn't wait until we stopped. I don't know why those two mountain men were angry about the girls— they weren't that good-looking!"

"Well, they weren't at first, but after a couple of pitchers of beer they looked beautiful to me," John chuckled. "But I'm like you. I'm glad we travelled almost twelve hours today. Why don't we make a division of labor for the rest of the trip; you catch the fish and I'll handle the game. The map seems to indicate we're still in the mountains; there are a lot of trees along the river. When we stop tomorrow, I think I'll see if I can get a deer or maybe a turkey while you're fishing."

They had the breakdown of the camp and loading of the canoe now down to thirty minutes each. After six hours in the canoe, the river seemed to end in a small lake. They found a good place to make camp. There was enough light for John to hunt for a few hours. While Jimmy gathered the gear in the canoe and set up camp, John went into the woods surrounding the small lake. Jimmy was sure there were fish in the lake; he set up three lines and went about getting some wood for a fire.

John had been on several outings with Jimmy and his father and had learned from them how to spot game's tracks. In front of him was a small trail where deer or other animals travelled to the lake for water. He set up a blind with a clear view of the trail and waited. Two hours later, a deer walked very deliberately down the trail as though it sensed someone was watching. John took aim, fired his Springfield, and the doe fell. He rushed to finish the kill, but his shot had been on the mark; the animal was dead. It was a small one—he estimated it weighed nearly ninety pounds. John was a slender young man, standing about five feet ten inches tall, but he was strong. His father had seen to it that his son worked while he was growing up, both in the cotton fields and at the wharf, where he loaded cotton bales onto outbound ships.

He decided to carry the deer back to camp and skin it there, which was about a quarter of mile away and directly across from their camp site. It was cumbersome, but he willed his way to the lake's edge and called out to Jimmy to bring the canoe over. It took a few minutes of yelling before James heard him and brought the canoe to where John sat with his kill.

"Hail the conquering hunter! That's a beauty! I can't wait to have some venison. I've got enough wood for a fire."

There wasn't enough room for the deer and the two young men in the canoe, so John walked back to camp while Jim rowed across the small lake with the deer. John arrived soon after Jim had tied the canoe to a tree and helped pull the deer into camp. Unfortunately, one of the hoofs had rubbed a small pinhole in the side of the canoe, and it had to be patched.

"While you're skinning the deer I'll patch the canoe," Jimmy said. "I don't want to wait until tomorrow."

He dragged the canoe out of the water and placed the torn side near the fire to heat the area and force out any water that had permeated the skin. He skinned a second layer of bark from one of the indigenous trees, and after sanding the affected area of the canoe, he placed the thin bark over the torn area. Next he rubbed sap over the entire surface inside and out and left it to dry. He'd put the boat in the water early the next morning to check the seal.

He and John had learned to skin a deer at the Catawba camp last summer. By the time Jimmy finished patching the canoe, John had skinned the deer, wrapped the meat in a cloth, tied it to a tree and placed it in the river. The deerskin was stretched out to dry around the fire, while all the organs were buried. Now they had enough meat for a least a week. Couple that with the fish Jimmy had caught, and they'd have a healthy diet down the river.

"Let's turn in early," John suggested. "I'll take the first watch."

Three hours later there was a noise, and he saw a black bear come into camp. The bear began pawing at the ground where the waste from the deer was buried. John grabbed his weapon and fired at the animal just as the carnivore charged him. He hit the animal in the chest, but the bear struck him across the side of the head, and John went down with the bear on top of him. He tried to fend off the animal as best he could while trying to shield his face, but he was bitten several times on the arms. The noise awoke Jim and he rushed over with his gun, firing point blank into the bear's back, but it continued attacking its victim. Jimmy brought his rifle butt down on the enraged mammal's head, but that only seemed to make the beast more aggressive. John's face was covered with blood and his sleeves were ripped and saturated with blood. John retrieved his knife from his boot and was puncturing the animal with it, to no avail. Jimmy picked up his axe, and with both hands brought it down as hard as he could on the bear's head. The animal's skull split open, and it fell dead on top of John.

It was a major effort freeing John from the dead animal. Jim helped him to his feet, led him to the river, and eased him down the bank. He took some clean cloths and wiped John's face and head, trying to see the source of the bleeding. There were four deep gashes in his forehead. He put some liniment on the wounds and bandaged the area. He helped John off with his shirt and cleaned the wounds on his arms; blood was still oozing out of the gashes. He washed John's arms and bandaged two significant cuts. "How about your legs? Did he get you there or any other place?"

"No, just my head and arms, but I'm a little groggy."

They had brought along a first-aid kit of sorts andsome willow bark tea for pain, so Jimmy gave him some tea and helped him to his feet. "I think you need to lie down. I washed the cuts and bite marks thoroughly and put some liniment on the wounds. I don't think there'll be an infection. Sleep is the best cure for you right now."

Jimmy reloaded both rifles and leaned them against rocks at opposite sides of the camp, so that no matter where he was in the camp, he'd have a rifle handy. The dead bear was the next problem he would have to deal with. He estimated the animal to be about two hundred fifty pounds. He wondered if he could bury the animal, but decided against it, so he skinned it by the fire.

It took him nearly an hour to get the coat off, and then another forty-five minutes dissecting the animal. He dug a hole about three feet deep and nearly as wide, near where they had buried the deer parts, threw the cut-up parts in the pit, and covered it over. It took longer than normal to dispose of the carcass because he'd stop every few minutes to look around to see if anyone was nearby. Even if he was tired, he couldn't sleep; his adrenaline was working overtime. He checked in on John, but found him asleep and breathing normally. John was rugged, and Jimmy knew that he'd survive. As he sat down and leaned against a rock, he heard wolves in the distance. *That's all I need,* " he said to himself.

CHAPTER FIVE

At dawn, Jimmy checked on his patient, but he was still asleep. He wanted to use this time to check the exit in this small lake to see what obstacles they'd encounter making their way downstream. He rowed to the end of the lake and pulled the canoe onto the bank. Walking to where the water was flowing swiftly, he saw a small waterfall with a five-foot drop they'd have to portage. Further along the bank, he could see that they'd need to carry the canoe about sixty yards before they could reënter the river. It was obvious he couldn't accomplish the task by himself. The question was, how long before John would be able to continue?

Meanwhile John had awakened; he tried to get up but his head hurt. The willow bark was out of his reach, and he felt too weak to get out of bed. He stayed in bed until Jimmy returned. "How about something to eat?" Jim asked him.

"I'm not hungry. What I need is some more willow bark to ease the pain in my head and arms."

"Okay, but you need to eat something. I'll cook a little meat and give it to you."

"I understand, but right now I have to sleep some more. Maybe later I'll eat something."

Jimmy knew that he would have to move their equipment as well as their food stores around the rapids and waterfall. He went over in his mind how he was going to accomplish these tasks if John was too weak to help. He might have to make four trips. The challenge was how to move the canoe along the bank without damaging it any further. He remembered the travois that Aaron had fashioned, and wondered if he couldn't make something similar, but one that he could pull himself.

Aaron had left them a large knife that he used to cut small trees restricting their movements. While Jimmy hated to leave John, he wanted to see what obstacles would be in his way if he pulled the canoe over the ground. The patch on the canoe was holding as he paddled to the end of the small lake and tied it to a tree. There were only a few trees that he'd have to cut down along a path that he felt was suitable to pull the canoe with the travois strapped to his shoulders.

John was awake when he returned, and was feeling a little hungry. Jimmy explained what the exit of the lake looked like and what his plan was. He then cooked some of the meat, and he and John sat down for lunch.

"I'm feeling better, but my arms are really sore. Come to think of it, so is my head."

Jimmy took the bandages off John's arms, washed the wounds again, added liniment, then rebandaged the areas.

"You don't know how much I appreciate you and what you're doing, but you can't go on without any sleep," John pointed out. "Why don't I stand guard for a few hours so you can rest? Even if it's just for a couple of hours, you'll be better off, and so will we."

They passed the remainder of the day alternating sleep between the two. John would stay up as long as he could and then he'd change places with Jimmy. The next morning John felt better, so Jimmy took the large knife and went to the lake exit and cleared a path for the canoe. Jimmy's plan was to move the equipment first, then the food supplies, then John and finally the boat. He'd cut two slender poles about twelve feet long and fashioned some leather straps for his shoulders.

With the equipment, John, and the food supplies moved to the end of the lake, James fashioned the travois to the canoe and John helped strap it to Jim's back. Since John felt that he could walk, Jimmy put his plan in motion. With John watching the equipment and food supplies, Jimmy started walking slowly while pulling the canoe behind him. The walk was difficult and the straps cut into his shoulders, but he was able to drag the canoe along the bank to a place where they could put it in the water.

"Look, Jim, you need to stay healthy if we're going to survive—you've got to get some sleep! I think I can stay awake four hours; if I can stay up longer, I'll let you sleep some more."

John stayed awake for eight hours. It was tough on him, but he needed to get Jimmy some relief. It was midnight when he tapped his partner and asked him to switch places. They hadn't made up the tent; all the gear had been stowed in the canoe in case they had to make a hasty escape.

Jim was still groggy when he got up; he dunked his head in the river and wiped himself off with a towel. It was then that he saw the light—a light that came from a spot near their last camp site, if not from the actual site. The first thing that entered his head was that it must be some kin of the two that Aaron had killed. In their present condition, he and John wouldn't be able to stay ahead long, or even fight it out. He had to think of something that would even their odds.

Leaving John, he headed toward the light, making his way over land with his axe and large knife, until he reached their old camp site. It took him nearly an hour, but when he came upon the clearing, he saw two scruffy men with long beards fast asleep on the ground around a fire. He also spied a couple of open jugs lying near the sleeping men. Each had a rifle on the ground next to them, and there was a canoe tied up on the bank. When Jim was sure that there were no other individuals besides those two—and especially no dogs—he made his way back to camp, took off his boots and entered the water.

He'd always been a strong swimmer, ever since his first vacation at the Catawba reservation. He and the young braves used to swim in the river for hours, mostly against the current. He knew what had to be done. He swam most of the distance to their old camp, with the last twenty feet underwater. Coming up on the side of the canoe, which was partially in the water, he took out his big knife and cut four holes in the bottom and the side of the canoe. He felt his hair standing on end when he heard one of the men talking in his sleep, but when he was sure they were asleep, he swam back to where John lay asleep; it would take them a least a day to repair their craft.

He nudged his friend until he was awake. When he was sure he was coherent, he told him what he had found and what he had done.

"John, we have to leave now. You can sleep in the boat. I'm sure I can handle the canoe at night; it's clear and the moon is out. We need to cover a lot of distance before sunup."

He put John in the front of the craft and covered him with a blanket. Just as they pushed off from the bank, he heard some shouting coming from the area he'd visited earlier.

"Just in time, Jim—you called this right."

* * *

Charlie and young Willie had gone after the two Americans, thinking they'd be easy pickings. When they didn't return in two days, their pap told Brian and Sean to go track them down. They found the camp, and although it had been cleaned up, they saw some spots on the ground that could be blood; they searched around the camp site until they found the two graves, which they dug up and confirmed that it was indeed their two younger brothers. When the two went back and reported to their father, he was distraught. He screamed and yelled at them for two hours before he settled down. Then he gave them a four-day supply of food, with instructions to go out and bring the three back—dead or alive.

"No one is going to kill an O'Neal and get away with it!" the father stormed.

Brian and Sean were sure they were gaining on the two when they came upon this camp site; they could see some used supplies and knew that an animal had been killed here; they confirmed it when they saw the hole Jimmy had dug to hide the carcass. Now, since they'd been travelling hard over the past week, they decided to relax with some white lightning, confident that they'd catch the two soon.

When Brian got up to relieve himself, he sensed that something was wrong with the canoe—it was submerged! He pulled it out of the water, and that's when he saw the cuts in the bottom.

"Get up, Sean—somebody's been here and slashed our boat!"

The younger brother was still half asleep when Brian pulled him to his feet and showed him what had been done to their canoe.

"They must be close, Brian. I'll bet they're just at the other end of the lake, where the river starts again. They must have done this just after we went to sleep. I told you not to light a fire. That's what they saw and decided to attack."

"Get your gun, Sean—we may be able to catch them before they start downstream."

The two brothers ran to the small waterfall at the end of the lake, but they'd just missed Jimmy and John. They could see where their boat had entered the water.

"They think they're pretty smart," Brian smirked, "but they won't be so smart when we catch up to them. Let's get back to camp and repair the canoe. We have a long night ahead of us."

"Why don't we just go back and tell Pap that we couldn't catch them?" Sean wanted to know.

"I'd rather fall into a pit of rattlesnakes!" retorted his brother. "We're not going back without them."

Meanwhile, Jimmy had paddled as fast as he could, never stopping until it was daylight. "After I check your bandages, I need to get a couple of hours of sleep, and then we need to move on. I heard them yelling; they're not going to be happy until they catch us."

After redressing John's wounds, Jimmy tied up the canoe, grabbed the bear skin, and lay down on the bank. In the front of the boat, John stood alert with his rifle ready.

He was feeling a lot better, and the wounds on his forehead were starting to close. The bites in his arms still hurt, but the bleeding had stopped.

"You should be a doctor, Jimmy. You certainly have taken good care of me."

John let his companion sleep until noon. After a quick lunch, they continued down the river, wanting to get as far as they could before stopping for the night.

"I think we can light a fire, cook some of the venison and all the fish, and get a reasonably good night's sleep," Jimmy figured. "I don't know about tomorrow night, so I want to have enough food cooked so that we can eat while we're on the river. They're probably mad as hell and will be coming after us as soon as they patch their canoe. From what I can remember, they have a larger boat, but that shouldn't slow them any."

"What happens if they catch us?" John asked.

"I don't know what you mean."

"I think you do. They're planning either to kill us or to take us back to Asheville, which is tantamount to death. Are you willing to wait until they're upon us before striking back?"

"I don't know *what* I'm willing to do. I've never killed anyone; in fact, I've never even thought about doing away with someone."

"The chances are they'll catch us before we get to the end of the river. There are two of them, and there's only you. I can shoot, but I wouldn't be much help for handto-hand fighting. We need to come up with a plan to trap and kill them."

"There's no doubt that what you say makes sense, but I was raised not to kill. It's hard to ignore what I believe."

"I respect you as an individual and as a friend, but I don't intend to die at the hands of some mountain men. I just don't want you to get in my way if I have to take action. Are you okay with that?"

"We'll see."

John took the first watch of eight till midnight and Jim took over for the next four hours; they changed places for the last two hours. They were on their way at six-thirty in the morning. John was feeling a little stronger, and the sleep had refreshed Jimmy. John made sure that both rifles were loaded and that he had plenty of ammunition available.

Meanwhile, their adversaries took the entire night and all the next day to patch their boat; then they spent four hours drying it out by the fire. Sleep was their first priority: they'd check out the repairs at first light. They were a day or two behind, but they could make up most of that deficit by rowing until sunset. They were hardy young men, and the fear of their father made their desire to catch the two ahead of them even greater.

They tested the cuts. Everything seemed to be sealed, so they loaded their gear and pushed off, stopping at the end of the lake and removing all their supplies and gear. Following the trail Jimmy had made, they carried the canoe between them before setting it back in the water. After reloading their food and supplies, they started down the river, with both men paddling.

Both John and Jim knew that a confrontation was inevitable. They had to prepare as best they could for that eventuality. Jimmy was torn between his faith and being practical. John was steadfast in his belief that they must get the upper hand when the two groups met, or it would be disaster for them. Jimmy figured that their pursuers wouldn't catch up with them the next day, but the day after that would probably be the showdown. John could stand guard and shoot, but all the other duties would fall upon him. They took out their map and estimated where they'd be on the river the following evening. Then they looked for some sort of curve where they could hide out and surprise the two who were tracking them.

John pointed to a spot on the river. "This looks like a place where we could ambush them, if we agree that's our plan."

"It looks like the river narrows to less than a hundred feet," Jim concurred. "My suggestion is that we leave early tomorrow before sunup and stop at this spot. What I'd like to do is tie a rope to some solid trees on both sides and wait for the mountain men. As they approach, we can tighten the rope, and they won't be able to pass unless they cut the rope. Maybe we can reason with them, and it won't be necessary to get into a shootout. If not, we can do it your way."

John was able to walk around the camp, although he was still in considerable pain. He stood guard while Jimmy fished and caught some bass, skinned them, and cooked the remaining venison over the fire. John checked both rifles and made sure the spare ammunition was available and ready. He didn't seem nervous.

"Jim, the bandage on my forehead is itching like hell. Can you take a look at it and see if I can discard it?"

After Jim cleaned the wound and applied some more liniment, he threw away the used bandages. "I think it looks good; maybe some air will help it heal even faster."

"Do you think there will be a permanent scar?"

"I think you'll be as irresistible as ever with the women. Your blond hair will cover most of it. Women like men they think have been in a battle, even if it was only with a cuddly little bear."

John faked a punch, and Jimmy laughed out loud. It was the first time they'd been able to have a laugh since leaving Asheville. To them, it seemed like the whole population of the Blue Ridge Mountains was after them.

They were up before dawn, cleaned up the camp, and pushed off from the shore. Their rendezvous was two hours down the river, and they were especially alert for any danger from behind. When they reached their planned landing spot, Jim paddled to the opposite bank, jumped out of the canoe and tied a rope to a stout tree while holding onto the rope secured to their canoe. He then paddled over to the opposite bank, took out their gear and pulled the canoe out of the water. They hid everything in the bushes behind them. Jimmy tied the rope to a tree on this side and allowed to rope to lie just under the surface of the river. There was some brush along the bank and John set up there with both guns while Jimmy was moving the gear.

About three hours later, John tossed a small rock in Jimmy's direction and signaled him to be quiet: their pursuers were within sight. Jim picked up the rope, ready to pull hard as the canoe neared it. John had his rifle ready with extra ammunition in the pocket of his jacket. When the boat was within a few yards of the rope, Jim pulled hard and wrapped the strong cord a couple of times around the tree, fastened it quickly and picked up his rifle. He could hear John say, "We have you covered and we'll shoot both of you unless you give us your word that you'll turn back and not follow us."

Jim moved next to John, picked up his rifle, and aimed at the men in the boat. He heard the bigger man say, "Cut the rope, Sean, they're not going to shoot."

The man in front leaned into the water and started cutting the rope; John shot him in the back. He fell into the water, capsizing the boat, and before Jimmy could shoot, the other fell backward into the water and went under. John reloaded his rifle and took a shot where he thought the survivor might be, but it didn't appear that he hit anything. With the boat submerged in the water, neither John nor Jim could tell if it had passed under the rope and was heading downstream with the current. Where the river had narrowed at this section, the current was swifter. Jimmy didn't feel capable of swimming against the current to locate the canoe, so they stayed there for some time and just watched.

Now they had a bigger problem. They weren't sure whether one of the mountain men had survived the river and was now trying to find his boat. "John, I suggest we leave immediately. The big guy probably survived and will be coming after us. Maybe we can reach the Catawba village before we have another shootout. These guys have a lot of kin throughout the western Carolinas—he may go back for more help."

"You're right. Let's go."

John stood guard while Jimmy loaded the gear and food supplies, and then Jimmy said, "I know you're tired, so why don't you get in the front again and go to sleep. My adrenaline is working, so I've got a lot of energy and can put a lot of miles between us and the mountain man."

True to his word, Jim rowed in the swift current for six hours, took a short thirty-minute break and continued until just before sunset.

"I think I can start doing my share now," John offered. "I still hurt, but my arms are working fine. You're a great friend; I'm a little embarrassed at all you're doing to keep us alive—I won't forget it."

"You'll have your chance tomorrow. I'll take most of the watch this evening and sleep in front tomorrow. The current is swift enough, so all you have to do is steer the canoe."

"The big guy is not going to let us be," John speculated. "If I were him, I'd follow on the opposite bank and wait until we let down our guard. We have to assume that he has a weapon and probably some ammunition."

"My feelings exactly," Jimmy said.

The next three days passed without incident; it was the nights that made them apprehensive. Jim couldn't sleep. The thought of the surviving mountain man kept him alert, even though John stood guard. John was nearly back to normal, though he still had some bandages on the bite marks on his arms. The scar on his forehead had healed, and the sun obscured most of the wound. They confirmed that the mountain man was still alive; John thought he saw him hiding behind a tree on the opposite bank yesterday and the day before. He still had to cross the river, but there were parts up ahead where the river narrowed. They had to be careful.

One day out of their rendezvous, they set up camp along a straight stretch in the river. It was narrow, but the river current was swift; anyone trying to cross from one side to the other would have a very difficult time. This wasn't their first option, but they were tired, not from the physical part of the trip, but from the stress of being a target for their entire leg home. They decided not to unload the canoe. They would sleep on the ground next to a fire. With John standing guard, Jimmy went in search of some kindling for the fire.

•   •   •

When Jimmy was eight years old, his father had taken him on a field trip to visit one of the reservations he was responsible for. That was Jim's first experience with young Indian males near his age. He became acclimated to their life style, joined in their games, and went hunting and fishing with them. Jimmy was what was known as a total outdoorsman. He especially liked his companions at the Catawba village and spent part of each summer at the camp, sometimes with his father, other times with his grandfather. He became a skilled hunter and was particularly adept at throwing an axe. He and three of his Indian friends would have a contest to determine who was more accurate at throwing the axe at targets ranging from twenty to sixty feet. Raining Dog was best at sixty feet, but at the closer distance, Jimmy had no peer.

He and the Indian boys went bear hunting one weekend armed only with axes. He was reluctant at first, but the others shamed him into going. When they came upon a bear, the four young teenagers circled the animal and threw their axes at him. While others distracted the bear, those who threw their axes retrieved them. Soon they wore the animal down and it succumbed. Jimmy was scared the entire time.

Now, as he walked back into their camp site, he saw John on his knees, with the older mountain man holding a rifle pressed against his back.

"Get in here and throw down the wood," he shouted at Jimmy. "If you run for it, I'll kill your friend. I'm going to take you both back to my Pap. He'll decide your fate for killing three of my brothers. Now get over here and tie up your friend."

Jimmy was carrying the axe on his rear right side. He tossed the kindling to the ground, diverting the mountain man's attention for a split second, just enough time for Jimmy to grab his axe. In one fluid motion, he pulled it up by the handle and hurled it directly at Brian O'Neal. The man let out a blood-curdling scream as the axe imbedded in his chest, and fell on his back. John was up quickly and kicked the man's gun away, but it wasn't necessary. The mountain man was no longer moving.

Jimmy's worst concerns had come to fruition: he'd killed a man. All his earlier training was about the sanctity of human life, and on this trip he'd violated those teachings.

John patted him on the shoulder. "Jimmy, you had no choice," he told him. "They were going to kill us—if not here, then back in Asheville. You saved my life, and for that I'll always be grateful. I don't think anyone needs to know about the two we killed. Let's keep it between ourselves."

CHAPTER SIX

To say that they were glad to see Aaron at the terminus of the river would be an understatement. To Jim and John, their nightmare seemed to be over. They greeted the Catawba brave but were reluctant to share their experience with him. They wanted to relax, have a good meal and think about what had happened before they shared their ordeal with others.

Over the next two days they sat around the fire, occasionally smoked the peace pipe, and, more than anything, they slept. On the third day of their return to the village from where they started their adventure, Jimmy asked John if he would like to go hunting, just the two of them. Both felt that things needed to be said, and it was better if they shared it only with themselves. Aaron offered to guide them, but John said he and Jimmy wanted to get away by themselves for a day.

Catching game was not their object. Each shared with the other that they half expected to see the mountain men's kin stroll into the Catawba village and start shooting. They found a spot on the bank of a small creek, connecting to the Catawba River, and sat down.

"I guess I've recovered enough from the trip to share with you some of my thoughts. First, I'm grateful for your friendship, John, and especially how we worked together. It seems as though we knew what the other was doing and wanted. I will never forget this trip. You're like a twin brother to me, and I couldn't like you any more if we were related. I don't know what the future holds for us, but I hope you are part of my life."

"You saved my life, not once but twice. You took care of me and doctored me until I was well enough to assist; yet, you continued to do most of the work. I'm forever in your debt, and as long as I live, I'll be there for you. I don't think anyone knows another human being until they meet adversity and overcome whatever they faced. I couldn't believe my eyes when I saw that axe swish through the air and hit that jackass in the chest. I thought we were goners, and I had almost starting saying my prayers. I don't mind telling Aaron about the trip, but I don't think I want to share it with others, even our family. I want this to be between us two and only us two."

"We can make up a version of the ride down the Catawba for our parents and friends, because they're going to ask us; you're right, this is ours," Jim answered.

"My parents are going to wonder about the scars, but I think we can tell them about the fight with the bear and you saving my life by killing the bear and then taking care of me on the trip home. I think that's enough for them. They need not know anymore. I agree that Aaron has a right to know, because you never can tell what the future may bring. Some day, their kin may visit the village and want to know where we are. If I told my father, he'd hire some irregulars and go to Asheville and clean out the whole clan. I think there's been enough killing to last me a lifetime. There's not too much time left before we go off on our separate ways. I don't think we'll see each other very much over the next four years, but I'll write to you at the University. And by the way, just because you'll be in this area the next four years, that doesn't mean you can spark Louisa. I proposed to her before we left, and she accepted. We're getting married the day after I graduate from West Point."

"That's pretty sneaky of you! Boy, did I have you worried! I like Louisa, but not the way you do. I wish you the best."

They left the bear and deer skins with Aaron and headed home. John's parents had planned a welcome home party for him and invited Jimmy, his father and grandparents. John's mother was shocked when she saw her son's face and the bite marks on both arms, but his father was so proud that his son got those scars killing a bear. He couldn't talk enough about it to anyone who would listen. The boys had agreed to tell everyone that they both killed the bear.

John's parents, along with Louisa Harrison, who was sporting a large engagement ring, met them as they arrived. She looked so much older than her eighteen years. You could tell that both parents were proud of the future marriage. When she had Jim alone for a minute, she gave him a passionate kiss.

"Hey, I thought you were an engaged woman. That kiss was very provocative."

"It was meant to be. See what you missed for being too slow."

"Don't give me that! You and I both know that you always had John in mind as your future partner. I was just around to make him commit."

"You think what you want, Jimmy Harris, but you'll never really know."

John joined them. "What are you doing? Are you trying to take my fiancée from me? I might have to challenge you to a duel—but it sure as hell won't be with axes. Why don't you and I go have a couple of beers? I know a place."

"John William, don't you dare go down to that shack where all the shanty town girls hang out," Louisa pouted.

"How do you know about places like that? A sheltered southern girl shouldn't know about things like that! I'm shocked that you think so little of me and Jimmy to think we would go there."

"Don't give me that! I'm telling you that if I find out you went there, I might use a knife in the right places, if you know what I mean." Louisa walked away, but managed to shake her bottom so both boys would notice.

"Boy, is she mad! We better not go there," Jimmy said, and both boys laughed.

The two young men downed their beer and took off for the shanty town hideout, as it was called.

John seemed to be known by many of the young men and women who frequented the bar-like structure. It was a wooden shack with a few tables inside, one of them serving as a bar; there were only two picnic tables outside. Kerosene lamps provided just enough light to allow you to see who you were talking to. There was a smooth dirt section that everyone used as a dance floor. A three-man combo took care of the so-called music. The two boys were having a beer, talking to one of the other young men, when a beautiful dark-haired young woman about eighteen came up and hugged John William. "Jimmy, this is Maria Garland."

"I haven't seen you in here before," Maria smiled at Jimmy. "Which plantation does your daddy own?"

"You have me confused with some of John's other friends. My father is an Indian agent, and we're not rich— but I like girls if that's what interests you."

"Well, a young man with a sense of humor!"

"It's my turn to ask if you belong to the plantation set?"

"My father is the overseer at Magnolia. Want a job picking cotton?"

"No, but I'd like a dance. What do you say?"

"I'll give it a try. If your father doesn't own a plantation, what do you do?"

"I just finished school in Charleston, and in September, I'm attending the University of South Carolina. I plan to major in History. Are you impressed?"

"Why yes, young sir, but that won't get you too far with me." She gave him the widest smile; he could feel the heat on the back of his neck.

"I guess the real question is why?" she asked.

"My grandfather taught at U.S.C. and feels that this country's future success will come with better relations with other nations. He feels that past history shouldn't be forgotten, because it repeats itself."

He moved in closer and kissed Maria on the lips and then spun her around.

"You're pretty sure of yourself, aren't you?"

"I wanted to see what your reaction would be. I'd like to see you again. What about you?"

"I haven't made up my mind. Why don't you come out to Magnolia next week? Perhaps we can go on a picnic down by the bayou—unless you're afraid of gators!"

"Of course, I'm afraid of gators! Who isn't?"

"How about Wednesday? Papa will be back from Charleston and will probably want to see who's going to try to deflower his daughter."

"I can hardly wait."

Jimmy spent the remainder of the weekend with his grandfather and grandmother, helping around their small cottage. He was delighted to see that his father was visiting this weekend. Grandfather Hendricks had a fertile mind, and his father wasn't far behind. It was at the evening meals that the conversation was lively; Sunday evening was no exception.

"I was at Rosebud last evening, and the discussion between many of my contemporaries was of secession," Jimmy ventured. "Is it slavery that's driving the movement?"

"I don't think the issue is based entirely upon the question of slavery," his grandfather replied. "Most of the commerce between America and other nations emanates in the South. They grow the crops that are exported abroad. However, the financial structure of the nation lies in New York City, which is basically the clearing house for all international financial transactions. The South has a colonial period type of economy, and many of its profits are drained by northern middlemen. Still, the number of things that both North and South have in common, forces both sides to compromise and try to make the best of the situation. How long that will last is beyond my grasp."

"Although the majority of citizens above and below the Mason and Dixon line have good rapport, the issue of sectionalism cannot be ignored," his father chimed in. "The almost complete monopoly of banking in the North has been a thorn in the side of the southern states for a long time. Contrast that with a view of many in the North, that the feudalistic South dominates national government issues, promotes delaying tactics in Congress and therefore holds up progress."

"My question has always been, is slavery economically profitable for all the states?" Hendricks extended a questioning hand. "If not, what should those states in the South do that want freedom from slavery? Will they be forced to go along with the firebrands who'll use slavery as an issue to stoke the fires of secession?—Now I'm dominating the conversation. What are your views?" He directed the question to James.

Before he could respond, his father broke in. "I've not sensed a desire in the North to break up the Union. Many in the business community travel extensively to the South and don't encounter any animosity on their trips. I travel to the many reservations in the South, and although some newspapers publish provocative editorials, the masses go about their business as though there is no issue. The big plantations may have a different view from most in the South. They see slavery as paramount to their economic future, and they won't make any effort to see if their business can be profitable without the slaves." Cameron looked to Jimmy.

"I don't know if I know enough about either issue to discuss the problem intelligently. I think slavery is morally wrong. Having the power of life or death over a group of people who have no rights seems perverse. I've listened to John William and his father justify their position. I don't argue with them, nor do I openly challenge their views; still, I don't like it. My problem is, I haven't reached the point where I'll cut off any dialog with them. I like them both and I like being with them; I consider them my friends. That's the issue; I'm unwilling to take a position."

"Don't beat yourself up. I talk a lot, but, like you, I haven't taken a definitive position." Hendricks smiled at his grandson and son-in-law. They raised their glasses to salute each other.

• • •

Magnolia Plantation was eight miles from Charleston. Jim rode his horse to the entrance and asked for Maria Garland. He was directed to a medium-sized home about two hundred yards from the main residence. Her father was having lunch with the family when he arrived. Jim was invited him to join them, and he graciously accepted. Besides Maria and her father, there were Maria's mother, Alice, and her grandmother, Coleen, enjoying a lunch of ham and potato salad. "My father would like to give you a tour of the plantation after lunch, if you're interested," Maria told Jimmy.

"I would very much like to see the operation. I worked in the cotton processing plant at Rosebud two summers ago, and I'd like to see if the approach is similar."

When lunch was over, the two men left the women at the house and walked to where the slaves were picking cotton. "We have seventy slaves on Magnolia. Forty are males, twenty are female adults, and there are ten children. During harvest, we bring the cotton to the processing plant in carts pulled by mules."

The processing plant was similar to the one at Rosebud, where the seeds and impurities were separated from the raw cotton and baled. There were at least a hundred bales stacked outside the plant. "We ship about two thousand bales a week," said Garland, and then turned to face Jimmy. "I understand you're going to the University in Charleston this fall?"

"Yes, sir. My grandfather taught there for thirty years before he retired."

"Didn't you and John William go on a trip just recently?"

"We went to the Blue Ridge Mountains and returned on the Catawba River before we stopped at the Catawba reservation."

They spent about three hours on the tour. "Let's go back and have some lemonade at the house. My wife makes the best lemonade.

"Unless you were planning to head back tonight, we have plenty of room, and I would like you to stay. We seldom get visitors, and I think my daughter would like to spend a little time with you. By the way, do you play chess?"

"Thanks for the invitation—and yes, I'd like to stay over and yes, I play chess. My grandfather taught both my father and myself."

The women had seen the men approach and had set up the kitchen table with some cookies and a pitcher of lemonade. "What do you think of my father's operation?' Maria asked.

"I was impressed. I think it's as effective as Rosebud's, even with less acreage and less help."

"Did you know that I picked cotton alongside the slaves when I was twelve?"

"No, but I can picture it. I bet you didn't let anyone pick more than you!"

"You think you know me pretty well, don't you! Dinner is at six, so why don't I show you the mansion. All the Harrisons are in New Orleans and won't be back for a week."

"Lead on, fair maiden!"

The butler let them in. "You know your way around, Miss Maria; I'll be polishing the silverware in the dining room if you have any questions."

James Stephen had been in the mansion at Rosebud, but it didn't have anything on Magnolia. After looking through all the rooms on the first floor, Maria took his hand and led him to the second floor and the master suite, which looked out over a lush garden. "Have you ever seen anything as lovely as their four-poster?" With that, Maria ran and jumped on the bed. "Getting any ideas, young man?"

"You can't be serious! What if someone comes in? They'll tell your father, and he'll kill me!"

"I think you're timid."

"Yes, I am. You can stay, but I'm leaving." He could hear Maria laugh as he walked down the stairs and out of the house.

Her father was a good chess player, and it took only two hours before he checkmated James. "You have a nice game—you just need to play a little more, and you and I can have a really good contest."

Dinner was stimulating, mirroring the discussion that James and his grandfather had had over Sunday supper. Everyone was equal and joined in the conversation, though it wasn't as heavy a discussion as those he was used to at his home.

He decided to leave at about three o'clock the next afternoon, so he asked Maria if they could go on an early picnic. He was surprised to find that she had anticipated the idea; she'd gotten up early, fried some chicken and made an apple pie that morning. James hitched up the one-horse carriage her father used, and off they went to the pond at the southern end of the plantation. "You haven't said much to me since yesterday afternoon," Maria said. "Are you shocked?"

"No, I just didn't want to make a fool of myself and have other people, besides you and me, witness my embarrassment."

They found a spot under an old elm tree where they spread out the blanket, set the food on it, and then walked to the pond, which was about two hundred yards across. There was a slight breeze in the air with a modicum of humidity. "There really are alligators in there," Maria told him. "When I was young, we swam in it, but always stayed close to the shore because those gators can really swim fast. My daddy always had his rifle handy just in case they came out of the water and tried to run us down."

Jim hadn't had a large breakfast, and, being a young man, he devoured the chicken, between mouthfuls telling her what a great cook she was. He didn't know if he had enough room for the apple pie she had baked, but forced himself to have two pieces. "I could use a nap after stuffing myself like this. You're a great cook!"

"Compliments are always nice to receive, young sir."

He lay down on the blanket while she picked up the food that was left and put it back in her hand basket and set it aside. She lay down next to him. "Kind of cozy, isn't it?"

James rolled over and looked down at her. He kissed her on the cheek, and when there was no resistance, he kissed her lips and she moaned slightly. He could see her nipples pressed against her dress, and he touched them lightly. When she didn't say stop, he squeezed them carefully, and that's when Maria kissed him back. Feeling emboldened, Jimmy placed a hand under her dress and began moving it up her thigh. She grabbed his hand and said, "That's far enough! No one is going where you want unless there's wedding ring attached to my hand."

"Hey, I'm too young to get married! I've never had a real job—I couldn't even support myself. I thought you wanted to have some fun!"

"I do, and I did, but I know when to stop. So, if you can't abide by the rules, go back to those Indian girls who'll let you do it to them." Maria got up from the blanket, yanked it so hard that Jimmy rolled off, and then put it in the carriage. "I'm ready to go back," she said. She had her arms folded across her chest and there was a scowl on her face.

"Hey, don't be mad," Jimmy exclaimed. "I like you a lot—I just wanted to see how far you'd go. You kind of shocked me yesterday, and I wanted to see what you had in mind."

"Well, now you know."

"I sure do. Can we talk for a minute? I liked kissing you, and I think you enjoyed it. I really want to visit you again; your family is great. Can I have another chance?"

Maria smiled, walked over to Jimmy and kissed him on the lips. "I look forward to the next visit."

On the way back to her house, Jimmy asked, "What did you mean about the Indian girls?"

"I overheard your friend John tell a couple of his friends what a stud you are and how many Indian girls you've slept with. Of course he didn't word it that way. They were all really embarrassed when they saw me close by. You know his parents are giving him a going-away party very soon. Are you going?"

"Are you going to be there?"

"Yes."

"Well, so am I."

CHAPTER SEVEN

Second Lieutenant P.G.T. Beauregard, or Pierre, as he was known in the family, asked for special permission to be relieved from maneuvers to attend his cousin's going-away party. Needless to say, his uncle's influence with the two senators from South Carolina could have helped. The party at Rosebud had a twofold purpose. One was to give John a large send-off, and the second was to announce the engagement of Louisa Harrison to John William Beauregard.

Pierre looked superb in his military uniform. Although short of stature, he had a look in his eyes that attracted those of the opposite sex. Such was the case this evening. There were at least three young women hanging on his arm from the time he arrived. He'd taken John under his wing before he left for the academy, and he felt a sense of pride that the young man was going to follow in his footsteps. He wouldn't have much time for John this evening; they planned to go fishing tomorrow. Besides, the pretty young girls were making him feel like a hero already and he didn't have one campaign under his belt.

James had been at U.N.C. the entire morning, setting up his schedules of classes. He realized he was running late. The going-away party for John was at six, and it was already noon. His father and grandparents had been invited and were anxiously awaiting him. He took the train to Charleston, cleaned up quickly, and off the four went in a carriage. The party was in full swing when they arrived, but John, who'd been keeping an eye out for them, came over to greet them.

"The food is going fast. I suggest you go over to the serving line, because in forty minutes, Louisa's father is going to announce our engagement; we can talk later."

When the time came, Mr. and Mrs. Harrison got up on a makeshift stage in the center of all the tables where people were sitting. With their daughter and John William by their side, and his parents close by, they announced the engagement. There was a receiving line for everyone, and then, as was the custom, the betrothed walked to the dance floor and waltzed to the applause of all. "I loved you from the first moment I saw you and knew that I wanted to be with you for the rest of our lives," John whispered in her ear.

"I feel the same way. I hated your teasing at first, but soon I looked forward to seeing you. I especially liked to watch you when you least expected. I'd hoped it would be me that you would choose."

"What about James?"

"He was someone I liked a lot, but it was you I wanted to marry. James was just someone I wanted to spend a week with, nothing more. He's not going to marry Maria Garland. I can see it in his eyes; he has plans for the future and he's not going to deviate until he realizes his goal. His sights are set much higher than Maria. The woman he marries will be one of quality and will have a stature equal to his. I hope you can handle my frankness?"

"I wouldn't have it any other way. I always saw him as a rival; I guess I was wrong on that point."

"Yes, you were—he was never your rival. I *liked* him, but I loved *you*."

Everyone had been seated during the announcement and the subsequent dance by the betrothed couple; now many were leaving. His grandparents saw a couple they hadn't seen in some time and excused themselves to walk over to the other table. His father was talking politics to two men who shared their table, so Jimmy got up and wandered around the perimeter of the festival. He was standing next to one of the kerosene lanterns, shooing the insects away, when suddenly he yelled out—someone had grabbed his rear!

It was Louisa Harrison who had come up behind him and squeezed his bottom.

"What the hell are you doing?" he demanded. "You're supposed to be engaged. Besides, that wasn't very ladylike, if you want to know!"

"Oh, come on. What's a little pinch between friends?"

"You're my best friend's betrothed. You can't play games with me any more!"

"Well, whose fault is that? You could have made your intentions known."

By this time John had walked up to the two. "What's going on here?" he asked, with a smile on his face.

"Well, Louisa is acting like a teenage girl, if you know what I mean."

"Did she pinch your butt?"

"How did you know?"

"She told me she was going to do it."

"Thanks a lot, you two."

John wasn't the only one who'd been waiting for Jim to arrive. Maria Garland excused herself from the group she was with and walked over to the three who seemed to be having a good time. "Well, Jimmy Harris, when were you going to come over and pay your respects to me and my family?"

"How about right now?"

Maria smiled at Louisa, grabbed Jimmy's arm, and led him toward the table where her father and mother were sitting. "Still carrying a torch for Louisa?" she asked, casting him a sidelong glance.

"Now, why would you even *think* that, when I'm with the prettiest girl at this party?"

"You do have a way of escaping from difficult situations, don't you?"

After spending some time with her parents, the young couple mingled with the guests, but their route took them to a small grove of trees. James pulled her to him and kissed her firmly on the lips. "Don't hold me so tight, young sir, I won't run away from you."

He leaned her against one of the trees and kissed her again, and she responded with her body pressed to his. "Let me get some air," Maria said finally, and moved away from him.

"Are you going to visit me while you're at that school?"

"As much as my studies will allow."

"Well, you say that now, but once you meet some of those girls who hang around that school, you're not going to come back here as much."

"I don't understand the problem."

"Of course you don't. You can move around as freely as you want, but I can't. You can court young women, but I can't court any young men. I have to wait for you or some other suitor to come calling; I don't like it. How'd you like to be restricted because of your gender?"

"Well, I guess I wouldn't like it. What is it that you want of me?"

"I'd like some sort of commitment. Louisa has it from John. Why can't I have it from you?"

"We've just met; they've known each other for ten years. I like you a lot and I'm going to visit you as much as you'll let me, but I don't want a commitment now, or at least until I'm able to support a wife."

Before she could respond, John and Louisa walked up to them. "You two look like you're having a very serious conversation. Are we interrupting?" John asked.

Her anger passed quickly. Maria never wanted to show any emotion in front of Louisa. She was but the foreman's daughter on Louisa's father's plantation. Although the girls were about the same age and had played together while growing up, Maria knew her place, and as long as she lived at Magnolia, nothing would change that. "No, what would you two like to do?"

"Let's take a walk down by the pond. There are no alligators in it. Maybe we could go skinny-dipping?" John laughed.

"No, we can't, John William, and I'm shocked that you'd let another man see your fiancée naked!"

"Oh, I was just kidding." John winked at James.

Before James went home with his relatives, the two young men spent about thirty minutes together. "Life is going to change for us, some of it good and some not so good," John mused. "I've known you for four years, and I couldn't ask for a better friend. I don't like it that we're going in different directions from now on. I guess that's life, but it makes me sad. I hope that Louisa hasn't made our relationship weaker. "

"I'm happy for you and Louisa. I will always look back on that trip down the Catawba River as a turning point in our lives. I'm grateful that I got to share it with you. I like Louisa, but I knew from the start that she was meant for you, so I always looked upon her as a sister or a cousin." The two friends shook hands and parted.

Pierre G.T. Beauregard, recently graduated from West Point, wanted to impart some words of wisdom to his cousin while he had a chance. After Jimmy left, Pierre and John took a walk down by the pond and sat on one of the benches under a large sycamore tree.

"You're an aggressive young man, John, and that's a plus. At West Point, you need to show your aggressiveness, but not overtly. Try to keep your opinions to yourself unless asked. You're going to be baited by some who view southern cadets as nothing but slave owners. Try not to lower yourself to their level. Since every congressman can nominate someone to go to the academy, chances are that there will be more Northerners than Southerners in your class. You'll make lifelong friends—and perhaps lifelong enemies. Try to restrict the latter, and you'll do fine. Any time you need some words of wisdom, contact me. Any chance I get I'll come and visit."

John had wanted to have a military career from early on. His father François had also had dreams of a military career, and went to West Point, but after his first assignment, he found that it wasn't for him, and he came home to run Rosebud. Ambrose was ecstvtic and hoped that his grandson would make the same choice.

CHAPTER EIGHT

The plan was for Louisa and John and both sets of parents to travel by train to New York City. They left two weeks before John was to report, and would spend four to five days in Gotham. This was to be an engagement present to the young couple and a pleasure trip for the two sets of parents. Train travel was in its infancy, but the young couple saw it as an adventure, and enjoyed each experience on their way to New York City.

They booked rooms at the prestigious Cairns Hotel on 42nd Street in mid-Manhattan. The hotel was within walking distance of the theater district and the good restaurants surrounding the playhouses. On the first day, they took a boat trip around the island and had lunch in one of the many fish houses that dotted the edge of the river. On another outing, they had a picnic in the Battery, which was at the end of Manhattan Island. In the evening they dressed in their finest and attended plays at the Park Theater, the Bowery Theater, and of course Sans Souci. The four days seemed to fly by with lightning speed; soon John would have to leave for West Point.

Louisa's mother relented and allowed the young couple to spend their last day together unchaperoned; they chose Governor's Island. The hotel fixed them a picnic basket and off they went in a horse-drawn carriage down the length of Manhattan and then by boat to the island. Louisa was dressed in a summer dress with a wide-brimmed hat; she was carrying her normal parasol. John wore a blue suit with a top hat and carried a cane. They looked like an affluent young couple. "We haven't been alone since we were children," Louisa smiled. "I'm glad mother trusts us."

"I think she trusts *you*," John returned wryly. "I overheard her tell your father that if I laid a hand on you, she'd kill me."

"Well, mother was always blunt—but I think she likes you."

John had his hand on her knee as they rode in the carriage and was slowly moving it up her thigh when she grabbed his hand and pushed it aside.

"Do you love me?" Louisa asked.

"Of course, you know I do."

"Well, I'm not going to be one of those girls who gets pregnant and has to go away to Aunt Suzy's or to Europe until she delivers. There's no way you can hide those things from nosy people, and I'm not going to try. The next four years are going to be tough for both of us. Remember, you asked to marry me. So let's get some ground rules established. You can feel my breasts if you're discreet, you can pat my fanny, and you can kiss me as much as you want, but nothing else. If that's not okay, we're going to get unengaged as of this minute."

John put both hands around her face and kissed her softly on the lips. "We'll do it your way, and I'll be happy about it. You're the only one for me."

They'd hired the carriage for the day; the driver would wait with the carriage until they returned. The main attraction of Governor's Island was the circular building in the northwest part of the island called Castle Williams. The building was part of America's coastal defenses, featuring guns that would rotate 320 degrees to cover the south end of the island. After touring the building, they found a picnic table under some willows and laid out their lunch. "What are you going to do with yourself while I'm at the academy?" John asked.

"My father wants me to learn the cotton business. I know most women are for show, but my father wants me to be self-sufficient in case something happens to my husband, should I marry, which I assume will be you."

"I hope you don't plan to work after we get married."

"Why not? I'm not dumb. If my father dies, who's going to run the plantation? I'm not turning it over to someone else just because I'm a female."

"What if we have children?"

"I'll take care of them. Perhaps I'll have help; they'll be my main responsibility, but so will Magnolia. What are you afraid of? Do you think someone will think you're less of a man because I have a business? John, no one who knows you could ever say you're not a man, and that you're not comfortable with yourself." He smiled and kissed her hand.

When they returned to the Battery, they notified their driver that they wanted to walk around the surrounding area. They found some dilapidated buildings and an unused pasture. Louisa stumbled and asked John to wait a minute while she took a pebble out of her shoe. She leaned against one of the old vacant buildings with her left foot off the ground; John stooped down and took off her shoe, discarded a small stone and put her shoe back on. Before they could start back to their carriage, they were approached by three scruffy young men. "Give us your wallet, or we'll take your woman, and you won't like what we'll do to her," sneered the largest of the three.

As John looked at the three, one of them moved closer in a menacing way. Rather than wait for them to attack, he decided to take the initiative. He struck out with his foot and kicked him in the groin; the man went to his knees. John backhanded the one on his right with his cane, catching him alongside the head, and he fell forward with blood pouring from a wound on his head. Seeing the other two fall, the third man turned and ran off. Just then two policemen came up to the couple, hauled the fallen two to their feet, and took them away. "Sorry this had to happen to you, sir. A couple of days in the pokey will make them think twice before they do this again."

Their driver had seen the confrontation and signaled for the police. John's reward inside the cab on the way home was a very passionate kiss. "You're my hero, young sir."

"If you don't mind, Louisa, let's not tell our parents about this. It will only worry them and make them more protective."

"I know you're fearsome, but where did you learn to defend yourself like that?"

"Jimmy Harris taught me. He learned the art of self-defense from the Catawba Indians and passed it on to Pierre and me. I'm a little stronger than Jim, but he's much quicker. I don't think he and I would ever want to face off against each other."

When they arrived at the hotel, their parents asked about their day. "Nothing unusual happened. It was just a nice summer day," Louisa responded.

Everyone enjoyed the vacation in New York City, but the time had come for John to leave for his processing at West Point. He and his father talked that evening and came up with a plan. It wasn't necessary for everyone to deliver him to the academy. His father would travel with him while the others remained in the city until the father returned. There was some resistance at first, especially from Louisa, but when his father explained that John wouldn't have any time for them once he reported to the academy, they finally agreed to the plan.

Louisa cried and clung to John until the last minute. "Mother and father will bring me up there during your Christmas break. I know you can't come home the first year, but you'd better write to me weekly. I love you and **can't wait to be your wife."**

It took them a day to reach the site of old Fort Putnam. John hugged his father and thanked him for being considerate to his desire to be an Army officer. "I have great faith in you," his father told him. "You will do us all proud. It is an honor to be your father."

The first part of processing was a series of exams which weeded out twenty potential candidates. Subsequently, John's hair was cut short and he was issued several sets of uniforms. He and his classmates were hustled to the East Barracks where all the plebes, or first-year cadets, would reside for the next two months. Cadets were entitled to thirty days leave per year, but plebes wouldn't have that privilege until their second year at the academy.

Over the next two months, John learned about the Honor Code, demerits, and the massive amount of memorization required of all first-year cadets. He was so focused on everything that was expected of him that he didn't have time to learn the names of any of his classmates. Initially, all he was trying to do was survive the hazing. His instructors were extremely critical of everyone, though John felt they were concentrating on him. His shoes were never polished enough; his brass was too dull and he didn't shave close enough. He felt that if he shaved any closer, his skin would be peeling from the razor!

He also learned that if he didn't respond quickly enough to an upper classman, he'd get a demerit, and if he got too many in a week, he'd ride a cannon for a few hours. The ride wasn't on a smooth surface, so it was not only an effort to stay on, but it was an effort to walk when he got off. He finally had time after a month to speak to the cadets in the bunks next and above him; there were four to a room. James Longstreet was next to him on the other bottom bunk, with Abner Doubleday on top. William Rosecrans had the bunk above him. The four seemed to be compatible. There were others he liked, but he spent most of his early cadet years with those three.

Rosecrans, from Ohio, had little formal education and almost no financial aid. He had petitioned Congressman Harper and was surprised when he secured the appointment to West Point. An avid reader, he excelled in all aspects of engineering. Doubleday, from New York State, was keen of mind but short in stature. Longstreet, born in South Carolina, would be as close to John as any individual at the academy. Raised on a plantation in Georgia, he had received his appointment from an Alabama congressman. He was a poor student and always seemed to have excessive demerits. Therefore, most of the time, he could be seen walking tours, cleaning up the horse stalls, or riding the cannon around the compound as a form of punishment.

After the first two months, the upperclassmen returned from leave, and the plebes moved to permanent housing. Rosecrans roomed with Doubleday and John with Longstreet. The first two months were but an introduction to what was to come. The returning upperclassmen came back with a sincere desire to make life as difficult as they could for those in John's class of 56 cadets. Longstreet and John were the main recipients of their attention. In particular, Cadet Sergeant William T. Sherman seemed to make life miserable for each southern plebe. John wondered whether he would react the same way, if and when he became an upperclassman.

The seasonal holidays were fast approaching. John had only a few demerits, and was therefore assured that he'd be able to host Louisa and her family at the Plebes' Parents Weekend, hosted in early February. This was the one weekend when they'd have the post to themselves, their family and friends; all the upperclassmen would be away.

John's parents and future in-laws found accommodations in the neighboring town of Highland Falls and then met John at the main entrance on Saturday morning. Under the watchful eyes of their instructors, the greetings were dignified. John told Louisa later that he wanted to pat her butt, but was afraid to get more demerits. With both sets of parents, they walked the grounds, visited his room, and talked to several of his instructors. He and Louisa couldn't find a moment to be by themselves. Lunch on that day was served in the cadet mess hall, and John squeezed Louisa's hand before an instructor walked up to their table and engaged the family in conversation.

Late in the afternoon, the two families and Louisa returned to their accommodations to prepare for the evening's formal ball, called a hop. The women wore ball gowns, and the male guests were in formal dress. John had on his Class A uniform. Louisa kissed John on the cheek when they returned to the main hall for the banquet. He'd been able to acquire extra tickets from those cadets who didn't have family coming that weekend, so both sets of parents could attend. They found their seats, listened to opening remarks by the commandant, and had a dinner of roast beef. Both he and Louisa were nervous when they got up to dance. It'd been eight months since they'd been in New York City. She pressed herself to him and he nearly lost his breath. "I really missed you, Louisa. Your letters helped me get through these past months."

"I love you, John, and I miss you every day. I don't know if I can wait another three and a half years before we can get married. I may have to find a boyfriend!" She laughed out loud and squeezed his shoulder.

"Thanks a lot, Louisa. I really needed that."

"You don't have to worry. It's you and only you that I want." Whether it was acceptable or not, he kissed her on the mouth—and held the kiss for a long time.

His father and mother and Louisa returned the next morning, and after lunch at the mess hall and a walk around the campus, they returned to their lodging and took the boat back to New York, some fifty miles to the south. John had a strong inner spirit and felt that the visit of his loved one would carry him through until he was able to come home on his first leave.

After his first year, the hazing subsided. The upper-classmen, including Sherman, had their sights set on the new set of plebes, and John went about his studies. This was perhaps the finest engineering school in the country. For a short time, in its infancy, it was the *only* engineering school. At the end of John's second academic year, he came home for thirty days in July.

CHAPTER NINE

The first two years of college passed more quickly than Jimmy expected. This year he'd planned to spend the summer in Savannah, working for a cotton broker. The previous summer, he worked at a cotton clearing house in Charleston and lived with his grandparents. John's father had taken a distinct interest in his son's close friend and set up the position in Savannah. Jim wasn't sure that any aspect of the cotton business was in his future, but it helped defray his educational expenses and gave him an entry into the business world.

Needless to say, James' visits to Magnolia to see Maria Garland were limited to twice a year. She knew that he wouldn't give her a commitment, but she hoped that he'd give some indication that he cared and would be making an offer after college. Jim had no intention of making any such gesture to Maria. He had a goal in life, and that was paramount. Besides, he didn't think he'd ever marry the girl; she was not only too aggressive, but her mood swings gave him pause.

Just after Christmas of his second year, he invited Maria to a weekend at the University which included a formal dance. He'd tutored some students and saved up enough money for her to travel by train to Columbia with her mother and stay at a hotel in town for the weekend. She was excited about the invitation and was extremely pleasant throughout the weekend; Jimmy enjoyed her company. He wasn't a proficient dancer, but Maria's grace and fluid movement more than made up for his deficiencies as a dancer. He could tell how impressed his classmates were with her.

At intermission, they went out to the porch surrounding the auditorium where the dance was held. "You look especially pretty tonight. Your gown is magnificent. I can't think of another time when I've enjoyed myself so much." James kissed her softly on the lips.

"I like your friends. How often do you have dances?"

"Once a quarter, but this particular one comes but once a year. You're seeing my friends and me at our best."

He danced with Maria for the remainder of the evening. He felt very warm holding her in his arms and one time nearly told her he loved her. Though neither had professed their love, Maria made it very clear that she wanted to marry James.

On the drive back to her hotel, he stopped in a grove of trees and pulled her to him. He'd had a couple of glasses of the punch that his classmates had spiked with liquor, and he was feeling flirtatious. He kissed her passionately and fondled her breasts. Her breath was coming fast until he reached under her dress. That was her signal, because she pulled herself from him and sat upright in the carriage. "We're not going there. I like you a lot, but not enough to go any further until we're married."

Nothing was said between the two as they reached the hotel. He helped her out of the carriage and escorted her to her room; her mother was awake. He tried to kiss her goodnight, but she turned her head and walked into the room and shut the door.

He got up early the next morning and drove to their hotel in his rented carriage. He'd planned to have breakfast with Maria and her mother, but they'd already eaten when he arrived. He took their bags, put them in the carriage, and drove them to the railroad station, where he waited until their train arrived. There was very little dialogue between the three.

As they were boarding, Maria turned and met James' eyes. "When will I see you again?" she asked.

"I'm busy the next two weeks with exams. How about three weekends from today? I'll come down, and perhaps we can spend the weekend together."

"If that's the earliest you can make it, I guess it'll have to do."

He didn't want to pursue the issue any longer. Although she was very pretty and he really liked her, he wasn't sure he'd want to spend the rest of his life with her. There was no kiss goodbye, and no request for him to write to her.

James felt a great deal of apprehension about his next visit to see Maria in three weeks; he passed all his exams and made preparations to visit her. He took the train to Charleston and rode his old horse, Saxon, to Magnolia, where he was surprised to learn that Maria and Louisa had gone riding. Her father wasn't aware that James was visiting this weekend, but he was a gracious host. "She probably planned to be here when you arrived, but when she's with Miss Louisa, they usually lose track of time. How about a game of chess while we're waiting? You know, when you're married, you'll spend a lot of time waiting for your wife, and you'll never understand why."

His mind wasn't on the game; Thomas Garland easily beat him. "How about another game, James?"

He didn't need to respond, because at that moment Maria and Louisa drove up in a carriage. They jumped out like two young girls and ran into the house.

"Don't blame Maria for not being here when you arrived; it was my fault that we were late," Louisa apologized. "We were talking about my wedding plans and we lost track of the time. Please say all is forgiven." She kissed James on the cheek.

"Why don't you entertain James while I change into something more comfortable?" Maria said to her.

Louisa took him by the hand and led him outside, where they sat in the rockers. "She's mad at you. Why don't you want to marry her?"

"I didn't say I didn't want to marry Maria. All I've been saying is that I'm not ready to support a wife. You and John have something special, and you both come from wealthy families. My family's finances are not in that category, so I must plan for the future. I don't think I'll be ready until I'm in my midto late twenties. There's so much more that I want to accomplish before I take on more responsibility. I'm thinking of going to Europe after I graduate from college. John will have an assignment and a career; I'll still be trying to find a profession."

Maria joined them on the veranda. "Am I missing something?"

Louisa didn't want to cause a confrontation between her two friends, so she told a little lie. "Jimmy and I've been talking about John and when he's coming home this summer."

Jimmy decided to return to his grandparents' home before dark rather than stay over until tomorrow. Maria was disappointed and let him know it. "I waited for three weeks for you to come down here, and now you leave after a couple of hours! Why do you bother coming down here? It doesn't seem as though you want to."

"That's not fair. I have a job, and that's to get good grades. My father and grandfather are paying my way, and I owe it to them to do my best. I like you very much, but every time I come to visit, you pressure me about marriage. I'm not ready, and won't be ready for many years. If your timeline is earlier than that, I suggest you start seeing someone else."

"Who, if I may ask? Very few eligible young men, or men of *any* kind, come here. You're someone I could easily love, and I thought you felt the same way. I don't want to wait for many years. I'll be an old maid—and what if something happens to you, or you change your mind, where will *that* leave me?"

"I'm sorry, Maria, but I have to go back." He knew he was being a coward by not facing the situation head on, but he didn't want to tell her that he didn't want to marry her; and that was the truth. There was no reason to visit her again. Although she wrote him each month during the summer, asking when he was coming to Magnolia, he finally responded that he could come the week before college resumed.

But he didn't ride out to Magnolia to visit Maria until the weekend. She waited three days for him to come, and when he didn't show up, she had one of the slaves drive her to his grandparent's home in Charleston to see why he hadn't come. The two young people apparently missed each other in transit. When he found out from Thomas Garland that Maria had gone to Charleston, Jimmy decided to see if Louisa was home, so he walked to the main residence. When she answered the front door, she gave him a big hug and kiss and escorted him to the porch. She asked the butler to serve them something cold and sweet.

When Maria returned home, her father told her about Jim's visit and said that he was up at the residence visiting Louisa. Maria was furious. She stormed over to the main house and knocked on the front door. The butler answered and escorted her to the porch, where Louisa and Jimmy were laughing at pictures of John in his cadet uniform riding a cannon, which was what happened to cadets who received too many demerits.

Jimmy got up from his seat and offered it to Maria. "I thought you were coming on Monday," she fumed at him. "When I didn't hear from you this week, I rode to your grandparents' house to see if you were sick. That's when I found out that you were *here!*"

"I'm sorry. I got home last weekend from Savannah and was planning to come here on Monday. But it rained that week and my grandparents' roof leaked like a sieve. I had to fix it; they're too old to get on the roof, though grandfather wanted to. I finished yesterday and came this morning. I apologize for not sending you a message. I hope you'll forgive me."

"I don't know. It depends."

They excused themselves and went back to her house. She asked if he was hungry.

"I had some cookies and lemonade with Louisa."

"Dinner's at five. Perhaps you can play chess with my father while I help mother with dinner. Father has been waiting all week to play with you. So I'm not the only one you've disappointed this week!"

In spite of the discomfort raised by Maria's comments, Jim had a fine time playing chess with Thomas Garland. Jim wasn't at his level yet, but his game was good enough to make the older man take his time and calculate each move. When he declared "check mate," Thomas reached over and shook Jim's hand.

"Your game has really improved. It won't be long before I'll have to concede that you're a better player. I really enjoy your company. I don't know how you and Maria are progressing, but you can visit me any time that you want a game."

"That's very kind of you, sir."

Most of the conversation at the dinner table was between Jim and Maria's father. Maria was quiet, and didn't seem interested in discussing anything. After dinner, her mother suggested that they allow Maria and Jimmy to have the parlor.

They sat across from each other and were very quiet. "I know you're unhappy that I didn't send word that I couldn't make it here as planned. That was an oversight on my part, and I apologize. Can we put this behind us, or is it going to permeate our entire evening together? I suggest we go for walk and talk it out."

It was still light out as they made their way past Louisa's home; she was out on the front porch and waved to them as they passed by. When they got to the picnic area in a grove of trees, they sat down. He tried to put his arm around her, but she shrugged it off.

"I can only say I'm sorry so many times. I'll say it one more time, if you're interested, but that's it. This silence is making me uncomfortable."

"I accept your apology. I'm not mad any more. I'm just resigned to the fact that you don't care enough for me to let me know you wouldn't make it here as planned. I really looked forward to your visit; I was sincerely afraid that you were ill. I wanted to have something between us that would last a long time. It's not to be. Even if you made a commitment now, I wouldn't be able to rely on it. You're never going to marry me. I accept that now and will look for someone else. I'm sad that it's not you. Let's go back. I'll fix you breakfast in the morning before you leave. You were my first love."

She had said it all. There was nothing he could argue with. He really didn't want to marry her. She was a very pretty young woman, but not for him. He wondered who would come along for her. He sincerely hoped it would be someone who'd appreciate her. He rode off in the morning knowing that he wouldn't be coming back to visit her again. He waved to Louisa as he left.

CHAPTER ELEVEN

College seemed to fly by for James. He came home the first summer and worked in Charleston at a cotton clearing house. His employers were so impressed with his work ethics that they offered him a permanent position, but he respectfully declined. "I promised my father and grandparents that I'd complete college before seeking full-time employment."

College was an absolute joy for him. He found that his chosen field of study, History, with some subjects in International Relations, was interesting and relevant in the late 1830s. His studies were enhanced by the lively conversations he had with his grandfather and some of his classmates who were from England, France and Spain.

Maria Garland had found someone she liked and who was interested in making a commitment, which James himself was not. They had quarreled on his last visit to Magnolia, so Jim spent part of the day with Louisa, catching up on what John was doing at West Point. He knew that Louisa's father was having some aging pains, and with no male siblings, it fell to her to manage the cotton plantation.

As a Southerner, he was expected to defend the South's position toward slavery and secession whenever there was a class discussion concerning those issues. He understood the position of many of his southern friends, but it was absurd for anyone to think that just because a person was born in South Carolina, he would favor his state's view on that subject. But what was rewarding to James was the fact that the more he argued for the southern position, the more he was convinced that he had a northern or European view. Luckily, he was able to disguise his real views. During his second year of college he was on the debating team, and they hosted a team from the University of Pennsylvania. A panel of professors representing both universities introduced the premise, "The South is being cheated out of their wealth by the North."

The Pennsylvania team of three students, including one from London, England, was tasked with defending the premise, while James and two other students took the opposite view. They worked together and had one week to prepare their arguments. The winning team was assured a grade of A by their respective University.

On the day of the debate, four professors, two from each school, volunteered to determine the winner of the debate. The team defending the proposition started off.

The first speaker argued that "economic inequality of the South results in the majority of banking, shipping and international trade being concentrated in the North. Therefore, the marketing of exports is centered in New York City. Any southern planter sending his cotton to England receives a Bill of Exchange from a northern financial institution, to be paid in sixty or ninety days. Waiting out the sixty to ninety days is, in many cases, an imposition; therefore, the planter generally exchanges the Bill for ready cash. With the market for this transaction in New York City, the result is that he receives a discounted amount on the money owed to him."

The second speaker continued the argument. "If the demand for the Bill is low, the planter suffers because the value of the Bill is depressed. The planter also feels that if the demand for the Bill is high, some speculator in the North will buy the note and pay the par value to the planter, thereby reaping a profit. Southerners feel that there is a vicious speculative cycle in the cotton market, and in each case, rewards the North."

The final speaker for the premise argued that "the North is in complete control of the banking system, and this works a hardship on the South. Heavy tribute is paid to the North's shipping interests, who carry the bulk of the goods internationally. The South needs to be free of this northern dominance. Banking and manufacturing must be brought back to the South. We want New Orleans as the banking capital of America. The ports of Charleston, Savannah and Mobile should be used as the terminus of European lines, not only Boston and New York. There is a migration of wealth from the South to the North, which makes the South subservient to their whims; whenever there is a panic in the North, we must suffer.

"In summary, we produce King Cotton; yet, we're at the mercy of the banking interests in the North and the speculators who function as our middlemen. We provide the raw materials for the manufacturers in the North even though we are the great wealth-producing section of this country. American commerce, whether incoming or outgoing, should begin in the South."

James was the first from his group to argue against the premise. "The South has essentially an agrarian economy, based on a vast use of slaves, to maintain a plantation style of living and make cotton King. The North seeks a liberal immigration policy to provide an abundance of cheap labor, and a sound monetary system to provide improvements in roads, canals and harbor facilities which are blocked by southern votes in the congress. These southern congressmen use their voting power, inflated due to the three-fifths rule, to control committees and thereby stymie federal legislation. They want a status quo."

James could feel the passion and intensity in the other group's arguments, and sympathized with them, but if the South wasn't willing to allow immigration of cheap labor to stimulate investment in factories, they would be married to slavery forever. Though it wasn't an issue in the discussion, James voiced his concern whether the majority in the South really thought that slavery was economically sound. He wondered if they weren't tied to a social framework they were reluctant to discard or perhaps come out against. "The South is on a runaway train that won't stop or slow down to allow the moderates in their region to get off."

At the end of the debate, those supporting the premise were declared the winners. He wasn't the least surprised.

CHAPTER TWELVE

Near the end of his third year of college, Jimmy knew that he wanted to study abroad. He'd made many acquaintances with other students from England, Spain and France who were in his classes. He expanded his major to include International Relations. He and Maria were no longer seeing each other, and from what he heard from John, she was smitten with James Longstreet, his classmate from West Point.

When the school year ended, Jim returned to work in Savannah. His position was that of a clerk. But in his second year with the company, he was allowed to expand his duties. He entered into several factoring contracts on small lots. He was also involved in a myriad of small transactions, from purchasing cotton from clients to buying odd lots for others. He handled some financing, provided supplies to plantations, and passed on advice relating to economic conditions of the market to their customers. Sometimes he was asked about the advisability of selling or withholding the product to wait for better market conditions. Knowing his limitations, he forwarded those requests to more seasoned agents.

Because of the number of questions posed by clients, he was tasked to write an advisory letter on economic conditions of the cotton market. He wasn't so naïve as to think that his opinion mattered, so he'd prepare the newsletter and have his supervisor correct or add to it before sending it to their clients. Subsequently, this document was furnished to plantation owners in the area and to financial markets in New York City. Soon, he was wired directly by cotton factors and financiers seeking his opinion; he always responded after making sure that his manager approved of the advice he was forwarding. He liked the action in the market. Previously, he'd ruled this out as his future profession; now it seemed to have some merit.

One day, a gentleman he'd never met was escorted to his little desk at the rear of the clearing house. He introduced himself as Franklin Dexter Lee. "I hear you write a newsletter summarizing the conditions in the cotton market."

"Yes, sir, but I have a lot of help in developing the opinions stated in the journal. Is there a problem?"

"Not unless you won't give me a copy." He was smiling at James. "How often do you make up this type of document?"

"Initially, it was an annual publication, but recently my employer wants it published on a monthly basis while I'm here. I leave near the end of August and return to the University of South Carolina, where I'll be a senior. So I'll only be involved in one more edition after this one."

"I'm hosting a party at my home next Saturday. I'd be honored if you'd accept my invitation. Just so you know, there'll be about ten young women around your age, and if I don't say so myself, they're all real beauties. What is your name, young man?"

"James Stephen Harris."

The social life in Savannah for a young man of twenty-one was fantastic. There were so many young women in the city; James was invited to many parties held in some of the most fabulous homes that he'd ever seen. Previously, his only exposure to large homes was at Magnolia and Rosebud. While the mansions on the plantations were grand and fashionable, Lee's home was plush. The tapestries, the paintings and the furnishings were magnificent. James self-consciously wiped off his boots as he entered the large entryway. The party was in full swing as he and another clerk from the factoring company made their way to the main room. Black men and women were serving champagne and appetizers to the guests. Being young men, the two helped themselves to the food. Mr. Lee saw James enter and walked over and greeted him. "Let me introduce you to some of the young women. I know you don't want to talk to old folks like me."

There were three young women standing by the stairs talking to each other as Lee and James walked up to them. "Ladies, this is James Harris, a student at U.S.C. and a clerk for a factoring company in town. He's a bright young man, and good-looking to boot. I'll leave you here, young man, and let them introduce themselves to you. See how you navigate with three women. If you can, you're really a good man." He laughed out loud as he walked away.

One of the women had red hair, another was a blonde, and the third a brunette. The young redheaded woman introduced herself as Sarah Ann Lee.

James looked surprised.

"Yes, I'm my father's daughter," said the redhead, "and he was correct, you *are* good looking."

James smiled. The other two women were Jane Muirfield and Alicia Jones. James didn't have much time to get acquainted with either, because he was led away by Sarah Lee. "You don't think I'm going to share you with those two vultures! My father told me about you. It seems that you have an admirer in him as well." She squeezed his hand to accentuate her position.

He wasn't much of a dancer, but she more than made up for his shortcomings and glided beautifully in his arms as they waltzed around the dance floor. She was wearing a flowing pink dress, and to Jim, she was by far the prettiest woman at the party—and she definitely knew it. He was flattered that she would take an interest in him.

"You obviously could have your pick in this crowd— why me?" he asked her.

"Why, sir, you're too modest. My father told me a good deal about you, and I wanted to get to know you. Are you shy because I'm so forward?"

"Not in the least. I enjoy a spirited woman, and if she's as pretty as you, I'm more than delighted to be with her. May I get you some punch?"

"Don't use the bowl in the middle of the table. It has nothing in it. The one on the right has the *real* punch." She pointed to a bowl monitored by one of the black waiters.

She wasn't where he had left her when he returned with the punch. He walked around for a few minutes and found her seated on a couch in a large sitting room. There was only one other couple in the room, but they were admiring one of paintings on the wall. As James entered, they strolled away and he and Sarah were left alone.

"This is a beautiful room. I've not been in one that is this outstanding."

"Oh, I don't want to talk about the weather and things like that. I want to know how long you plan to be in Savannah."

"Until the end of August."

"Have you been to Savannah before?"

"Yes. I was here last summer working for the same company. If my employer agrees, I'll come back next summer. I'm fascinated with financing. I'd like to learn a little more about international financing, and hopefully make that my profession in life."

To her question, James told her about his early life, his parents, and his best friend, John William Beauregard.

"Do you have a girl friend?"

He laughed and had another sip of his drink. "I feel as though I'm interviewing for a job. No. I had a girl friend, but we drifted apart—and since you're going to ask me why, I'll tell you. I wasn't ready to make a commitment, and she felt she wanted one."

"Will I see you again?"

"I'd like that very much, and next time I'd like to know a lot more about *you*."

"That's fair enough. I'm away this week, but I'll return next Saturday. Would you come to dinner on Sunday evening? It's formal, but if you don't have formal clothes, a nice suit would do for the first time."

She leaned into him on the couch, and he kissed her firmly on the lips; she didn't break away. In fact, she put her hand around his neck, opened her mouth, and met his tongue with hers. "That was delightful. I enjoyed it very much. Can I count on you next Sunday at six p.m.?"

"I *do* have dress clothes, and yes—I'll be here."

He hadn't realized how quickly the evening had passed. It was eleven o'clock, and her father entered the room just after their kiss. "Sarah, our guests are leaving. I wonder if you'd join me in saying goodnight to them."

"I'll be right there, as soon as I say good night to Mr. Harris."

She led him out to the entryway and told him to remember about Sunday; then she joined her father at the door wishing their guests a nice evening.

Outside, the other young man who had come to the party with Jimmy was waiting for him. His name was Francis Limon. "I have two passes to the Deluxe House of Pleasure downtown. How about you going with me and see what we're missing?"

Normally James would have declined the invitation, but after three glasses of champagne, he was receptive. "Lead the way!"

Whereas the Lee Mansion was elegant, The Deluxe Pleasure House was ornate, gaudy and plush. The house, in a modest section of town, had a bar room to the left of the entryway, a plush parlor directly ahead, and a room beyond that, where a gentleman could relax with a cigar. Twelve rooms were on the second floor. The walls on the first-floor rooms were covered with pictures and paintings of nudes in suggestive sexual positions. The carpet was deep red, and the chairs and lounges were covered with a blue satin material. After presenting their letter of introduction, both boys went to the bar room and had a glass of champagne. There were seven different women in the room who were either sitting on a couch or resting against a wall.

Most of the hostesses were in their early twenties, except for one woman, called Madam, who appeared to be in her late thirties. James recognized some of the customers of his firm and at least one local politician. When his acquaintance said he was going upstairs, Jim said he'd wait in the lounge. Soon a young woman sat down next to him and asked if she could pleasure him.

"I'm sorry, miss, I've never been here before, and I think I just want to watch. Maybe when I come back, I might want to be—*pleasured,* as you call it."

He knew that condoms were being used, but from what he heard, they didn't protect anyone from disease. Most of these pleasure houses had a physician on call, but Jim didn't want to take a chance. Syphilis was common in the South.

The first time he had experienced intercourse was at the Catawba village when he was sixteen, with one of the maidens from the village. He and she had gone swimming at a remote lake in the village where many of the young people were swimming in the nude; they immediately joined in, and he wasn't the least embarrassed. Later in the afternoon, the others drifted back to the village, and when they were alone, he and Maiden Magic had intercourse. Why she didn't become pregnant was a mystery to him. It seemed that the girls in the village became aware of sex early in life and seemed to have a method of restricting pregnancy. Whatever they did was all right with him; he thoroughly enjoyed his stay there. When he returned the next summer, he was happy to see Maiden Magic, and they enjoyed many of these "swimming sessions," as she called them.

CHAPTER THIRTEEN

Charleston had a significant harbor and was therefore a large exporter of cotton to Europe. Annually, the ultimate purchasers and sometimes middlemen came to the South Carolina city to have a conference on the cotton market. One of these men, Harold Phelps, came for another reason. His son, George, was a classmate of James, and when he came to America, the father took the two young men out to dinner several times. His son, like Jimmy, was studying International Relations and Financing. But unlike Jim, he'd go home for the summer and work in his father's manufacturing plants, learning the business. Mr. Phelps was surprised that his son's friend was also the author of a monthly newsletter out of Savannah that was valuable to men in his profession.

During one of their outings, Mr. Phelps asked James how it was that he, a college student, had such an insight into cotton futures.

"I've worked one summer in Charleston and the past two summers in Savannah. I really have a lot of help in developing the opinions. They're not all coming from me."

"I appreciate your modesty, but I don't believe your employer would trust you with this task unless you were up to it. What are your future plans after graduation?"

"I haven't finalized them yet, other than the fact that I would like to pursue International Relations and Financing as a career."

"I have a suggestion for you, young man. Why don't you do your post-graduate work at Oxford in my country? There's no finer educational institution in the world for the profession that you seem to be choosing. Our family owns a home in Oxford with several guest cottages. We can provide housing for you if you decide to attend. George is also planning to complete his education there. I think he'd enjoy it if you'd come over."

"I appreciate the offer, and that's something to consider. I'll talk it over with my father and grandfather."

The dinner was, as Sarah Ann had indicated, very formal. There were ten people in attendance. The two main guests were the U.S. senators from South Carolina, who came with their wives and aides. Making up the remainder were Jimmy, Sarah Lee, her father and the mayor of Charleston. Jimmy knew that he was out of his element here, so he'd just have to make the best of it. After dinner, the men adjourned to the smoking room and the women to the parlor.

The two U.S. senators were amiable; they asked James what he was doing and didn't attempt to patronize him. When told of his writing about cotton production, the Charleston mayor asked James what he thought of the future of the South.

"There are men here tonight who are better qualified than I to discuss this subject."

One of the senators was so impressed with his response that he insisted that Jimmy share his view. "My grandfather taught for several years at the University of South Carolina. He was an expert in the field of foreign relations. If you don't mind, I'll give you my grandfather's view. Cotton is king in the south, and the plantations are making enormous amounts of money. His concern about sustainability would be on several levels. First, the overuse of the land for cotton could take all the nutrients from the soil and leave the South with poor crops until the land replenishes itself; their economy would thereby take a serious hit. Second, while the South is moving toward world dominance in cotton as the basis of their economy, the North is industrializing. New England, for example, is becoming a textile giant. Factories are springing up and non-agricultural jobs are being created. If the South is to prosper, it should try to industrialize to protect its future. Why not build textile factories here? They'd be closer to the raw product."

The men in the room were stunned. They didn't expect such a candid view from someone who was only twenty-one. "I can see what our host sees in you, young man. I don't agree with your grandfather's argument, but I like the analysis that you made. What was your grandfather's name?" one of the senators asked.

"Frederick Hendricks."

Sarah Ann had overheard James' argument, and she was pleased, but she realized that he was in over his head and decided to rescue him. "Father, you're monopolizing my escort. Do you mind if I have some words with him alone?" She smiled to all the other men in the room and was rewarded with comments on how beautiful she looked.

"I heard your speech, James. Those men don't really care what you have to say—they've made up their minds years ago, and you can't change it. But I do admire how you were able to hold your own in such distinguished company. I've become more impressed with you since the last time we met. How about giving me a spin around the porch? Nobody will miss us."

He squeezed her hand. "Make it somewhere secluded. I haven't kissed you in a week!"

When he left for Charleston at the end of the summer, it was with the understanding that Sarah Ann would write to him at his college. He didn't realize that she'd write every week, and when the Christmas holidays arrived, so did she and her father for a week. He introduced them to his father and grandparents and was able to share Christmas Eve and Christmas Day with her and her father at his grandfather's modest home before they returned to Savannah.

He'd applied for Oxford and was accepted just before graduation. He decided to spend the summer in Savannah to make some money and be near Sarah. By this time he was in love with the beautiful redhead and hoped that she felt the same way. The problem was still the same as with Maria. He didn't want a commitment until he was sure he could handle the responsibility; he wasn't sure Sarah would wait. There were too many beaux who would make the commitment to her now.

John and Louisa's wedding was a couple of weeks off and Jim asked Sarah if she'd accompany him to Magnolia for the wedding. "There's plenty of room at the plantation, and Mr. and Mrs. Harrison assured me that they'd act as chaperons for the weekend. If that isn't convenient, you can stay at my grandparents' house and I'll stay with a friend. We'd go up on Friday and come home on Monday. What do you think?"

"Do you think father could come? In that way, there'd be no need for a chaperon. I think we could get accommodations in Charleston and therefore we wouldn't be a bother to Louisa's parents. They have enough to do without having some house guests. Would I get to meet your old girlfriend?"

"Probably, but why would you want to?"

"Just checking out the competition, that's all."

CHAPTER FOURTEEN

Louisa looked so beautiful coming down the aisle on her father's arm. Jimmy remembered the first time he saw how spirited she was, and he wondered if his friend John knew what was in store for him. Jimmy was the best man, and newly commissioned Lieutenants James Longstreet and William S. Rosecrans were the groomsmen. Someone Jimmy had never met was the maid of honor—John said she was a distant cousin. He was surprised that Maria Garland wasn't part of the wedding party. Right after the wedding, Jimmy could feel the tension when he, Longstreet and Rosecrans had their photographs taken with the bridal couple. That's when Maria and Sarah came face to face. Though they were cordial, it was obvious they were giving each other a critical examination. Jimmy smiled when he saw Louisa looking at Sarah and then back at him. There was a huge smile on her face.

The guest list was a kind of *Who's Who in the South.* Magnolia was an economic powerhouse in the Charleston vicinity, and anyone who was anyone was there. Jimmy's father and his lady friend, Abigail Stanton, the widow of the British ambassador to Washington, as well as his grandparents had all been invited by the Harrisons. When they were alone, Sarah said that Maria was very pretty, but seemed cold. She waited for a reaction from Jimmy, but he was smart enough to change the subject. But it was the kiss that Louisa had given James that brought the best comment. "That woman has designs on you!"

"We're just good friends. She's my best friend's wife now, and both of us respect that. Once you get to know her, you'll like her spirit. Her father is turning over management of the plantation to her."

"How is that going to work?"

"I really don't know, but they've loved each other since they were teenagers, so I think they'll figure it out."

Sarah was looking around to see who else was there, and spotted her father with a handsome woman. "It looks like my father has found a companion for the evening. Are you going to ask me to dance?"

"Absolutely!" They walked over to the dance floor installed in the middle of all the tables near where the guests were sitting.

Jimmy held her tightly, and she put her hand around the nape of his neck. His temperature began to rise. "I like it when you hold me this way," she murmured, pressing her body close to his.

It was inevitable that Longstreet and Maria would be on the dance floor at the same time. It was also inevitable that when the music stopped, they would approach Jimmy and Sarah on the floor. "Jimmy, aren't you going to introduce your friend to Lt. Longstreet and myself?"

When introductions were made, Maria asked Sarah, "Where are you from, Miss Lee?"

"I'm from Savannah—that's where I met this handsome man I'm with tonight." Jimmy stiffened.

Luckily the music started again, and Longstreet navigated Maria to another side of the dance floor. Jimmy felt that he had dodged a bullet.

"She still likes you," Sarah declared, watching them go.

"What difference does it make? I'm with *you*—and I like you better than her or Louisa. If you were concerned about me, don't be."

"Oh, I wasn't concerned in the least." She reached up and kissed him on the lips. Other dancers turned and looked at the handsome young couple.

As they started to mingle with other people, Louisa mounted the stage that had been made especially for the wedding and prepared to toss her bouquet of flowers. As the band struck up a tune, she tossed them into the crowd. Sarah Lee was strategically placed among the young women hoping to catch the flowers, and she snatched them out of the air just as Maria Garland reached for them. As she headed back to James, she smiled at Maria.

"You are more amazing every time I see you," James told Sarah as she walked up to him with a wide smile on her face.

"Am I amazing enough to love?"

"Yes, you are."

"Am I amazing enough to want to spend the rest of your life with?"

"Sarah, I've been waiting to tell you that I have been accepted to Oxford University in England for two years of graduate studies in International Financing. I leave on the fifteenth of August. I don't have a job yet, and I'm not ready for marriage for at least two years. I can't ask you to wait that long!"

"London would be a fantastic place to have a honeymoon! I love you, James. What's the problem? I don't want to wait two more years; that doesn't make sense, unless you don't love me."

Just then Franklin Lee came up to the couple and told James how delighted he was that he had been able to secure an invitation to the wedding for himself and his daughter. He had apparently overheard part of their conversation, and asked James if they could talk in private.

"I learned from your father that you've been accepted at Oxford for their graduate program. I know that your finances are limited, but your father seems to think that he and your grandfather can handle it. I also understand that your employer has an office in London and wants you to work there the two summers you're abroad. I know you love my daughter. The main question is, would you marry her, if your finances were sufficient?"

"I love your daughter, and I would like to marry her, but not until I can support a wife."

"I admire your code. However, I have a business proposition for you that would make it feasible for you to marry Sarah and still go to school. I'll lend you fifteen thousand dollars toward an employment position in my firm in Savannah. The term of employment is for ten years. You'd be expected to repay the debt out of your wages, spread over the entire ten years. Now that's a sound business proposition that I believe you can't turn down—unless my daughter says no."

"Sir, before I give you my answer, I'd like to talk it over with Sarah."

"You're smarter than you look, young man!"

He found Sarah sitting with his father and Abigail. "We wondered where you've been," Abigail said as he sat down next to his father. "We've been fascinated talking to your pretty friend."

"I've been wrestling with a problem and trying to figure how to solve it. I wonder if you and Dad would mind if Sarah and I went off by ourselves for a bit. We'll be back shortly."

He led her to a bench that circled one of the large trees on the plantation, where he sat down and asked her to sit with him for a bit. "Sarah, I'm very much in love with you, but I didn't think there was a chance for marriage until your father gave me an option today.

"What he said to me didn't change my feelings toward you—you are beautiful, bright, and fun to be with. What he pointed out was that I may be foregoing happiness when I don't need to." He paused and took a breath. "I know I'm making a mess out of this, but I want to marry you and take you with me to England!"

"You're right," she agreed, her cheek dimpling. "You tried to mess it up—but you didn't! I love you with all my heart, and I'd be proud to be your wife. We're going to have a great life together. What a wonderful place to have a honeymoon! A week on the boat, and whatever time we have in England, is a dream come true! I have great faith in you. My only regret is that my mother isn't here to share in this wonderful occasion. Let's find our parents and tell them the good news." She grabbed his hand and pulled him up.

It was Jimmy's father and his lady friend who were the first to be told, and they were delighted. "I knew this was going to happen once I met Sarah," Abigail Stanton said.

Sarah's father cried openly when they told him their decision. "I liked you from the first moment I was introduced to you," he beamed, "and it was I who told my daughter about you."

"You don't know how happy I am that you did," Jimmy assured him. "She's wonderful. I'll be the best husband I can be, and I'll cherish her forever. I'll always try to make you proud to be my father-in-law."

This was John and Louisa's day, of course, and Jimmy didn't want to tell them about the new plans he had with Sarah. It still hadn't sunk in, anyway. He had been certain he was going to lose Sarah, because he couldn't see how he could have her and pursue his goal at the same time, but her father's offer had been generous and fair, and he was happy that his future father-in-law had suggested it.

CHAPTER FOURTEEN

Louisa looked so beautiful coming down the aisle on her father's arm. Jimmy remembered the first time he saw how spirited she was, and he wondered if his friend John knew what was in store for him. Jimmy was the best man, and newly commissioned Lieutenants James Longstreet and William S. Rosecrans were the groomsmen. Someone Jimmy had never met was the maid of honor—John said she was a distant cousin. He was surprised that Maria Garland wasn't part of the wedding party. Right after the wedding, Jimmy could feel the tension when he, Longstreet and Rosecrans had their photographs taken with the bridal couple. That's when Maria and Sarah came face to face. Though they were cordial, it was obvious they were giving each other a critical examination. Jimmy smiled when he saw Louisa looking at Sarah and then back at him. There was a huge smile on her face.

The guest list was a kind of *Who's Who in the South*. Magnolia was an economic powerhouse in the Charleston vicinity, and anyone who was anyone was there. Jimmy's father and his lady friend, Abigail Stanton, the widow of the British ambassador to Washington, as well as his grandparents had all been invited by the Harrisons. When they were alone, Sarah said that Maria was very pretty, but seemed cold. She waited for a reaction from Jimmy, but he was smart enough to change the subject. But it was the kiss that Louisa had given James that brought the best comment. "That woman has designs on you!"

"We're just good friends. She's my best friend's wife now, and both of us respect that. Once you get to know her, you'll like her spirit. Her father is turning over management of the plantation to her."

"How is that going to work?"

"I really don't know, but they've loved each other since they were teenagers, so I think they'll figure it out."

Sarah was looking around to see who else was there, and spotted her father with a handsome woman. "It looks like my father has found a companion for the evening. Are you going to ask me to dance?"

"Absolutely!" They walked over to the dance floor installed in the middle of all the tables near where the guests were sitting.

Jimmy held her tightly, and she put her hand around the nape of his neck. His temperature began to rise. "I like it when you hold me this way," she murmured, pressing her body close to his.

It was inevitable that Longstreet and Maria would be on the dance floor at the same time. It was also inevitable that when the music stopped, they would approach Jimmy and Sarah on the floor. "Jimmy, aren't you going to introduce your friend to Lt. Longstreet and myself?"

When introductions were made, Maria asked Sarah, "Where are you from, Miss Lee?"

"I'm from Savannah—that's where I met this handsome man I'm with tonight." Jimmy stiffened.

Luckily the music started again, and Longstreet navigated Maria to another side of the dance floor. Jimmy felt that he had dodged a bullet.

"She still likes you," Sarah declared, watching them go.

"What difference does it make? I'm with *you*—and I like you better than her or Louisa. If you were concerned about me, don't be."

"Oh, I wasn't concerned in the least." She reached up and kissed him on the lips. Other dancers turned and looked at the handsome young couple.

As they started to mingle with other people, Louisa mounted the stage that had been made especially for the wedding and prepared to toss her bouquet of flowers. As the band struck up a tune, she tossed them into the crowd. Sarah Lee was strategically placed among the young women hoping to catch the flowers, and she snatched them out of the air just as Maria Garland reached for them. As she headed back to James, she smiled at Maria.

"You are more amazing every time I see you," James told Sarah as she walked up to him with a wide smile on her face.

"Am I amazing enough to love?"

"Yes, you are."

"Am I amazing enough to want to spend the rest of your life with?"

"Sarah, I've been waiting to tell you that I have been accepted to Oxford University in England for two years of graduate studies in International Financing. I leave on the fifteenth of August. I don't have a job yet, and I'm not ready for marriage for at least two years. I can't ask you to wait that long!"

"London would be a fantastic place to have a honeymoon! I love you, James. What's the problem? I don't want to wait two more years; that doesn't make sense, unless you don't love me."

Just then Franklin Lee came up to the couple and told James how delighted he was that he had been able to secure an invitation to the wedding for himself and his daughter. He had apparently overheard part of their conversation, and asked James if they could talk in private.

"I learned from your father that you've been accepted at Oxford for their graduate program. I know that your finances are limited, but your father seems to think that he and your grandfather can handle it. I also understand that your employer has an office in London and wants you to work there the two summers you're abroad. I know you love my daughter. The main question is, would you marry her, if your finances were sufficient?"

"I love your daughter, and I would like to marry her, but not until I can support a wife."

"I admire your code. However, I have a business proposition for you that would make it feasible for you to marry Sarah and still go to school. I'll lend you fifteen thousand dollars toward an employment position in my firm in Savannah. The term of employment is for ten years. You'd be expected to repay the debt out of your wages, spread over the entire ten years. Now that's a sound business proposition that I believe you can't turn down—unless my daughter says no."

"Sir, before I give you my answer, I'd like to talk it over with Sarah."

"You're smarter than you look, young man!"

He found Sarah sitting with his father and Abigail. "We wondered where you've been," Abigail said as he sat down next to his father. "We've been fascinated talking to your pretty friend."

"I've been wrestling with a problem and trying to figure how to solve it. I wonder if you and Dad would mind if Sarah and I went off by ourselves for a bit. We'll be back shortly."

He led her to a bench that circled one of the large trees on the plantation, where he sat down and asked her to sit with him for a bit. "Sarah, I'm very much in love with you, but I didn't think there was a chance for marriage until your father gave me an option today.

"What he said to me didn't change my feelings toward you—you are beautiful, bright, and fun to be with. What he pointed out was that I may be foregoing happiness when I don't need to." He paused and took a breath. "I know I'm making a mess out of this, but I want to marry you and take you with me to England!"

"You're right," she agreed, her cheek dimpling. "You tried to mess it up—but you didn't! I love you with all my heart, and I'd be proud to be your wife. We're going to have a great life together. What a wonderful place to have a honeymoon! A week on the boat, and whatever time we have in England, is a dream come true! I have great faith in you. My only regret is that my mother isn't here to share in this wonderful occasion. Let's find our parents and tell them the good news." She grabbed his hand and pulled him up.

It was Jimmy's father and his lady friend who were the first to be told, and they were delighted. "I knew this was going to happen once I met Sarah," Abigail Stanton said.

Sarah's father cried openly when they told him their decision. "I liked you from the first moment I was introduced to you," he beamed, "and it was I who told my daughter about you."

"You don't know how happy I am that you did," Jimmy assured him. "She's wonderful. I'll be the best husband I can be, and I'll cherish her forever. I'll always try to make you proud to be my father-in-law."

This was John and Louisa's day, of course, and Jimmy didn't want to tell them about the new plans he had with Sarah. It still hadn't sunk in, anyway. He had been certain he was going to lose Sarah, because he couldn't see how he could have her and pursue his goal at the same time, but her father's offer had been generous and fair, and he was happy that his future father-in-law had suggested it.

CHAPTER FIFTEEN

Louisa's parents had booked a room for themselves at the Charleston Hotel for three nights, so the bridal couple could have the Magnolia Mansion to themselves.

The big surprise to John and Louisa had been the young woman whom Jimmy Harris had brought to the wedding— he hadn't mentioned the red-haired beauty to either of the newly married couple. They wondered if she was a cousin of sorts, or was it someone serious? Louisa wondered why Jimmy didn't introduce the girl to them. She did, however, catch Maria Garland glaring at the young woman.

It had been a long engagement period for the couple, and after the bride threw the traditional bouquet of flowers to her maids of honor, the couple quietly left the party and went directly to the main house. John carried Louisa up a flight of stairs to her parents' room, which was redecorated as a bridal suite. "Do you realize how long I've waited for this?" Louisa said as he set her on her feet in the room.

He kissed her for a long time and then started to undress her, but he was all thumbs as he tried to undo the tiny buttons on her dress. "Stop that—I'll do it," she smiled at him.

Louisa didn't show the embarrassment of a normal bride as she let the last piece of clothing fall to the floor. He couldn't control the astonishment on his face as he looked at his beautiful young wife standing before him, completely nude. He wondered how he had been so lucky. She put her arms around his neck and kissed him with an open mouth. He couldn't get his clothes off fast enough, and finally he lifted her in his arms and carefully laid her on the bed. "You are so beautiful," he said.

He stroked her thighs; she spread her legs and moaned as he touched and fingered the spot between her legs while sucking on her nipples. When he finally entered her, she screamed as she felt the delicious pain for the first time. Unsure of what to do, she followed his moves and mirrored his rhythm. When she surrendered to the throes of excitement, she held on to him as though she'd never let go. When he climaxed shortly after her, they lay in each others arms for nearly an hour until the mood presented itself again. This time John took his time and Louisa enjoyed her climax even more. "Is that what I've been missing all these years?" she whispered.

"I hope so," he murmured in her ear. She laughed and squeezed his arm.

"I don't know where you learned all those things you did to me—I really don't want to know! I'm just glad you knew more than me. I've watched some of our slaves do it, but they don't know anything compared to you . . . you devil . . ."

The next day, they walked around the plantation holding hands. Those who came upon the young couple gave them a wide berth and didn't try to intrude on their time. Dinner for two was in the main dining room, sitting at opposite ends of the table. "Tomorrow, I'd like to take a ride out to one of the ponds on Magnolia," she told him afterwards. "I want to do it on the ground somewhere, and especially in a carriage. You can humor your wife's fantasy, can't you?"

He grinned. "I'm more than obliged."

"I want to it do as much as we can while we're young. I just know I'll get pregnant soon and be expected to behave like a lady once I become a mother, and then there's Magnolia that I must manage."

"You can always hire someone to do that."

"Not on your life! Women aren't given the opportunity that I have, and I'll not give it up for anything."

They found a secluded place a half mile from Magnolia and parked under a shady tree. Louisa peeled off all her clothes and walked around the carriage like a free soul. "Come join me under the tree. Don't worry if someone comes by—they'll be more embarrassed than us. This is a once in a lifetime for us, so let's enjoy it!"

He knelt down in front of her and held both her breasts in his hands, feeling them, kissing each and then sucking on them until she yelled, "Do it!"

"I love you, John. Don't you ever forget it!"

Soon she rose and knelt down in front of him. "I watched one of the plantation girls do this, and her male friend went crazy. I hope you enjoy."

She grabbed his penis, kissed the top and gradually, as though teasing him, sucked it until he gasped. "My God, Louisa, you're going to be the death of me—but it's going to be a sweet death."

"You know, I like walking around without any clothes on. Let's do it when we get back to the house. I'll have all the servants leave and we'll be alone. I'll tell them not to come back until breakfast tomorrow. Maybe we can think of a few more ways to do it. I've watched our plantation people do some odd things. Maybe we can do the same."

Before leaving, they made love in the carriage, and when the sun started to go down, they drove back to Magnolia. Louisa had a pensive look. "What kind of assignment do you expect?" she asked.

"It isn't official yet, but I've been led to believe that I'll join Longstreet and be on General Winfield Scott's staff in Louisiana. I think P.G.T. Beauregard is there. With an engineering degree from the academy, I hope my assignment is in that field. My grades were high in all aspects of engineering. It was the military subjects that I was deficient in; still, I finished fifteenth in my class. I don't know whether I want to be apart from you very long, so I hope to come back within six months and take you with me."

"Let's not quarrel, but I can't leave Magnolia for very long. I can only visit you for a month at a time. We're expanding right now, and I must be here to make sure that what I put in place is accomplished."

"Okay, no quarrelling on the honeymoon. Let's go back so I can see that beautiful butt of yours. I'd like to bite it!"

CHAPTER SIXTEEN

Three days later the newly engaged young couple, with the future bride sporting an engagement ring, drove out to Magnolia and met the recently married John and Louisa. Sarah couldn't control herself, and just blurted out that they were engaged. Jimmy had always seen his fiancée as cool and collected, but she showed an emotional side that was fun to watch. He hadn't realized that she wanted to marry him so much. How could he get so lucky? That's what John said when told of the news. They were spared a confrontation with Maria, who heard the news from one of the servants who attended the lunch the two young couples were enjoying.

John had known Jimmy for eight years. They had spent summers together, shared dreams, and had gone on that adventuresome trip to the Blue Ridge Mountains. They were best friends, but now he was thrown for a loop when he found out that Jimmy was going to marry Sarah Lee that very summer and go to England on their honeymoon. "You never let on that you and Sarah were serious," John told Jim. "In fact, this is the first I ever heard of her!"

"Well, it's not a surprise to me. I've loved her for almost two years, but I thought that my finances were such that I couldn't afford to take the next step in our relationship."

"Boy, talk about a close-mouthed individual! You could carry the nation's secrets, and no one would know anything," Louisa said.

"I know both of you are talking about me," Sarah interjected. "I've loved Jimmy from the first moment we were introduced in my father's home. Jimmy has spent the last three summers in Savannah, and we've been seeing each other, maybe not exclusively at first, but for the past two years I've not dated any other men. If he wouldn't marry me, I was going to shoot him, so I guess he had no choice." Louisa couldn't control a wide smile. She knew what Sarah meant.

"But this creates some problems with us," Louisa frowned thoughtfully. "John wants to be James' best man. He hasn't received an official assignment yet, but he's been told that he'll be on Gen. Winfield Scott's engineering staff in New Orleans. John has thirty days' leave. We were going to spend ten days here and then go to New Orleans. What we'll probably do is go to New Orleans early, check into the post and see if they'll allow us to come to Savannah for your wedding. We won't know the answer until we get to New Orleans. Have I summarized that correctly, John?"

"I couldn't have said it better myself."

"I understand your problem," Jimmy acknowledged, "and yes, I want my best friend to stand up for me. But Louisa has been my friend, too, and I don't want to leave her out. The wedding date is set, but I can wait until the last minute to select the best man, if that'll help."

"Do you think Pierre can help us?" Louisa asked. "He's on Scott's staff as well. Maybe we can wire him to see what he advises. Besides, he'd probably like to come as well."

Jimmy asked George Phelps, his roommate at college, if the guest house in Oxford was still available, and whether it was big enough for himself and his bride-to-be. He also asked him to be in his wedding party, and, if necessary, to be his best man. George agreed to be his best man if John couldn't make it. He sent a letter to his father asking about the cottage. Two weeks later he received approval and made Jimmy aware that the cottage was indeed large enough for two—even three or four.

John wired P.G.T. in New Orleans, who followed up on his assignment, and yes, it was in New Orleans. He and Louisa cut their honeymoon short so they could personally seek General Scott's permission to attend the wedding in Savannah. With tensions with Native Americans in Northern Texas rising, General Scott wouldn't issue leave for anyone. In fact, John and his cousin Pierre Beauregard were temporarily assigned to a Texas garrison on the Louisiana-Texas border, leaving Louisa in New Orleans with her long-time maid. Subsequently, Louisa found out that she was pregnant, and her doctor advised against any travel. She wrote Jimmy and told him the news.

His old employer was surprised when Jim told him about his arrangement with Mr. Lee. He hated to lose the young man, but he understood

Jimmy and Sarah were married on August 14, 1842, in the Lee home in Savannah. Sarah had her hair piled on top of her head; her white wedding gown had a train of about ten feet. It seemed to James, who was standing by the altar, that the dress would never make it to the altar! Most of those in attendance were Sarah's friends and family; only Cameron and Abigail and his grandparents, from Jimmy's side, were able to attend. George Phelps was best man and his father was the groomsman.

Sarah's father had arranged transportation to England for the couple on a cargo ship that had been modified by adding two staterooms next to the captain's. The ship would leave Savannah and sail directly to Liverpool; the crossing would take ten days. Her father smiled when he told them that he had a majority interest in the vessel.

There were more surprises for young Jim before he sailed. He learned from his bride-to-be how wealthy her family actually was and that she had an annual allowance. In addition, a husband-and-wife team of servants would travel with the couple, preparing their meals and cleaning up after them on the voyage. This was Franklin Lee's wedding present. "I hope you're not going to worry that your wife is richer than you and has her own money," Sarah confided.

"The amount of money your family has was indeed a problem for me, until your father made me that proposition," Jimmy said. "I have great faith in myself, and I believe that I'll repay your father the money and justify his faith in me. You and I will love each other whether you are rich or poor. Right now, we don't have a problem with the cottage the Phelpses are lending to us; it can handle the maid and butler you're bringing. But what if you become pregnant—what happens then? Believe me, Mrs. Harris, you're going to be pregnant as quick as the parson says, I do." He placed his hands around her face and kissed her softly.

Surprisingly, neither was nervous on the day of the wedding, but when he undressed her in bed on their wedding night in her family's home, he was all thumbs. He slowly explored her body and kissed her passionately before they consummated the marriage. Her body was soft and curvy, her breasts were small but her nipples were sensitive to his touch, and when he kissed and sucked them, she let out a moan. There wasn't much dialog between them as they each explored the other's body. When he was ready again, he took more time so that they could orgasm simultaneously. "I dreamed about what this would be like, but I never dreamed it could be so wonderful," she breathed. "Thank you for being patient with me. Some of my married lady friends have told horror stories about their wedding night . . . I prayed it wouldn't be that way. You were wonderful. I want to do this as much as you want."

Their onboard cabin was small and aft on the main deck; the captain's was forward. Franklin Lee had had the staterooms added for his wealthy friends so they wouldn't have to travel to New Orleans or New York City to sail in comfort to England. He'd used the ship twice before, and knew that his daughter and her new husband would enjoy the trip.

They ran into a rainstorm the second day out and the ocean was rough, so Jimmy and Sarah spent most of the day in their cabin—which for a newly married couple wasn't an imposition at all. "I don't care if it rains every day and I don't care if the crew knows what we're doing," Sarah teased. "Just keep the champagne coming and keep that staff of yours up!"

"Wow, what a tart you've become!"

"Does it embarrass you?"

"Not one bit."

Their male servant did the cooking in the galley and stayed with his wife in another cabin on the other side of the Captain's. By the third day, the rain had stopped and the ocean was calm. Sarah and James walked around the deck after each meal and then read some of the books they had brought with them. Both were avid readers, and after making love, they'd stay awake in bed with a kerosene lamp to read by. Before he turned out the light on the fifth night on board, James leaned over to Sarah and said, "If you're not pregnant by the time we reach England, then I don't know how to do it."

"Maybe we'd better do it again just to be sure."

The next day he walked around the main deck, talking to the captain and some members of the crew, while Sarah spent most of the day writing thank-you notes and a long letter to her father. "Will we have any time in London before we have to be at Oxford?" she asked him that night.

"I think we can spend ten to fifteen days someplace after we land and before I sign in at the University. We could stay in London or go to Paris—whatever my wife desires."

"I desire *you*—and I desire you right this instant!"

They landed in Liverpool in a downpour and waited for an hour before departing the ship. Soon their carriage arrived, and they made the short trip to the railroad station, arrived in London three hours later and registered at their hotel. The concierge made reservations for the couple traveling with them at another hotel. Sarah told them they could have a ten-day holiday before she and James would travel to Oxford.

James had planned to pay for their ten-day stay in advance, but the manager assured him it wasn't necessary. If they wanted to leave before the ten days was up, it was fine with the hotel. They spent most of their first day in their room, and only went downstairs for their meals. The wind and the rain didn't make it a pleasant day for vacationing. They seemed unconcerned.

By the third day, the rain had stopped, and although it was cold and foggy, they hired a hansom cab and started touring the city. For lunch they found a sidewalk café, and although it was still quite cold, it didn't seem to bother them. "Let's spend two more days here and then go to Paris for four or five days. What do you say?" Sarah asked.

"If that's what my bride and love of my life wants, then we'll put the plan in motion."

Paris was everything that Sarah had read about. They did a day trip to Versailles, visited Montmartre, and spent two days on the left bank browsing for paintings from the many artists that frequented the river. For a few francs, an artist they admired painted a portrait of Sarah in watercolors. Back at their room, Sarah took off all her clothes and paraded in front of Jimmy. "What do you think of my beautiful dress, young sir?"

"It's how I always want to remember you!"

"I hear there are some naughty shows at the theaters in town. Would you think it appropriate if we went?"

"I'll ask the desk to recommend some plays, and ask them which would be appropriate for a refined young lady from the South."

The concierge recommended two plays and warned them against two others. According to the clerk, they were too risqué. "Well, pick one of the two that he said not to go to, and have him make reservations," Sarah said firmly. "I want to find out about all the things that young women have been cautioned against or forbidden to see. You're my husband—I expect you to educate me. I don't want to be naïve about the world!"

James pulled her to him and kissed her softly on the lips while he fondled her breasts. "That's exactly what I'll try to do."

They found the play to be amusing. Two of the women in the show displayed their breasts. During intermission, in the lobby for a glass of champagne, Sarah whispered in Jim's ear, "Mine are as big as those two women on stage."

"Bigger!"

Before going back to London, they decided to climb the Eiffel Tower steps. When they bought their tickets, they were advised not to go all the way to the top; the fog was heavy, and although there was an observation platform up there, the visibility would be nearly zero. The climb was exhausting, and the dampness made it even more of an effort, but they were undismayed and eventually made it to the top. "I think we'd better go, Sarah," Jimmy said. "There's nothing to see."

She caught his arm. "I've always fantasized about making love on the top of the Eiffel Tower. Well, we're here, and there's no one else around, so I want to be humored!"

"You've got to be crazy! What if someone came by? How would we explain it? And then there's your clothes, you couldn't put them back on in time! Let's go."

"I planned for it. I'm not wearing any underclothes except for two slips. We don't have to take our clothes off. Jimmy, I want to do this. One of my girlfriends did it on top of the Empire State Building, and she never forgot it."

He knew it was useless to argue, and besides, he was intrigued as well. He reached down, lifted her dress and petticoats, and exposed her from the waist down. She was so much smaller than he. He had no problem in opening his pants and entering her while he held her under the buttocks. She let out a cry as she orgasmed. As he set her back on her feet, she leaned against the interior wall and straightened her skirts.

"That was magnificent. I'll always remember this day and what we did here for the rest of my life. Thank you for satisfying my fantasy. Now I can become the good little wife that you expect." She placed her arms around his neck and kissed him with an open mouth.

James led her to the steps and they took their time going back down. It was cold and nearly five in the evening. He really felt married at this moment, and, like her, he'd remember this moment for the rest of his days. "Sarah, I'd rather have you this way than a dowdy, compliant companion."

After nearly a week in Paris, they returned to their hotel in London for a few days before reuniting with their help and travelling to the University at Oxford. The direction George Phelps had given him to their cottage was spot on. His father had stocked the pantry with wine and champagne, some caviar and a lot of crackers. It wasn't as spartan as described by George; it was an English home with three bedrooms, a kitchen, dining room and drawing room. Best of all, they were only ten to fifteen minutes by foot from the Oxford campus. "James, you can have one of the bedrooms as a study," Sarah cried excitedly, "and Nickolas and Mary can have the other room. We are going to have so much fun here. Our honeymoon may never end!"

• • •

They weren't the only newly married couple faced with changes in their life. After getting to New Orleans and being refused leave in August to attend the wedding of James and Sarah, John and Louisa found an apartment in the French quarter that was large enough for the young couple and Louisa's long-time servant. John reported to his new commander and was assigned to an engineering division working on the dikes surrounding the city of New Orleans. By the time of James and Sarah's wedding, Louisa was pregnant, and her doctor had suggested that she not travel to Savannah. She gave birth ten months after her wedding to a seven-pound little boy with blue eyes and blond hair; they named the child James Stephen Beauregard.

Louisa's father was ill, and she had hated to leave Magnolia, but she had a child and a new husband to attend to. It was left to the overseer to carry on the work. They lived in the apartment with her maid for the first year and then found a home to rent. They weren't sure how long John would be assigned to General Scott's Army in New Orleans, so she couldn't make any formal plans.

There was a lot of unrest in the state of Texas. Indians were travelling through the state to attack the northern parts of Mexico. Surprisingly, the Mexican government encouraged U.S. citizens to immigrate to Texas to act as a buffer to the marauding Indians. There was a contingent of infantry and some cavalry at Fort Sabine on the border of Louisiana and Texas, but they had limited engagements; troops rotated six months at a time. After a year and a half in New Orleans, John was sent to Fort Sabine under his cousin Captain P.G.T. Beauregard.

With John's rotation to Texas, Louisa decided to take the boy and her maid back to Charleston. Her father's health was stable, but the day-to-day management of the plantation was putting an undue burden on him. Thomas Garland had retired, the new overseer wielded a heavy hand with the slaves, and production was way down.

Louisa had a confrontation with her new manager on the second day after her return. "I've been doing this type of work for twenty years," he said. "Just let me run the plantation and we'll be back on schedule."

"I don't see how your way of managing is getting the job done. Cotton isn't being picked, and we've not shipped enough to satisfy our commitments. I have a different way of looking at things. If you leave today, I'll give you two weeks' severance."

Louisa knew where Thomas Garland was living. She had one of the slaves hook up the carriage, and the two went into Charleston. Mrs. Garland was at home, and although the welcome wasn't warm, it was courteous. She asked Louisa to come in while she fetched her husband, who was taking a nap. As he entered the parlor where Louisa was sitting, he smiled. "Why, Miss Louisa, how nice of you to come out to see me!"

"Thomas, you look well."

"Can we offer you some lemonade?"

"Yes, and I wonder if my boy can have some too? It's a warm day."

After her driver had been taken care of, they sat across from each other in the parlor. "I wonder if you could come back for three months until I hire another overseer. I fired the latest one this morning. The place is run down and we're behind. I'll pay you a bonus plus your regular wages. I would appreciate your help."

Thomas Garland hadn't quite gotten accustomed to being retired, and he welcomed the idea of having something to do. "When do you want me to start?"

"The sooner the better."

Two days later Thomas Garland returned to Magnolia with his wife. "We've talked it over, and my wife and I will stay as long as you'll have us. I know I'm getting older, but I still know how to get the cotton in. Is our old home still available?"

"Yes, it is, and you can have all the time you need to move your furnishings from your current home here. I know this isn't the way things are done, but with your accord, I'd like to have one of our slaves act as your assistant and take some of the work off your hands. Which one of the workers do you see who could do the job and get the others to follow him?"

"I have just the man in mind. With your permission, I'd like to be the one to hire him. Do you plan to pay him?"

"I do. Give me your recommendation. Starting next Monday, I want a meeting with you and the new assistant every Monday morning to bring me current on what needs to be done and what we can do to improve things here at Magnolia."

Soon after her return, Louisa's father had fallen and broken his hip. He was recovering, but at a much slower pace; it gave his daughter some concern. Her mother spent most of the day looking after her husband and the grandson, putting an additional burden on the elderly woman. Louisa wasn't sure how long her mother could keep up this pace.

During the next year, John came home on leave, and it was always sad when the lovers had to part. Louisa was determined to run the plantation and not spend her life traveling from one fort to another. John hoped that he'd be assigned closer to her and his parents. Being apart from his wife for the better part of a year was preying on his mind. His father asked him if his career was worth the separation.

Louisa had been an accomplished equestrian during her teenage years, competing in dressage and jumping in many of the local events. She and John went on trail rides when he was home on leave, either at Magnolia or at Rosebud. Their love seemed to grow in spite of the constant separation.

"Father isn't well enough to run Magnolia," Louisa confided. "He knows it, and so do I. I love you very much, but I have to take care of my family. How important is your military career? It isn't as though it's the only thing you can do, and then there's Rosebud; you're their only child. What are they going to do when they're too old and need your help?"

"Let's not quarrel. I only have so much time to be with you, and I don't want to waste it on negative thoughts. Let's go for a trail ride and take a picnic basket with us. We haven't made love in the woods in a long time. What do you say?"

"I'll get the cook to prepare a basket. Let me change while you're saddling the horses."

They rode out past the cotton field to the pond they had used so often in their youth. "Do you think anyone saw us skinny-dipping when we were young?"

"If they did, they never said anything, Louisa."

"I wanted you so much then. I told my mother, but she warned me not to let you touch me, and especially not to go swimming in the nude with you."

"I'm not sure I knew what to do, but I wanted to do it. I was afraid you'd be mad if I touched you and I didn't want to make your mad."

"Well, we're here now—we can always eat later. Want to go in the pond?'

"I thought you'd never ask," John said.

They both rushed to take off their clothes and jumped into the pond. "Look, Louisa, no alligators!"

Louisa had brought a couple of towels, which they used to dry off and wrap around their bodies as they sat on a blanket, eating lunch and savoring their wine. The horses, untethered, were grazing around them as they ate. They hadn't been this alone since their marriage, and they couldn't stop looking at each other. "I've missed you, John. You have got to come home. You're missing out on so much."

"I recognize that I'm losing out, but whose fault is that? I understand why you left to come home, but you could come back now; the plantation is under control again. The main question is, why should I give up my career goal so you can satisfy your desire to be an entrepreneur? You created this problem. I had no idea that when we married, I would become the wife and you the husband."

"That's not fair!"

"What's not fair about it? My wife doesn't want to follow her husband; she wants *me* to follow *her*. My parents are getting older, but you don't see them requiring me to come home and run Rosebud. You either want a husband or you want a career, and you're going to have to make that decision. I'm going back to Louisiana, and I expect you and my son to come with me."

"Don't put me in that position. Why can't you see how *I* feel? I was sitting at home in a place foreign to me, with a new child and no husband. Why shouldn't I come home where I have friends, where I wanted to be, and where I'm needed?"

"You are needed at our home, not yours. You're cheating us out of a life together and taking my son away from me. I won't stand for it, and I don't have to."

"I never would've believed that you would act this way toward me!"

"Of course not. You've been catered to all your life, and you feel as though you're still living with your parents. This is what married life is like, and, as the minister said, it's for better or for worse. I wanted you as my wife—but with me, not someplace else. That's not marriage, and it's certainly not something I intend to put up with."

Louisa put her hands to her face and sobbed. "Please don't leave me, John. I don't want to be without you. I've loved you for a long time; I don't believe I could be without you. Can we discuss this calmly? If I come back with you to Louisiana, will you consider resigning your commission and moving back to Charleston to be near our families?"

"I will think about it at the end of three years and then decide whether that's my calling. That's the most I'll agree to."

Louisa dropped her towel and climbed into his arms, kissing him passionately. "Let's not quarrel like this ever again."

"I agree."

Her parents were upset when she told them she was joining John in Louisiana, and that they were leaving the day after tomorrow. "Why so soon?" they asked.

"We need to be alone with young James. My husband feels that I abandoned him, and in a way, I did. I'll not do that again. I love you both, but he's my husband and my future."

"But what about Magnolia?" her father asked.

"I'll keep monitoring its progress through Thomas, who plans to stay on indefinitely. John said he would evaluate his military career at the end of three years. That's only a year and a half away. I hope he decides to resign, but if he doesn't, I'll follow him."

"Your goal in life was to run Magnolia. What about that?"

"That'll have to take second place to making sure my marriage lasts. My husband comes first."

CHAPTER SEVENTEEN

It had been nearly two years since James and Sarah had left Savannah on a cargo ship to Liverpool, England. Each was excited about coming home, even though both had thoroughly enjoyed their stay. The social contacts would stay with them for many years. But it was the business contacts that had James made while there that would eventually prove to be very beneficial. Since Sarah wasn't pregnant, she had had a pleasant experience with the English elite in Oxford, Cambridge, and even as far away as London. James had attended some of the dinner parties, but it was Sarah who had had the free time and made the most of it.

When they arrived home, her father was waiting at the dock as they walked down the gangplank onto American soil. All three were so excited that they were constantly interrupting each other. Finally they got in her father's carriage and drove to his mansion. The home had six bedrooms, of which two were master suites; one was on the first floor and other on the second. Her father had already laid claim to the downstairs suite, with an adjoining bedroom functioning as his office. Jimmy and Sarah had the help move their things to the second floor and occupied the master suite on that level.

"Dad, we're planning to spend two days here and then go by train to Charleston to visit Jimmy's grandparents and hopefully his father. When we come back, you and my husband can talk business, but not until then. Is that agreed?"

Dinner was formal. and Sarah was delighted to be sitting at the big table in her dining room with her husband and father. It was comfortable being served in her childhood surroundings by their long-term maid and butler, who'd come home with them from England. The next day Sarah met many of her girlfriends at a welcome-home luncheon in her honor. Jimmy used the day to move the considerable collection of books that he had accumulated in England into one of the upstairs bedrooms. He then used the rest of the time to reflect on his future, and wondered if he'd be happy working for his father-in-law.

His previous employer had been easy to work for and had gradually given James more and more responsibility. He wondered if he'd be constrained, and how that would impact their living relationship, since they were staying in her father's home. He'd honor his commitment to his father-in-law, but beyond that, he wasn't sure. He enjoyed the factoring business, but he knew that his goal was to own an international financing company. He knew it would be possible to move the Lee Company that way, but he couldn't make that decision; he wasn't the owner.

He also wondered why Sarah wasn't pregnant. It wasn't from a lack of sex! They'd had sex as many times as they could, and in some pretty peculiar places, to satisfy his wife's fantasies. Whatever her lady friends did, she wanted to try. The Eiffel Tower on their honeymoon was mild compared to other locations that she fancied. Doing it on the grounds of Windsor Castle scared him the most. They were never caught in the act, but it was close!

They traveled by train to Charleston and were impressed with the style of architecture that seemed to blossom after the disastrous fire of 1838, while Jimmy was attending college. His grandparents' home had been partially destroyed, but they'd been able to extinguish much of the fire, and only the outhouse and part of the roof was damaged. Jimmy's new wife couldn't tell that the property had been damaged; his grandfather had done a remarkable job of restoration.

They stayed in his mother's old room. After dinner they retired early, but Sarah wasn't sleepy. "Jimmy, I'm concerned that I'm not pregnant. Now, I'm not an expert on the subject, but it would seem that the amount of sex we've had should have paid off!"

"What do you suggest?"

"I think I need to see a specialist, but I don't know where to start."

"What does your doctor say?"

"I think he's too embarrassed to talk much about the subject."

"You seem to enjoy the sex. Am I missing something?"

"No, I like all of it. I think we're using every method there is to get pregnant. When I hear my lady friends talk about the subject, they indicate they have sex about once a week. You and I have it nearly every day. Boy, are they missing something! Do you think it's possible that it could be you and not me? I don't mean it like that. I was just wondering out loud. I wouldn't hurt your feelings for the world."

"When we get back, I'll talk to a doctor client of mine and tell him the problem and see what he suggests, and if it's me, then I'll deal with it." Sarah reached over and hugged him.

They hadn't seen his grandparents in two years, and although they had aged a bit, they were as alert as ever, and the two days they spent with them at the old house was something Jimmy and probably Sarah would remember forever. "What have you learned at Oxford, my son?"

"I've learned a great deal about International Financing, about trade with other countries and what the European perspective is about our country. Many of my classmates were from France and Spain. Their views were similar to those of England."

"How do the English view the rising tensions between the North and the South?" his grandfather asked.

"They have a dual view. On the one hand, they think it's immoral to rely on slavery, but on the other hand I think they'd side with the South if there's an armed conflict. They like their cotton."

"A good analogy, my son."

"I didn't realize that there was probably some deep-seated animosity between the two American sections much further back in time. I learned that there was a North-South conflict during the American Revolution. Many of the southern militias owed their allegiance to England, because that's who they traded with. Tensions in the South were so high that there was an armed conflict between the southern militias and Washington's forces in the South."

"That's true. It's possible that the seeds of discontent may have their origin much earlier than present-day disagreements."

"I understand you're going to work for Dexter Lee," Hendricks ventured.

"I'll probably start next week. I agreed to a ten-year term to pay back the money he loaned me. There's nothing in writing, but that wouldn't matter. I like my father-in-law, and I'll honor my commitment. I don't think it's something for my future, but I have time."

Two days later, they were back in Savannah; Dexter Lee and Jimmy sat down to discuss his employment. "You know a good bit about factoring, so I don't want you to start there. What I want is to expand my operation. We're kind of sectionalized, and I'd like to spread out. Whereas we concentrated my efforts in the Savannah area because there was only one of me, I like to go further south, since that seems to be where the cotton crop is headed. I have enough money to expand; I just need someone who sees things as I do and will help me accomplish my goal. What do you think?"

"It's certainly doable. Why don't I come up with an initial plan and run it by you, and then we can change it as necessary. I like the concept. My only reservation is that factoring ties up a lot of cash if we're unable to sell the paper quickly. Perhaps we can do what the northern bankers do: we can act as middlemen in the transaction. It's safer and there's a huge upside. It's also more in line with how I see my future. But first, I'll look at an expansion plan."

During Jim and Sarah's time in England, John's company had been sent to the Texas and Mexican border after negotiations broke down between President Polk and the Mexican government over a disputed portion of the border. John had been transferred from General Scott's army to Gen. Zachary Taylor's. The army he was assigned to was camped on the north side of the Rio Grande when General Taylor received intelligence that the Mexicans were crossing the border. Taylor split his forces, sending a detachment down river to intercept the Mexicans and another upstream with the same mission. John was working under Captain Seth Thornton, and their squad went upriver. Within a half day, his entire group was overwhelmed by a superior enemy force twenty miles from Taylor's camp. Eleven of his fellow soldiers were killed, six wounded, and he and the remainder were captured.

The prisoners were taken back across the river and thrown into a fenced-in stockade. There was a bucket in one corner for water and another in the opposite corner for waste. John looked around and saw only two men from his company. The fifty in the wired-in stockade were guarded by ten Mexicans; one sat in a rundown shack and four patrolled around the camp. John assumed that they took twelve-hour shifts. When dawn broke, John could see that they were outside a small village, and there was no cover from the sun for himself and his fellow prisoners. It was summer, and he knew they wouldn't last long under these conditions.

Escaping from the stockade wouldn't be easy, but the alternative was unacceptable. He walked around the interior of the makeshift prison and took note of the guards as they patrolled the perimeter, going through shift changes. He wanted to see if any of the fenced area was vulnerable. At noon, they were given rations of dried bread and tepid water. This was to be their only meal of the day. He had to make a move. Should it be a mass escape, the Mexicans would probably send troops after the prisoners, but a lone escapee might not be considered that important.

On the second night, he noticed that the guards were becoming complacent and weren't continuing their patrol around the entire camp; they'd go a quarter of the way around and then return to the fire they'd made in front of their shack. Around midnight, the four guards were sitting around a couple of logs, smoking and drinking.

When they performed the same ritual the next evening, John asked Captain Thornton if he wanted to escape with him. The captain said his leg was injured and he'd only hold John back. Several of his comrades stood in front of the fence while John dug under the barrier at the opposite end from the guard's fire. He crawled about a hundred yards and then made his way toward the Rio Grande River. He rushed to reach the river before daylight, but he had to be careful. He didn't expect any of the guards at the camp to pursue him; it was the robber bands that roamed on each side of the river that were the problem.

He reached a tree line about thirty yards from the river, then stopped quickly and dove for cover. Soon he heard riders in the distance, and he pulled some fallen branches around him. About fifteen minutes later, four riders came up to the river from the direction he had travelled and looked around. The four were having a serious discussion; John didn't speak Spanish, but he sensed they were looking for him. They had probably followed the tracks he'd made in the sand.

Two of the riders got off their horses and started toward him. He reached down and pulled a short piece of branch toward him. It wasn't much against a gun, but it'd have to do. The two came up to the tree line, stood for about five minutes, looked around and yelled to the other two on horseback. John thought it was all over, but when the two walked back to the others, got on their horses and crossed the river, he breathed a sigh of relief.

The moon was out, and he saw the riders cross the river, go up the sand dune on the other side and disappear over the horizon. He knew that he'd be a sitting duck if he crossed now, but he didn't have an alternative. He knew it was near sunup, so he dashed to the edge and jumped into the river, which was fairly shallow at this point. The days when he and Jim used to swim against the swift stream on the Catawba River paid off. He made it across.

His headquarters was about twenty miles from where he was. The question was how to get there without running into bandits or being shot by his own people. There wasn't much cover on the American side, though he found some rocks and lay down behind them to rest. He thought his best chance of survival was at night. He hadn't eaten for over two days, but he was able to get some moisture from the cacti that inhabited the desert. The sun was already starting to beat down on him, but he was free—at least for now. He found shelter behind some rocks and waited until dark.

He knew he had to travel northeast to reach his lines. He'd studied the stars at West Point, so he used the North Star as a guide. He'd gone about two hours after sundown and that's when he heard horses. He dived behind some sagebrush, put his arms over his head, and kept as quiet as he could. Four riders passed within thirty feet of him but didn't stop; he assumed they were going back over the river. He waited until his heartbeat slowed down and then continued on, finally reaching an American camp just before daybreak. He credited the ordeal down the Catawba River as the reason for his escape.

At the camp, John was subjected to about thirty minutes of intense questioning by a major before he was accepted as an American soldier. He gave them the location of the camp where he had been held, and asked the senior officer to rescue the other prisoners. While waiting a day before returning to his command in New Orleans, he asked the major several times when the rescue party was going to be sent over the border, but he never found out if there was an attempt at rescue.

After returning to his command, John was granted leave, and he reunited with his wife and children, who had moved to Baton Rouge, Louisiana, while he was in enemy hands. Louisa had rented a home in the center of town, and when John arrived she breathed a sigh of relief. She had been told of his possible capture, but nothing of his escape.

"You scared the hell out of me! Initially, I thought you were dead—there was no word. Finally we got a list of those who were killed, wounded or captured. I know you don't want to talk about your prison time. But if you need someone to talk to, who knows you better than I?"

"Other than a lack of food and water and lousy accommodations, I was able to get through it without any scars. However, I had a lot of time to think about our future during the short period I was held by the Mexicans. I'm not going to make any decision about my military career until the war ends, but I'm having second thoughts. All I could think about was you and the children. I love our life together, I love where we grew up, and I loved that life style. I know you're ready to go back to Magnolia, but bear with me a little longer—I just can't quit while the fighting is going on."

Louisa held him tightly and stroked his head. "I know you'll do best by us. What I want won't work unless you want the same thing."

P.G.T. Beauregard came to see them in Baton Rouge and was wearing Major's leaves; he and John spent time talking about the conflict. "You know the Mexicans are going to lose, and they're going to lose big," Pierre told him. "I'll bet we get the rest of New Mexico and all of California from them. From what I've read in the northern papers, Polk has this doctrine of Manifest Destiny, and he's not going to stop until the United States reaches all the way to the Pacific Ocean."

"Do you think the new territories coming into the Union will be able to have slaves?"

"If our southern senators have their way, they will."

After his leave was over, John was reassigned to engineering duties on Winfield Scott's staff. He'd come full circle now, going from Scott's army to Taylor's and back to Scott's. His task was to develop a plan for the invasion of Mexico. After three months, the plan was accepted by Scott. It called for an amphibious landing at Veracruz and a subsequent march on Mexico City.

Since John was one of the architects of the plan, he was allowed to be part of the assault force at Veracruz. The

Mexican army held out against several artillery assaults, and the Americans dug in for a planned siege. They were in the second week of the siege when John spied a fellow officer walking near him. "Hey, Jim, you've grown a beard!"

James Longstreet turned and greeted his fellow classmate. The two shook hands and walked to the officers' mess for a cup of coffee. "You look good! How's Maria?"

"I think she's pregnant again—this will be our third. Sooner or later we're going to find out how it's happening! I haven't seen you since your wedding. How's Louisa?"

During the rest of their conversation, John learned that Longstreet's friend U.S. Grant was with the amphibious assault team, and so was Major Robert E. Lee, whom John had met when he was at the academy. "Do you hear from Rosecrans and Doubleday?" John asked.

"No, I think both are serving up north," Longstreet responded. "My assignments have been primarily down south, so I haven't seen a lot of our classmates."

They agreed to keep in touch, and moved on to their respective companies. After twenty days of siege, Veracruz fell. The assault team then began a march to Mexico City. John was assigned to his cousin's company and was in charge of his own squad of ten, mostly made up of Southerners.

General Santa Anna wasn't conceding anything to the Americans, and he made one last bold attempt to impede their advance to Mexico City. With nearly three thousand troops, Santa Anna made a dash to cut their lines and seal them off from the coast. Coming under heavy enemy fire, John and his squad retreated to an arroyo and dug in. They were taking fire from both sides. Two of his men were seriously wounded and another was dead.

"Hey, Lieutenant, we've got to get out of here!"

"Not with two wounded. We have to wait it out, Corporal Jones, but thanks for the suggestion."

Throughout the first night, they traded fire with the enemy; their position seemed defensible and the Mexicans hadn't charged. At daybreak, the enemy sent two men to try to flush out some of John's men, but their movement in the bush was heard by John and his men. "Brown, you and Moore move about ten feet to your right," John ordered. "I think we have visitors."

When several shots rang out, his men returned fire, but this was only a decoy, because there was an immediate attack on their left flank. Some of the Mexicans were on higher ground firing down into the ditch. John hit one of the infiltrators in the stomach and he fell forward. Two of John's men returned fire and shot a second and a third intruder; they died instantly. After intense fire from both sides, the enemy retreated to their former position. "I guess they realize they can't overrun us, but they'll soon figure out that all they really have to do is wait a while and we'll be out of ammo," John speculated. "Brown, check to see if we have any more casualties."

"Christopher is dead, but no one else is wounded. We're down to six now, Lieutenant."

"I want an ammo check. We need to make every shot count."

It was at that instant that John realized he been shot in the leg. He called Smith, who was acting as medic, to take a look at the leg.

Smith cut John's pant leg up through the thigh. "You've been shot in the thigh, Lieutenant, just above the knee. I need to put a tourniquet on the leg to stop the flow of blood."

Once he was able to stop the bleeding, Smith washed the wounded area. "I can't get the bullet out. I'll do the best I can, but you need to be in the hospital."

His leg hurt, and they hadn't eaten for two days. As John leaned back against the side of the ditch, someone yelled out, "We're not going to make it out of here!"

"Whoever said that, cut it out!" John snapped. "We've got a good chance of being rescued. Brown, I want two men on watch at all times. Set up a schedule for the six of us, me included."

There was sporadic firing from the other side throughout the next day. It was as though the Mexicans were trying to entice John's company into an all-out clash. But John had enough discipline in his men to hold them back, and they survived to the next day. Around noon, it appeared that the enemy was pulling out. And that's when he heard a lot of commotion coming from the road to Veracruz—the relief column had arrived!

Dehydrated and hungry, John's men were rescued and transported to Veracruz. John was placed in a wagon, along with the two other wounded members of his team, and taken directly to the hospital. A surgeon examined his leg and directed that he be operated on immediately— there was a fear that the leg might have to be amputated. Luckily for John, the doctor performing the operation was a gifted surgeon, and although there was some infection, he saved the leg.

While recuperating in the hospital, John received a medal for valor from General Scott, with Longstreet and Grant in attendance. When he was well enough to walk, even though with a serious limp, he was sent to New Orleans for further treatment. Louisa and the two children joined him.

Louisa had written to Sarah about John's wound and told her that he was recuperating in New Orleans. Sarah spoke to her husband: "Jimmy, I'd like to visit Louisa and John, if you can spare the time."

"I'll talk to your father. I'd like to see both of them. I can probably do some business while we're there."

Jimmy and Sarah arrived in New Orleans by boat in the fall and were picked up by the Beauregards' carriage. They were transported to their friends' home in the French Quarter and were greeted by Sarah and John, who was still using a crutch. "Well, I heard that you were promoted to captain and received a medal for gallantry," Jimmy grinned. "Nice going, old friend!"

"Well, they were shooting at us and we shot back, that's all. I didn't do anything heroic other than try to defend myself and my men—and oh yeah, I got shot."

"If I know you, John, you're just being modest. I'm sure you deserved the promotion and the medal."

"Well, that's all behind us now," Louisa broke in. "John has resigned, and as of this morning we're civilians. We're headed back to Magnolia and Rosebud."

"I'm not really surprised," Jim said, "but whatever you decide to do, I know you'll make a success of it."

"I was contemplating leaving the Army after I was captured by the Mexicans, but I figured I'd wait until after the war was over before making a final decision," John explained. "The leg did it. It was treated quickly and became infected while we were under fire on the road to Mexico City; I'm lucky that I didn't lose it. The prognosis is good; I'll eventually recover full use of it."

"We knew you and Jimmy were coming, so we waited to spend some time with you in naughty New Orleans," Louisa jumped in. "We know where there're some great restaurants and shows that are little risqué for the normal Southerner, but they're fun. Now, enough about us— what have you two been up to?"

Jimmy and Sarah told them about their time in England, their travels to France and Spain on holidays, and finally the expansion of their business interests, which included new offices in Mobile, New Orleans and Charleston. "Why don't I show you our New Orleans office while the girls go shopping?" Jimmy suggested. "I know Sarah wants to buy some things before we go back. Besides, I promised my father-in-law that I'd check on the office while I was here. I hope you don't mind?"

"As long as we have time to talk, we can visit whatever you want."

The next day, Jim and John rode to the docks and found Jimmy's office, which was staffed with five employees. The manager, George White, was more than gracious to show the owner and his friend around. There were at least two customers in the office the whole time they were there. Jimmy had to excuse himself for a few minutes to give approval for a large outlay of cash that exceeded the manager's authority.

"Does that happen often?" John asked.

"About once a month, I receive a wire or letter asking for an approval. If it's a long-term customer, I'd grant it immediately, but if it's a new customer, I'll look for some collateral; as you know, I'm a little cautious. Cotton is a hot commodity, and if I have to call the note, we won't lose much, provided we can take back the cotton. I don't know how long this boom will last, but it's making my father-in-law rich."

"What about you?"

"Well, he's very generous to me, and since Sarah will inherit the business, I guess I'm getting rich. Of course, I'm not in *your* bracket, but I'm working on it!" They both laughed as they got in the carriage and headed off to a club that John frequented downtown.

"I assume many of your clients are members here," John said. Jimmy nodded. They were led to a small table by an attractive waitress who took their orders. It was midday, and only a few patrons were here.

"What are your plans, now that you are a civilian again?"

"My father wasn't disappointed when I went to the academy; yet he hoped that I wouldn't make a career of it. On the other hand, I never saw myself running a plantation. I know he's looking forward to my return and taking over from him, but that's a last resort. With my military career over, I've been thinking about politics. I've talked to a few plantation owners in the Charleston area and they think I could win their district's congressional seat. It helps to be a veteran."

• • •

Sarah and Louisa went shopping in the town after lunch. "What are you looking for?" Louisa asked.

"Nothing in particular. I thought Jimmy and John wanted to get away by themselves for a day, and I wanted some girl talk with you!"

"I noticed how much weight you've lost. Is everything all right?"

"I've been to several doctors in Savannah, and they recommended various tonics to put on weight. I've tried them, but they don't seem to help."

"Is there something you're worried about?"

"No. Jimmy and I love each other and travel together when he visits his offices up and own the coast; the sex is still great. The problem is that I seem to be more tired than I can remember. I take a nap in the afternoon, so that I can be up and have dinner with Jim every evening. After dinner, we have a nightcap, talk about everything from business to politics, and then go to bed. I'm up in the morning to see him off. I've a great life but no children. I don't know about you, Louisa, but we have sex nearly every day, but I still can't get pregnant. You'd blush if I told you some of the positions we use, but they don't seem to work either. Jimmy went to a doctor to see if he was sterile; he isn't. We want children but I can't get pregnant. But enough about me—what about John? Is the leg okay?"

"He says its okay, but there are times when he doesn't know I'm looking, that he grimaces when he walks. He and I talked about going back to Charleston nearly two years ago, but he wanted to give his military career a chance. I don't know whether he was told that the leg would prohibit him from advancement or he really was tired of the Army. I just don't know what was behind his decision. I'm just delighted to be going home, so I'm not questioning his motives. Both of our parents need us. It may be difficult running two plantations, since John is talking about going into politics. We may have to sell Rosebud somewhere down the road."

The two couples spent the next five days going out to dinner every night and seeing a show afterward. There seemed to be more color in Sarah's face, but she still took an afternoon nap. During her siestas, the other three would go horseback riding along the bayou. When the vacation was over, they agreed to meet at least once a year, and especially when James visited his office outside Magnolia.

Over the next year, Sarah and John went home to Magnolia, where she resumed management of the cotton plantation. John met with his father and an aging grandfather and told them his plans to run for office. They were disappointed and tentatively agreed to sell the plantation when François could no longer run it.

Jimmy's father-in-law succumbed in early 1850; he'd realized his dream to expand his business, and had once told Jim that he was more than the son he'd always wished for. In his will, he left everything to Sarah and James. But it was Sarah's health that took most of Jimmy's time these days. She lost the color in her cheeks and became very listless; she spent most of her time in bed. When she couldn't even come down to dinner, Jimmy had the maid prepare the meals and take them to their bedroom. They ate together, with Sarah propped up in bed. He had the best doctors in the area come to treat her, but they couldn't determine what her problem was. When he had to visit his offices, he'd hire full-time nursing care to be with her. But it was to no avail. She passed away on her thirtieth birthday, with Jimmy at her bedside. The last words she spoke to Jim were, "I've had a great life with you. Thank you, my love."

John and Louisa came to Savannah and stayed with Jim after his wife died. He was so distraught that they didn't know what he'd do next. The business didn't seem to interest him—all he could think about was the woman he had lost. They stayed with him for a week and then went back home after promising to visit again in a couple of months. John was planning to make a run for the U.S. Congress, while Louisa was happy making all kinds of plans for Magnolia.

CHAPTER EIGHTEEN

The incumbent congressional representative from the first district in South Carolina was Charles Gray. He'd been in office for four terms, and his backers, composed largely of the business establishment in and around Charleston, seemed to be confident that he'd be reëlected. He was a moderate on most issues, especially on states' rights. Since he wasn't a slave holder, he was mostly ambivalent on that issue. Secretly he abhorred the institution, but didn't voice his sentiments in public. He served on the House's Foreign Affairs Committee and seemed to have a good grasp of the nation's foreign policy. His opponents in the previous four elections concentrated on his age, as well as pointing out that he hadn't sponsored any legislation for his constituency.

John and his backers knew that they would have to create an issue in the campaign, because Gray was well liked and equally well respected. Heading his election campaign was his father, François Beauregard, who raised significant money for John's campaign from the plantation owners. Sensing the rise of the abolitionists in the North, they wanted a slave owner in their district's seat. Ten of the plantation owners met at Rosebud to discuss John's campaign. In addition to the Beauregards, there was Hamilton from Magnolia, Stephens from Cypress, and six others. "John, are you willing to get in and mix it up in the campaign?" Stephens asked.

"You can count on it! I've felt the fire in real life and survived. I think I can give him a real run for his money. This is something I want. The economy of this entire country is based upon cotton. We as plantation owners are providing that wealth, and we are not being well represented. The North is getting fat over our sweat, and the northern bankers have strangled our flexibility. My family and my wife's family are slave owners, and I don't want some northern bureaucrat deciding how we live our lives. Gentlemen, I will not yield on this position."

Hamilton said, "Gentlemen, do you agree that we have a viable candidate?" The answer was in the affirmative from all those present.

François became John's official campaign manager, Robert Harrison his financial manager, and William Stephens his marketing manager. The others who attended would act as advisors. They agreed on several initial steps. They wanted pictures of John in his uniform posted throughout the district. Next, they set up informal talks to civic groups and business organizations, and finally, they wanted the Gray camp to agree to several debates—preferably three.

Apparently Gray, a seasoned campaigner, didn't see much of a threat in John William; he readily agreed to the three debates. The first of the three was cordial. It was as though the two candidates were trying to size up each other. Both made introductory remarks and stuck to a code of conduct that was gentlemanly in all aspects. When John and his group met two days after the first debate, they analyzed the results. "You didn't even make him blink, John. He was able to control the debate by the rules that were set up. You tried to be a gentleman, and you lost. If you want his seat, you have to make him uncomfortable; you need to put him on the defensive. He's treating you with indifference, as a candidate who doesn't know anything about the issues. He's taking your argument away from you by ignoring it and turning to his own talking points. You need to disrupt him." Stephens, the marketing manager, was extremely critical of John's performance.

François had raised John to see the truth, no matter how hard it was. The second debate was what John's campaign was counting on to turn defeat into victory. During the two weeks between the two debates, he appeared every day before a variety of civic and business groups and listened to their questions and criticism. By the time of the next debate, he was ready for a rematch with his opponent.

It took place at four in the afternoon on the steps of the courthouse, with at least three hundred people in attendance. After Congressman Gray presented his opening remarks, John got up to speak.

"This election is about representation, and my opponent, who's been in Congress for eight years, does not represent this district. Our rights are not being preserved by you, Mr. Gray. You vote as a Northerner and ignore your constituents' desires and needs. You say that the Constitution was meant to be perpetual and to maintain the life of liberty. I say to you that the Constitution is a document of consent, and any rights not delegated to the Federal government are reserved to the states. Where does it say in the Constitution that the Federal government has the right to invade a state, if we disagree? The right to govern and make laws rests with the voters. Too many of our rights are being slowly eroded by northern congressmen and southern politicians, like you, who are aligned with them." A huge roar emanated from the crowd gathered in front of the courthouse.

In rebuttal, Gray fell right into John's trap, echoing the feelings of politicians in the North, and was roundly booed by the crowd. To top off the debate, John accused Gray of being a northern puppet. The more Gray tried to defend his voting record, the more John painted him as a northern sympathizer. The press covered the event, and the Charleston newspaper printed John's speech word for word. The word *slavery* was never used, but the crowd knew what was being discussed.

After the debate, John made several appearances to the businesses in Charleston, looking for support. On one of his visits, he had an encounter with Bruce Gray, the congressman's grandson, who owned a local printing office and was a staunch supporter of his grandfather. He openly criticized John on how he spoke about his relative. John tried to placate the young man, citing that the debate wasn't personal—it was just politics. But Gray pressed him: "Sir, I think you're a coward, and you're hiding behind your wound."

"I'm not looking for a fight. What I said was true for many of our citizens. If they don't feel the same as I, then they can vote for your grandfather."

John started to leave the establishment, but the young man grabbed him by the arm, spun him around and slapped his face. John retaliated immediately, striking him under the chin, and the younger man fell to the floor. He reached down to help Gray up, but his hand was pushed away.

"You can't get away with this!" Gray lashed out. "I demand satisfaction. You can name your weapon."

"Now wait a minute! Aren't you carrying this a little too far? You want a duel just because I'm running against a relative of yours? That doesn't make sense!"

"Name your second, and I'll have mine arrange the time and place."

"I'm not doing any such thing, and I'm not having a duel with you."

"Then I'll tell everyone you're a coward and unfit to hold office."

John punched his adversary in the stomach. "That's my answer."

When he told Louisa what happened, she was irate. "They know they're going to lose and are just trying to provoke you. Don't you dare go through with a duel."

"I don't intend to."

It wasn't that easy just to forget about it. Gray's grandson went to the papers, calling John a coward, and stated that he shouldn't be elected to Congress. Louisa was angry and spoke with her father, who, though getting on in age and recovering from a broken hip, was still a fiery competitor. They got in the buggy, drove to Congressman Charles Gray's office, and demanded to speak to him. A half hour later, they were ushered into Gray's office and sat down facing the congressman. "Good to see you, Robert— it's been a long time," Gray smiled.

Louisa told Gray about the incident and asked the congressman what he intended to do about his grandson. "I'll talk to him, but he's young and impulsive, and I may not be able to stop him. Of course, if your husband doesn't want to have a duel, he doesn't have to show up."

Robert Harrison, though in his sixties, was still an imposing figure. He'd fought several duels in his youth, and was still considered by many to be formidable. He got up from his chair, walked over to the congressman, and slapped him in the face. "Your manners are repulsive, sir. You have ridiculed my family; I demand satisfaction." Harrison stared coldly at Gray.

Charles Gray turned pale. "It's against the law to fight a duel," was all he could say.

Harrison slapped him again. "If your grandson can call out my son-in-law, then I can call *you* out."

"Get the hell out of my office or I'll call the police!" Gray shouted at the two.

"Call this duel off now, or so help me God, I'll shoot you on sight the next time we meet, and that'll be within days. Either way, you've served your last term, either by the voters or by me."

Two weeks later, John was elected by a narrow margin and the party was on at Rosebud. The duel had been called off by Charles Gray, who gave a statement to the newspaper that there was no need for a duel, because that would deprive him of the satisfaction of beating Beauregard in the election. Jimmy made a token appearance at the party to congratulate his longtime friend, but he didn't stay long; he was still in mourning. Louisa begged him to stay with them, but he refused. "I'm not good company. I'll come back when I'm not feeling so sorry for myself."

Louisa put her arms around Jimmy and muffled a cry. "Jimmy, please stay with John and me. We want you with us while you're going through this, and we love you so much." She kissed his cheek, but he broke away and left.

It took three months for the sale of his business to be completed. James Stephen Harris was now a very wealthy man. For some time, he had wanted to go back to the Catawba village and just fish and hunt with Aaron, the late Chief Running Deer's son; now he had the time. His grandparents were still alive, and after he sold his home in Savannah, he stored his personal belongings at their place, bought some equipment and a horse, and made his way to the village. He hadn't been there in nearly fifteen years.

He was received warmly by Aaron and shown around the village. "I made room for you in my lodge. Tomorrow we'll take a canoe and go fishing."

The morning for the Catawba started much earlier than what Jim had grown accustomed to, so they didn't get started until eight in the morning. They trailed the canoe on a travois attached behind their horses until they reached the river. In a little over an hour they were paddling to a spot that Aaron said would have a lot of fish. They tied the canoe to a tree on the bank, walked into the shallow water, and cast their lines. Aaron got the first strike, but Jimmy wasn't far behind. They fished for two hours, catching six good-sized trout, and decided to have them for lunch with something cold to drink. "I always remember that trip the three of us took to the Blue Ridge Mountains," Aaron said.

"Don't remind me about that trip. I'd like to put it behind me forever. I still have dreams of the two brothers chasing us, let alone the first two that you did away with. I never thought that I could kill anyone, and when I did, it was the worst thing that ever happened to me."

"If that's what you want, it's okay with me, but I just wanted to tell you one thing. Their kin came looking for you in our village shortly after you returned."

Jim looked at him, startled. "Now you've got me wondering! Tell me what happened."

"There were five of them. I think one was the father of the four who didn't come back, and the others were nephews or cousins. One of our braves saw them coming down the river and ran to tell my father. I'd told him the story, so he sent two braves to inform your friend's father. Two days later, François Beauregard, Robert Harrison and six other men came to our camp and asked about the mountain men. They weren't there at the time. We'd told the men from Asheville to look in a town north of us; they said they'd be back. Beauregard's group arrived a day after they left and decided to camp about a mile west of us. We told them we'd send word if the mountain men came back. Two days later the father and four others returned and started questioning my father again. He'd sent word to the plantation owners, and they came upon the five and surrounded them."

"You mean there was a confrontation?"

"It was more than that; it was deadly serious. The older of the men from the mountains said four of his sons never came back after they chased two boys down river toward the Catawba village. He wanted to know what happened to his sons, and he wasn't leaving until he found out."

"I can't figure out why Beauregard and Harrison came with some armed men."

"We were the ones who let the secret slip out. My father told Mr. Harrison what happened on the trip one day when he came to our village. He didn't mean to tell him, but he let something slip, and Harrison asked enough questions until he found out everything. He must have told John's father."

"What happened next?"

"One of the younger men from the hills said he was sure that you and your friend had killed them all. At that moment Beauregard turned, shot that man in the head, and he fell over. The men with Harrison raised their weapons and aimed them at the remaining four and told them to drop their weapons to the ground."

"My God, he killed him, just like that!"

"That wasn't the end of it. The father of the missing boys screamed at Beauregard and said they'd come back with more men and find them. He was going to kill them all, including the two boys, who he assumed were related to them. One of the other three turned to the older man and said, 'Uncle John, we came with you because we thought your boys were hurt. We didn't come to kill anyone; I think we should go back.' But the older man yelled at him to shut up and said no one was going to kill his sons and get away with it.

"Harrison shot the father in the chest and the man fell over dead. The question was posed by his friends what to do with the remaining three.

"The one who tried to get the father to withdraw spoke. 'We don't like what you did here, but if you let us leave, we'll not come back, and neither will any of our kin. We didn't want to come after our kin because we knew what our four cousins were like. We have women and children at home. I give you my word that if you let us leave, it will end here.' Beauregard turned to the other two and they repeated their cousin's vow."

"Did they let them leave?"

"Yes, and that was fourteen years ago, and we've never seen any of the three or their kin."

"I didn't want this to happen, but I don't know what else we could've done! First the two came to rob us and more than likely kill us. Next their brothers came and actually tried to kill us. I'm still troubled with the one I killed. I'm also sorry that it put your people in harm's way."

"They knew better than to try to harm us. We made it clear to them, the first time they came looking for you, that we would kill them if they brought any harm to our village or any of our people."

Fishing and hunting for five days didn't take his mind off what he'd lost. For all practical purposes, he and Sarah had grown up together, learning about life, sex and what it took to make a marriage work. He'd wanted children, but it wasn't to be. He wondered if he'd ever learn what had taken his wife. He was grateful to her and her father for a good life, a wonderful opportunity, and the fact that he was a very wealthy man.

His father had remarried and was living in upstate New York. He'd retired from the Interior Department two years before, but was still called on several times a year to handle problems in some of reservations he had previously managed. Occasionally, he and Jim would spend a day together when he was in the Charleston area.

Jimmy had been busy with the factoring business, but not too busy to see what was happening in southern society, and he didn't like it. Holding slaves was morally wrong, yet he socialized with people who held slaves. His best friend's families were slave holders. Besides that, John had given an impassioned speech defending slavery in his debate for the congressional seat. It was obvious how John felt about the issue. Jimmy wondered if he'd be happier in Europe or in the north.

CHAPTER TWENTY

Jimmy sailed home on the *Velvet Starr* and used the time onboard to look at his options. Starting a bank was at the top of the list. The obvious question was, where should he establish it? He was a true Southerner and could see that somewhere in the South would be his first choice. After landing in New York, he spent a day with his father and left the next morning on the train to Charleston, a city that was certainly one of his choices, along with Mobile and New Orleans. It was early afternoon when he arrived, so he rented a carriage and rode to Magnolia to see what John and Louisa thought about his plans.

They were having a nap when he arrived—at least that's what Louisa said was going on. He'd wired them that he was coming, but was unsure what day he'd arrive. Louisa hugged and kissed him several times; John hugged him and then shook his hand. "It's good to see you, old buddy. We have a lot to talk about while you're here."

"I know that you've been elected to Congress for two terms, and I hear you're running unopposed for a third term."

"For someone who hasn't been here for some time, you have a good feel for what going on. I assume I'll run unopposed this time, but it was my initial run that caused all the problems. I won two of the three debates, but soon thereafter, my opponent's grandson called me out and challenged me to a duel. I punched him out."

"I assume you either won the duel or it got cancelled."

"I'll let Louisa fill you in on that."

"When I heard about the duel, I was frantic and didn't know what to do," Louisa said. "I know John; he's not someone who'll back down from a challenge, and he was either going to be arrested for killing his opponent or he was going to be dead. The newspapers were having a field day. There wasn't a day that went by that they didn't insinuate that John was a coward. I couldn't leave it at that, so I called upon my father, who'd been in five duels. He and I drove to Charleston and called on the current congressman. My father told him that if he didn't call off his grandson and issue an apology, he was going to challenge him to a duel. To make his point, my father slapped him in the face twice—I thought the old congressman would wet his pants!

"My father's reputation is a legend in these parts. No one, and I mean *no* one, wants to be in a duel with my father. Well, the congressman didn't issue an apology, but he put out a statement that there was a misunderstanding and no reason for a duel. After a few days, the newspaper moved on to something else."

"You married well, John. Not only do you have the most beautiful wife in the entire South, but you have a father-in-law who will shoot any of your opposition," Jimmy laughed.

"I understand that you're considering establishing a bank here."

"I intend to look at it thoroughly to see if it's feasible. As to where it'll be, that hasn't been decided. I intend to look at Charleston, Mobile and New Orleans. I'll meet with the civic leaders in those cities during the next thirty days."

"What about Savannah?"

"The sad memories are too near. I don't know if I could operate in that city and not think of Sarah all the time. I think I need to move on."

"Have you been seeing anyone?" Louisa asked.

"I dated a nice woman in England, but it's too soon for me to get serious about anyone—maybe in a year or two."

"We understand." Louisa put her hand on his arm.

"John, I'd like to get your perspective on whether or not the movement to secede from the Union has any teeth."

"I honestly don't know. I think the southern politicians have been using it as a club to beat back the abolitionists, but the problem is more complex than that. The population in the South is substantially less than in the North. I think they have six million more people than we do. Our fear is that new states coming into the Union could be anti-slavery, thereby making the differential in population even greater. We've been enjoying control of congressional committees based upon the fact that our slaves count as three-fifths of a person when determining how many congressmen we can elect. If the differential changes such that the House and the Senate have enough support to pass a slave emancipation law, it will be an economic disaster for our way of life. Those of us elected from the South understand the numbers game, and we'll do everything we can to protect the status quo. My guess is that secession will be an option in the future."

"That's a very sobering analysis."

• • •

Young James Stephen Beauregard was the spitting image of his father, though he had his mother's complexion. The boy was starting to ride, and John had bought him a horse. Louisa wasn't as timid as John's mother, but she still had moments when she felt that the boy was the reincarnation of John. There wasn't anything that the young lad wouldn't try. John had taken him to the Catawba village the summer before; he wanted him to have the same perspective that he and Jim grew up with. Young James liked the village and asked his father if they could go back the following summer.

Rosebud had been sold, and John's parents were living in a small house at Magnolia. Both were in failing health. François had lost considerable weight, and Jerome was helping him walk. Jimmy went to their home to visit the older couple. They were gracious, and the three reminisced about the old times when he and John were teenagers. Jimmy always liked the couple—they were like second parents to him.

He left two days later, with his first stop in Mobile. He met with several of his former clients, who gave him strong encouragement for the enterprise. Most wanted to be included as investors in the project. The reception and feedback he received in New Orleans mirrored what his friends in Mobile said. When he broached the subject of secession, all seemed to think that it wouldn't come to pass. Armed with this information, he came back to Charleston and met with his grandparents; his old room was still available.

His grandfather had been retired for years, but his mind was still as sharp as ever. Jim told him what his acquaintances in Mobile and New Orleans had told him and what John Harris had said.

"The people in Mobile and New Orleans have an agenda. There isn't a national bank in the South. and they see your venture as a boon to their cotton industry. Your friend gave you a chilling and somewhat accurate analysis of what you have to look forward to. I would love to have your bank in Charleston, but I'd be remiss if I didn't tell you that the moderate element in the South has gone into hiding; it's the vocal minority that rules the day. Let me ask you a question, Jim. What's your view of slavery?"

"I'm opposed. I think I've been the moderate who's put his head in the sand. I've never taken a position on the subject, even though I have friends who own slaves. Do you think there are a lot of people like me in the South?"

"I do. With King Cotton our most profitable export, no one wants to upset that industry by suggesting to the plantation owners that they free the people who do the work in the fields. Emotions run mostly hot, and no one wants to be called out as a slave lover. There have been a few in this area who voiced opposition to the slavery movement. They were visited at night by some thugs. Soon, they either retracted their views or became silent. Two that I know even went to the hospital."

Cameron and Abigail greeted him as he got out of the carriage he'd taken from the train station. Their threebedroom home was in the center of Manhattan. He'd always liked the city and wondered if this wasn't the place he should consider for his business operations. After a discussion with his father and Abigail, he decided to see if he could find a suitable location for the bank, and if so, then he'd purchase a home. Money wasn't an issue. George, Michelle and his Parisian friend Pierre were committed as investors. John and Louisa wanted to see where he'd locate before they'd commit. Even without those two, he had enough investors to push forward.

A week later he made an offer on a vacant lot on Wall Street, and when it was accepted, he applied for a charter for a national bank. He selected the name Harris National Bank, and hired an architect to draw up plans. He hadn't been this excited in two years!

One year later, the bank held its grand opening, and Jimmy was amazed at the number of clients he was able to obtain in a little over three months. During this period, he kept in contact with Claire, who suggested that she visit America, since he was so busy with his new startup. Actually, it was Abigail who had suggested that she become aggressive and force Jimmy to make a decision on their relationship. With both women working on him, it was a wonder he any chance at all!

Cameron and his wife met Claire at the harbor in New York and escorted her to their home. They would be her chaperons while she was visiting. Jimmy was in Philadelphia when she arrived and wouldn't be back until the next day. Abigail set up a dinner for the four the following evening. Jimmy brought wine and flowers and kissed Claire on the cheek when he arrived. "You look as lovely as ever," he told her. "I'm glad you made the trip. I've cleared my schedule over the next few days so we could spend some time together, if that's okay with you."

Over the following few days the four were inseparable, going out to dinner, taking ferry rides around the island, and taking in plays at various theaters along Broad-way. Jimmy and Claire enjoyed each other's company but longed to be alone for a day. This finally came to pass the following day, when they took a cab to the museum, had lunch near the Harris National Bank, and took a carriage to Battery Park. They asked the driver to wait as they walked around looking at the skyline of Jersey City across the bay.

"I missed you, James."

"I feel the same way. I couldn't wait until you came."

"I know you think I'm an aggressive female, but I generally know what I want, so what's the problem with saying it out loud? I think you and I would make a good match. I don't want to compete with your late wife; I just think we have enough in common that we could be happy. Are you shocked?"

"Not in the least. Once I saw you at my father's home, I knew that I was going to propose. You just beat me to it. I missed you very much and would be proud if you'd be my wife."

Claire was facing him, so he leaned over and kissed her on the lips. She reciprocated and moved her hips against his. This sent a sensation through him, and he was aroused.

"I accept," Claire said simply.

"There is one little caveat to my proposal. After we tell my father and Abigail, I want to travel to Charleston and tell my grandparents and then my two closest friends, John and Louisa Beauregard."

"I accept. Any friends of yours will be mine."

Abigail had anticipated the announcement and had champagne cooling in the icebox when they returned. The four got a little tipsy from all the toasts they made at dinner that night. Two days later, the couple took the train to Charleston, hired a rig for four days, and went to see his grandparents, who were fascinated with Claire. When they heard her play the piano, they fell in love with the young woman. Claire slept in James's room and he slept on the couch; it seemed like old times for him.

James did have time to shop for a ring, and Claire couldn't help but show it off to his grandmother. Claire wanted to be married in her home in Hertfordshire, and Jimmy agreed. Jimmy invited his grandparents to sail with them to England, but they declined due to age. This made him sad and he nearly shed a tear; Claire saw it and grabbed his arm. As they were leaving, the grandmother cried and made them promise to come back after the wedding.

John was waiting for them when they rode up to the main house at Magnolia. "I understand that your wife runs a six-hundred acre plantation while you're a U.S. congressman," Jimmy greeted him.

All of a sudden they heard a voice from outside. "Did somebody say, 'Let's go skinny-dipping?'"

Louisa came out to the porch from the kitchen. Claire eyed the beautiful woman, who stuck out her hand and said, "I'm Louisa Beauregard. Welcome to Magnolia."

Awestruck, Claire stammered a hello. Here was a self-assured woman who could dictate the conversation. All Claire could think of to say was, "What's this about skinny-dipping?"

"When we were young I used to watch Jimmy and John go swimming in the buff. I always wanted to go in with them, but they wouldn't allow me. Some day, and I hope not too far in the future, we may just do it."

Claire was not used to such a self-assured woman. Those in her circle were very discreet. Then again, she hadn't met any woman who was running a large cotton plantation with nearly 100 slaves!

"Why don't we let the men talk, and you and I can get acquainted. Let's go to the kitchen—I'm going to have a glass of wine. How about you?" Louisa asked.

They passed idle talk for a few minutes and suddenly Claire asked about Sarah.

"She was a lovely flower and I'm sure Jimmy loved her very much," Louisa began. "She died too young; I don't think they know what killed her. She was a lot like you— nearly the same size. I gather you're quite outspoken when someone gets to know you. That's how Sarah acted with Jimmy. She pushed the romance. Not that he was reluctant, but she knew what she wanted and made sure he knew it."

Claire couldn't help but smile as she remembered how she had pushed Jim into a proposal.

"I'll be very blunt with you," Louisa continued. "I love Jimmy almost as much as I do John. I don't want him hurt."

"He won't be. He'll be taken care of with a great deal of love."

"I'm going to tell you some intimate details of James and Sarah's life. I want you to succeed. Sarah was quite uninhibited. She had Jimmy make love to her on the observation deck of the tallest building in New York City. She was equally bold in a carriage in Central Park in the daytime. Jim was always in wonder what she'd want next! Now, you're older than Sarah was when she married. My advice is not to have children immediately. Have some fun with your husband; think about a family in a couple of years. There are new contraceptives that are sold now, so you shouldn't have any problem remaining childless until you're ready." Claire blushed and couldn't look at Louisa.

"I'm sorry if I offended you, but these are the facts of a good marriage. I'm trying to help you."

"Yes, I'm embarrassed, but you don't know how much I appreciate your candor. I hope you won't be offended if I look upon you as a sister."

Louisa gave Claire a hug. "Here's to a long friendship. I hope we'll be invited to your wedding. Where's it going to be?"

"The wedding and after-party will be held in my home in Hertfordshire, England. And yes, you are invited. I hope we can travel over the Atlantic together!"

Jimmy booked passage for six on the *Belle Starr* steamer, with departure in ten days. Travelling to England would be Cameron, Abigail, John, Louisa, Jimmy and Claire.

The steamer was more of a luxury ship than the one he had returned on two years ago. There were only fifty cabins, with a large room on the main deck that served as a restaurant and recreational area. The first night at sea was rough. The winds were blowing hard and the ocean was choppy. Most of the passengers had dinner served in their cabins; Jim and Claire were no exception.

The second day was calm, and at dinner, the captain invited Claire and James to join him at his table, but the couple declined. They were having too much fun. Louisa was keeping everyone in stitches telling those at her table about all the funny things her slaves did while they were working. The captain was shocked that someone would decline his invitation, so he asked the purser to check on Claire and James. He got another surprise when he learned that Claire Temple was the stepdaughter of the Prime Minister of England and that she was a renowned pianist.

After dinner, the captain stood up to make an announcement, stating that they had a celebrity on board. "Claire Temple, the stepdaughter of the Prime Minister, is an accomplished pianist. Let's give her a hand, and perhaps she'll reward us with one of her piano specialties."

"Go for it, girl!" Louisa encouraged her to perform.

Claire strode to a movable stage near the captain's table and addressed the audience. "I'll play one of Chopin's piano concertos and dedicate it to my fiancé, James Harris, whom I'll be marrying in two weeks. This is for you, Jimmy—I love you."

At the end of the performance, Claire bowed to loud applause, turned, and there was James, ready to help her down from the stage. "You're wonderful," he murmured in her ear. "I love you, Claire."

Back at the table, everyone hugged and kissed her. Other passengers came over to congratulate her; some asked for Claire's autograph. "I didn't know you were so accomplished," Louisa said. "What I've accomplished pales in comparison to you!"

"On the contrary! I excel in things that are feminine; you, dear Louisa, excel in things that are normally maledominated. It is *I* who feel admiration for *you*."

Then she turned to Jim and suggested, "Let's go for a walk on deck." She grabbed his arm and snuggled very close to him. "Jimmy, I'm so full of love at this moment that I don't want it to end. I would like to be a virgin on my wedding night, but I want to spend the night with you. I've never felt this close to anyone before."

"Let's walk some, and when there's no one looking, we'll go into your cabin."

Ten minutes went by before they felt that it was clear enough to risk it. As they entered the cabin, Jimmy said. "Let's leave the lights off and keep as quiet as we can."

As he slowly undressed Claire, she shivered at his touch. When she was completely nude, he kissed her on the mouth, then moved on to her breasts and her thighs; she put her hand to her mouth to keep from crying out. Then he lifted her in his arms and placed her on the bed, quickly undressed and climbed in alongside her. He pulled her on top of himself and slowly explored the softness of her body. She moaned as he touched her breasts and massaged her buttocks. When he moved her onto her back alongside him, he asked her to spread her legs, and she quickly complied. He put his hand on her vagina and slowly massaged a particular spot until she had an orgasm. When she started to cry out as she climaxed, he put his hand lightly over her mouth. They fell asleep with her head in the crook of his arm and her leg over his body.

At six the next morning, James awoke, quickly dressed, and looked out the door of Claire's stateroom. When he was sure he was alone, he exited, went down two doors and entered his room.

But James wasn't the only one who was up early that morning and wanted to smell the ocean breeze. Cameron and Abigail had been unable to sleep, so they got a cup of coffee and went on deck. They sat in deck chairs for a while, but the breeze was a little too strong, so they pushed the chairs behind one of the exterior walls such that no one could see them as they relaxed. But they did see Jimmy coming out of Claire's room, and smiled at each other.

At breakfast, Louisa looked at Claire, who was still flush from her night with Jim. "I think you got lucky last night, girl," Louisa remarked.

Claire reddened and turned to Abigail, who smiled. She whispered in Abigail's ear, "My God, does *everyone* know?"

Abigail whispered back, "Louisa is only guessing. But Cameron and I saw Jim leave your cabin this morning. It happens to everyone. Before we were married, Cameron and I were staying at the English ambassador's home. Cameron visited me that night, and when he went back to his room the next morning, the ambassador's wife saw him and laughed. She had probably had the same problem some time in her past."

The Hertfordshire estate had thirty rooms, of which fifteen were bedrooms. Emily Temple met the entourage at the front door and immediately took charge. She directed the servants where to put everyone's luggage and what the schedule would be for the next few days. The wedding was but five days off, and the Prime Minister wouldn't arrive for another three days. Cameron and Abigail wanted to go to London for a few days and do some shopping while Jim, John and Louisa wanted to ride on an English hunt. They would hardly see Claire until the wedding. She and her mother would be busy with all the planning.

The hunt was in two days, and Emily sent one of the servants to ask permission for the three to ride. The next day they received the invitation. All three had brought riding attire and boots; Emily furnished hunting hats for all. On the day of the hunt they rose early, readied their horses and rode over to Hertford Castle with Emily. She introduced them to the Master, Lord Barrington, and the Huntsman, Sir William Beedle, and begged leave to return to her home. Before she left, an issue was raised by the Master: Louisa was not riding sidesaddle as did the other women on the hunt. Emily interceded, telling the Master that it was too late to go back and change saddles and that Louisa was the best rider of the three. All Lord Barrington would say was, *"Humpft!"*

They were led out through the granite archway at the entrance to the castle by the Huntsman, with the hounds trailing behind him. Louisa turned to Jimmy. "If that old fart isn't careful, I'll run all over him!"

James couldn't help but laugh, but his horse sensed something unusual and started to bolt; it took Jimmy about a minute to rein him in. They rode over grassland and stone fences separating separate parcels for over an hour without seeing any game. It was yet another hour before the hounds got on a scent and the Huntsman yelled, "Tallyho!"

All the riders urged their horses to a gallop, following the hounds over several stone divisions before they could see the fox in the distance. The Master was in the lead, but another rider was on his left side, rather a breach of etiquette; it was Louisa. She was hell-bent to get to the fox first! As the hounds gained on the fox, the animal made a ninety-degree turn to the left to avoid them, but Louisa made the same maneuver and nearly ran over the animal. The pack caught the fox near another stone fence and the Huntsman completed the kill. It was the Master's choice to award the souvenir of the tail, head and feet to someone on the hunt. He smiled and handed them to Louisa. A cheer went up from the other riders, and Louisa beamed her pleasure.

When they arrived back at the castle, Louisa curtsied to Lord Barrington, who seemed to blush as he looked at the beautiful young woman. All the way back to Hertfordshire, Louisa said she would give Jimmy and John lessons before they returned. She was on a high, and it carried through dinner, especially after she had had a couple of glasses of wine.

Two nights later, Viscount Palmerston, the Prime Minister, arrived at Hertfordshire, and Cameron and Abigail returned from London. The dinner conversation that evening was lively, and the Prime Minister and the other three men adjourned to his study for brandy and cigars. Since Cameron was the oldest of the three, the Prime Minister directed his initial question to him. "Do you think hostilities are imminent between the North and the South?"

"Sir, I've lived in the North for so long that I can't answer your question with any degree of knowledge. My son has spent considerable time in the South, both as a boy and a businessman. His friend John is a U.S. congressman from the state of South Carolina. They should be the ones to answer."

The Prime Minister turned to John, who carefully thought about his response before answering. "The South is like a second son in a wealthy family. He's been enjoying the benefits of being in the family, but when the patriarch dies, he has no control over his life; everything goes to the oldest son. I and my fellow Southerners want to be able to live the life we have led up until now. We see, however, a change on the horizon. With new states coming into the union as a result of the Mexican-American War, our percentage of representation is slowly decreasing, and the North's is increasing. To answer your question, I would say that unless the South can be assured that our way of life is protected for posterity, we must look at all options that will grant us our rights."

As the Prime Minister looked to James to ask him a question, Jimmy turned the tables on him and asked, "I think it's only fair to ask what your government's position is relative to these hostilities."

"Personally, I'm opposed to slavery but sympathetic to the South's cause. But as Prime Minister, I'm opposed to intervention, and I don't believe France or Spain will interfere unless we take the initiative. . . . Shall we join the ladies in the parlor?"

James hadn't seen much of his intended, but as he sat next to her in the parlor, she kissed him on the cheek, squeezed his arm, and whispered in his ear. "It'll all be over soon and we can be together like that night on the ship." He smiled.

CHAPTER TWENTY-ONE

The wedding plans called for the service to be held in the parish church at ten in the morning, followed by a reception at Hertfordshire Manor. James, John, Louisa and their friends walked to the church, which was about a half mile away. Claire, her mother, and the Viscount went in a carriage pulled by a grey horse, which was considered to be luck for the English. James had purchased the ring, with their initials and the date of their wedding engraved inside, and now gave it to John to hold. Due to Claire's stepfather's position, several members of Parliament and his entire group of ministers attended. John was best man, or first groomsman, while Abigail served as Claire's maid of honor. After the wedding, James and Claire signed their names in the wedding book; she signed her maiden name.

Since there were many dignitaries, the servants pushed several tables together to handle thirty guests at one table and twelve at another, including the clergyman and his family. As per tradition, James paid for a carriage to transport them from the church to Emily's home where the reception was taking place. Claire wore her wedding dress until after the meal was over and toasts were made to the wedded couple.

The newlyweds made their exit at one o'clock in the afternoon and planned to spend their wedding night at the luxurious Great Northern Hotel in downtown London. They arrived by train and had a small meal before retiring for the night. Claire had looked forward to her wedding night ever since meeting James and deciding he was the man for her. Thir suite was on the top floor, with a view to downtown London. The chambermaid had turned down the covers, while hotel management provided a bottle of champagne. Jimmy popped the cork and filled two glasses. "Here's to you, Claire. I love you very much, and will do everything in my power to make you happy. If I don't, please let me know."

"Here's to you, James Harris. I've loved you from the first time we met, and I will be a good and loving wife for all the rest of your days."

They emptied their glasses, and Jim kissed her on the lips as he slowly began to unfasten the tiny buttons on her dress. Claire helped. When she was completely nude, he lifted her in his arms, kissed her on the mouth, and laid her on the soft feather bed. He took his time bringing her to a high state of arousal before he entered her. He had massaged her vagina until it was wet before intercourse, and she gasped and nearly screamed as he pushed inside. "Don't stop, please," she moaned.

He didn't stop, and after they both climaxed, they lay side by side, and finally she laughed. "That was so great— let's do it again!"

They did, and when she climaxed again, she felt as though a load had been lifted from her shoulders. "Can we do this again in the morning? Right now I'm exhausted and I want to fall asleep in your arms."

They didn't wake until nine o'clock the next morning, and per her request they did it again. "I'm starved!" Claire said. "How about you? I think this lovemaking makes me hungry. Can we call for room service?"

They left two days later by train to Dover and then by ferry to Calais. Their honeymoon destination was the southern part of France, after a short stop in Paris. Claire wanted to do some shopping, and like a dutiful husband, James was there as she tried on different outfits at several luxury dress stores. After ten days in Nice, they headed back to London for a week in order to say their goodbyes before departing for America. It was a tearful parting with her mother at Hertfordshire, but the Prime Minister had remained in London: there was a crisis in the government.

After a ten-day trip across the Atlantic, Jimmy and Claire arrived in New York and were met by Cameron and Abigail, who'd been home for ten days. After a dinner prepared by Abigail, Claire and James took a carriage to Jimmy's home, just off Seventh Avenue. "Why don't we live here for at least three months while you become acclimated? If you're not comfortable with this home, we can look for something else."

Over the next two years Claire and James had two children, a girl named Emily, after her mother, and a boy named Cameron, after his father. But Claire was restless. Though she had adequate help, she missed giving recitals, and she felt that Jim was ignoring her. She didn't want any more children, but she wanted the intimacy that they'd shared when they first were married. Jimmy was busy with the bank, which had shown a profit the second year and by the next year was in a very stable financial condition. Over dinner one evening, Claire asked if they could go off for a few weeks without the children. "Perhaps Abigail and Cameron would look after them while we're gone."

"Where do you want to go?"

"I'd like to visit Magnolia. I haven't seen Louisa in years. She has a way of cheering everyone up."

"Are you unhappy?"

"Not with you, but it seems as though we've gotten into a rut, and I think a change of scenery would be good for both of us."

Two weeks later, after receiving an invitation from John and Louisa, they took the train to Charleston. A visit with the grandparents was in their plans while they were in town. John was at home when they arrived; Louisa was still in the cotton fields. After they freshened up from their long trip, they went downstairs and sat with John on the porch. There was a small breeze, with a slight overcast in the skies, and the temperature was pleasant. "I understand you're running for the Senate?" James asked John.

"Yes. Senator Butler is finally retiring and giving me his endorsement. I don't think I'll have much competition; his word carries a lot of weight around here."

"It seems that I heard something about an altercation he was in. What was that all about?"

"Well, he wasn't directly involved. A local congressman, named Preston Brooks, took exception to what Senator Sumner said about slavery, and especially about Senator Butler's view on the subject, and he caned Sumner in front of a lot of people."

"You mean someone spoke his mind and was beaten for his views? I thought we had free speech in this country!"

"Some issues are very volatile and bring out the worst in some of us. I don't condone what Brooks did, but he's from South Carolina, and it's as if my friends can do no wrong."

"That's not like you, John."

"I'm trying hard to navigate a moderate stance and at the same time represent my constituency, which is proslavery. Let's change the subject. Tell me about your banking ventures."

"Well, we opened in New York City three years ago and Boston last year. I'll probably open a bank in Chicago, maybe some time next year."

"Are you lending strictly in the North?"

"No, we have some customers in the South. I did want to talk to Louisa while I was here and see if she'd be interested in shipping some of her cotton to New England. The textile industry has taken hold there, and many of the manufacturers are our customers."

Louisa rode up, tied her horse to the hitching rail, and rushed in to greet her guests. "My, don't you two look prosperous! You don't know how much I've missed you. Why don't we let the men talk? Come with me while I bathe and clean up. Dinner will be at eight and very casual."

After the two women left, John poured James another glass of wine. "The last time we talked was at my wedding. You were quite forthright with the English Prime Minister. Do you still think that there's enough support for secession?" Jim asked.

"Is this a business or a personal question?"

"My bank has considerable money invested in some plantations in the South, so yes, it's business, primarily."

"There is no doubt that South Carolina is the center of a secession movement. Contrast that with the North, where the abolitionist movement has taken hold. The more the abolitionists grow in strength, the more rabid the secession movement becomes. It's like the old question: which came first, the chicken or the egg? Both groups are gaining more members. I think that armed conflict is inevitable."

"Where will you stand if there is secession?"

"With my people—where else would I be?"

"I can't believe that you aren't a voice for caution."

"Those people get tarred and feathered down here, or don't get reëlected to office. When you're a politician, you can't afford a high brand of ethics; you represent people and what they want."

"Do you believe the majority of your constituents want secession?"

"I don't believe they do. It's the power brokers who want secession. Theirs is the only voice that's heard in this area."

"But your views must carry some weight. Why not talk caution? You may have more support than you realize."

"I think I know the temperature here much better than you do, and I'm not going to take a strong stance.... Look, let's not discuss politics. We haven't seen either of you for so long, and I don't want to have any friction while you're here. Okay?"

Jim smiled and nodded his head.

Later, Jimmy asked the hosts if they'd mind if he and Claire visited his grandparents for a day.

"We expected that you would want to spend time with them," Louisa said. "You could leave early in the morning and be back at night."

The couple spent a day with the grandparents and promised that they'd bring the children next time. "Is it possible for you two to come by train to New York City and stay with us?" Jim asked.

"If you're asking us to move there permanently, the answer is no. We are Southerners, and we love this area even if we disagree with what's going on."

"I must admit that I was being selfish. I *was* asking you to come live with us. I remember how it was when I was young—I wanted my children to see you more often. It's a shame that we don't live close. Is it possible that you could visit?"

"I appreciate the thought, but I think the trip would be too hard on my wife."

They returned to Magnolia late that night and went directly to their room. The next morning at breakfast, Louisa asked them what they'd like to do for the day. Before anyone else could say anything, Claire blurted out, "I'd like to go on a picnic by your old swimming hole and go skinny-dipping!"

James almost gagged on his eggs and brought his napkin up to his mouth. "Claire, you can't be serious!"

"I'm very serious! If we're ever going to do it, now's the time. The weather is great and we're healthy. What's the problem?"

"It's not proper," Jim said.

"I'm for it," Louisa jumped in. "I say let's go! What about you, John? You're not going to be a prude, are you?"

"I forbid it," Jim said firmly.

"Then Louisa and John and I will go," Claire fired back.

Jimmy looked at his old friend John, who burst out laughing and shrugged. "You people are all crazy!" Jim sounded defeated.

"Well, what's it going to be?" Louisa pressed. "Will there be three or four in the pool in the altogether?"

"The wine had better be good—I think we're all going to need a stiff drink to get through this day!"

James nodded his agreement.

They drove out to the pond, unloaded the carriage, and spread a blanket; they'd unwrap the food later. Louisa looked at Claire, and almost on cue, they started to disrobe. James' face turned red, but John just smiled and joined the ladies. When all four were nude, they ran to the edge and jumped into the pond.

Once in the water, they seemed to relax and the nudity didn't seem to bother them. After thirty minutes they returned to the blanket and dried off. James started to dress.

"No, no, we're going to have this picnic in the nude as well!" Claire had gotten out of her shell and was enjoying it immensely.

They sat, ate and drank for two hours before deciding it was time to go back to the house and have a nap. The four didn't talk much on the way back, but once the Harrises were in their bedroom, James kissed Claire passionately and they made love for the next hour. "You look positively ravishing today. I love you, Claire."

The next afternoon, Louisa asked Claire how she had had the nerve to go forward with their little adventure. "To tell you the truth, I was kind of desperate. James hadn't made love to me in months. He's only been interested in his bank. I was trying to shock him out of middle age. I especially took notice of him watching John giving me the look. He could see that another man found me attractive."

"You know, it didn't hurt my love life either," Louisa responded. "We did it last night and early this morning. I owe you one!"

The next day, John was at his office in Charleston for the morning, and Claire wanted to sleep in, so it was Louisa and James who shared breakfast. "Have you considered shipping your cotton to New England?" he asked her.

"I've had contracts with certain factors for a long time. I'd be afraid to make a change after so many years."

"If I could show you that you'd be saving money, would you be interested?"

"My factor has lent me money when we had a bad crop and when the textile manufacturers were slow in paying."

"My bank would, in essence, become the factor and make sure you were paid on time if you went to New England with your cotton. You know you ultimately pay for shipping across the Atlantic. Think how much cheaper it would be to go to New England instead of Europe!"

Louisa produced her records for the previous five years, and James showed her that there would be about fifteen percent more profit for her if she made the change.

"I hope that we're close enough friends that I can raise another issue. It's apparent that no more slaves will be introduced into the South, and many in this area are moving further south, where the majority of cotton is grown. If you want to maintain a viable business, you have to have labor that you can count on. If you lose your slaves, you'll have a big problem. If I can guarantee you an additional fifteen percent, will you free a portion of your slaves and hire them back for wages?"

"You're a God-dammed abolitionist!"

"No, I'm a businessman. Look at what I've shown you and what I've said about labor. Think it over. You may be able to compete down the road while your contemporaries are stymied for lack of labor. If you pay your help, they'll stay. You're a smart woman. Look at it logically and not politically."

"That's easy for *you* to say. I'm living with a future U.S. senator who is pro-slavery and will probably lead the fight to secede from the Union."

"John is a pragmatist. Talk to him, show him the numbers and ask what *he'd* do. He certainly would be an asset if you decided to go the route I've suggested."

When they left, the four hugged each other as though it would be for the last time. They had been friends before, but now they shared an intimacy that few couples dared. Louisa whispered in James's ear, "I'll let you know after I talk to John."

On the way to the train, Claire asked him what Louisa had whispered in his ear. He smiled and told her about their conversation and what she had said when they left.

"She's in love with you!"

"Nonsense. From the first time I met her, she let it be known that John was the one."

"That doesn't mean that she doesn't love you. She told me that she did."

CHAPTER TWENTY-TWO

Jimmy and Claire enjoyed their children and their life together. Their only problem was that Jimmy was restless unless he had another project to work on. With Boston and New York banks showing a profit and his investors happy, he turned his thoughts to Chicago and a third bank in his empire.

Cameron and Abigail loved the two children and were happy to watch them while Jimmy and Claire went to Chicago to look for a new site. The train ride to Chicago took nearly a day, but their stay at the Illinois Plaza, a new hotel in the downtown, more than made up for the inconvenience. The next morning they met with the mayor and told him what they had in mind. He suggested a real estate company, an architect and a builder, who had good reputations. Jimmy told him he'd look at their resumes. Three days later he and Claire found a site on Main Street that met their specifications, put down a deposit, and talked to the architect the mayor had recommended. Preliminary sketches would be available in a week for them to review.

Since their visit to Magnolia, Jimmy and Claire were sharing an intimacy that they hadn't experienced for two years. Their sex life had improved, but better than that, Jimmy was including her in all his business decisions and Claire finally felt like an equal partner. Having Cameron and Abigail close by was especially fortunate; the two of them could travel when they wanted to, while his father and his wife looked after the grandchildren.

There were several circulars in the businesses in town touting the debates between Abraham Lincoln and Stephen Douglas. The newspaper carried the entire narrative from the previous debate. Both Jimmy and Claire read the newspaper accounts and were excited to see that the next debate was in a few days at Freeport, about an hour by train from Chicago. James wanted to meet Lincoln, so he and Claire went to Lincoln's law office in downtown Chicago and asked the male receptionist if they could meet with

Lincoln in Freeport. "I'll see what I can do. Is there a particular reason why you wish to speak to Mr. Lincoln?"

"I find his approach to the slavery issue very refreshing, and I'd like to pursue some dialog with him. We plan to attend the debate in Freeport and then come back by train."

"I'll be at the debate. Once it's over, come to the stage and I'll see what I can do."

The debate was two days hence, and Jimmy and Claire travelled by train, had an early dinner there and were at the Freeport site before six o'clock that evening. The stands were set up with a large stage in front. They were lucky to get a couple of seats near the front; it was estimated that nearly fifteen thousand people had turned out to hear the two men. The first speaker had sixty minutes to make his case and the second speaker ninety minutes for his speech and rebuttal. An additional thirty minutes was awarded to the first speaker. Lincoln went first.

He went on the offensive immediately, responding to the seven questions from the previous debate that Douglas had insisted he hadn't responded to. Next Lincoln asked four questions of his own for Douglas. It came down to a ploy on Lincoln's part to box Douglas into making an error. The main question Lincoln posed was whether Douglas favored the Dred Scott decision, which said that slaves could not be excluded from U.S. territories, or the Kansas Nebraska Compromise, which left the slavery question to the voters of those territories.

In the past, Douglas had supported the doctrine of Popular Sovereignty, which said that squatters had the right to decide the slavery issue; this was termed the Freeport Doctrine by the newspapers. This would later prove to be an obstacle that Douglas couldn't overcome and expect any support in the South for his Presidential run.

At the end of the debate, James, with Claire in tow, pushed his way through the crowd to get to the stage. When they saw Lincoln's assistant, they yelled out his name until he turned and waved them over. "I know you've come a long way to meet Mr. Lincoln, but he's busy with newspaper reporters, and I don't know when he'll have time to see you. He'll be in his office in Chicago in four days. Come around noon and you can have a chat while he eats lunch. That's the best I can do for you."

The timing was good for them because they still had to review the preliminary sketches on their new bank project. They arrived at Lincoln's office on time and were told by the assistant that his boss would be available in fifteen minutes. Soon they were ushered into a small office, where they met Lincoln, who towered over them. Sandwiches and lemonade was provided for all three; neither James nor Claire declined. "We've not met before, that I can recall, so please tell me why you wanted to meet me."

"We heard your speech the other night in Freeport and liked what you had to say. To let you know a little about us, I'm James Harris. I'm the chairman of two national banks in New York City and Boston and this is my wife Claire, who is the stepdaughter of the Prime Minister of England. We came to Chicago to see if it's feasible to establish one of our banks here. Both of us read the newspaper article on your first debate with Mr. Douglas, and each of us wanted to meet you."

Lincoln stopped eating his sandwich and stared at the two before he spoke. "I'm not looking for financial assistance."

"I grew up in the South; I have many close friends living there, and now we live in the North. I'm concerned about the conflict between our two sections of the country and what the future holds. Like many of our contemporaries, we would like to find an equitable solution before the unsaid conflict gains too much momentum and secession is the only alternative."

"And you, Mrs. Harris, what are your views?"

"I find slavery abhorrent and believe it should be abolished. But, like my husband, I believe that a compromise of some nature is what needs to be done. Have you considered running for a higher office?"

"At times I have, but I'm afraid that I haven't been too successful of late, so I don't know whether that vocation is on the horizon."

"If you decide that you want to run and do need financial support, we'd be glad to help. In the interim, please visit us at our home in New York City when you're in that area and bring Mrs. Lincoln; we have plenty of space," Claire said.

• • •

Claire had a keen eye for detail, and she made some minor changes to the drawings that the architect presented to them the following Monday. James made a deposit to purchase the land and asked Lincoln's office to follow through with the transaction.

Nine months later, he and Claire returned to Chicago for the grand opening of the bank. James had promoted one of the vice-presidents from the New York bank to be the Chicago manager. In the interim, Lincoln and his wife had visited them in New York City on two occasions. Although the subject of running for political office came up in their conversation, Lincoln wasn't ready to throw his hat into the ring. He was, however, making speeches all over the North for Senatorial candidates and those running for the House of Representatives. Throughout this time, he avoided the rhetoric of the extremes and used a common-sense approach to the problems of the day. This endeared him to those candidates who were successful, and when it came time to pick a nominee for the Republican Party, he had substantial support. The only serious competition within the party was from William Seward, who was an uncompromising foe of slavery.

The Harrises travelled to Chicago on a quarterly basis to evaluate the branches' progress. Each time they visited the Windy City, they would allocate time to meet with Lincoln. This visit was no exception; they had an appointment in Lincoln's office the day after they arrived. Both smiled when they saw sandwiches and lemonade set up for three.

"Due to a suggestion by some influential members of the Republican Party," Lincoln told them, "I've decided to run for their party's nomination for president in the 1860 election. Thanks to you two, I have sufficient financial backing to make a good attempt to win the nomination."

"What else can we do to help?"

"Nothing, at this time. But if I secure the nomination, I may ask you to go south and check with your former friends and acquaintances to see what kind of support I could expect if I campaigned there."

Significantly, Lincoln won the nomination at the Chicago convention on the third ballot, with Senator Hannibal Hamlin as his running mate. The Democratic convention was to be held in May 1860 in Charleston. John Beauregard would be a delegate to the convention, and had managed to get on the rules committee. However, he and two other southern senators were a minority on the committee.

The southern delegates to the Democratic convention held a caucus before meeting at Charleston. John was chairman of the committee and gave the opening speech before the assembled body. "Gentlemen, there are several issues that we must insist upon: first will be the platform. I believe that we must have a federal slave code for the territories as part of the plank. I know that the northern delegates will strongly resist our initiative, but if we aren't able to prevail on this issue, then our way of life is in jeopardy.

"The second issue is who the nominee will be. Douglas, with his ridiculous Freeport Doctrine, cannot be supported. I suggest we vote for John C. Breckinridge of Tennessee. He has admirable credentials, is the current Vice-President under Buchanan, and is a candidate we can rally around."

When the Democratic convention convened, it was obvious that a confrontation was brewing, and when the platform as proposed by the southern delegates was defeated, John and fifty other delegates stormed out of the hall. Douglas, thinking he'd have smooth sailing now that the more rebellious delegates had left, was nonetheless unable to secure the nomination, nor could anyone else, and the convention adjourned to meet again in Baltimore six weeks hence.

John went back to Magnolia. He planned to meet the following week with the fifty who had bolted the convention.

"I don't understand why you walked out," Louisa said. "It seems to me that it would be better to stay in the convention and try to rally some of the northern delegates to your way of thinking. Your strategy could backfire!"

"Well, you weren't there, and therefore you can't understand what our strategy was. Douglas was unable to gain the nomination after fifty-seven ballots, many of which occurred after we bolted. I think we were correct to use that maneuver. The convention will reconvene in six weeks, and I'll be there with the others who walked out."

"I thought you were one of the *moderate* voices among the delegates!"

"I am! We played by the rules, and were using a strategy that we thought would work. We want Breckenridge as the nominee. I believe that if we keep up the pressure, we can get Douglas to capitulate."

"Will they let you back in the convention?"

"They'll have to, since I'm a delegate from the state of South Carolina."

John was present when the Democrats reconvened in Baltimore. There was no doubt that a great deal of animosity remained between the northern and southern delegates. When the platform came up for a vote, John and the other southern members of the platform committee introduced an amendment to that platform. They wanted to have the federal slave code in the territories added as part of the plank. The Douglas group prevailed, and John and his fellow southern delegates walked out of the convention once again and held their own convention in another part of town.

This wasn't what John wanted, but he was a Southerner at heart, and he and the delegates nominated Breckinridge as their presidential nominee, with Joseph Lane of Oregon as his running mate. John returned to Magnolia and told Louisa what transpired.

"How can you possibly win with Breckinridge?" she snorted. "No one from the North will vote for him. All you've done is alienate yourself from the established Democratic party, and you'll be on the outside of the power structure. I hope this isn't a prelude to secession."

"If Lincoln wins, he'll set the slaves free. How are you going to run Magnolia without slaves?"

"I've been moving away from slave labor for some time. Right now we're fifty percent free and fifty percent slave labor. By sending my cotton to New England, I've bypassed the factor, and I'm saving about fifteen percent. I don't have to rely on the excess charges imposed on us in the past, especially if there is a time delay between delivery and getting paid. Jimmy has shown me a way to basically modernize my operation," Louisa said.

"Why didn't you talk this over with me before you freed some of the slaves? Do you know what position this puts me in?"

"What difference does it make if the South secedes, unless you're still going to be a Senator from South Carolina?"

"I forbid you to free any more slaves!"

"Magnolia belongs to me. You've never wanted to be part of this operation, and therefore you have no say."

"I can go to court and take Magnolia from you."

"You'll never do that, and both of us know it. I have something else we need to discuss. Jimmy has three banks up and running, and all three are showing a profit. I'm concerned about what's happening in the South with the threat of secession. What are you going to do with the money you received from the sale of Rosebud?" Louisa asked.

"I have it invested locally, but it's fairly liquid. What's your point?"

"I think we ought to invest with Jimmy. His investments are about sixty percent in northern industry and thirty-five percent in Europe. The remaining five percent is in the South. I'd like you to consider taking the money invested in the South and put it with James. We need to be sure that our children will be taken care of."

"I don't know if I can do that. It would be like selling out the South. It's as though I don't believe in our cause."

"What is our cause?"

"To live our lives on our own terms, without northern interference."

"My God, John, you've gone too far. We don't have any interference at Magnolia from the North, and you know it. So who are you fighting for? Certainly not you and me!"

"I don't know why I'm discussing this with you—you're a woman!"

"Well, I'm one smart woman, and I'm your wife. That's why you're discussing it with me."

•   •   •

There were other parties rearing their heads during that political season. One of these was formed by disenchanted members of the old Whig Party and some members of the American Party. They held a convention and nominated John Bell of Tennessee for President and a former Senator from Massachusetts, Edward Everett, for Vice-President. Their platform recognized the constitution and the preservation of the Union.

The other was a more sinister and secret movement called the Knights of the Golden Circle, founded by Dr.

George Bickley. Its original goal was to form a circle of slave states to include Mexico, the Caribbean, Central America and the southern states below the Mason-Dixon Line. Their membership was limited to southern sympathizers both in the North and the South. They held a convention in Raleigh, North Carolina, and proposed an agenda of one big slave empire.

Presidential nominees didn't generally campaign in those days; they had their surrogates do the actual campaigning. Soon after he received the nomination as the Republican candidate, Lincoln met with Jimmy in New York City and asked him for a favor. "You're someone I've come to rely on. I haven't decided whether to have a campaign in the South or stay strictly in the North. Since you were in business in many of the southern cities, I wonder if you'd make a trip for me to assess how much support I'd have in the south. My understanding is that you had offices in Charleston, Savannah, Mobile and New Orleans. What do you think of my idea?"

"I'd be delighted to make the trip. I still have some investments in the South, and it'll give me an opportunity to check on them at the same time. I could leave next week and be back in ten days."

Claire had a recital scheduled for the following week in Philadelphia, so she was unable to accompany Jim on his trip. He took the train to Charleston and stayed with his grandparents for two days before riding out to Magnolia.

His grandparents were totally mesmerized by his success. "Jim, I think moving north was a smart move. I understand that you've invested heavily in New England," his grandfather wondered.

"New England has many advantages when it comes to textile manufacturing. There are plenty of rivers to produce hydroelectric power; there's an abundant educated workforce, and it's given women an opportunity to work. In the South, the emphasis is on agriculture, and there's a lack of manpower to expand and or to go into manufacturing. So yes, we're investing where the action is."

His friends were home and welcomed him to Magnolia. They hadn't seen each other since he and Claire visited and all four went skinny-dipping. At dinner that evening, the conversation turned to the election on the horizon.

"Are you supporting Lincoln?" John asked.

"As a matter of fact, I am. The purpose of my trip here is twofold. The first is to see you and Louisa, and the second is to get a feel for Lincoln's chances in the South, especially if he campaigned here."

"Jimmy, he has no background to be president. He's really a country bumpkin running for the highest office in the land. I don't think he's ever written a coherent sentence!"

"Why don't you tell me what you *really* think, John? I read the *Charleston Mercury* before I came here. They certainly aren't supporting his candidacy, but portraying him as a ugly duckling is carrying it a little too far. From what I've seen of Mr. Lincoln, criticism about his appearance falls off him like water off a duck's back."

Louisa laughed out loud. "He's got you there, John!"

"Well, whatever you think, he doesn't have a ghost of a chance down here. In fact, he'd better stay out of the South, if he knows what's good for him!"

"Sounds ominous to me. Do you really think there's a realistic threat to him?"

"I do."

"Let's change the subject and talk about you, *Senator* John Beauregard. That has a nice ring to it! I'm proud of you, John. I'm also proud of Louisa. How many women have the courage not only to run a large plantation, but to free some of her slaves and hire them back as free laborers."

"Well, that's not going over too well on the other plantations," Louisa responded. "The owners accuse us of subverting the southern way of life. John hasn't been invited to a couple of functions. On one occasion, a constituent of his asked him whether *he* was the man of the house, or was *I*. John punched him out, and he hasn't been asked that question again. But Jimmy, what you proposed makes a lot of sense, and I've found that those who work as free men work almost twice as hard, and my profit has increased."

"Are any of the other plantation owners taking your lead and trying it?"

"There are none that I know of. There's a lot of intimidation in the South if you step out of the norm. I've faced some of that, but with John's position, they leave me alone. I haven't had any midnight visitors to show me the errors of my ways yet, but some have. How long are you staying with us?"

"I'll leave the day after tomorrow for Savannah. It'll be the first time I've been there since Sarah died."

"John and I want to talk about some potential investments."

"Okay."

"We've invested the proceeds from Rosebud locally, and we're wondering what *you* could offer us."

"My banks use our money to support local enterprises, invest into the textile industry in New England, and have interests in linen manufacturing in France and England. We can provide you with solid investments, or some with a certain amount of risk. My advice, as a banker, would be to put half of your money into a solid investment and half into a little riskier one."

"I'm not comfortable with moving all of our money out of the South," said John. "I'd feel like I'm not supporting our cause. Let's put half of our money with Jimmy and invest the other half locally as we did before. I like your idea of half in solid investments and half with a little risk. The money is for our children, in case something happens to us. And Jim, I hope we're good enough friends that you'll keep this transaction between us. It could prove embarrassing if the word got out."

• • •

Jim took the train south to Savannah, where he stayed at the Chestnut Hotel. The next morning he looked up one of his old acquaintances, an individual who ran his former office downtown. Franklin Fontaine was happy to see him after all these years. "I've got about an hour's worth of work to do, but I'm free for lunch. Can you wait?"

"I have an acquaintance at Morton's I'd like to visit. I can be back by noon. Does the old Morse Saloon still serve great fish?"

"I'll meet you there."

Franklin had been very helpful during the last days of Sarah's life when Jim wasn't in the office very much. When he had sold his factoring business, he made a provision for Franklin with the new owners. At the saloon, they passed the first thirty minutes catching up on each other's life and then ordered lunch. "I've been asked by Abraham Lincoln to look at the feasibility of running a campaign in the South. You've always had your hand on the pulse of things in Savannah, so I'd like your opinion."

Franklin looked around the room as though trying to see who was there and who could overhear what they were discussing. "These are tough times. The secessionists are on a mission, and I don't know what or who can slow them down. If you're a moderate and try to voice your opinion, you are either shouted down or they try to intimidate you. It's working. I believe most of the South doesn't want to secede, but that makes no difference. We seem to be in a boat without oars, and it's carrying us all downstream fast. If I were Lincoln, I wouldn't waste my time, especially in South Carolina and Georgia—those are the hot beds of secession. Jimmy, the most common theme down here is, if the Yankees want a fight, we'll lick them in a month."

"I guess you've answered my question. I got the same from my old friend who runs Morton's."

"Are you staying long?"

"Too many memories. They were good, but I've remarried, and I need to move on with my life. Savannah was always good to me. I hope it's the same for you, Franklin."

Mobile and New Orleans gave him the same feedback, and he returned to New York with a message to Lincoln that was not very encouraging. Claire had returned from Philadelphia and was excited about the reception she had received. She had an agent now and was looking forward to more concerts. Since his last visit to Magnolia, Jim realized how much he missed John and Louisa. He feared that the South was on a course that couldn't be altered and he wondered what would happen to them. After his tour of the four major cities in the South, he wasn't sure that Lincoln, with all his wisdom, could keep the Union together. He also wondered if and when he'd see his old friends again.

CHAPTER TWENTY-THREE

The national election of 1860 was contentious, to say the least, but in the end Abraham Lincoln had the prerequisite number of electoral votes and was elected President of the United States. Douglas came in behind Breckinridge and Bell; he only won one state. After the election, Lincoln began forming a cabinet and hiring a series of assistants. He and Mrs. Lincoln came to New York City and stayed with Jimmy and Claire. They stayed but a day, but the question Lincoln asked James would make a change in his and Claire's life.

"James, I'll do everything possible to keep the Union together, but slavery has to go. I'm not sure what the South will do, but I know that whatever they do, it will depend on their main asset, which is cotton. They ship the majority of that commodity to Europe. I don't want to have my policies kidnapped by the Europeans. I need an administrative assistant who understands international financing and has the ability to talk to those in power in England and make them understand that we will not tolerate any interference."

"You mean my wife's stepfather."

"Yes, that's who I'm talking about."

"This would require a move to Washington, turning my banks over to some form of consulting company and probably making frequent trips to some European capitals. Did I read the position correctly?"

"You're a very astute young man."

"I need to talk this over with my wife. Can I have a few days?"

"I'll give you a week. That should be enough time for you to decide if it's feasible for you."

Claire asked a lot of questions about the offer, but the main one was, "Is this something you want to do?"

"I admit that I do. I never gave much credence to working for the government, but what he's suggested is something I can do and I believe, I'll do it to the best of my ability."

"I gather that I and the children must move to D.C.?"

"I don't want to be there without you, and I won't accept the position unless you agree."

"You and I have a wonderful life together. Banking is something you enjoy, and being here in New York giving piano recitals is something *I* enjoy. It would be a shame to drastically change our lives for something that someone else could do just as well. Can I hedge my approval by saying that the children and I will move to Washington with you, but I don't want to buy a home until we're sure? I'd like to retain our New York home as security. Do you think we can rent adequate housing for all of us?"

"I do—and thanks for your approval. I love you very much and want us to be a family above everything else."

"Jimmy, is there anything else that needs to be done before you give him your answer? The thing that comes to mind is the three banks. You've done a remarkable job for us and your investors. I don't know if you can find anyone who will give it the attention it needs."

"There are two things I need to square away. The first is management of the banks, and the second is the three significant investments I've made to some plantation owners around Charleston. I'm not comfortable with the way the situation is unfolding between North and South."

James had someone in mind who he thought would be able to fill his shoes. The manager of his New York bank had shown a great deal of ingenuity and stability as Jim opened the other two branches. When he met with William Sampson, the man was as humble as he could be when Jimmy laid out what his new duties would be. "I won't let you down, Mr. Harris. When you're ready to come back, I'll turn everything over to you in the same shape as though you were running the operation."

It was late November when he made the trip south again. He could tell that his grandparents had aged, and he wondered how many times he'd be able to see them in the future. He begged them to move to New York City to be close to Cameron and Abigail, but they refused. "We appreciate your concern, but we've lived here all our lives and here's where we want to stay," his grandfather said as his wife looked on.

John and Louisa were at home and were happy to see him, even though John was angry that Lincoln had won the election.

"I don't have much time to spend with you, so I'll get directly to the point. I'm taking a position with the Lincoln administration to handle some aspects of international financing and relations with Europe."

"Being the son-in-law of the Prime Minister of England didn't hurt you, I see!" John was ribbing him.

"I'm turning the banks over to William Sampson, an associate of mine in the New York branch. There are three loans in this area that I need to address, and one of them is with Magnolia. You've never been late, but I need to reduce the principal. I know this may be too sudden for you, so I'd like to hear what you have to say."

"I can't repay the debt at this time," Louisa responded. "I could pay it down nearly thirty percent, but beyond that, it may not be possible for at least a year. I've always made payments on time, so what's the problem?"

"The conflict is increasing, and with Lincoln's inauguration about four months off, I'd like to alleviate any future concerns for Sampson."

"So are you going to foreclose on me?"

"No. If you can't, you can't. I'll make other arrangements."

"You mean that you'll fund it out of your own pocket."

"That's one option."

"I'll pay down thirty percent now and twenty percent more by the end of next year, and then we'll see where I am. Is that acceptable?"

"Thank you. I knew you'd understand."

The President-elect was at home the first week in December when James sent him a telegram saying that he'd accept the position in the new administration. He and Claire travelled to the nation's capital, and after a few days found a suitable home they could lease for a year.

But the events that exploded on the scene caught the new administration in a peculiar position. They had to deal with the secession of South Carolina on December 20 and five more states within the next month; yet, they couldn't deal with it directly. James Buchanan was still the President and would remain so until March 4th. Prior to that date, Texas approved secession and Jefferson Davis was elected Provisional President of the Confederate States of America. When Jimmy told Claire, she was astonished. "What do we do now?"

"Lincoln is coming east to meet with his cabinet appointees, probably here in New York. Since we've plenty of space, I suggested he stay here while he's in New York. I hope you don't mind?"

"Are we still moving to Washington? This secession movement puts things in a different perspective. I wonder if we should move now? You could go to Washington, if you must, while I and the children could stay here until this all settles down."

"There's nothing to worry about. I got your approval before I accepted Lincoln's offer. I want to be there for the inauguration. I suggest we start moving this month, soon after Lincoln's meeting here." Claire didn't respond.

Meanwhile, John Beauregard and all the South Carolina congressmen and senators resigned from the U.S. government soon after their state seceded. John was sitting at home when an officer rode up in the rank of Brigadier General of the Confederate States and tied his horse to the rail out front. John and Louisa raced out of the house to greet John's cousin, Pierre Beauregard, whom both of them hadn't seen for some time.

"My, you look handsome in that uniform! Give me a hug," Louisa said.

"The last I heard about you was that you were superintendent at West Point, but that was a Union position," John commented.

"I'll make it a short story. As soon as some of the southern states started to secede, the War Department said I had southern leanings and perhaps it wouldn't be wise for me to remain as superintendent. I resigned my commission shortly thereafter and was appointed as a Brigadier General in the Confederacy; now I'm in charge of the South Carolina militia, commanding Charleston harbor."

"This is very disturbing, and it hits close to home. My son James was planning to be at West Point this year. I nominated him before I resigned from the Senate, and I was looking forward to having you mentor him while he was at the academy."

"What about V.M.I.? It's not as prestigious as West Point, and he wouldn't be able to follow in his father's footsteps, but he could be commissioned in the Confederate Army. Many of the lads who planned to go to the academy have already applied to V.M.I. I can help if necessary."

"I'll have to talk to James. He had his heart set on West Point. You think war is coming—don't you?"

"I do."

"James is not going to take this lightly. From the moment he could talk, he wanted to be a soldier like his father. I really don't know how he'll take this. Why don't you men talk, and I'll see how dinner is coming along. You're staying, aren't you, Pierre?" Louisa asked.

"You bet I am! I heard you were a fabulous cook."

The two men went out onto the porch and John poured Pierre a glass of wine. "I can give you something stronger, if you wish."

"This is fine. Why don't we go for a walk? I have something confidential that I want to pass on to you."

When they were about fifty yards from the residence, Pierre stopped. "I have orders from Jefferson Davis to attack Fort Sumter if they don't surrender on April 12th."

"You can't be serious. That would mean war!"

"I have my orders in writing. Davis asked Lincoln to vacate three installations in the South, but he refused."

"Who's commanding the fort?"

"It's Major Anderson."

"I know him. I was at the academy with him."

"I'm keeping all this information close to my vest, but I'm inviting you to come to the Charleston harbor on April 12th and watch me take it down. Why don't you bring your son? And by the way, what are you going to do now that you're no longer in Congress?"

"I'm going to Richmond next week to see what our new President has for me. I knew him for a short time while he was in the Senate; we had dinner a few times. They couldn't have chosen a more worthy individual to take charge of our new nation."

"You're assuming that all the southern states will secede."

"I count twelve for sure, and two on the fence. Those two may wait a while and then do the same as the rest of us."

John travelled to Richmond and met with several of Davis' assistants, and finally, at the end of the week, he had a meeting with the man. "Good to see you, John. I'm sorry that I've kept you waiting, but this cause is moving so quickly that I don't seem to have enough time to do anything. I hope you won't take that as a slight, because what I'm offering you is a position that's as important to our cause as fighting a battle."

"I'm anxious to hear what you have to say, Mr. President."

"I want you to take over our Signal Corps and build it up so that we have a first-class intelligence agency. We have many spies already contributing to our cause, and I want you to give the agency a rudder and some direction."

"You know that I don't have any experience in the art of spying."

"You were a soldier, and a darn good one, and a firstclass legislator. I know your views, and I know that you're a man who gets the job done. What say ye?"

"I'm honored that you have this much faith in me. I won't let you down. I accept."

"We have a man in place right now, by the name of William Norris. He's been told that he'll report to you. I think he can show you what's been done, and he'll be a good second in command."

John wondered what Louisa would say about the position that Davis had offered him. He also wondered if she would move to Richmond and leave Magnolia. Well, he might as well go home and tell her the news. He waited until after dinner while they were sitting on the porch having a glass of wine before he raised the issue. "You haven't asked me what Jefferson Davis wanted to see me about."

"I figured that you would tell me in good time. It's obviously not good news, or you would have told me already."

John smiled. "He's offered me the commander's position in the Signal Corps. In essence, I'd become the new Confederate states' chief spy. What do you think of that?"

"You can't be serious about accepting that position! You were a U.S. senator, and if the South is going to have its own country and laws that mirror the one they left, then you should be a senator from this state. Have you already accepted the position?"

"I have, and it requires us to move to the new capitol, Richmond."

"You mean *you*, not *us*. I can't pick up and move at a moment's notice! This is our livelihood, and I'm not abandoning it."

"I didn't mean initially. I figured it would take you six months to find someone to run the plantation and then you and the children could follow when it was convenient."

"No, it's not convenient at *any* time. This is pure folly, John. I know you want to help the cause, but this is our home! Our children will still need direction as the conflict escalates. There is no better life than the one we have. Why do you want to destroy it?"

"I was asked to fill an important position in our new nation, and I intend to do just that."

"*What* new nation? All that's happened is some states have seceded. Who's to say that the two sides can't get together and reach a compromise—say, somewhere in the middle? Why does it have to be either or? I understand you want to make a point—just don't stab yourself with it!"

"You're a woman. How could you understand the grand scheme of things? I don't know why I'm even discussing it with you."

"You're discussing it with me because you don't know whether you're right or wrong, and because I'm your wife and I've stood by you all these years."

He got out of his chair and walked to her end of the table, putting his hands around her face and kissing her tenderly. "You're right on one point. I do love you, but I'm taking the position."

A tear dripped down her cheek.

Before leaving, he wanted to speak with his son James. He found him in his room; they'd been very close. They had been hunting and fishing companions each summer, and twice they had gone to the Catawba village and stayed a week. John remembered how in his youth he and Jimmy had stayed there with Cameron Harris. Those summers had been the happiest times of his life. It was no wonder that he wanted to share the experience with his oldest son! John respected and loved his father François, but the man was always busy with the plantation. They spent *some* time together, but it was Cameron Harris whom he emulated.

John and his son were sitting in James' bedroom, talking about West Point. "James, the appointment to West Point doesn't seem to be very stable now," John said.

"You mean that the appointment was conditioned on your staying in Congress?"

"No, I think you still have a slot. There is nothing I'd rather see than you following in my footsteps at the academy. However, tensions are so high at this time that the Union commandant may ask you to leave. My cousin was superintendent at the academy and they asked him to vacate that position. We don't have to make the decision today. Here's what I'd like you to do: meet me in front of the entrance to Fort Sumter at noon on April 12th."

"What's significant about that date, Dad?"

"I'd rather not say, and I'd appreciate it if you didn't mention our meeting on that day to anyone—and I mean *anyone.*"

"No wonder you're the South's chief spy now, Dad!"

Well, Louisa was right about one thing. He wondered if the South really was going to carry through with secession— or was there a compromise to be made? He'd heard rumors that Davis had sent a delegation to Washington to meet with the President-elect. He wondered what they'd discussed, and whether Jimmy Harris was involved. Secession was predicated on Lincoln winning the election, but Buchanan was still the president for almost two more months. A lot could happen in that short time.

John was shown to his office in the Richmond Capitol and immediately went about learning his job. He had an initial briefing from Major Norris and learned about his Washington cell, which would play an important part in the future.

"Who's my counterpart in the North?"

"Allen Pinkerton has that position, though I know there's a signal corps headed by a cutthroat named Lafayette Baker. From his background, I believe he's more dangerous to the Union than to us," Norris said.

"What else?"

"Your main problem will be in consolidating information coming into the Confederacy. It seems that both sides are in the spy business and have their own agents. Sometimes we don't know who's working for whom. Rose Greenhow and her group work for us. She's set up secret routes between the Union capitol and Richmond that are changing on a daily basis. One of the major spy activities at present is under the Naval Department. James Hudson and about ten soldiers have been dispatched to Liverpool, England, to set up a base of operations. From what I've been told, he's coordinating the shipment of cotton to Europe and is initiating contracts with private boat companies to build blockade runners for the South. Hudson hasn't been coordinating his actions with me. You may have a lot more clout than I do, and you may be able at least to be in the loop on what he and his men are doing abroad."

What John didn't have, as yet, was an objective, and a comprehensive plan to implement. If the North would accept secession, then any plan would have to take into account that the North was a bordering country and probably a friendly one. If hostilities broke out, then the job of the signal corps would take a different route and any spying would be proactive. He set up a meeting with Davis to get some guidance.

Major Norris appeared at his office two days later. John could tell he had something serious to tell him. "Have you ever heard of the Knights of the Golden Circle?" Norris asked.

John smiled. "Yes. I know about their grand plan for a vast empire that would be pro-slavery. I always thought they were crackpots."

"They're not, I can assure you. They came to me with a plan which I approved before you took over. I wasn't sure they had the resources to implement it, but now I believe they can."

John was attentive. "Tell me what they plan."

"They're going to blow up the train that Lincoln will ride to his inauguration in Washington. They plan to blow it up in Baltimore."

"And you think they can pull it off?"

"I give them a better than even chance of success."

"This could be a game changer! With Lincoln out of the way, Davis could probably negotiate a settlement that would favor us, and there'd be no war. Do they need anything else from us?"

"If they do, I can't reach them."

Jimmy was travelling with Lincoln on his way to his swearing in by the Chief Justice of the Supreme Court. They planned to stop in Baltimore, greet the crowds lining the route, and then, after an hour's delay, continue on to Washington. Jimmy was sitting with Lincoln in the smoking car when the train suddenly came to a halt. Just then Allen Pinkerton came into the car and spoke softly to Mr. Lincoln. Lincoln looked at James. "Mr. Harris, we must change trains now. There's been a change in our itinerary, and we must proceed with due haste."

Pinkerton ushered the party off the train and onto another train that had its steam up. As soon as Lincoln and his party stepped aboard, the train got underway. Jim asked Pinkerton what this was all about.

"We have reason to believe that there'll be an attempt on Mr. Lincoln's life, so we switched trains."

"How did you find out about the plot?"

"We had a credible source inside the group that was plotting the assassination."

John waited all day for any news of the attack on Lincoln. Toward the end of the day, Norris came into his office and informed him that Pinkerton had gotten wind of the plot, and Lincoln had changed trains. "He's now in Washington and has probably been sworn in as President."

Rentals were in high demand, but John got lucky and found a three-bedroom home close to his office. It came with a housekeeper who came in every morning but was off on the weekends. John wrote to Louisa and asked her to change her mind and come to Richmond with the children. To date, she'd not responded—and he was lonesome.

The decision on which plan to initiate was almost made for him, even though he couldn't get an appointment with the Confederate president. First, Lincoln was inaugurated, and then, with the state of Virginia leaning toward secession, it was almost certain that eleven or twelve states would secede. Before he knew it, April had arrived, and P.G.T. Beauregard called upon him at his office, again asking him to come to Charleston on April twelfth. Beauregard was going to give Fort Sumter an order to evacuate on that date. "You know if you fire on Sumter, that'll mean war," John said.

"I think Davis was rebuffed in Washington, and he's ordered me to take the fort," Pierre said.

"No wonder I couldn't get an audience with him!" John mused.

On April 12th, James Beauregard was standing in the Charleston harbor looking at Fort Sumter. His father and his cousin, General Beauregard, were at his side. The South

Carolina militia under Beauregard had given their allegiance to the South and were prepared to take the fort. Supplies ships from the North had been turned back, leaving the defenders short of supplies and food. Major Anderson had declined Beauregard's order to surrender and the fort flew the Union flag; sentries manned the walls. Beauregard walked over to his battery commander and ordered the South Carolina militia to initiate an artillery attack. After an hour of bombardment, the walls of the fort were crumbling, but Major Anderson refused to capitulate. The militia continued the bombardment for the remainder of the day. Major Anderson surrendered the fort the following day.

John stood by his cousin's side; he could feel the enormity of the situation. They were going to war against the northern part of their country, against people who looked like them, spoke like them, and in most ways lived like them. "You look sad, John," Pierre noted.

"I *am* sad. Yes, I fought for a pro-slavery platform and yes, I'm for states' rights, but I never envisioned that we would go to war!"

"They have no stomach for a long, drawn-out fight; we'll win this within six months and get everything we want. You'll see."

"If we get what we want, will we be able to enjoy it?" John responded.

James spoke up. "I can see why you asked me here today. I agree that West Point seems out of reach now. What do you really think about V.M.I.?"

"It's a fine school—perhaps not in the same class as West Point—but you'll be proud to go there."

"Could I apply there and make up my mind by the first of August?"

"You think there may be peace yet?"

"Perhaps not—but what do I have to lose?"

John and James went back to Magnolia, where John tried to get Louisa to reconsider; however, she was adamant and wouldn't even discuss the issue.

"We're a peaceful country. Who are these idiots that decided we all want war—was it you?"

"No, it wasn't me. I'm as shocked as you are, but the difference between us is, my country has made the decision to go all the way for our freedom. I must honor that decision and go back to Richmond; I have a job to do."

"But your country is *America*," Louisa said. "You've deserted your country for another one."

CHAPTER TWENTY-FOUR

James and Claire Harris had been in their new home in Washington for nearly a month when the news came that Fort Sumter had surrendered to the South Carolina militia. Lincoln called an emergency meeting with all cabinet heads and James present.

Prior to the firing on Fort Sumter, General Winfield Scott had initially proposed a plan that he believed would bring the South to its knees. It was called the Anaconda Plan. The first part of the plan called for sending gun boats, with sixty thousand Union troops, down the Mississippi to secure the river from Chicago to the Gulf. The second part was a blockade of the eastern coast. It would in essence put the South under siege, and allow those Southerners who were against secession to pressure their government to surrender.

Feelings were mixed about the plan; there was a fever up north to move quickly and finish off the South in a series of quick victories. The Anaconda Plan was too deliberate for the more vocal group of cabinet members. However, Scott's plan for a blockade of the eastern and southern seaboards as far as New Orleans was approved. Lincoln turned to Scott. "Do you mind if Mr. Harris reviews the plan from his perspective? He's owned and operated cotton factoring companies in Charleston, Savannah, Mobile and New Orleans harbors. He doesn't have your military background, but he might have an insight from first-hand knowledge how the southern ports work."

Scott smiled. "I look forward to having Mr. Harris serve on the Blockade Strategy Board."

The initial blockade plan looked at three main issues. The first issue was the number of serviceable ships needed to perform blockade duty. There were fewer than fifty seaworthy ships to patrol over three thousand miles of coastline. The second dealt with the blockade runners. It was conceivable that smaller, faster boats would be difficult to intercept. Large supply ships could be waiting in ports in the Bahamas and the island of Cuba to offload to the runners. The third issue would be how to deal with European nations who sympathized with the South and would aid or abet them in breaking the blockade.

While a blockade of the main ports of the South was more than feasible, once the Navy was able to put sufficient ships to work, the third part of the plan took into consideration all the small sites where the runners could load and offload goods. The chairman of the committee turned to Jimmy. "Mr. Harris, I wonder if you would look at the actions of foreign nations in trying to help or hinder our operation of the blockade plan?"

"I will."

The task was enormous. He wondered if he had bitten off more than he could chew. The question was how to start. He wasn't naïve. Men and nations would find a way to use this conflict to make enormous sums of money. The Union could deal with that, but what if some other nations got involved and offered support to the South? To Jim, his initial focus should be to work with the Secretary of State to convince other nations to remain neutral and not give a wink and a nod to these groups that wanted to profit by running the blockade. He knew deep down that his country's main concern was Great Britain; Lincoln knew that France and Spain would not initiate anything without the British, so it was important to keep the British from initiating any action that would incur unforeseen problems.

With John residing in Richmond, Louisa's work day was from dawn to dusk. All of the slaves and free workers were nervous. They knew that the war was in its infancy, but they were afraid that Union soldiers would come south and kill all of them. Louisa acted calmly, but she wasn't with them all the time.

One day Pierre Beauregard showed up at Magnolia and went out to the fields where Louisa was supervising the picking. "What a pleasant surprise! What brings you here?

You must have your hands full with the two forts in the bay."

"I promised my cousin John that I would check in with you periodically—so here I am."

"Let's go back to the house and have lunch; you can tell me what's going on."

Before they could head back, several of her overseers came up to General Beauregard and asked him if South Carolina was going to be invaded. "To the best of my knowledge, it won't happen. The Yankees seem to be primarily interested in blockading the coast and don't have the stomach for a face-to-face confrontation." That seemed to appease the group, and he and Louisa rode back to the house.

They went out to the porch. There was a slight breeze, and she offered him some lemonade. "Tell me what you're working on," she prompted.

"I've reset the fortifications for the two forts on Port Royal. The Confederate command believes the North is going to try to blockade the coast, and we'll need a staging place. It'll be either Sumter in Charleston or Port Royal, a little to the south. I won't be in this area to see this through. I'm being reassigned to form the new Army of the Potomac, near the Union Capitol. I hope this is a prelude to invasion; I think the timing is ripe. How are you surviving?"

"Well, it's lonesome without John, but I can't move to Richmond and leave our cotton plantation. If they blockade the coast, how will I survive? I've been sending my cotton to New England, but that's been cut off entirely. Now I must sell to England again. To do that, I had to make a contract with a new factor, since my old factor wouldn't take me back. I don't know what's going to happen to us. Do you think there a way to get through the Union blockade? Then there's the question of financing. Jim had arranged financing for me, but he's working for Lincoln and turned his banks over to someone I haven't met. I have a note due at the end of the year and may not be able to pay it."

"I can't help on the financing, but as far as shipping your cotton is concerned, I offer you this. They can tie up the major ports, but we have so many settlements along a thirty-five-hundred-mile coastline that they'll never be able to shut us down."

"I hope you're right."

"We've been told that the British have built a series of small, speedy craft that can outrun the Union Navy. You may have to think about shipping from some of the small ports where a runner can get in and out before the Union Navy is aware of their presence. I know the smaller ships can't carry as much, but they can make multiple trips. I think you may be able to use Wilmington. That could be a way out for you."

"Have you seen my husband and son?"

"I saw them when we took Fort Sumter, but I haven't seen John since that day. I probably won't see you for some time. As far as I know, James is getting along well at V.M.I. Take care, and if you see your husband, tell him I said hello."

Initially, John Beauregard felt that he was in over his head, trying to figure out what assets he had and what his long-term objective was. Davis had outlined a strategy with which he could develop an objective. The South would fight a protracted war. They would retreat in the face of a superior force, counterattack when feasible, and above all, avoid full-scale engagement. Davis was constrained by two factors. The first was that the governors wanted each section of the Confederacy defended, and that tied up a large portion of the South's forces. The second was the mentality of the South. They felt that they could whip any number of Yankees, and objected to the idea of waiting for the North to attack. The southern press was clamoring for an attack on the Union Capitol in Washington, and they couldn't understand Davis's tentativeness.

John set up initial objectives to have his assets infiltrate the Washington scene, develop contacts and try to ascertain troop movement and strengths. His prime asset at this time was a woman by the name of Rose O'Neal Greenhow, a wealthy woman living in the Union Capitol.

Born on a small farm in Maryland, northwest of its capitol, to a slave holder father, Rose and her sister were orphaned early in life and moved in with an aunt who ran a boarding house in Washington. When she was twentytwo, she married Robert Greenhow, a doctor and lawyer who worked in the U.S. State Department. Early on, she was a protégée of Dolly Madison, the former president's wife who was known for her lavish parties in the capitol. The courtship of Robert and Rose was blessed by Washington society. The couple thrived in that atmosphere.

Her husband's position required constant moving to places such as New Mexico and San Francisco, where he was killed in an accident. His death didn't seem to alter her position in society; it was as though nothing had happened at all.

The passing of her husband rekindled her sympathy with the Confederate way of life. Many in the nation's capitol were sympathetic, and she became insulated in her beliefs. She soon became a friend of Senator John C. Calhoun of South Carolina, and shortly thereafter was recruited as a spy for the southern cause. Her handler gave her a cipher for encoding messages.

John knew that each side wanted to engage the other and win. The South felt that a win would make the North back off and they could continue on as a separate country. The North hoped for a quick victory to bring the belligerents back into the fold. General Mc Dowell led his Union troops toward Bull Run, where P.G.T. Beauregard was camped with his Army of the Potomac. The heightened fever in the North led many to believe that the war would be ended with one swift victory. Hordes of people made the over twenty-five-mile trip to the hills overlooking the town of Manassas to see the rout of the rebels.

The North was unaware that P.G.T. Beauregard had received a message from John's spy in Washington. She accurately laid out Mc Dowell's battle plan and his troop strength. The end result was a rout of the Union forces, and the citizen observers went scurrying back to Washington.

When James Harris came home that evening, Claire was waiting for him. "Are the rebels going to attack Washington?"

"I don't know. The administration had several meetings that I attended this afternoon, and they weren't sure what was going to happen. In spite of having superior numbers, our generals were out-maneuvered. I don't say the army is in disarray. I just think they don't really know what to do. I'm concerned."

"I think the children and I should go back to New York. I want our children to be able to play and sleep without fear of an invasion. Are you aware that the soldiers who came back from Bull Run are milling around in the streets, acting as if they're lost? All I can see is supplies pouring into the city and troops everywhere. I've had no training in military affairs, but I don't have to be a soldier to see that we're preparing for an attack on the Capitol."

"I think you're being a little premature. There's nothing imminent at this time. Perhaps we can discuss this, if things heat up."

"We're discussing this *now*, not later. I have no allegiance to either the South or the North. I don't want to take any chances since we have a beautiful home in New York, miles away from the conflict. I married a banker, not a soldier. I'm not interested in being someone who has to be here because you're here—especially since you don't need to be."

"I made a commitment to Mr. Lincoln. I can't just tell him, 'I'm sorry, but my wife doesn't want me to be here.'"

"You made a commitment to *me* that should take precedence over anything you made to *Lincoln*. Since you're new in your position, you can't be that indispensable. Let someone else carry the load—you're needed at home!"

"If I sense that there's a potential invasion, I'll take you and the children to New York myself. Now, if you don't mind, I have to get some sleep. I've got an early meeting tomorrow on the blockade plan."

As Jimmy left the room, Claire threw a book at him. It landed at his feet. Rather than continue the argument, he continued to his bedroom.

The Secretary of the Navy was working diligently to get as many serviceable ships as possible on line in a short amount of time. Starting with less than ten, they were up to fifty after a few months. Whether they were combatready wouldn't be known for some time. To compound the problem, the Navy's task was not only to find serviceable ships, but to train men to sail them—and that couldn't happen overnight.

After another exhausting day, Jim arrived home at eight that evening. He called out as he came in the front door, but no one answered. Even the maid didn't respond. He started through the downstairs rooms and then went upstairs. He checked the master bedroom first; there was no one there. He went to the children's room and checked their closet. All their clothes were missing. Now he was worried! He went back to his room and checked the closet. His clothes were there, but Claire's were not.

He sat on his bed and put his head in his hands. What was she thinking? Did she return to New York? Or worse, did she go back to England? He walked down the stairs and went into his office. There was a note sitting on his desk. He opened the envelope and sat down in one of his overstuffed chairs to read what was on the sheet of paper inside.

It was Claire's writing. "I've given this considerable thought. The children and I are moving back to our home in New York, where it's safe. You're a wonderful man, and I love you very much, but I don't think you understand what you've done to the family by taking a position with Lincoln. I assume that you will provide sufficient funds for us while we're living separately. I've wired your father and told him we're coming. I don't want this to be the end of our relationship. I just want you to understand that a marriage is not one-sided. Both sides have to be heard. Love, Claire."

He decided not to do anything about it right away. He'd write her a letter and see if they could compromise. But tomorrow, he had a heavy schedule. He had no reason to leave his position. The country was in turmoil and he owed an allegiance to Abraham Lincoln. He believed in what he was trying to do and was thoroughly disappointed in Claire. He could force the issue, of course, but he decided that would be better to let a little time elapse and then go to New York and bring them back.

Two weeks after the battle of Bull Run, General Beauregard was in Richmond, where he called on his cousin John. "That was a timely message we received on McDowell. In fact, it was essential. Was that you who sent it?"

"Congratulations on your victory! The newspapers are calling you Little Napoleon. The information came from an agent of ours in Washington called Greenhow. She's been active in D.C. society for many years and has cultivated some important people. I think she got the information directly from a northern Senator who is sweet on her."

"With those kinds of resources, we should win the war in a couple of months," Beauregard exclaimed. "We need to move on Washington now that their army is in disarray. Davis and I don't get along very well, so I need you to see if we can get him to move. The time couldn't be better than right now."

"I'll try, but he's receiving a lot of pressure from the governors to make sure their states are sufficiently protected. They want troops stationed in every state, but we have only so many people under arms. The President is trying to satisfy everyone, and what we're left with is a defensive/offensive strategy. I'm seeing him tomorrow. I'll bring it up, but he's a little short of temper these days and I may not be able to argue the point."

"I went to Magnolia a month ago and talked to Louisa. She's not very happy with the situation. Can't you do something?"

"Pierre, I'm working seventy hours a week to get my network up and operating. Louisa was asked to join me. She could direct her overseer to manage the plantation, but that's her baby and she won't relinquish control. What was I to do? I can't spare the time to go back there now."

It was August before John could get a moment with Jefferson Davis. He hadn't seen his superior in nearly a month and was shocked at his appearance. "Mr. President, General Beauregard indicates that our major victory at Bull Run could give us an advantage to attack the Union's capitol as soon as possible. He feels their army is in disarray and they are extremely vulnerable at this time."

"That pompous piss-ant is reveling in his press clippings! We don't have the manpower to strike. The Union is heavily defended and we can't afford a loss. Is that all you wanted to discuss?"

"I have bad news. Our main spy in Washington was Greenhow. She's been arrested, and they're holding her under house arrest. My sources say it's only a matter of time before she's put in prison."

"Is there anything we can do?"

"I have other assets in place, but none who are as competent as she was. We're still receiving significant information on troop movements and their strengths. It seems that McClelland has sent Pinkerton down south to determine our capability. He told the general that our strengths were greater than we have; consequently, McClelland wouldn't move. We should take advantage of his overly cautious behavior. I know you don't want to hear it, but this is a great time to attack Washington."

"I've given you my position. Good day, sir."

At about the same time, Jim took the train to New York and went directly to his home. Claire was there and kissed him as he came in the front door. "I'm so happy to see you," she said.

He barely acknowledged her greeting and went directly to the children's rooms. They were awake, and Jim read them a nursery rhyme before the two fell asleep. Then he went downstairs and saw that the dining room table had been set for him. "I know that you must be hungry, so I heated up a casserole that the children and I had," Claire said. "Will you open the wine? I'll join you for a glass."

"I should be angry with you for leaving without any discussion."

"Well, we discussed it, and I wasn't happy with the answer you gave. Just because the southern generals haven't attacked the capitol yet doesn't mean that I was wrong."

"You took my children from me! If it hadn't been for my father, I wouldn't have known where they were. This is America. You're not some privileged dignitary who can do what you wish. The law is on my side. I can take the children with me when I go back to Washington, and there's nothing you can do about it. That's what I intend to do unless there is some civil dialog and what we do next is a joint decision. I thought marriage was between two people. It seems as though you think it's only about you."

"James, I love you very much and don't want to lose you or the children. I was scared and you didn't seem to understand my fear, nor were you willing to address it rationally."

"I love you, but the main thing that holds a marriage together is trust. I don't trust you! I don't trust you even a little bit. The first thing you need to do is come back to Washington with me; we need to see if we can repair this break. If after six months it looks like an invasion is imminent, or you don't want to continue with the marriage, then we'll address that."

"I don't want to go back there, and I don't want the children to see what's happening."

"There's no choice. Either you're coming back with me and the children, or you can stay here. I'll provide for you as long as you stay here."

"You can't force me—I'm a British citizen!"

"You're correct. But the children are *American* citizens, and they're going to be with their father. Whether they're with their mother is your option."

"You can't do this!"

"I stopped by my father's home before I came here. The children and I will spend the next two nights there; we'll leave for Washington the day after. That will give you a couple of days to come to your senses. You may come, or you may stay in this house for as long as you want. I'll provide a line of credit for you at my bank, so you'll not want for anything. Tell the housekeeper I want to see her."

James directed Mrs. Green to dress the children and provide him with four days of clothing for each. Recognizing that Claire might be difficult, he had a carriage waiting outside. The children were crying as the housekeeper brought them down the stairs. He knew it was going to be difficult for the next few days, but his wife had given him no choice. Claire was crying and yelling at him at the same time; Mrs. Green stood to the side. As he went out to the carriage, he turned toward Claire. "I want my family together, and there's no reason why they can't be."

"Have you thought this through?" Cameron asked his son when he arrived with the children.

"I know what's right and what's wrong. I've identified what's wrong and hope that it can be rectified. If my method is crude, it may be the only way I can communicate with my wife."

"If you don't mind, Abigail would like to go over and see Claire tomorrow. Perhaps she can mediate your dispute. If you do mind, she's going anyway."

Jimmy smiled. "Let's hope it works."

Cameron and Abigail invited Claire for dinner the following evening. She came early and read to the children until they went to sleep. She was dressed in a summer dress with a purple wrap. James couldn't help notice how attractive she was. The dinner conversation was tense at first, but gradually became cordial. It was Jimmy who tried to come to some accommodation. "I didn't get married to be a bachelor, and I didn't sire children so someone else could enjoy them. If I know one thing, children need both parents. Even at this period of our lives, I still love you, Claire, and I want you to be my wife and the mother of my children."

"You have a poor way of showing it! You take my children and tell me I can come with you or stay in New York. What kind of love is that?"

"I'm doing the best I can. What about you? I come home and you and the children are gone. What am I to think? There was no word you were leaving and no word where you went. What kind of marriage do I have?"

Abigail interceded at this point. "I want you to know that Cameron and I look upon you as our daughter. We care a great deal for you, but taking the children without warning and without telling your husband where you were taking them is hard for us to understand."

"I was scared there was going to be an attack on Washington and my children would be injured. I voiced my concern to my husband, and he practically ignored me."

"It seems to me that your husband is the Administrative Assistant to the President of the United States. Don't you think he would know when an attack was imminent? Do you really think your husband would leave you in harm's way?" Abigail responded.

"No, I guess not."

"I think you need to decide what you want out of life. Is marriage in your plans, or are recitals and concerts what you want? Being married takes work. Each person needs to communicate with the other. If you disagree, then both need to seek a resolution that's in the best interests of the marriage. These are tense times in America, and your husband is supporting his Commander-in-Chief. You both need to support each other. It can't happen if one goes to extremes."

"I don't want to be without my husband *or* my children. I also don't want them in harm's way. If I come back with you, will you promise that we'll leave if D.C. is under attack or an attack is imminent?"

"I'll promise that, and I'll also promise that I'll take you and the children back to New York as soon as it's feasible." James got up from his chair, walked around the table and kissed Claire on the lips; she cried and held onto his arm.

"This calls for champagne. Let's drink to a long reconciliation." Cameron was smiling as he made the toast.

CHAPTER TWENTY-FIVE

Back in the capitol, they slowly went back to being a family. There was still some tension when James and Claire were alone, but it was better than being separated. His work was his consolation. Lincoln called upon him more each day to review some action or other that he contemplated. And he was still a member of the Blockade Committee, headed by Secretary Welles, who was doing an admirable job in putting together a navy. The blockade runners were still getting through, but the capture or kill rate, according to the Union Navy, was close to fifty percent. Jim didn't know how valid those statistics were since the South was consistently being supplied with armament and munitions.

They were in a cabinet meeting in Lincoln's office when word came that the American Navy had intercepted a British ship and boarded her. Captain Wilkes of the Union Navy took two Confederate envoys from the ship and then released the vessel. Almost immediately, the English Ambassador requested a meeting with the Secretary of State to make a strong objection to the boarding and the taking of those two men, who were now in Union custody. The ambassador's message was that he wanted an immediate apology and the release of the two Confederate envoys, Mason and Slidell.

As soon as the President was aware of the situation, he provided the information to those assembled and asked for their input.

Secretary Seward spoke. "Mr. President, I believe that American citizens will think this was a good maneuver on the part of Captain Wilkes. I don't think we should release Mason and Slidell. They were on a mission to Britain and France to seek support and recognition of the South. Many in the English Parliament are openly supporting the rebels. In addition, most of the blockade runners are being built in England, and the English government is turning a blind eye to British citizens trading with the South."

"The British haven't tried to break the blockade, have they?" Lincoln asked.

Secretary Welles responded to that one. "Well, technically they haven't, but it's English captains or English civilians who are commanding the blockade runners. What they're doing is offloading their supply ships in the Bermudas, the Bahamas, and the island of Cuba. The swift blockade runners have no trouble reaching those depots, offloading cotton and tobacco, and then loading as much as they can hold before sailing to a small port in the South. The Crenshaw brothers of Virginia have established a blockade company that delivers tobacco and cotton to English ships in those ports. Although we've set up a coastal blockade, aiming at the major cities of Charleston, Savannah, Mobile and New Orleans, it's the city of Wilmington, North Carolina, that's become the major port for the exchange of goods. Our problem is that we don't have enough ships to stop them. Most sail when it's late at night with no moon, and they come in without any lights on. It's common for them to pass close to our ships and we miss them."

"Can't you blockade the city and port of Wilmington?" Lincoln asked.

"The city is uniquely located thirty miles up Cape Fear River. It's difficult to access, because of the Confederate guns up and down the river. My suggestion is to make it a priority to attack the city and blow up its harbor," Welles responded.

"Mr. Harris, what's your take on English neutrality?"

"To the best of my knowledge, Prime Minister Palmerston is following a policy of neutrality, though I know from personal experience that he supports the southern cause. If it weren't for his distaste of slavery, I believe he would have come into the war on the side of the rebels. Our other problem is how outspoken Lord Russell and Mr. Gladstone have become. It seems that the Tories and the Whigs in England favor entering the war on the side of the Confederates," Jimmy responded.

"Palmerston sent ten thousand troops to strengthen the Canadian forces. What do you make of that?" Lincoln asked.

"I believe he's responding to a threat from us," answered Secretary of War Stanton. "They're nervous that we covet Canada and fear that we'll use any incident as provocation to act. But the prime minister has a huge problem. Many in Britain fear that the troops he sent may desert to our side. The other problem with his deployment is that we have the only serious warships in the Great Lakes. St. Lawrence freezes over in the winter, so he can't provide reinforcements to Quebec City by water if he wanted to; his only road in that area parallels ours in Maine. An amusing sidelight to this deployment is that many of his officers had to land in Boston and take the train to Montreal to reach their troops."

"I know that we've explained to the prime minister that support in any way to the South will be considered an act of war, haven't we?"

"I personally made a trip to England and told him that," Seward said. "Officially they're neutral; unofficially, they're aiding and abetting our enemy."

"He obviously didn't take your suggestion too seriously, Bill," Stanton responded. "Our people confiscated a briefcase containing a discreet battle plan belonging to one of his officers who landed in Boston. The scenario called for Palmerston to send twenty-one ships under Admiral Milne to the western Atlantic, along with the *Great Eastern* luxury liner as a troop-carrying ship. Their plan calls for bombarding both Boston and New York. They believe that if New York City is neutralized, it will paralyze our commerce and make us vulnerable such that we'll seek a negotiated settlement with the South."

"We're at a crossroads, Mr. President," he went on. "England is at the peak of its power. Their Navy rules the waves, and with Napoleon's troops, they could be a formidable adversary. I think we have to prepare for war with them."

"I only want to fight one war at a time," Lincoln said grimly. "What about Spain?"

"I don't believe that Spain is a player in this," Seward replied. "France has eyes on Central America, but they'll act only if England makes a move. Britain doesn't trust Napoleon—they see him as too adventurous. I believe our strategy should be to convince Great Britain that we don't want them to intercede, but if they consider it, they must be apprised of our power to repel any expeditionary force. I know they've been angry since the war of 1812, but over the past ten years our relations have improved. We should use that as the basis of our strategy."

"I believe the South views the ship-boarding incident as an entrée for them to seek diplomatic recognition from England, France and Spain," Lincoln said. "Unofficially, I like what Captain Wilkes did, but we need time to assess how intense the English reaction will be. Let's reconvene in three days and come up with a response or some action that we can take. Mr. Harris, what are your thoughts?"

"I'm not an expert in maritime law; I can only look at this through the British eyes. I believe that there will be many who propose war with us. Their sovereignty has been violated, whether rightly or wrongly. They are a proud nation, and I believe that whatever action you take, Mr. President, it should be firm, but with a carrot stick."

"Thank you, Mr. Harris. Gentlemen, what are we to do about all these blockade runners being built in England and France? It seems that the South has issued letters of marque, and that's created an industry of privateers seeking wealth," Lincoln said.

"I have three suggestions, Mr. President," said Secretary Wells. "I think we can stop many of the blockade runners off the coast of England and France. We could send two or three warships to patrol the waters outside the legal limit, and when they appear, we blast them out of the water. To do all that, we need to know where they're being built and we need a port that can resupply our ships. I suggest we send a team to the British Isles to determine which ship-building companies are helping the rebels. The third suggestion is to pressure the British to stop building ships for our enemy."

"Are there any nations that support our action against the South?" Lincoln asked.

"Switzerland has supported us, and so have Russia and Prussia," Seward said. "I'm sure you remember that it was Alexander II who alerted us to the fact that Britain and France were trying to encourage him to enter the war on the side of the Confederacy. But Alexander has his own problem; there's a labor revolt in Poland. Since his loss in the Crimea War, he's concerned that France and England will think that Russia is vulnerable and intercede on the part of the Poles."

"Thank you, gentlemen; we'll reconvene at this same time in three days. Mr. Harris, please come to my office."

Lincoln was talking to his secretary as Jimmy entered the Oval Office. He sat down and waited for Lincoln to finish. He rose as the president entered. "Please don't get up. I have a task that I think you can handle. I'd like you to go to England and France and see if you can determine where the blockade runners are being built and who's building them. Find out what it'll take to get them to stop. My instincts tell me that if we can't stop them, the war will go on longer than necessary with a greater loss of men and property. In addition, I'd like to know how large a spy network they have in England."

"I'll certainly go if you ask, but I don't think I have the qualifications for the assignment. Someone with naval experience would be better suited to the task."

"James, you know England and France better than any one of us. You at least can talk to the prime minister, and you have friends who will help you with unmasking these builders. It could be dangerous, especially if someone from the Confederate side knows what you're up to. I'm not going to order you—you need to volunteer—but if you take the assignment, I'll send Navy Lieutenant Stephen Lawler with you. He, like you, studied in England."

"I'd like to run it by my wife, if you don't mind. She's an English citizen, and she understands the mental makeup of her countrymen."

James waited until after dinner before he raised the issue of his assignment. Their relationship bordered on one of tolerance. He wondered if they'd ever be able to bridge the situation caused by her leaving with the children without telling him. She was pleasant and willing to help, but it didn't appear that she'd go beyond what was expected of her. They were intimate on a weekly basis, but Jim didn't feel the passion of their years before the incident.

They were having an after-dinner drink when Jimmy got her attention. "Claire, Mr. Lincoln has asked me to go to England to see who's building the blockade runners. I suspect many of them are being built around Liverpool."

"Are you considering taking me and the children?"

"No, I'm not. A Lieutenant Lawler is accompanying me."

"I could be helpful, since I grew up in England and know many people on the island."

"Perhaps the next time I go, you and the children can accompany me."

"Jimmy, I'm not comfortable in Washington. Would you object if the children and I go back to our home in New York while you're gone? I miss Abigail and your father; he's a great source of support and comfort."

"When would you plan to leave?"

"I'd like to leave at the same time you do."

"If you can get ready in three days, I'll escort you to our home in New York and leave from there. It'll give me a chance to see my father again. Do you think that'll work?"

"I think that'll work. Mrs. Gibbons can get us ready in three days."

James accepted Lincoln's assignment. He then contacted Lieutenant Lawler, asking him to come to his office. When Lawler was available, Jimmy explained what their assignment would be and suggested that he carry a firearm while they were abroad. On the third day, Jim went into his office early, met with Lawler, and the two went to Jim's home. They, his wife and children took the train to New York and stayed overnight at their home. At around noon the next day, Jim and Lawler left on the ship *Emerald Bay* for Great Britain.

CHAPTER TWENTY-SIX

His college roommate, George Phelps, was waiting when they came down the gangplank after the boat docked in Liverpool, England. He and George spent a few minutes embracing and telling each other how great it was to be together again. Lieutenant Stephen Lawler was introduced, and after Phelps' driver secured their bags, the three took the train to London and then drove out to the Phelps Manor. James had been here before, but Lawler was overwhelmed with the structure and the beauty of the grounds surrounding the manor. All the help had retired for the evening, so George offered them pot luck in his massive kitchen. They dined on cold chicken and room-temperature English ale.

"I hope you won't think poorly of me, but the help has been running back and forth to my London residence. They're exhausted, so I'm not going to wake them."

"We're happy to be off the ship and finally sitting down to a stable platform!"

They took their trays into the game room and sat down facing each other.

"George, we're here on a confidential mission and I don't know how much I can tell you. Perhaps I could ask you some questions to see where your allegiance is, and then maybe we can be more candid."

"Do I understand that you're a special assistant to Mr. Lincoln?"

"Yes. I've had that position since his inauguration. He's a fine man who's trying to fix a difficult problem."

"You know that feelings are mixed over here. The gentry want to come in on the side of the South, but the average citizen is more in tune with the Union's position."

"How is the war affecting your textile business?"

"It's played hell with it. I've had to shut down three plants since this conflict started. Oh, we've received this year's allotment of cotton, because most of it was shipped before hostilities started. But that's changed now. I'm being told that we'll only receive about twenty percent of what they'll produce next year. That number could be lower depending on whether the blockade runners get through. Many in my industry have to look elsewhere for cotton or else go out of business. To date we haven't found a source that could supply enough cotton to keep all the plants going."

"I thought you had diversified, so that you wouldn't be put out of business if you stopped getting cotton from the South."

"You're correct, but I don't like losing money, no matter what I do. I don't know what you're here for, but we may not be on the same side."

"We'll always be friends, George, but perhaps it would be better if Stephen and I found other accommodations tomorrow."

"Many of my associates would be hostile to you if they saw you; I won't tell them you're in England."

James was sure that Michelle Grand and his friend Pierre from Paris, both in the linen manufacturing business, would feel the same as George. He'd have to be careful where he went in France. Oh, they'd welcome him and dine with him, but he couldn't confide in them. His mission was too important.

Jimmy decided that London should be their base of operation. He knew that Liverpool was probably the center of the British-built blockade runners industry, but with train service available, they could go out each morning and come back in the evening and be less conspicuous. After registering at the hotel and having their baggage placed in their rooms, they checked in with the American embassy and did much of their research in one of their conference rooms. They narrowed down the shipbuilder list they were going to target to the following companies: Jones, Quiggin and Company; W.H. Potter and Sons; William C. Miller and Sons; and the Laird Brothers. Significantly, the ambassador, Mr. Long, provided them with the name of James Hudson, a Confederate agent operating in England.

"Mr. Harris, I believe that Hudson has at least seven or eight agents working for him with a secret headquarters in the U.K.," the ambassador said. "He's the one who's negotiating for the blockade runners with some of the companies you've identified. Here's a photograph we took of Mr. Hudson without his consent. If I were you, Mr. Harris, I'd also have a look at Clydeside in Scotland. I've heard that a builder named Govan is building some ships for the South there.

"Another issue you should be aware of is that there's a company in Liverpool called Fraser, Trenholm & Co., who're cotton merchants both here and in Charleston, South Carolina. I believe they're the Confederacy clearing house for purchases in Europe."

"I know them well—I had dealings with them for over six years. Before my position with Mr. Lincoln, I was the president of three Harris National Banks located in New York, Chicago and Boston. After the war, I plan to return to the banks. For your information, I was born and grew up in Charleston, and my grandparents still reside there. Before my banking interests, I was a cotton factor, with offices in Mobile, New Orleans, Savannah and Charleston. Now I can't go to Fraser and Trenholm and tell them I'm in London, but I'll have my bank do some research to determine what their assets are and how they're funneling money to the rebels. What are our chances of stopping the building of these blockade runners?"

"I believe there is little chance that you'll have any success," the ambassador frowned. "The English government's position of neutrality is a complete sham. There's too much money being made building ships for the Confederacy. In addition, the linen manufacturers are calling upon the government to do something to break the blockade. To compound the overall problem, the boat builders are also entering the lucrative venture by using their own ships to break the blockade. They see that the business can produce significant profits with only moderate risks; they're really lining their pockets. I heard that the margin of profit is so great that if they can sneak by our ships twice, they've more than paid for the vessel.

"Before you go, I want to be sure you're aware that the Confederacy has a substantial mission here. Not only do they have spies, but they have activists who are constantly pushing the South's position. James Spence, a British citizen, writes articles and hires speakers to promote the South's cause, and also bribes journalists to push articles applauding the South. The pro-Confederate organizations are the Liverpool Southern Club and the Manchester Southern Club; other English cities have similar organizations."

"Are there any pro-Union clubs or organizations?"

"The Union and Emancipation Society and the British and Foreign Anti-Slavery Society are among some. Some black Americans, such as Frederick Douglass and William Andrew Jackson, have lectured throughout the country about the sins of slavery and have drawn significant crowds. Since the South hasn't been recognized by the British government, their supporters are hoping that the more vocal their pronouncements are, the more Britain will take notice of their cause."

It was Secretary Welles who had suggested that Lt. Lawler accompany Jim on this mission. Lawler came from a seafaring family; his grandfather had been a commodore in the U.S. Navy during the War of 1812. Prior to this assignment, he had been serving on a Union ship that had significant success in stopping the blockade runners; in fact, his ship had captured three so far. Subsequently, they had confiscated the goods on board and sold the boats. Through first-hand experience, he knew what they looked like, how they were built and what their shortcomings were.

Lawler was a pleasant companion, and Jimmy was sure the young man could hold his own in any encounter. He stood six feet tall and weighed one hundred eighty pounds, had blond hair and a hawkish face, and his file indicated he was an excellent shot with handgun or rifle. Jimmy and Stephen were issued handguns, to be returned to the embassy before they departed the country.

"I think we should go to Liverpool soon to meet with the builders and try to determine whom they're selling their runners to. I know they won't readily give us any information, but let's try. In order to make our appearance more credible, I want to contact a boat designer and get a set of preliminary plans."

"Sir, I would suggest that we present ourselves as ship buyers. It's my opinion that people wanting to sell something give as much information as necessary to complete the sale. I'm familiar with the class of runners being built, and I think I can ask enough questions that they're bound to let some information slip," Lawler responded.

"Whom should we say we're buying the boats for?" James asked.

"I'd say it would be my company, Lawler, Ltd. You can be the representative of Harris National Bank of Chicago, my main investor. I want to have two fast boats for shallow rivers in Honduras and Guatemala to service the banana and rubber plantations."

"Do you know anything about those countries, or about the banana and rubber industry?"

"I worked on a banana plantation in Honduras for about six years before I came back to the States."

"We'll probably only be able to contact two or three of the four shipbuilders that we've identified as being in the Liverpool area. After we contact the second, word will be out that maybe we're into a different game other than buying ships."

They contacted Daniels and Hagan Engineers, told them what they wanted, and asked their advice. The managing partner, John Daniels, was more than glad to set up meetings with W.C. Miller and Sons and the Laird Brothers in Liverpool. "I know both of these builders have the capability to satisfy your needs. Have you a design in mind?"

"Not at the moment. We were hoping that you could provide that expertise, based on our needs. The boat must be sturdy, be able to travel down shallow rivers and be fast enough to escape some serious situations." Daniels smiled when Lawler added the last bit of information.

"I recently designed such a boat for an unknown client."

"It must have been difficult when you didn't know whom you were designing for."

"It wasn't that difficult. They gave me the specifications and a substantial down payment. I didn't have any problems at all, other than that I wanted to go on the test sailing, but I wasn't invited. I know that my client paid for the plans, but we can use theirs as a starting point."

They looked over the plans and Lawler made some immediate changes, both in length and draft. Daniels indicated he could easily make the changes and have a preliminary sketch in two days. He wired the Laird Brothers and W.C. Wilson and Sons and set up the first appointment at 10:00 a.m. with Wilson and Sons four days hence, and the day following at the same time with the Laird Brothers. Daniels asked if they wanted him along. "We were hoping that you'd be available," Jim responded.

Wilson wasn't available when the three arrived at the shipbuilding company in Liverpool. The construction supervisor, Peter Wright, gave his apology for Mr. Wilson but said he could answer any of their questions, and if they were serious, Mr. Wilson would be available to complete the contract. "Where would you gentlemen like to begin?"

Daniels took the initiative and gave Wright a sketch of what he thought would satisfy Lawler's needs. "Peter, I know that you've built a boat along these lines; perhaps we could see it or the drawings."

"I think that's possible. I have such a boat that's nearly complete. We can walk down to the wharf and look at it and see what design changes would be needed."

As they were walking to the shipyard, James got in a discussion with Wright about the testing of the craft and where it was done. "Sir, you have a distinct southern accent. Are you from the Confederate states?"

"You're very observant. I was born and raised in Charleston, South Carolina, but now make my home in New York City. Here's my card. I'm the representative of Harris National Bank, with locations in Chicago, Boston and New York City."

"Then you're not purchasing a boat."

"No. My bank is the principal investor in Mr. Lawler's company. It's he who wants the boats. If the price and terms meet the investment profile, then we'll fund the purchase. Mr. Lawler's father and I are past business associates. He asked me to help his son."

"You're a lucky man, Mr. Lawler," Wright observed.

They continued down to the docks. There were three dry docks, each with a ship in various stages of completion. Peter steered the group to the first dock. "Here's a boat that's nearly finished." He pointed to a blockade runner.

"When completed, it'll be able to handle 1,800 tons fully loaded. It's two hundred eighty feet long and thirtysix feet across the beam. There are two oscillating engines, four boilers, and two side wheels that generate three hundred fifty horsepower; it can do sixteen knots fully loaded. The draft is 8.5 feet, which is good for shallow water. Would something like this meet your specifications?"

"I wonder if the three of us could board the boat and get a good look at her?" Lawler asked.

Led by Daniels, they surveyed the entire length and beam of the remarkable boat, and when they were finished, James asked the superintendent how long it would take to build two of these boats, with some modifications.

"I don't want to commit to anything without Mr. Wilson's approval, but my guess—and I don't want to be held to this estimate—is that we can build both in six months' time, condition on financing."

The next morning the three left by train for Liverpool once again to keep their appointment with John Laird, the son of William Laird, founder of the shipbuilding company. Daniels again took the initiative and explained to Laird what the two Americans wanted. Again, Jim's southern accent was noticed by Laird. "Some of your people were here last week to look at some of my designs."

"And who would that be, sir?" James asked.

"A Mr. Hudson seemed to be the spokesman for the team, though a Mr. Surrey and a Mr. Thomas, who were with him, had significant input."

"I don't know these gentlemen," Jimmy said. "It's my southern accent that has you confused. Mr. Lawler and I are from New York City, where I represent the Harris National Bank; here's my card. I've lived in the North for nearly twenty-five years, but I haven't been able to lose my southern accent. You see, I was born in the South."

"Sorry for the confusion." From that point on the conversation was courteous but restrained. Jim suspected that John Laird was uncomfortable with him and Stephen.

There were no runners to inspect. Laird looked at the drawings that Daniels had drawn up. "I think you gentlemen would be best served by the Wilson Company here in Liverpool. Our emphasis has been on metal-hull ships. My father discovered that the principle used in shaping the ship's boilers could also be used for the ship's hull."

The message was clear to James. Laird either didn't want to do business with them, or he suspected that they weren't legitimate buyers. When they returned to London, Jimmy left a small deposit with Daniels to provide preliminary sketches for Lawler to approve. Back at their hotel, they went to the lounge to have a drink and went over their next step. "I think Laird is suspicious of us. It's obvious that he's communicating with Hudson and may already be contracting with him. We got as much as we can from the two builders in Liverpool. I think we should go north to Clydeside and see if Govan is doing business with the rebels."

"What are you going to do about Wilson and Laird?" Lawler asked. "It's obvious to me that they're building ships for the South."

"When we're ready to go home, I'll have a talk with the prime minister."

"Do you think you'll get an audience?" Lawler asked.

"He's my father-in-law! Yes, he'll see me."

Laird knew where James Hudson was staying in London, so he wired his hotel, asking him if he knew James Harris and Stephen Lawler. Subsequent discussion by wire told Hudson that there was a northern spy operating in England, who was checking on the blockade runners. He wired his supervisor in the Confederate Navy, who talked to John Beauregard from the Confederate Signal Corps.

"Do you know a James Stephen Harris or a Lieutenant Stephen Lawler?" John was asked.

"Harris is the special assistant to Lincoln, and Prime Minister Palmerston's son-in-law. My advice is to do everything you can to block his inquiry, but no physical violence should come to him, or we'll alienate the British. I believe they already know who's building our blockade runners, and there's nothing they can do about it."

Jim and Lawler took the train to Glasgow the next morning and checked into the Windsor Hotel. They wanted to visit the Govan Shipbuilding Company and see if they were building ships for the South. In addition, they wanted to see the area around Clydeside. Daniels wasn't with them, but he did wire the shipbuilder and received confirmation of an appointment for them.

They rented a rig and drove to Clydeside. The shipbuilding office had two rooms and was located about a thousand yards from the water. They could see one boat in the water, tied to a dock. They were in time for their appointment. As Laird had done, the owner, William Govan, noticed Jimmy's southern drawl. "Are you part of Mr. Hudson's group?"

"We came separately. Have you seen him this morning?"

"He's down by the river. They're testing a new blockade runner. Perhaps you'd like to join him?"

James had to think fast, or his mission would be compromised. "I would like to conclude our business with you first, and then we'll go down there and meet with the other members of the team."

An hour later they excused themselves, and although Govan wanted to accompany them, Jimmy assured him that they could find the other members of the team.

"What are we going to do now?" Lawler asked.

"Let's go down to the river and see who's there!"

They recognized Hudson from his picture, but not the other three who seemed to be with him. Jimmy drove about halfway there, just past where the road forked, and pulled the carriage to a stop. When he did that, Hudson and the others turned to see what was going on, but they didn't move. Jimmy didn't hesitate; he backed the horse up to the fork in the road and took the lane to Glasgow. "Do you think they saw our faces?" Lawler asked.

"It's unfortunate, but I think they did. We now know who's building their ships. What we don't know is where the Confederate headquarters is in the U.K.," James said.

"Okay, what do you suggest?"

"Let's go back to the hotel and check on the train schedule. They're either staying in Glasgow or someplace close. I think we ought to split up. You should stake out a spot on the road into town. I believe there's a small pub on the left side of the road, just as you turn into the main street. I'll drop you there; you can have a brew while you watch for them. I'll check to see if they're staying at any of the hotels in town and then return to our rooms. If you spot them, come back to the hotel and get me; then we can figure out what to do."

An hour later, Hudson and two men rode past the pub, through the town square, and stopped at the train station. They tied up their rig and went inside. Lawler had to take a chance; he wandered over and checked the train schedule on the big board outside the station. The next train to Aberdeen was leaving in twenty minutes. He quickly left the station and ran back to the hotel; Harris was in his room. After Lawler told Jimmy what Hudson was up to, they both went to the station, purchased tickets for Aberdeen, and waited inside to see what the Confederate and his acquaintances would do.

They didn't have to wait long. Hudson walked across the street into the station; he and his two men boarded the first car of the train to Aberdeen. James and Lawler boarded the second car and took seats that would give them a clear view if anyone left the car. "I wonder why they're staying so far from Glasgow," Lawler wondered. "It doesn't make sense to me."

"I know. Perhaps they're meeting some of their party along this route."

Fifty minutes later, the train stopped at Stirling, and Hudson and his associates got off the train. James and Lawler waited to see if they'd reboard. When they didn't, he and Lawler jumped off the train just before it got underway.

The Confederate group split up, with Hudson renting a carriage and leaving town on the north road. The other two went into a pub in the middle of the small town.

"We'll have to split up," James said. "Why don't you follow Hudson, and I'll keep an eye on the two who went into the pub. And Stephen, don't take any chances!"

Lawler walked to the livery stable to rent a horse; it was on the main road about a hundred yards from the depot. The road north was flat, and Lawler had an easy time keeping track of Hudson in the rig ahead of him. He stayed back so it wouldn't be obvious that he was following the Confederate spy. Thirty minutes later Hudson came to a crossroad and took the fork to the town of Bridge of Allan; Lawler followed. It was a typical sleepy English village, with a church, general store and pub. Hudson parked his carriage in front of a small house about two hundred yards from the building housing the pub. Lawler felt out of place, so he decided to go into the pub, where he could keep an eye on the house Hudson entered.

The Fiery Lantern Pub had a bar, four or five chairs around each of the four tables in the small room, a potbellied stove and a dartboard. Over the bar, which took up one wall, was a picture of a rugged prize fighter. Lawler took a table near a small window with a view of the town square and the house Hudson had entered. Thirty minutes went by. He didn't see any movement in or out of the cottage. The rig was still parked in front.

Subsequently, two men entered the pub and joined a small group that was throwing darts, while two other men at another table started singing. As Lawler turned to see who was singing, he was suddenly hit on the head from behind, and he fell to the floor.

As soon as Lawler fell, the bartender rushed to his side, but was pushed aside by one the burly Confederates. "You mind your business, if you know what's good for you! He's coming with us."

Lawler was alert enough to know that some people were pulling him to his feet, and he sensed that he was going out a door into the cool afternoon air. He wasn't conscious long before he was hit several more times and passed out.

Meanwhile, James followed Hudson's men into the pub and sat nursing a glass of ale for two hours. The two men he was following were engaged in conversation and didn't give any indication they were leaving. He was getting worried because Lawler hadn't returned. Finishing his brew, he went outside; the two men, one tall and thin and the other short and burly, followed him.

"Who are you looking for?" the taller of the two men asked, with a distinctive southern accent.

"No one in particular," Jim responded. "I just took a ride to see what the town was like."

"I think you're following us," the shorter man replied. "I saw you at Clydeside in a carriage with another man. He followed our friend north."

"I don't know what you're talking about. Now if you don't mind, I'll bid you a good day."

"We don't think so. You're going to stay right here until our friend returns, and then we'll find out why you're following us."

"You're absurd! I'm leaving at this moment."

The tall man charged at James, who sidestepped and put his foot out. The man landed on his hands and face and was slow to move. The shorter man then charged; Jimmy hit him two quick rights on the side of his face and he fell over. The tall man had gotten to his feet; Jim kicked him in the groin, and the fellow lay flailing on the ground crying out in pain. The shorter of the two was unconscious.

Jimmy checked them for identification. One was a sergeant and the taller one a lieutenant, both in the service of the Confederate States of America. He now was able to verify that Confederate spies were indeed working in England. But what of Lawler? Jim was worried. One of the spies was wearing suspenders. Jimmy dragged him behind some bushes and tied his hands behind him with his own suspenders. He pulled the other man to the same spot, but this time used the fellow's belt. The livery where Stephen had rented his horse was but a short distance away; they had one rig left to rent. James drove north on the road Lawler had taken.

When he got to the fork in the road, James chose the road to Bridge of Allan. He inquired at the store whether anyone had seen Lawler; nobody had. Next he went into the pub and asked the same question; they denied seeing Lawler.

Either Lawler hadn't come to this town, or someone was lying.

James was really worried now; he backtracked to the fork in the road and chose the other route. When he got to that next village, he asked the same questions at the pub, which was the only place open, and got the same answers. It was getting late, so he asked where he could board for the night. He was directed to the grey house across the street. The O'Neals had a room available and were happy to have Jimmy. "Your horse can stay in the paddock in the back. Breakfast is at six in the morning; after six-thirty, you'll have to find breakfast someplace else."

Over breakfast, Mr. O'Neal filled him in on the towns in the area. "I know your young friend didn't come by here yesterday. If he had, everyone would know it. Now the town of Bridge of Allan is a different story. There's some foreigners living there—maybe ten of them. Oh, they try to pass themselves off as Scotsmen, but the way they dress and the cigars they smoke give them away. They talk like you, Mr. Harris."

"Is there any law in the surrounding area?"

"Aye. There's a constable in Stirling."

James rode back to Stirling and found the local constable, William McGregor, sitting in his one-room office. He told him about his experience of the previous evening and the disappearance of his young acquaintance, Stephen Lawler.

"I didn't find any men tied up in the brush as you say, Mr. Harris. I walked by there before I came to the office. Could you be having a bit too much to drink and then made up this story?"

"Mr. McGregor, I'm not making up any story. Two men attempted to assault me; I got the better of them. I dragged them behind the hedge on the side of that house we're talking about and then tied them up. It's possible that someone untied them. Just so you know who I am, seven years ago I married Claire Temple, the Prime Minister's step-daughter. It was in all the papers."

"Sure and I'm Queen Anne's adopted son. Get off with ye, or I'll put you in the lockup!"

"I can see that you're going to be a lot of help. Is there a place where I can place a wire?"

"I have one in my office, but you can't use it. Go to the railroad station down the street. Maybe if you tell the operator about the prime minister, they'll wire your message for free!" McGregor laughed out loud.

James had wiring instructions for the Viscount and insisted that the operator send the wire. Two hours later a wire came into the railroad station and the operator jumped up and handed it to James. He didn't have time to read it before the constable came running into the station. "Why didn't you tell me that you were related to the prime minister?"

"That must have slipped my mind. Can we go to Bridge of Allan and see if we can find my acquaintance?"

"I'm ready, but I'll have to get my horse."

"Why don't we use my rig? It's ready to go."

CHAPTER TWENTY-SEVEN

James told the constable as much as he thought necessary about the Confederate group and why he had been following them. They went back to the pub in the center of Bridge of Allan and James followed the constable inside. "We're looking for a young man with blond hair who came in here yesterday—and don't tell me that he didn't, or I'll have about ten from the constabulary in London here tomorrow looking at your operation!"

"He left with two men."

"By himself, or with help?"

"They picked him up off the floor and took him out the back."

"How did he get on the floor?"

"I don't know. I wasn't looking."

"Who were they?"

"I don't know."

"You know every man and child in this area—so *who were they?*"

"It was a couple of those foreigners who live in the house down at the end of the street."

"Do you know what they did with the young man?"

"No."

"Have you seen any of those foreigners today?"

"I think all of them left town. I saw a carriage pull up in front of the cottage and two men loaded some bags, got in and left."

"If I find out that you saw the young man get hit in this pub, I'm coming back and put you in the lockup. Do you hear me?" The owner nodded.

They walked down to the blue-trimmed white house with the small porch in front and knocked. When there was no answer, they tried the door; it was locked. They went around back and tried that door; it was locked too. The constable found a window that was partially open. He pushed it open and crawled in. Soon, he opened the front door, Jimmy came inside, and he and the constable searched the rooms. Lawler was lying on a bed in one of the bedrooms; he was unconscious. Jim checked his pulse and breathing. He had a weak pulse and his breathing was sporadic. There was a severe wound on the back of his head and his pillow was saturated with blood.

"Is there a doctor in the area?"

"There's one in Stirling. We have to take him there."

They carefully loaded Stephen into the back of their carriage; the constable drove and Jimmy sat with Lawler. It took about thirty minutes to get to the town of Stirling. "I'm sorry, Mr. Harris. If I'd believed you at first, we would've gotten here sooner and maybe saved his life."

"He's got a good chance if the doctor is any good."

"Do you know the people who did this to him?"

"The only name I have is Hudson—he may be the leader of the group. It looks like they left the cottage clean. They're probably long gone by now and have a new hideout."

Doctor Wellington was at home when they arrived with Lawler. He had a one-room office in the rear of his home where he met patients, did some lab work and operated when necessary; his wife was his nurse. Jim and the constable carried the young man inside and set him on the padded table in the doctor's office. They were told to wait outside while he was being examined.

The wait was extremely exhausting for Jimmy—he felt responsible for Lawler. If only *he* had followed Hudson and let Stephen watch the other two! Two hours later, the doctor came out of his office and said that his patient had regained consciousness, but he wasn't lucid.

"My expertise is not with head injuries, but I believe he has a severe concussion. I wired the London Hospital and consulted with Doctor Freden. He's willing to see the patient as soon as you can transport him there. The railroad is probably the fastest; it runs every hour. Would you be willing to accompany him to the hospital?"

"I will."

"I'll have two men put him on a gurney and push him to the station to help put him on board. Someone from the hospital will meet you."

"I'm ready as soon as you can transport him to the station."

Within thirty minutes, James was escorting Lawler by train to the London Hospital. When they arrived, there was a wagon with a hospital logo on it waiting outside. Jimmy got off the train and directed the two hospital orderlies to move Lawler into the wagon, and then accompanied them to the hospital. James met with Doctor Freden and was told to come back the next morning. In the interim, Stephen would be undergoing a serious of tests and several examinations until late in the day.

"We won't have a prognosis until tomorrow. I want to see if the swelling goes down and then see how coherent he is after a good night's sleep."

Jim rented a room at the London Arms, cleaned up, and contacted the prime minister's office to see if the Viscount was available for dinner. He hadn't seen his father-in-law since he and Claire married, and it would be good to get his perspective on the Civil War. He was in his room when the bellboy brought him the answer. He was to meet the prime minister at his club at eight-thirty.

The Regency Club was in the heart of London's Financial District. James presented himself at the registration desk, and eventually one of the waiters escorted him into a lounge where the prime minister was talking to several of the other members.

"There you are, James! Gentlemen, this is my son-in-law, James Harris, the special assistant to the President of the United States. James, this is Mr. Harvey and Mr. Tesler, both politicians for the other party." The Viscount gave a hearty laugh. "I must be back at my office in one hour, so we only have time for a quick meal and an afterdinner drink."

They were escorted into the dining room and seated at a table away from the other diners. "They always give me this table so I can speak without being overheard," said the Viscount. "I got your message about Mr. Lawler—did you find him?"

"The Stirling constable and I found him unconscious in a cottage rented by a Mr. Hudson and several of his Confederate friends. He'd been beaten badly and is now in the London Hospital, where Doctor Freden is handling his case. He's conscious, but not coherent. I'm to return tomorrow morning and meet with the doctor. Thank you for taking the time to assist me. If you hadn't, Lawler would be dead by now."

"I was more than happy to be of assistance to my favorite son-in-law. Have you completed your mission? Or should I say, Mr. Lincoln's mission?"

"I found out a great deal."

"Can you confide in me as to what you've found out?"

"We found that the C.S.A. has a number of spies in the United Kingdom and they're actively purchasing ships for the Confederacy. I saw first-hand one of the blockade runners near completion and spoke with other shipbuilders in Liverpool and outside Glasgow."

"Are these private citizens?"

"I believe that to be the case. They have a lucrative business enterprise that directly affects my nation, and I object that your government is allowing it."

"My government's position is one of neutrality. With that being said, we don't encourage these shipbuilders, but they're not breaking any law."

"Sir, I believe your position of neutrality is mostly a sham. You tell us you won't interfere; yet, you allow the making of war machines for our enemy that could impact and kill many people. In fact, these blockade runners being built in your country will prolong the war and lead to more casualties. I feel that Lord Russell and Mr. Gladstone are determined to have your government intervene on the side of the South."

"James, sometimes things are not black-and-white, but mostly grey. You must know this from your own personal experience. Claire has written her mother many letters telling us how unhappy she is, how cold you are to her, and how insensitive you are to her concerns about living in Washington. Now, I know that sometimes people embellish what really is happening, and the truth may lie somewhere in the middle. I like you very much and I believe you're trying to be a good husband to Claire, but it's something only you can address, and the answer may not be easy to find."

James was stunned. He was living with someone whom he didn't understand, and with whom he obviously wasn't communicating very well. "Mr. Prime Minister, I thank you for spending some time with me. I believe we've given each other a message, and I, for one, am going to take your comments seriously. I hope you reciprocate." The prime minister smiled and shook Jim's hand as he left the club and returned to his office.

Lawler could tell that he was in a hospital, but he didn't know why. He was awake, but his head hurt. The nurse gave him some medicine, and he remembered the doctor making his rounds. Yesterday was a fog. He had a sense of moving from room to room, but nothing registered with him. He thought of Harris and wondered where he was. Would he know where to find him?

Harris waited outside Lawler's room until Dr. Freden, making his rounds, stopped to talk to him. "Mr. Lawler has a severe concussion. I believe that we should keep him in the hospital for the next week before you depart for the States. The wound is behind his right ear and his hearing is affected. That should only last for a few more days; I just don't know about the concussion. Have you determined how his injury happened?"

"Not really. I believe he was hit from behind as he was having a beer in a pub in a small town. Subsequently, he was dragged from the saloon and left in a cottage about a hundred yards from where he was hit. It's possible that he was beaten again. The constable from that area is following up; I suspect he won't make an arrest."

"I know you're concerned about your young friend, and I'll allow you to visit him, if you keep it within thirty minutes. You can come back each day, and perhaps then I can allow you more time."

"Thank you, doctor, for all your help."

Lawler was lying on his side, and Jim wasn't sure whether he was awake, so he sat on a hard chair by the bed. When Lawler moved and opened his eyes, Jimmy felt relieved. "I won't stay long. I just want you to know I'm here and won't leave without you."

Lawler smiled. James leaned back in his chair and stayed until the nurse said his time was up; the whole time, Lawler looked at him but didn't speak. This went on for three days, and finally, on his fourth visit, Lawler was sitting up eating some custard. "Good to see you're up and eating," James said.

"I think I'm ready to go home. What do you say?"

"The doctor wants you to stay a week, and that's what we're going to do. Life's too short to take any chances. I'm sorry I didn't go with you—I feel responsible for your injury!"

"Mr. Harris, I think they were on to us and they set me up. It's hard to believe they didn't have a go at you! I think we're lucky to be alive."

"Well, let's get you up and running. I'll tell you about my confrontation on the boat. We've accomplished our mission. We know where the boats are being built, where they're being tested, who's engineering them and who's financing them. I don't think it's necessary for us to go to France, especially with the condition you're in. It's up to Mr. Lincoln to go beyond what we've determined."

Claire and the children had been in New York City while Jimmy was in England. Cameron and Abigail were constantly coming by to see the children. One time they stayed until late in the evening while Claire gave a piano performance for some visiting dignitaries. She knew that Jimmy had owned the house before they were married, but it was a lovely home, and close to everything important to her. She didn't want to go back to the capitol. The children, sensing her mood, seemed to be happier here. She knew that Jim would visit with the Viscount, and she wondered if her stepfather would say anything about what she had written. She talked to Abigail about her concerns, and knew that Abigail confided in Cameron, but neither would say anything about her feelings to Jim. But the Viscount was a more direct person, and he may have told Jimmy some of the things she'd said.

Why did he have to take the position as Lincoln's right-hand man? There were others more qualified. He had a good life and a family that loved him; yet, he seemed to give that all away for some feeling of patriotism. She was fearful about what the future might bring to them. What if the South attacked the capitol? Would he honor his pledge and move them to New York City?

Then Claire received a wire that said Jim was scheduled to return in two weeks, and she knew that he expected her and the children—or at least the children—to return with him to Washington. What was she to do? She'd established a life *here*. This is where she felt comfortable; this was where she performed in concerts three times a year; this is where she felt alive. How could she leave?

CHAPTER TWENTY-EIGHT

Louisa had just come in from the fields. She was feeling the heat and humidity and wanted a cold glass of lemonade. Thomas Garland was aging; much of the overseeing of the slaves was now left to Jerome, who was technically John's slave. Sensing Louisa's need for help, John had left Jerome with her during his absence. As she sat down on the porch, she saw a rider come up the drive. He tied his horse to the rail and came up to the front door. It was François Renard. He, she and John were childhood acquaintances, but she hadn't seen him since the wedding.

She went to the front door and greeted him. It was nice to see and talk to someone other than her workers; she had been quite lonely after John's departure. "I hadn't seen you at any of the parties, so I thought I'd come by to see if you were okay."

"That was nice of you! Why don't you come in and have some refreshing lemonade?"

"Thank you, but if you have something else, I'd prefer that."

Louisa smiled. "I have bourbon and scotch. Which would you prefer?"

"Scotch in a glass would be fine."

She poured some scotch in a glass, handed it to Renard, and escorted him out to the porch, where they sat facing each other. They talked about the war and the impact it was having on their plantations. "I understand that you freed half of your slaves, and that you're paying them wages to do what they did in the past," Renard said.

"I tried it as an experiment, but I found that it was economically feasible. My free slaves produce almost twice as much as those who are still slaves. The freed ones seem to be more content, and my profit margin is higher. As time goes by, I'll probably free all of them."

"Your neighbors are offended by what you've done. Our way of life is threatened by the North, and now you are undermining what we are fighting for. I came here today as a member of a group that would like you to reconsider your stance and put everything back to the way it should be. How can your husband allow such a thing to happen while he's serving the Confederacy?"

"Don't worry about John. He's man enough to handle it. Is yours a request or a demand?"

"It's a request by your neighbors. They fear that what you've done could cause a slave uprising, or encourage many to run away. Our troops are tied down and can't be spared to go after runaway slaves. Any policing would be left to us. I hope you'll listen to your neighbors' concern."

"I won't promise anything until I talk it over with John."

"It must be lonely here on Magnolia for such an attractive woman. There's a dinner party this Saturday at the O'Neal plantation. Most of your friends will be there. Perhaps I could escort you."

"I don't think it would be appropriate for me to go without my husband."

As Renard got up to leave, he placed his glass on the table between them and walked back through the kitchen to the main entrance. As Louisa was walking him to the front door, he turned and put his arms around her, pulled her to him and kissed her on the lips. "I've always wanted you, Louisa—you're so beautiful!"

She tried to pull away, but he was too strong. She could smell the scotch on his breath as he kissed her again on the mouth and fondled her breast. Soon he was tearing off her clothes. He was slowly backing her into the drawing room where there was a couch. She struggled, but he was walking her backwards, and she knew what he had in mind. "John will kill you if you do this to me!"

"Who's going to tell him?"

"*I* certainly will, even if I have to go to Richmond this afternoon!"

"I was always a better shot than John, so if you tell him, then you'll be a widow, and I'll have you whenever I want."

With his hand firmly holding her long hair, Renard pushed her down on the couch and tore the remainder of her clothes off. He was very rough about it, and when her undergarments were off, she was completely nude. He pushed her legs apart and was about to enter her, when he caught a glimpse of someone walking into the drawing room; it was Jerome; he was carrying a pistol.

"I think it's time for you to leave, Mr. Renard," Jerome said, his gun pointed at Renard's back.

"Get out of here if you know what's good for you," Renard growled, turning his head to look at Jerome, who now had the pistol leveled at him. "I'm going to tell you one more time to get the hell out of here, or I'm going to take that pistol away from you and blow your brains out! Do you know what will happen to you if you shoot a white man?"

"Yes, sir. But I know what Mister John will do to me if I let you hurt Miss Louisa."

Renard pulled away from Louisa, stood up, pulled up his pants with one hand and took a step toward the black man. "Give me that pistol, or I'm going to take it away from you and beat you with a whip!"

Jerome, visibly frightened, turned slightly and backed away from Renard, who repeated his demand. Jerome continued to back away from his tormentor as Renard approached. But Renard was so intent on the gun that he didn't see Louisa rise, come up behind him and shove him to the side. Then she joined Jerome, who handed her the gun.

"You're right, Mr. Renard, I can't do anything to you, or I'd be hanged. But Miss Louisa doesn't have the same restrictions."

"I think I'm going to kill you, you degenerate piece of dung!" Louisa leveled the pistol at Renard and with her other hand cocked the firearm.

Sweat poured down Renard's face as he faced an angry naked woman pointing a gun at his genitals. "Louisa, we're old friends," he pleaded. "I got carried away—I'm sorry. Just let me go and I'll never return. Please, it was just a misunderstanding!"

He turned and started toward the front door, but Jerome had moved to the front door and blocked his path. Louisa was trailing behind him with the gun pointed at his back. Making a quick choice, Renard raced down the hall toward the kitchen and out the back door. Louisa and Jerome watched as Renard unhitched his horse, mounted it quickly, and rode off at a gallop. Louisa couldn't help but laugh.

"Miss Louisa, you have to put some clothes on before someone sees you and me and comes to the wrong conclusion. I may be hanged yet!"

"You're a great friend and I thank you." She started toward the stairs, but abruptly turned, walked back to Jerome, gave him a hug and kissed him on the cheek. "Thank you!"

She was still excited and angry as she sat down on the bed. She wondered what signal she'd given to Renard to make him act as though she wanted him. She hadn't had sex in three months, and she immediately thought of her husband and the times when they lay together in this bed. She lay back with her head on the pillow and fondled her breasts; her excitement was intense. She moved her hand down, spread her legs and touched the spot that always made her gasp. Soon she climaxed and felt a release of all the tension that had built up since the war started. "Damn you, John, for ruining our married life with your obsession about the southern way of life! What about *ours?*"

CHAPTER TWENTY-NINE

The information that the widow Rose Greenhow had sent to General Beauregard relative to the Union's troop strength swayed the Battle of Bull Run in the South's favor. She was the South's preëminent spy and the head of the Washington cell. Much of her information came from a U.S. senator who was one of the widow's many suitors; he happened to be Chairman of the Senate's Military Affairs Committee. But John was worried; his counterpart in the North would soon figure out that someone had furnished valuable information to General Beauregard's staff. It would be folly to think that your enemy was an idiot and didn't have the capability to uncover who was leaking information. He assumed that people were being interrogated, and it was only a matter of time before someone would come across information that would lead to Greenhow.

John sent word to her to be careful. But in less than two months she was detained, placed under house arrest, and subsequently put in the Old Capitol Prison, along with her daughter. She'd remain there for over a year. John needed to reinforce his network. His first step was to start recruiting while extending his sphere all the way to Canada. That country was sympathetic to the southern cause, and looked the other way as Confederate revolutionaries used their country as a base to make raids in the northern part of the Union. To compound the Union's problem, many Canadians had enlisted in the Confederate Army.

After setting up a small network, John went by boat to Canada to give some structure to the group and to initiate a recruiting and training program. While he was away, General Beauregard went to Magnolia to see what was happening to Louisa and the children. She was in the fields when he arrived, but her maid directed him to where Louisa was working. She was ecstatic to see him, and they went back to the house and had some wine. "Please say you're staying over, Pierre."

"I am, if you'll have me."

"Have you seen John?"

"I saw him last month. He's on his way to Canada to do some recruiting and training. He seems busy, but I know he misses you."

"Tell me about the war."

"Well, we won the first big skirmish, and seem to have the Yankees on their heels, but we didn't follow up. We should have attacked Washington immediately and brought the war to their front porch. My problem is with Davis. For a West Pointer, he's extraordinarily cautious. It's obvious to me that he and I have a problem, because he resented me telling him that we should attack the Union Capitol. We're fighting a defensive war; we need to bring the fight to their home. Sooner or later they're going to find someone to lead them who isn't as timid as McClelland, and we'll be beaten back and may lose the border states, including South Carolina."

"How's the morale?"

"Our boys have no quit in them. They're excited about all our other victories, including Manassas—or, as the Yankees call it, Bull Run. Do you know that thousands of northern civilians came to the battle site to have a picnic, and had to run home in fear of their lives after we thrashed them? I really wanted to follow those smug Yankees all the way back to Washington, but Davis ordered me not to pursue them."

"I hear that you're a hero—they call you the Little Napoleon!"

Pierre smiled and toasted Louisa. "That's what they say."

Before the general left the next morning, Jerome asked if he could have a moment with him in private. He proceeded to tell him everything that had happened when Renard visited. Pierre seethed inside, but he didn't let Jerome know that he was angry. "I'll take care of it," he said grimly.

He had played and partied with John and Renard when they were young, but he was sure that what Jerome said was true. There was a vicious streak in Renard, and he prided himself on being an expert with a handgun; many young men had been wounded or killed by him in duels. Although he had known Renard most of his life, he had never liked him, and then there was the fact that he'd never entered military service—or, at the least, the Confederate government. In fact, it didn't appear that he was doing anything to help the South; he was one of those who were going to wait out the war.

Wanting Louisa wasn't a sin. She was a magnificently beautiful woman. Renard had always been afraid of John, and that had probably curtailed his desire for her. With the war in full swing and John gone, Renard probably thought he could get away with seducing the man's wife.

Well, he was here, and he had a free afternoon, so Pierre decided to pay a call on his old acquaintance. The Renard estate was not as palatial as Magnolia, but it was above average for a plantation. The white home stood back about three hundred feet from the entrance, and one accessed the residence down a winding gravel road, bordered by cypress trees, which gave it a secluded feeling. Renard was at home when P.G.T. arrived, and seemed surprised, perhaps even apprehensive, at his visit.

Pierre was welcomed into Renard's home, and the two men went into the study to have a drink. Pierre could see a collection of handguns and rifles on one wall and pictures of Renard on a fox hunt on another wall.

"You must be a busy man—so what brings you to my home? I'm honored, but slightly curious."

Pierre decided to get right to the point. "I don't appreciate your visit to Magnolia the other day, and the way you took advantage of Louisa, especially while her husband's involved in our cause."

"Is that what she said?"

"She's too much of a lady to speak of your unmanly attitude, and, I must add, cowardly actions, while her husband is supporting our great nation."

Renard smiled. "She's a beautiful woman and very lonely. She led me to believe that my advances would be acceptable."

Renard was sitting in one of the plush chairs in front of the fireplace. His legs were crossed and he had a drink in one hand. Pierre had been sitting across from him, but now he rose and leveled a handgun at Renard's chest. "Stand up," he told him.

"Really, this is so frivolous! If you feel you have to defend the lady's honor, then I'll oblige you at any time, but I'm not going to stand up. However, if you leave at this moment, I won't take offense. You're a war hero. I don't want to kill you."

"I told you to stand! If you're not up by the time I count to three, I'll shoot you where you sit! One . . ."

"Oh, all right, I'm standing. What does that prove?"

Pierre shot Renard in the right knee. The man fell and cried out in pain. "My God, you've *shot* me! Are you crazy?" He continued to cry out in pain.

"I'll call your servants to take care of you before I leave, but if you want to satisfy your honor in the future, just call Confederate headquarters. They'll know how to find me. I'm not a doctor, but I believe you'll walk with a limp or a cane the rest of your life. I beg your leave, sir."

• • •

John Beauregard departed aboard a blockade runner in the summer of 1862 and went up the coast of New England. They sighted several Union warships, but their boat was too fast and easily stayed out of firing range. He was on a secret mission and only he, Jefferson Davis and his companion knew what their objective was. They sailed up the coast and turned west into the St. Lawrence River and then to Quebec, Canada. He and Gabriel Rains checked into an inn in the city. The next morning they walked to the address given to John by Major Norris, who was his second in command in the Confederate spy apparatus.

Rains had been introduced to him at a cocktail party in Richmond and the two became friendly. Mr. Rains, a West Point graduate, was an acquaintance of P.G.T. Beauregard, John's cousin. He'd served in the Union Army and distinguished himself in the Seminole War, where explosive land mines were first used. When John learned of the man's expertise, he asked him if he was amenable to helping John train some recruits in Canada; only later did he divulge his true mission to him.

They were to meet with five Canadian sympathizers who wanted to do something to help the southern cause. His contact, Jean Delac, a French-Canadian fisherman, was his liaison with the recruits. It was he who arranged the meeting at his home at one o'clock that afternoon. When the recruits arrived, John interviewed each individually to determine their qualifications and how they could be usable to the cause.

When he completed the interviews over a two-day period, he gathered the young men together and told them what his objectives were. His goal was to travel west to Lake Erie and then on to his destination. He wanted to free as many Confederate prisoners as possible from a Union stronghold on Johnson Island in Sandusky Bay, Michigan.

"If any of you feel timid about what I want done, now is the time to part company. I intend to use explosives to further our cause. What's your decision?"

Each indicated they were comfortable with the objectives, so John turned their training over to Rains, who showed them how to convert old artillery shells into land mines. He showed them how to plant bombs in buildings, around fences, in supply depots and in armory storage buildings. Throughout the next week, John taught them the clandestine methods they needed to gain access to Johnson Island and its stockade. Delac had secured a blueprint of the existing buildings, both inside the compound and those outside the prison. The armory and barracks for the guards were the ones outside the enclosure.

Gabriel J. Rains had invented the land mine, and over the next ten days he showed the recruits where to place it, how to set the fuse, and how to get away before the explosion. In addition, he showed them an ingenious device called a "coal torpedo," which was in essence a booby trap. It was a four-pound artillery shell shaped like a lump of coal and covered with coal dust. The hollowedout shell was filled with gunpowder and sealed with wax, making it look like the usual lump of coal. The coal torpedo was most effective when it was dropped into Union coal stockpiles. Although the charge wasn't strong enough to sink a warship, the blast it created could rupture a boiler, cause a leak, and put a ship out of commission for a period of time.

John had a Canadian map tacked to the wall and explained the route they'd take to the prison. "I'm assured by Mr. Delac that all our supplies and munitions will be waiting for us when we reach the small town of Chatham Kent in Canada." He pointed out the town on the map. "We'll be carrying hollow shells with us on our journey; the munitions will be available there.

"From Chatham Kent we'll travel by land until we're near one of the Canadian Islands north of Sandusky Bay. Johnson Island is fairly accessible by water; the only problem is the Union warship patrolling the lake. We've received their patrolling schedule from our Canadian allies. One of our jobs is to put 'coal torpedoes' in with their coal supply. Our intelligence indicates that they buy their coal in Canada at this point." He took a stick and pointed to the map.

"If you're worried about remembering all this, let me put your minds at ease—I'm going to cover it again at Chatham Kent. From our sources, there are approximately twenty-five hundred Confederate officers at this prison. If we can liberate a fair amount, we'll strike a blow for the Confederacy, and at the same time let the Yankees know that they are not untouchable."

It took them ten days to reach Chatham Kent. Soon after they arrived, John had a meeting with Delac. "I'm comfortable with what you and your friends have provided for us, but what about the boat that we and the prisoners will use to escape?"

"It's docked south of here," Delac said. "It's a slow steam-powered vessel. My cousin is the captain. It can carry about five hundred people, perhaps more if we have to. The Union warship must be out of commission before we depart for Johnson Island, and we have to be aware of some coastal batteries. It's risky but possible to complete the mission without being caught on the lake."

"The Union warship patrolling the lake took on coal this morning; we'll have to wait," Delac said. "I have people stationed along the coast who'll be able to see smoke and fire if there's an explosion; once they see it, they'll signal us to leave with our small barge."

It was about six o'clock in the evening when they heard a blast and could see fire on the horizon. Since the Union warship was the only one in the area, they had to assume it was the one on fire. Subsequently, this was confirmed by the Canadian lookouts. They gathered up their gear, walked the short distance to the shore, boarded the steam-powered boat, and shortly were on their way to Johnson Island.

Around ten o'clock that evening, John gathered the men in the dining room. He laid out a map of the Johnson Island buildings. There were approximately forty of them outside the compound. "Our plan is to make a quick strike to create havoc so that we can free as many prisoners as possible. There will two three-man teams. I will lead one with Mike and Carl; Frederick will lead the second with Peter and Joseph. Initially, my team will swim the last three hundred feet to shore. Our first priority is to neutralize the sentries. Mr. Delac has informed me that there are three guards patrolling the outer perimeter. Once we've disposed of them, we'll signal the boat to come closer to shore. The second group of three will then come ashore, put explosives on both barracks doors and the unmanned batteries and ignite them within sixty seconds. My group will put explosive around the perimeter of the armory as soon as we see the second team heading to the barracks. I want both teams to ignite the fuses at the same time. Use ninety-second delays. The second team will then put explosives outside the main gate and immediately ignite the fuses. Our intelligence says the prisoners have been alerted that a rescue attempt would be made this month; they've been instructed to run to the beach and board our boat as soon as they hear explosions.

"Explosives by themselves will create some havoc, but we must move fast. We're outnumbered, so it's imperative that we get in and out as soon as possible. The captain will be ready to move once I come back onboard. In the event that my group doesn't make it, I want Mr. Rains, who'll remain on the ship during our assault, to assume command and evacuate everyone as soon as possible and return to Canadian waters. My team goes ashore in thirty minutes. Are there any questions?"

There were none. "Since there are no questions, I want to thank you in advance for being part of this rescue mission."

At midnight, their steam-powered boat, aided by a slight fog and drizzle, moved to within three hundred feet of the shore; they hadn't been spotted yet. All six volunteers were dressed in black pants, black shirts, and black wool hats. Their faces were blackened and they were carrying their explosives in waterproof bags.

John and his team went over the side and swam the remaining distance to shore. When they were on the beach, the team gathered and they all took out their knives. From what John had earned from Delac, one sentry would be near the armory and the other two near the dock. "I'll take the one at the armory; you two take the ones at the dock and then come toward the armory. Once we're together, we'll signal the boat."

John found his sentry sitting down, leaning against a side wall of the armory building. He crept as close as possible, threw a small rock to divert the man's attention, and, as the man looked in the direction of the sound, John moved quickly and hit him over the head with his handgun. He had planned to kill the sentry, but since he was unconscious, he just tied him up, put a gag in his mouth, and hid him under some loose boards. Ten minutes later, his two team members arrived and signaled that they had been successful. John fired a small flare toward the boat while the other men in his squad placed the explosives around the armory. Soon he could make out the boat creeping toward shore, and then he saw three men drop into the water. He would wait two minutes and light the explosives.

"Okay, light the fuses. There's a large sand dune near where we came ashore. When we've completed the arming we'll go there and drop down behind it; I'll carry the prisoner. Let's go!"

John grabbed his prisoner, threw him over his shoulder, and hustled to the dune. His two companions were close behind him. Soon they heard a series of explosions as the armory blew up. He barely heard the ones igniting at the barracks, and never did hear the ones at the front gates of the stockade, but he had to assume that everything had gone as planned. Leaving the prisoner behind the dune, he and his team ran to the boat and got on board.

Explosions continued for over five minutes, and soon he could see men running toward the shore. He assumed they were Confederate prisoners and helped them on board; he signaled the captain to get up a head of steam. John didn't know how much time he had before the Union soldiers figured out what was happening and came running after the escapees.

That had nearly one hundred on the boat before he heard rifle fire. "We can't wait much longer, captain—let's move out!"

Soldiers were chasing the prisoners; some were hit and fell to the ground; others stopped in their tracks and put their hands up. John was helping as many as he could to climb on board, but they had to leave many in the water. If they tried to take others, they'd all be prisoners!

There was a line of soldiers on shore firing on the boat. "Get down! Get down! Come on, captain, get us out of here!" John ordered.

Three prisoners lay on the deck with blood pouring from their wounds. John checked them; all three were dead. Soon the boat was out of rifle range, and now their goal was to get away. Forty-five minutes later they were out of range and in Canadian waters. They still had to worry about the Union warship, if indeed it was back in commission.

They had rescued one hundred sixty-nine Confederate officers; only three of them had died after coming onboard, and they were buried at sea. Everyone was so happy to be free. The senior officer asked John what was to become of them. "We intend to get you to Canada. After debriefing and taking care of any medical problems, we'll get you back to your units in the South."

One member of the second squad had not returned. Still, they had made a quick strike on a Union prison compound, had rescued one hundred sixty-six prisoners, and had lost only one man of the six who went ashore. John got his group together and thanked each one for a job well done.

"We've struck a mighty blow for the South. We've shown the enemy that he's vulnerable even deep into his territory. The result is that the Union has to divert resources to bolster their garrisons and prisons. We should be happy tonight."

CHAPTER THIRTY

Instead of being gone for one month, as originally planned, Jimmy Harris and Stephen Lawler hadn't seen New York in two and one-half months. By this time, Lawler had completely recovered from his injuries, and he was looking forward to going back to his ship. Jimmy, on the other hand, wasn't sure what awaited him as he strode down the gangplank and saw his father and Abigail waiting for him. "Good to see you Jim; you're looking well. This must be Lt. Lawler," Cameron said as he shook hands with his son and the lieutenant.

"I'm not a suspicious man, but is there a reason why Claire and the children are not here to greet me?"

"There is. Why don't we recover your luggage, and we'll talk in the carriage."

"Sir, I see my mother is here to greet me," Lawler put in. "I'd like to be excused and join my family. I can be available for you in Washington when you need me."

"You go with your family. It was a pleasure working with you, and I'll notify your commander of that fact. I'll call your headquarters if I need more information. Have a nice trip home."

After they retrieved his baggage, they rode to Cameron and Abigail's home and went directly to their living room. Cameron poured three glasses of sherry and they sat down.

"The news is not good," he began. "From what we've been able to piece together, Claire and the children left for England four days ago. The way we found out is via a letter she sent to us as they departed New York City. When we found out what she had done, we didn't know exactly how to handle the situation, so we waited until you came home. There was also a letter for you—here it is." Cameron handed the envelope to Jimmy. He opened it and read:

"Dear James:

"I've had a great deal of time to look at our marriage and our relationship and have come to the conclusion that we are not meant for each other. I don't lay all the blame at your feet, but the ultimatum that you issued last year that I could either come back with you and the children to Washington or stay in New York was difficult to swallow.

"It was me, and not you, who carried my two children to term, and it was me, not you, who gave birth to the babies. I recognize your rights as a father, but they seem to pale in comparison to one who carried them nine months and went through excruciating pain to deliver them. As long as I'm in your country, my rights as a mother will be subservient to yours as a father. I find that unfair.

"I'm not trying to beat a dead horse, but we had a wonderful life in New York. You seemed to feel that it wasn't enough for you; for me, it was. I feel that with all the violence between the two sides, America is not the proper place to be raising children.

"It would seem that the only rights I have to my children are in my parent country. I'm sorry if you feel that my actions are underhanded, but it seemed the only way for me to protect my rights by acting while you were in transit and could do nothing about it.

"I'm going to live in Hertfordshire with my mother. The children will be enrolled in some of the best schools in the area. You are welcome to visit the children at any time, with prior written notice, but you will not be permitted to take my loved ones back to America. From this day forward they will be considered English subjects.

"Respectfully, "Claire."

Jimmy handed the letter to Abigail and sat down with his head in his hands. He was stunned. Not in his wildest dreams would he believe that Claire was capable of such devious action. He looked up at Cameron and Abigail, but they were anxious to see what he contemplated. "I'm tired.

I wonder if I can stay here tonight; perhaps we can talk again at breakfast."

He knew that he had to get to the Capitol to brief Lincoln on his trip and tell him what Palmerston had said; yet, he needed to make arrangements about his house in New York City. Tomorrow, he'd be able to think clearer.

He was up at six o'clock the next morning, and although he had tossed and turned all night, he felt renewed vigor, once again in charge of his life. At breakfast he asked his father to close up the New York house. "I don't intend to lease it. It's a fine home, and after my work is done in the administration, I'll probably come back here to live. I'm going to take the noon train to D.C., report to Lincoln, and then take a few days to see what my options are. I have a good attorney who has a license to practice in England. Claire may have given me no recourse, but I have enough assets to pursue this to what I hope will be a successful conclusion."

His father drove him to the train station and hugged him as they entered the concourse. "I'm sorry that you have to go through this. I'm always available if you want someone to talk to."

"Thanks, dad."

• • •

After several months, his anger still hadn't subsided. He'd corresponded with Claire and was getting nowhere. He decided to turn the situation over to his attorney to seek custody of the children and a divorce from Claire. To compound the situation, Claire had taken the maid, the housekeeper, and all the dishes and silverware from the Washington rental—just what he needed. He took a few days off, and Cameron and Abigail came down to Washington. It was she who hired a housekeeper for the residence.

Over the next six months, his schedule was intense. Lincoln appointed him to the Ironclad Committee, along with three Naval captains and Lt. Lawler. Although he was out of his element when it came to naval tactics, his knowledge of the British capability in Ironclads was extremely valuable. By November, the war was slugging along, but events were overtaking the military battles. The *Monitor* had been activated and became a serious threat to the wooden British warships. Although the English had ironclads of their own, they were not functional in deep water, and therefore couldn't sail across the Atlantic and make an attack on American soil. Not only that, but the American Navy was near full strength, and many felt it to be superior to the British Navy. This had to give pause to the firebrands in England who were encouraging the British to come to the aid of the Confederates.

Yet, in spite of the *Monitor*, the rhetoric from Lord Russell and Mr. Gladstone was heating up. The latter seemed to hate the Union, and praised Jefferson Davis in public. Each measure Gladstone put forward to intervene was met with stiff resistance from the English Secretary of War, George Lewis. To him, England's main concern was the loss of cotton due to the blockade. The subsequent layoffs of the linen workers was now more of a concern than gearing up for war across the Atlantic.

James was fortunate to have met many sons of English, French and Spanish aristocracy in his years at Oxford. He had maintained relationships with many of these men during his formative years. After Sarah's death, he had travelled to England, spent some time with George Phelps, and went to France and met the D'Orleans brothers as well as Alexander II, who was traveling in Europe at the time. He and Alexander were about the same age, and thus began a friendship that carried on through the American Civil War.

In November of 1862, Lincoln asked Jimmy to come to his office. "Mr. Harris, I recall from conversations we had before I became president that you were friendly with the Russian royal family."

"I met the Emperor in Paris in 1854, and we continue to correspond periodically. In fact, I received a letter from him just two months ago."

"Russia is one of but three countries that supported our stand against the South. I'm encouraged to learn that the Emperor has abolished serfdom and has spoken out against corporal punishment. We have a good relationship with Russia, and especially with their former ambassador, Eduard de Stoecki. I remember President Buchanan telling me that his predecessor, President Pierce, had nearly entered the Crimean War on the side of the Russians. They haven't forgotten that gesture. I believe that if Britain and France want to enter the war on the side of the South, a gesture from Russia about interceding on our side would probably stop the two nations permanently.

"It's my intent to follow in Alexander's path and issue a proclamation to free all slaves in the territories that we've taken from the South, sometime after the first of next year. I believe that our success at the battle of Antietam was the turning point of the war. I'm confident that we will soon be starting an offensive to take the war to the South and finish it once and for all.

"As Commander-in-Chief, I want to win this war quickly and with the minimum loss of life. I need to be sure that the English will stay on their side of the Atlantic so that I can finish the job. Last month, the British issued an ultimatum that we either agree to a ceasefire or there would be repercussions. The British see us as a threat to their world order, and France wants a foothold in Central America. I believe that Russia is the key to a quick and effective completion of our conflict. I want you to go to Russia, meet with the Emperor, and see how much help he and his nation can provide. Your mission has become a priority for me."

"But we already have an effective ambassador in Russia," Jimmy demurred. "I don't want to step on his toes."

"He's been advised of your personal relationship with Alexander and will be more than glad to set up some meetings. I have nothing to promise the Emperor other than our gratitude."

Winter in Moscow wasn't going to be much fun, but if he could encourage the Russians to help, it would pay dividends. This might be a good time to check with his attorney, who'd been in England the past month. The last news he had had from him was slightly encouraging. He desperately wanted to see his children and determine what his future was going to be with them. Although he'd written every two weeks, Claire had not responded in three months.

Lincoln was aware of Jimmy's personal family problems and encouraged him to seek some resolution while he was in Europe. He left two days later on the ten-day voyage across the Atlantic. His attorney had arranged for a visit with the children for the day after his planned arrival. The two men met at the London Regency to have lunch. "Give it to me straight," Jimmy said.

"The divorce is final as soon as you sign the papers. The best I could do was to insist upon unlimited visitation rights, conditioned on all visits being here in England, with twenty-four hours' notice. She doesn't want to see you, and I'm not sure she hasn't poisoned the children's minds against you. You can take them anywhere in England, but you must have the nanny along."

"You know what I think of that arrangement! I'm not going to accept it. I want joint custody and six months each year with my children in my home in America. Courts in both countries can enforce such an arrangement, but that's the minimum I'll accept. They don't know who they're dealing with! I can't go up against the government, but my financial holdings are such that I can make it painful for anyone who owes my bank money, or anyone coming to my country to borrow money."

"I'll see what I can do."

The two children, Mary and Cameron, were shy at first, but they soon got over it and enjoyed being with their father. He took them to the zoo and to a puppet show. They had caramel candy and some food from one of the vendors in the park. Mary was seven and Cameron six. They seemed like two well-adjusted kids. Claire wasn't available when he brought them home that night, and they asked when they were going to see him again. "I'm on my way to Russia. I'll stop back here in about two months. Perhaps we can be together for a longer period of time when I return."

He was unable to get an appointment with the Viscount; perhaps it had something to do with Claire. His only dialog was with the Prime Minister's secretary. "I'll be back in two months and will try again to see him. Perhaps the results of my meeting with Alexander of Russia will open up Prime Minister Palmerston's schedule."

He went by boat to France and then by train to Moscow and it was cold; there was no heat onboard the train. It wasn't unusual for the train to be stalled for hours while they tried to clear the snow off the tracks. On one two-hour stop, the passengers gathered some wood and lighted a fire, all taking turns getting next to the blaze. It was a lonely trip; he knew no one on the train, which was mostly filled with Russian peasants. Even at meals, most ate quickly and went back to their seat or compartment. Ten days later he was received by Alexander II for a quick audience; later in the day they'd have time to talk. James was staying at the palace, and over dinner they discussed geopolitics.

"My friend, the wolf is at the door. There's an insurrection in Poland and our friends, the British and French, want to intercede on the side of the Poles. The superiority of the English fleet has put the Russian Navy in peril's way. What am I to do? I believe we can put down the extremists in Poland, but if the British and French come to their aid, they may defeat or bottle up my Navy. What I'd like to do, and this is only for your president to know, is send six of our naval vessels to New York and six to San Francisco in the spring. In this way, our fleet is out of harm's way, and if you are attacked, our navy will defend your coastlines."

"I believe the President will be most grateful."

"My critics will say that my gesture is self-serving. I say, if it helps Mr. Lincoln and the Union, so what?"

The two toasted each other and withdrew to the drawing room, where the Empress was waiting. She didn't speak any English, but sat quietly as the two men talked of politics, laughed at some frivolous things, and spoke about the future. James spent a week with his friend, hunting, drinking good wine, and telling stories of their past. When it was time to leave, Alexander reiterated his promise to send the fleet in the spring. "I hope we see each other when your war is over. Have a safe trip home."

Instead of taking two months to complete his mission, he returned to England within a month and was surprised to learn that negotiations were complete. Pending his signature, James was to have the children in America during the summer months each year and Claire would have the children during the school semester; they would attend school in Hertfordshire. His divorce was final, and financial arrangements had been made for Claire and the children. She did not want to see James.

His attorney had a message for him from the Prime Minister when he returned to England. The leader of Great Britain hoped that the two could have dinner the following day, if it was convenient for James. He smiled. He assumed that the British ambassador to Russia had cabled his boss about Jim's lengthy visit with the Tsar at his residence.

The meeting was, as always, cordial between himself and his former father-in-law. "I'm distressed at the action Claire has taken. Emily and I looked upon you as a son. We both felt that you would be good to our daughter; we're heartbroken that it didn't work out."

"Thank you, sir. I appreciate your comments."

"Tell me about your visit with Alexander. I didn't realize that you and he were such good friends."

"We met years ago and continued the relationship. Mr. Lincoln asked me to visit him. I'm sorry that I can't divulge certain aspects of our conversation; I'm sure you understand."

"Yes, yes, I see . . . I do know that he has supported Mr. Lincoln at times. I hope that he's not going to furnish support to the Union!"

"Sir, you'll have to ask Alexander that question."

"I'm walking a tight line here. Some of my contemporaries feel very strongly about interceding. I'm doing everything to maintain our neutrality. I would hope that Mr. Lincoln will show good judgment and negotiate an end to this tragedy."

"Sir, I firmly believe he's doing everything he can to bring the South back into the Union. They can't sustain the fight they started, and they know it. I would hope that our two countries can maintain a cordial relationship. I don't think your country wants another war with America; it would be a disaster."

It felt like a chapter in his life was over. He still couldn't figure out why Claire had left. He knew they came from different backgrounds and different cultures, but there had to be more behind the separation. As the years passed, he realized that he had been partly to blame; perhaps he shouldn't have married so soon after Sarah died. Maybe she sensed that it was Sarah he still loved and she could never take her place in his heart. Well, he wished her well. At least he had two wonderful children, and he hoped that he'd be as good a father to them as his own father had been to him.

CHAPTER THIRTY-ONE

As spring made its way across the nation, the spirit in the South was unbreakable, but reality was sinking in on many and they wondered what the next few months would bring. Louisa was one of those people. Her finances were near the breaking point. The loans with Jimmy's bank were delinquent. The problem was that she had to negotiate the sale of her cotton produce not only with the factor but she had to take the entire risk that her cargo would get through the blockade; she was one hundred percent at risk. On two occasions she was notified by her factor that the Union had confiscated her shipment. Louisa wondered aloud whether it was her shipment or some other plantation owner's that was lost. And because she was a woman, she was easy prey to some unscrupulous factors.

John still hadn't come to visit. The only time she'd seen him was when she went to Richmond on business; it was only for one night and they had argued the entire time; then he was gone again. He told her that he loved her and wanted to be with her, but the South was hurting.

"We're short of supplies and ammunition. Many of our soldiers haven't been paid in months. Most of us have to work harder, or it's going to come down around our feet."

"Why don't you negotiate peace?"

"I wish we could, but Lincoln issued the Emancipation Proclamation at the beginning of the year, and we can't accept the thought of our slaves being free."

"Why not? Why do we have to lose everything just so you can hold that view? I don't feel that way. I'd like to go back to the life we had before the crazies attacked Fort Sumter. I've proved that we can be profitable by freeing the slaves and hiring them to work our fields. Why can't you and Davis see that?"

"If Davis adopted that view, he'd be lynched the next day. Someone else with more reactionary views would take over, and the war would still go on."

"You mean that you and Davis are not in charge? If not you, then who?"

"I didn't say that."

"My God, this is a bottomless pit that we'll all be swallowed up in! I've lost two shipments to the blockade and I need money. Can you spare some to keep Magnolia afloat? I have to pay the help, or they won't pick cotton."

"You got yourself into that fix by freeing your slaves and hiring them as wage earners. I told you it wasn't going to work!"

"Are you crazy? I'd still have to feed them. I'm running short of funds. Can you help?"

"You and I both agreed to give Jimmy half our funds to invest in northern securities and the other half in the South's cause. Why don't you see if he'll help?"

"I didn't agree to leave half our funds to be lost in the South. That's the only way I could get you to save some money for our children and not waste it on this cause. Do you have a way of contacting Jimmy to see if he can send me some money?"

"If I could, I wouldn't. He's Lincoln's right-hand man and he's been in England trying to shut down the shipbuilding for our navy. I could have had him killed while he was there, but I didn't. I'd like to eliminate him, but I don't want him dead. Do you know what I mean?"

"Don't you dare have him killed! That would be the end of us; I could never forgive you. Even if you did, it doesn't solve our problem. Do you want to lose Magnolia?"

"I can't think of it right now. What I'm working on is so much more important. I must go. The Union blockade of South Carolina will stop any future shipments of cotton from this area and you'll have to send them from some port farther south."

"Thanks a lot for all your help! What's more important than your home?"

John ignored her last comment. "By the way, my men in Great Britain tell me that Claire and James are divorced. She apparently left with the children while he was in England on a mission for Lincoln. He had to hire a lawyer and fight to gain joint custody. What do you think happened there?"

"I think he married too soon after Sarah died, and I think both of you are fools, giving up your families for something that will never fill the void it created."

John didn't want to lose Magnolia either. He'd been in Washington on many occasions to personally recruit spies for the South. It was tricky getting in and out, but his network was still intact.

•   •   •

Jimmy had just finished a meeting of the Ironclad Committee, and he and Lawler went across the street to the Beef and Ale Saloon to have a brew. He'd been in England one other time since he and Lawler identified who was building ships for the South. He personally talked to the older Laird brother and came away frustrated. The man told him point-blank that he was going to build ships for the South and there was nothing he or his stinking nation could do about it. James planned to go back at the start of the summer to pick up his children and bring them home until the start of the school year in Britain.

"What's your relationship with the prime minister since you and his stepdaughter are divorced?" Lawler asked.

"Not too bad and not too good. He won't see me as his ex-son-in-law, but he'll see me as Lincoln's emissary, after the ambassadors schedule a meeting."

"Do you plan to see him when you go back?" Lawler asked.

"Yes. I have a message from Lincoln which could be delivered by the American ambassador, but Lincoln likes my blunt way of saying things. Stephen, please excuse me. I've had two glasses of ale and I must relieve myself."

The men's room was at the rear of the saloon; there was only one other patron there at the time and he left soon after James entered. After he relieved himself and was washing his hands, he looked in the mirror and there was a man grinning back at him. He didn't recognize him at first because he had a least a month's worth of whiskers—but it was John Beauregard!

"My God, John, you're taking an unnecessary risk coming here! I won't turn you in, but I can't protect you either. You've got to be careful."

"It's good to see you! It's been too many years. Louisa sends her love. We need to talk."

"Well, it can't be here—I'm with a young associate. I'll send him on his way. Why don't you meet me at my home? There's no one there and you'll be safe. Here's the address. Can you make it on your own?"

"No problem."

A half-hour later, he opened the door to his childhood friend and invited him in. "I know you've not been here before, but my guess is that you've known where I live for some time. I suppose you come and go in our capitol as you please. What's on your mind?"

"Let's talk for a while and then I'll tell you. You seemed to have prospered, but then again, I always knew you would. I'm sorry to hear about Claire."

"That came as a surprise to me. I came home from the office one day, and she and the children had moved back to New York City without telling me or even letting me know where she was. When I found out, I went to New York, took the children, and gave her an ultimatum that she could either rejoin me in the capitol or she could stay there by herself."

"Boy, I'll bet she loved that! I can guess what her answer was, and I can also figure out what she'd do next."

"You always were smarter than I; I didn't see it coming. When I see what she did, I can almost smile. She reversed the positions and became the power player. I had to fight to even get visitation rights. I don't mean to bore you with my personal problems, but you're my friend and the only one I'd open up to."

"I've got my own family problems. I wanted to help my new country, but I've alienated the woman I love, and I wonder if I'll ever get her back. I don't want Louisa to leave me as Claire did you—not that I'd blame her. The situation is that I'm stuck: I can't walk away from what I've been doing and go home. My country needs and relies on me. By the way, I'm sorry about what happened to Lawler. When I found out, I immediately took action. I know what you've been up to, and I'll try to stop you, but not at the risk of your life. My people will not harm you."

"You didn't come here to tell me that. I know you, John—you have something else on your mind."

"This war is devastating my country, and my wife's plantation is in distress. She's lost several cotton shipments, either to the blockade or to unscrupulous individuals. She can't repay the loans to you and she needs money to stay afloat. You know that she has freed almost all her slaves and has hired them back as free laborers. I don't approve, but I admire her so much that I need to see if we can help her."

"What do you want me to do?"

"You invested half our funds into northern securities."

"You're not asking for them back so you can help the South, are you?"

"No—I'd like to have one thousand dollars for Louisa so she doesn't have to lose Magnolia, and then another thousand at the end of the year. Do you think you can do that for her?"

"I can have greenbacks for you tomorrow, if you want."

"I was hoping for gold, if possible. You're a banker; you should be able to access some gold. If our investment is sound, it should be no problem."

"I turned my banking operation over to a manager and I don't have access to any funds other than what's in my personal account. I can accommodate you with greenbacks, but I couldn't get you gold in a timely manner.

"As you know, the cost of war is more than either of us anticipated," Jimmy continued. "Lincoln didn't have any idea how much money was in our treasury and what it would take to wage war. We've issued a lot of greenbacks, and they'll be redeemed by the U.S. government when the war ends. But the redemption is not one-for-one. I have contacts up north, and they say the redemption is going to be like 100 to 160 gold. I'm sure your side has some of the same problems we have. You've issued greybacks and bluebacks. What is the South's redemption rate?"

"I don't think I'm willing to say. I'll take the one thousand any way I can get it. I have a place to stay this evening and could come by tomorrow around noon and pick up the funds, if that's okay."

"That's fine, but why don't you stay here tonight?"

"That would put you in jeopardy . . . but I have a second reason for coming to see you, and it's very confidential. I had a meeting yesterday with Jefferson Davis, and I told him I was going to Washington on business. He asked if I had a reliable contact in the White House. I told him I did. He gave me a personal letter for Lincoln. Could you see that Lincoln receives it? I'd like to stay in the area and wait, if there's going to be a quick reply."

"Would it be presumptuous of me to read it first?"

"Davis asked that it be opened only by Lincoln."

They had another drink and Jimmy made them dinner. "I've gotten pretty good at making my own meals. I'm not as good as Sarah or Louisa, but I've officially been a bachelor for nearly a year—even longer unofficially."

"It tastes good to me. Do you think of the life we had when we were growing up?"

"I loved that life. I knew there were slaves at the plantation, but I wasn't astute enough to see what it was doing to your society. You became so dependent on them that you couldn't see any alternative other than to fight to retain them."

"That's about the size of it. It wasn't the only reason we seceded, but it was the main one. I don't think any of us realized the commitment Lincoln had to Emancipation and how stubborn he was. It took us some time to come to grips with the reality that he would fight to keep us."

"I can see Lincoln in the morning if he's in the office. I'll present the Davis letter and try to get a quick response for you. Since I can only surmise what's in the letter, he may want to consult with his cabinet before he'll respond. That may take time. Where can I contact you?"

"I think I'd better keep my whereabouts confidential. Why don't we meet at the same saloon tomorrow at noon, and you can give me the money and perhaps Lincoln's answer? I think I'll leave you now. I promise that I won't do anything while I'm here that will embarrass you. I know what's in the letter, and I'm anxious. I'll see you tomorrow—go to the bathroom at noon." John couldn't help but laugh as he said the last bit.

His checking account had more than sufficient funds. The clerk raised an eyebrow when Jimmy said he wanted cash, and called the bank manager. When the manager saw who was making the request, he gave Jim the cash personally.

Lincoln wasn't available until eleven. When he was free, Jim presented the letter and told him about his visitor and his request for a quick response. Opening the letter, Lincoln read it twice, set it down on his desk, and looked at James. "Have you read the contents of this letter?"

"No, sir. The messenger asked that I not read it."

"Do you know who the messenger is? Is he reliable?"

"Yes, sir. He's the head of their Signal Corps; his name is John Beauregard. He and I were childhood friends. To be honest, he's still my best friend. I believe the letter to be genuine."

"Do you know where he is or how to contact him?"

"I'm to meet him, but I'd rather not say where or when."

"You grew up in the South, didn't you, Mr. Harris?"

"I was born in Charleston, went to school there, and my grandparents still live there. I married a woman from Savannah and I was in business with offices in Mobile, New Orleans, Savannah and Charleston. I still have many friends in the South, and I'm in sympathy with them, though I think they're wrong. If you remember, sir, I went south during the election season to see what sympathy there was for your candidacy. I'm wondering if many of them know that the route they've taken will never get them to where they want to be."

"I'm not implying that you're a southern sympathizer in any way. You've completed many tasks for me and I'm grateful for your dedication. My sources tell me that you've suffered in many ways; you've lost your family, and yet you stayed on. For that, I'm thankful."

Lincoln handed him the letter, and James read the three paragraphs on Jefferson Davis' stationery and handed it back to Lincoln. "I'm going to study the letter and meet with my cabinet," Lincoln said. "I assume that your friend is waiting around for an answer. I can't give him one at this time, but perhaps in a few days. Make arrangements for him to contact you in forty-eight hours and you'll have my answer. Please keep this between us—it will leak out, but not from you or me."

At the appointed time, James made sure they were alone before he handed John an envelope with one thousand greenback dollars in cash. "This should help in the short run, and I'll make sure she gets another thousand before the end of the year. Your investment account has grown by twenty percent; you and Louisa are not rich, but you're comfortable. I want you to sign this receipt. I took the funds from my personal account. This form will allow me to be reimbursed from your investment."

"You're a great friend—even if you *are* a Yankee. I don't know what's going to happen in the future, but I hope that all three of us can meet after it's over and resume our friendship."

"Lincoln wants you to contact me in forty-eight hours and he'll have an answer. He let me read the letter. Are you sure you can get a majority to agree to this settlement?"

"Jim, I'm only the messenger. I think the proposal has some merit, but whether Davis can deliver is not for me to say. I'm going to leave now—take care." They were both embarrassed as they hugged, and then John left.

•　•　•

It was May, and Vicksburg, Mississippi, was under siege. Lincoln had rejected a proposal from Davis to negotiate a settlement to the war. The basis of Davis' letter was to allow the South to reënter the Union, with the condition that slaves be allowed in six states: Mississippi, Texas, Louisiana, Georgia, Alabama and Florida. Other states that had seceded, the border states, those out West, and future new states, would all be free, and all slaves in those states would be emancipated.

There was a heated discussion within the cabinet concerning Davis' letter. Only one of the cabinet officers thought it had merit. Secretary Stanton summed up the majority view. "We're winning the war; we have them on the run, and their solution is to identify with a mini South of six states. Most of the slaves have moved south where the climate is even more conducive to cotton. What they're saying is that they can get along with fewer southern slave states because there are not many slaves in the other states; they offer us crumbs. Emancipation is for *all* the slaves; we should not give in."

Stanton prepared a one-page response with some conditions of his own—mainly that the South should surrender now. When John contacted him, Jimmy handed him the response and told him the Union wasn't buying the proposal. They parted after having a drink. He knew that John was as dedicated as he; he missed him already.

He took the *Empress Queen* to Liverpool from New York City, then the train to London, where he met with his legal firm. He was ready to take the children home.

"Mr. Harris, your ex-wife has added a new condition to the agreement. She wants the nanny to come to America with you and wants her to be with the children no matter what you do or where you go."

"In essence, she means that I can't be trusted with my own children."

"Yes, sir. That's how we read it. What would you have us do?"

"Go back to court and have the agreement enforced as we signed it. I know this is a different country than mine, but I believe the British rely entirely on the rule of law. Let's get it done. I'll wait until you're successful."

His was a respected firm, and it was able to gain an audience with a magistrate of the court and seek his advice. They petitioned the court to enforce the agreement. Two weeks later James was able to pick up the children and sail to America; he still hadn't seen Claire. He'd been given a leave of absence by Lincoln and would spend the summer getting reacquainted with Mary and Cameron Harris.

When they arrived in New York City, his father and Abigail were there to greet them. All six went to Cameron's home for a week while Jimmy took the children to the zoo, the museum, and made many trips around the islands in New York harbor. He so wanted to have his grandparents see the children, but it was too dangerous, and then there was Claire, always lurking in the shadows to restrict his visitations. He felt cheated on the amount of time he was allowed with the two young ones, forcing him to cram everything into such a short time. After a week the children were tired, and Abigail suggested they be allowed to play outside and not go anywhere for a few days.

The three of them were in Central Park when word came that Vicksburg had surrendered and that there were massive casualties at Gettysburg. Intuitively, he knew that the South had lost. He wondered how many more brave men they'd sacrifice before realizing it was over—and not on their terms.

Jimmy took all of them to Washington and the White House to show them where he worked. The children were shy around Lincoln; yet, they knew more about what was going on than they were telling. They thought Lincoln was the tallest man they had ever seen. When they were leaving, Lincoln asked for a few minutes of Jimmy's time. Abigail and Cameron took the children on a tour of the White House while the two men spoke.

"I understand you're leaving for England in the middle of August. I have another mission for you while you're over there. Those Laird Brothers are going ahead with the Laird Rams. If allowed to proceed, those rams would create havoc on our wooden fleet and destroy our blockade. See if you can get to Palmerston and make him understand that the war with the South is effectively over. If they permit those ships to be launched, we'll declare war on England. Our Army is mobilized, and our Navy is superior to the British.

"True to his word, Alexander has sent his fleet to America—one half went to San Francisco and the other half to New York. Palmerston and those two radicals, Lord Russell and Mr. Gladstone, must know that the Russians will fight on our side if we declare war on Britain. Don't mince words, Mr. Harris—I'm deadly serious."

They stayed in their cabin most of the way to England. One storm after another slammed the ship. Mary was sick, but Cameron was like his grandfather and stood up like a man. They were met by the American assistant ambassador: he and James delivered the children to Claire in London. She'd wanted to meet the children there so she could shop for their school clothes and supplies. But it was her mother who greeted Jimmy and the children. After he said goodbye and told them he'd see them next summer, Emily Temple asked for a word with him.

"I'm sorry that Claire is so stubborn. I still like you, and I can see that the children were happy with you. Perhaps we can have lunch while you're in London? Say next Thursday at Delmonico's. I've always liked that place."

"I'll be there at noon, Lady Palmerston."

He went to the embassy and met with Ambassador Herbert, who wanted to discuss the Laird Rams. His office was decorated with red velvet drapes, mahogany furniture, and pictures on three walls of the president and each cabinet member. On the larger wall facing the ambassador's desk were pictures of all the American ambassadors since the Revolution. James was greeted in the reception area and escorted into Herbert's office. "Thank you for coming so quickly, Mr. Harris. I know you've had a grueling trip. I'll try not to take too much of your time. Please sit down.

"Your appointment with the prime minister has been acknowledged; he knows why you're coming."

"Well, I have a written message from Mr. Lincoln, which I haven't opened. In addition, I plan to be very candid with my ex-father-in-law about the Laird Rams. Is there anything you wish to add?"

"Yes. Several members of my staff have been harassed, followed, and, in one case, spat upon. I've spoken to the foreign minister about the incidents, and he's beefed up some of our security."

"Do you know who or what groups are doing this?"

"I believe it's the Confederate group led by James Hudson. I know for a fact that Hudson was present when the spitting incident occurred at a pub. There have been incidents since the start of hostilities in the States that we've been able to take care of. But the situation is perilous now, and I fear that they may go to some excess and someone will be seriously injured—or worse."

"I'll present your comments and see what he has to say. I'm not surprised. My assistant, Lt. Lawler, was severely injured in a town north of Glasgow when I was here last. He suffered a concussion and took several weeks to recover."

James stayed overnight at the embassy, and after a good night's sleep was early for his appointment with the Viscount Palmerston, the British Prime Minister.

"So good to see you again, James. I hope you and the children had a wonderful summer; I'm glad that you and Claire were able to reach an agreement on custody. Children must have a relationship with both parents. But that's not what you came to see me about. I understand that you have message from Mr. Lincoln?"

He handed the envelope to the prime minister and waited until he had read it. "Have you read the message or been informed of its contents?"

"No, sir, but I assume it's about the Laird Rams."

"It is. I don't think your president understands that we are a democracy and cannot dictate to private citizens or commercial ventures, unless they break the law."

"Let me be quite candid with you, my Lord. It's 1863, and the South is being squeezed to a point where they have no alternative but to surrender. Oh, there are some diehards who will fight to the end, but the Union has mobilized to a point that we cannot be defeated. Our navy has transitioned from wooden to steel-hulled ships, and our ground forces are battle tested. This is not rhetoric to hear myself pontificate; these are facts. We cannot accept a response that you have no control over an enterprise that is leading you to war with the Union."

"These are strong words, James. I don't think I appreciate them. I think you are out of order."

"What is it you want from us? You think you can unleash these rams to impact our navy and our shipping and we're just going to let it happen? The rams can do grave damage, and we're angry that you're ignoring our concerns. It seems that two members of your cabinet, Lord Russell and Mr. Gladstone, are constantly talking about joining with France to intercede on behalf of the South, and you say I'm out of order because we won't take it lying down? Mr. Prime Minister, you need to take my words seriously. If you've been given different information by your advisors, then you should replace that group with people who will tell it to you straight."

The prime minister smiled. "I can't understand how Claire could let you get away. If you ever decide to live in England and want a job on my staff, I'd be more than willing to have you."

"I have one more issue that I'd like to discuss, if you have time, sir."

"Go ahead. I'm not about to stop you while you're on this roll."

"Tensions are high between the North and the South, and especially since the war is getting away from them. Our embassy has come under siege from Confederate spies and other groups loyal to their cause right here in England. I don't think it's in either of our interests to allow this to continue. My instincts tell me that the war in America will be over in a year or less, and your country and mine will normalize relationships. I don't think you want to create any more animosity because of these Laird Rams. We have a future together."

"I'll have someone take care of it. I'm meeting with my ministers tomorrow, and I'll raise Mr. Lincoln's concerns and your rhetoric with them. I wish you a good trip home, and I hope you'll call on me whenever you're in our country. Thank you, my boy."

They shook hands. Jimmy felt exhausted, but relieved. He believed that he had articulated Mr. Lincoln's position with the correct amount of candor.

Before leaving for home, he had lunch with Lady Emily Temple at Delmonico's; she had arrived just prior to him. "Thank you for seeing me, James. I miss our discussions since you and Claire divorced. I hope you don't think it presumptuous of me to invite you to lunch?"

"Not in the least. You're my main entrée into the children's lives while they're in England. I hope I can call upon you if I have any concerns?"

"It was my hope that you would ask me."

They spent the time telling each other about their lives, although in her case, Lady Emily shared with him what the children did while they were in England as well as what Claire was up to. When he left, he felt that he had gained a friend and a confidante in regards to his children. They promised to exchange letters until he came back the next June.

CHAPTER THIRTY-TWO

John didn't tell James that he'd been coming to Washington four to five times a year since the firing on Fort Sumter. His main task was making sure he had enough spies in critical positions and that the flow of information continued unabated. By this time, Greenhow had been released from prison and had fled to England. He was going to miss the spirited woman who had set his office off on such a good start.

Before she left the country, Rose was able to pass along information about a northern spy who had successfully infiltrated Richmond and points south. He'd been able to pass along critical information about troop movements and supply depots. His name was Simon O'Hara, an Irishman from Dublin who had come to America in 1855. After many different jobs, including work as a book salesman, he'd been introduced to Allen Pinkerton and recruited as a spy for the Union in 1861.

O'Hara was an avid reader, and in fact read some of the books he was selling for his publishing company. These included the three volumes of the *History of the War with Russia*. He loved to tell stories about the war; however, he tended to include himself in every episode. With a quick wit and the countenance of a story teller, he was able to infiltrate Confederate positions, have a glass of wine or whiskey with the commander, and come away with information about the installation that he could pass on to his boss, Allen Pinkerton.

On one such visit to Richmond, he plied Confederate officers with champagne, cigars, and wild stories about the Crimea. He proved to be so popular that he was invited to inspect the defenses of Richmond, and later, to dine with senior officers. John was among those in attendance. He became suspicious of the Irishman's story that he was a wealthy son of an Irish nobleman who just loved travelling in the South. John asked him to come to his office the next morning.

O'Hara showed up and tried to ingratiate himself with John by bringing a box of cigars and a bottle of whiskey. John wasn't convinced, and had the man detained while he sent two of his agents to inspect O'Hara's room at the hotel. An hour later, his men returned with several pages of notes found hidden inside the pillowcase in the book seller's room. The notes detailed encampment strengths, installation defenses, and locations of supplies and ammunition. When confronted with the evidence, O'Hara said it wasn't unusual for him to take notes; he said he was planning to write a history of the War Between the States.

John ordered him held at the hotel with an armed guard outside his room around the clock. O'Hara became ill shortly thereafter, and was attended to by a physician.

When Pinkerton heard about his protégé's illness, he sent two Union spies to talk to O'Hara and ascertain whether he had divulged any information to the rebels. When the two men arrived at the hotel, they talked to the doctor in charge of O'Hara to find out how serious his illness was. The doctor informed them that the man had a slight case of pneumonia. They asked to speak to the patient, claiming to be his two brothers. The guard allowed them into O'Hara's room. When they were alone, they asked him whether he had given the rebels any information; he shook his head no.

As the two were ready to leave, John walked into the room, followed by the guard. "Gentlemen, can you please identify yourselves?"

"We could if we knew whom we're speaking to," the older of the two men answered.

"My name is John William Beauregard. I'm the head of the Confederate Signal Corps. I'd like to see some identification."

Subsequently, the two men were identified as Lewis Long and Frederick Shortly, and were taken into custody and held in the Richmond Jail. John went back to his office and had his aide contact Michael Heaton and William Spain, two Confederate spies who had been caught in Washington and were subsequently released and sent back to Virginia. He and his two spies went to the prison and interrogated the two men who'd visited the Irishman. Long and Shortly immediately knew the game was up. Long had arrested Heaton the previous year in Washington.

All three men were tried as spies and sentenced to death. Although there was some hesitancy on the part of President Davis to carry out the sentence, they were eventually executed.

John had his network in place and was happy with the steady flow of information. President Davis was under increasing pressure to come up with some strategy that would have an impact on the war. He wanted John to expand his objectives to include some proactive initiatives, such as guerrilla raids.

Most guerrilla leaders for the South were well known, with the exception of John McNeill. Quantrill and Anderson were wreaking havoc on Union supplies, but there was another division that was having success against the Union without receiving the notoriety of the other two. John's introduction to McNeill happened inadvertently. He and an associate were traveling to Richmond after meeting with several of his spies in Washington. Before leaving, they mapped out a route that would take them through the western part of Virginia. They had used this route on three occasions and weren't apprehensive until they were stopped by a Union patrol.

They were traveling under false identifications as English cotton merchants when the patrol stopped them. John was using the name William Gibbons and his associate was John Henry. The squad leader of the eight-man Union patrol looked at their identification, asked a few questions, and was convinced they were southern sympathizers. He made them dismount and be searched. Since they'd left James Harris the previous day, John was carrying the money Jimmy had given him.

"Where did you get this money?"

"Our company gave us these funds to assist with our purchases," John replied.

"Why greenbacks?"

"We were in Washington when our supervisor gave us the job and the money. It wasn't my place to ask him why he gave us greenbacks. I must ask that you return our money and let us pass, so we can be on our way. It's getting late."

"I'm sorry, but I don't believe your story. We're taking you to our outpost, and I'll let them decide whether you're lying or not. It's a short walk. Some of my men will bring your horses. If I'm wrong, I'll apologize."

John McNeill and his raiders had just blown up a small bridge on the Ohio River and were on their way back to Richmond when they saw the Union patrol stop two men and put them under arrest. From ambush, they fired at the Union soldiers, who scattered. McNeill took John and his companion with him as his squad made their way east. When they stopped for the night, McNeill interrogated John and his associate for two hours.

"Captain McNeill, the main question I have is, can you prove that you're John Hancock McNeill? If you can do that, then I'll divulge who we are, but not until we reach Richmond," John said.

When they reached Confederate headquarters in Richmond, McNeill turned John and his associate over to the adjutant, who smiled. "Are you aware who these two men are?" McNeill asked.

"I certainly am, but I'm not going to tell you who they are. Just realize this: this man is on the president's senior staff." He pointed to John.

McNeill turned to John. "You said that you'd tell me who you were once we reached Richmond. Are you going to honor your statement?"

"Certainly, I'm John William Beauregard, and I'm the head of the Southern Signal Corps. Captain, you've done the

South a great service by saving their spy chief from the Yankees." He reached out and shook McNeill's hand.

John and his companion started to pull away when McNeill asked if he could speak to John in private. "I'm tired, but I'll spare you a few minutes, since you saved us," John said. "Come with me. I have an office in this building and we can speak confidentially, if necessary."

McNeill followed John to his office and sat in one of chairs facing him at his desk. "I'm glad to hear you out," John said, "but can we make it quick?"

"The Yankees use their railroads to move their supplies and soldiers east and west," McNeill began. "There are several key bridges over the Ohio River that, if damaged, could cut their supply lines drastically. I've presented a plan to my commanding officer to neutralize these bridges, but he hasn't seen fit to pass it up the line. I assume that you have enough clout to present my plan, if you think it's feasible. I have two hundred men, but my plan calls for more action than I and my men can handle. I believe the problem is that most commanders can't move men from another arena to put this plan into motion unless Jefferson Davis personally approves it."

"Let me have a copy of your plan. I'll read it, and if I think it has merit, I'll contact someone."

"I wasn't sure I should interfere when you were detained; I'm glad I did."

At his home in Richmond, John read the McNeill plan and was impressed, but it needed a sponsor. He was friends with a couple of Confederate brigadiers, and the next morning he showed the plan to both generals. William Jones and John Imboden said they would look at it and get back to John in a timely manner.

One week later, all parties, including McNeill, were available, and they met in John's office. McNeill thanked everyone for giving him an audience, and he presented his plan in some detail.

General Jones was first to comment. "I think you're thinking too small. I believe General Imboden and I could attack from two different directions and cut their supply lines as well as getting our troops some needed supplies."

"I gather that you and General Imboden have discussed this plan before you came here," John said.

"We think this plan has merit," Jones continued. "Here's what we suggest. I'll attack the Baltimore and Ohio Railroad between Grafton, Virginia, and Oakland, Maryland. General Imboden will attack the Union garrisons at Beverly, Philippi and Buckhannon. The objective will be to sever their supply lines, disrupt the B&O Railroad, perhaps gain some recruits and cripple the Union government in Wheeling. That's important, because the state plans to vote on whether the western part of Virginia will come into the Union or the Confederacy. Captain, you've given us an idea which we believe can put a severe hurt on the Union, if we expand your idea."

"Sir, if I can be part of the operation, I don't care if it's expanded," McNeill responded.

With recommendations from the two generals as well as John, President Davis gave his approval. General Jones' group would destroy two bridges near Rowlesburg, the more important one being the bridge over the Cheat River; the other was an iron bridge at Trey Rub. McNeill and his men, working under Jones, and another Confederate division would damage the B&O railroad bridge in Oakland, Maryland. John Beauregard was given permission by Jefferson Davis to function as an observer on this mission.

The Confederates arrived early in the morning at the hill overlooking the bridge over the Cheat River. There was a small Union detachment in town, and they had somehow gotten wind of the Confederate approach and alerted the townspeople. General Jones ordered the bridge torched; however, Union soldiers and the townspeople rushed to defend it. As the Rebels attacked, some of the townspeople, who had been hidden behind boulders and other impregnable objects, held off the invaders and eventually repelled them. Jones tried several other military maneuvers, but in each case his troops were stopped and forced to retreat.

McNeill, with John as his advisor, burned the Oakland bridge, so that part of the plan had succeeded. General Imboden was much more successful than his counterpart, General Jones. He captured Beverly and started toward Buckhannon, but learned that the Union had sent reinforcements to the town, so he fell back to Beverly. Subsequently, he moved on Buckhannon after the Union retreated in the face of his superior force.

In retrospect, John helped launch a mission that did accomplish some of its objectives. The number one priority had been to dismantle the bridge over the Cheat River; General Jones failed in that. However, part of his mission was successful, because some Union soldiers were killed, many prisoners were taken, and new recruits were added. The Confederates destroyed sixteen bridges and captured one thousand head of cattle and twelve hundred horses. John was given a citation by President Davis for having the foresight to bring the plan to his attention.

Initially, Rose Greenhow and her daughter travelled to Richmond after they were released from prison. John gave her several tasks to perform, which she accomplished admirably. They had enough agents in New England, so John asked her to travel to England and then on to France to influence the French on behalf of the South. Napoleon wanted to intercede, but unfortunately, France wasn't the engine, it was the caboose in the English/French agenda.

John's legion of spies was moving freely in the North and providing excellent information. To John, getting information wasn't the problem; the South's problem was resources. They had half as many people as the North to draw on, and cotton exports that fueled their economy were down nearly eighty percent. They were getting some loans, but not enough to fight the industrialized giant in the north. John was coming to the conclusion that if they couldn't break the blockade that strangled their shipping, they had to cause enough pain to the North to make them seek a negotiated settlement. Lincoln was the one who steadfastly maintained the position that the South must surrender and come back into the fold. John wondered out loud what would happen if Lincoln was not the president.

There had been a few attempts on Lincoln's life, but now it seemed to John that a better attempt should be made, or the South would be devastated—and he shuddered to think what that would entail.

With Charleston under siege, Louisa wondered how long she could survive. Magnolia was mortgaged to the maximum, and there would be no more loans on her crop, because of the uncertainty of being able to deliver. She received the money that Jimmy provided and immediately knew that she would need an equal amount in another six months. Her number of workers had declined from nearly one hundred to sixty, and soon she wouldn't be able to feed them. She felt sad for the slaves as well as her free workers—they had been thrust into something they didn't ask for. Without an education, the blacks were at the mercy of the economy. All their lives, they knew only one thing, and that was to obey their masters. Many plantation owners had stopped production and allowed their slaves to wander around the countryside to find work and food for their families.

Louisa was angry and wondered out loud who these idiots were who had ruined the economy and their way of life. They said they wanted a new nation to continue their old way of life, without any regard for what might happen if they lost. She put her own husband in that category. She thought she had married a man, but apparently what she had married was a ridiculous patriot—she didn't have a husband now. You would think that his main responsibility would be to his family, not running around the country trying to prolong the war. And she had no idea where her son was. He had gone to V.M.I. and left after one year, securing a commission as a second lieutenant in the Confederate Army. Her daughter, Susannah, was working on the plantation as hard as she was, trying to save their home. Thank God she had insisted that they take half their savings and send it to Jim! She knew deep down that as long as

Jimmy Harris was alive, they wouldn't be destitute, no matter what might happen to Magnolia.

Many in the South weren't entirely supporting their new government; they hedged their bets by not investing in the South. They invested abroad and cut their expenses at home. Some plantation owners had turned speculators. They fancied some of their neighbor's property, and when the less fortunate applied for bankruptcy protection, they were swift to buy the properties at distressed sales. Louisa had been approached by at least two of these men to see if she was interested in selling her plantation. When she asked what price they'd be willing to pay, they proposed a figure that was less than the amount she owed on the property. Louisa declined, even though she knew that Rosebud, which John had sold prior to the war, had been purchased by these same men.

"We'll be back in ten days to see if you've changed your mind. Our view is that the South is going to surrender within the next year, and there won't be a market for your cotton."

"I'm sure you're wrong. The English and French will be more than glad to continue purchasing cotton once there's peace."

"Our sources tell us that the Egyptians have become very adept at growing cotton, and there's not an ocean to contend with for the purchasers."

Louisa couldn't bear the thought of surrendering Magnolia to these cutthroats, but she wondered aloud if there was any truth in what they said about Egypt—or was it a scare tactic for people like her who were struggling?

Jerome had overheard Louisa's conversation with the two speculators, and he walked into the living room, where she was leaning back in one of their overstuffed chairs, just looking out the window. "Do you really think you'll be forced to sell?" he asked.

Louisa had freed Jerome, and he'd become her overseer after Thomas Garland had become too old to do the job. "I received some greenbacks and gold yesterday, and that should help for maybe six months, but we'll need another infusion of money if we're to keep operating."

"What about our workers? Most have lived here all their lives. This is all they know. I don't believe they can make it somewhere else. What will they do for food and clothing?"

"I don't know, Jerome—I wish I did. My only source of funds is the cotton crop. I don't believe that my benefactor, who lives up north, can help any more."

"Is that Mr. Harris?"

"Yes."

"The blacks you haven't freed won't know what to do; their whole life is here. The ones you freed may be able to find work elsewhere, but they'll feel betrayed."

"I know, Jerome; this isn't what I'd envisioned for us. But it's what we have, and we'll have to figure out how to cope with it."

"The residence is in disrepair. The columns on the back porch and the portico in front need work. If these people come back, they'll offer you less because of the number of repairs needed. I think you could sell some of the furnishings, such as paintings and Oriental rugs, to raise some money."

"Could you get some of the workers to fix the damage in front and back and perhaps paint the exterior? I know someone who's always wanted my two bronze statues. I'll see if I can raise enough money for the materials."

The next morning Jerome loaded the two bronze statues into a wagon. He and Louisa drove off to one of the neighboring plantations to see if the owners were still interested. Jerome waited in the wagon while Louisa went to the front door of the estate. The Phillipses were happy to see Louisa and invited her in. She told them the purpose of her visit, and asked them to come to the wagon and see if they were still interested.

They gave her approximately eighty percent of the full value in Confederate greybacks. "I understand your predicament, my dear," Mrs. Phillips said. "In the event your circumstances change, we'd be glad to sell them back to you. I know how much they meant to your mother."

They continued on into Charleston and purchased paint and some lumber. Jerome had given her a list of the materials they needed, and Louisa went into the lumber yard and purchased them. Although the harbor was blockaded, the town seemed to be thriving. Louisa paid in greybacks. The proprietor was happy to receive them and had her supplies loaded into her wagon. He said most people were buying on credit.

As she was leaving the yard, she saw Renard pull in with two of his slaves. They helped him down from the wagon, and he walked with a limp, holding on to a cane. "I wonder what happened to Renard?" she asked Jerome.

He turned to her and smiled. "General Beauregard shot him in the leg for what he tried to do to you. As I understand it, his knee is severely damaged, and he'll probably limp for the remainder of his life. He has to be helped in and out of a carriage."

Louisa was stunned. "How did Pierre find out?"

"I told him."

"I don't know what I'd do without you, Jerome! You're a good friend. I wish I could show more appreciation."

It was dusk when they returned with a loaded wagon of supplies and materials; Jerome had two of the laborers unload them. "We'll start early tomorrow morning with the repairs, and hopefully we'll have some material left over to repair some of the shanties. It's starting to rain much more, and several of the huts are leaking into the bedrooms. Perhaps the day after tomorrow, I'll have five of the hands do the painting. Since we don't have a ladder, I'll build a scaffold to reach the higher places. I hope the roof is okay, though I don't know what condition it's in after those two big storms last year. If you have a moment, there's something I want to talk to you about, Miss Louisa."

"You sound serious. Let's go in the kitchen and have a cup of tea."

"I've met someone, and I'm thinking of getting married. I don't want to take on a wife, and perhaps children, if the situation is bleak here at Magnolia, especially if you sell to those men who came here yesterday."

"Jerome, your guess is as good as mine. I don't want to give up the place where I was born, but there's very little money to keep it afloat. I don't know how long this war is going to last, and I don't know if the Union is going to invade South Carolina. They could come in and confiscate everything we have. I'm sure they'd like to conscript you and the other workers into the Union Army. Is the woman living here on Magnolia?"

"Yes. It's Mary Jones, though I'd rather she not know of my intention until I decide."

"That girl is a beauty. She'd be glad to have you. I'd like you to stay on, but Jerome, you're free and should lead your own life. I just don't know what's going to happen to Magnolia unless I can find a way to get more funds."

"Is Master John coming home soon?"

"I don't know that either. He's always gone someplace, but he doesn't come here."

"I'm sorry, Miss Louisa."

"So am I."

A week later the two speculators returned, accompanied by her neighbor, Renard. Louisa and Jerome were on the front porch. "You're not welcome here, Renard. I threatened to shoot you before; I guess I can do it now. Jerome, get my gun."

"Now, that won't be necessary," Renard replied. "I'm sorry for the misunderstanding, and I want to help."

Jerome had found the gun. Cocking it, he handed it to Louisa. "I said I want you out of here," she said. "Take your pick—either leave peacefully or with a bullet in your butt."

"I can't leave without the other two. Is it okay if I sit in the carriage while you transact your business?"

"You can sit in the carriage as long as you want, provided it's outside our entrance gate," Louisa responded.

One of the speculators got in the carriage and drove Renard to a spot outside the gate and then walked the three hundred yards back to where Louisa was waiting.

"We see that you've made some improvements to your home. I compliment you for the work—it's professional. I can only assume that you did the work to improve your bargaining position because you want to sell?"

"I haven't made up my mind. What's your offer?"

"How much do you owe on the property?

"Twenty thousand dollars."

"I don't know that we can offer much more than that. But then again, you may want to get out from under your debt and just turn the property over to us."

"This property, with a cotton crop and slaves, is worth over seventy thousand dollars. I know what we sold Rosebud for, so I know what the potential is here, once the war is over. Here's my offer for you. I will sell the plantation to you for forty-five thousand dollars, or you can lend me twenty thousand dollars, payable in four years, with interest accruing. If I can't repay the loan and accrued interest in the four years, I'll forfeit the property."

"That's an unusual offer. I don't know if we're willing to take that risk."

"Then we don't have anything more to talk about. If I can't repay the loan in four years, you pick up a piece of property that should net you thirty thousand dollars. So you aren't risking anything other than tying up some funds for four years."

"Will your husband approve of such a contract? We wouldn't move forward without his signature."

"We'll never know until we have a contract, will we?"

Renard was sitting upright as the other two returned to his carriage. "What did the bitch say?" Renard asked.

"She says she owes twenty thousand and doesn't want to sell on the terms we offered," replied the man named Smith. "What she'll consider are two options. She'll sell outright for forty-five thousand dollars, or she'll take a loan of twenty thousand for four years, and if she's unable to pay back the loan in that time, she'll surrender the property."

"My instincts tell me that she'll take less money and with a much shorter time frame," Renard said. "Why don't we wait another two weeks and call on her again and see what her terms are then. I think she's hurting and will make a deal. Let's do it on my terms."

CHAPTER THIRTY-THREE

Two days after the Battle at Gettysburg, Jefferson Davis called a cabinet meeting to discuss a strategy they'd employ in the future. General Lee was not present. One of the cabinet members asked where Lee was.

"He's leading the Army of Northern Virginia back to Richmond; General Meade is pursuing him," Davis told the gathered group. "After Gettysburg, he and the Army of the Potomac were nearly stranded on an island in a downpour, but they managed to escape before Meade arrived.

"Gentlemen, the day after Lee's withdrawal from the invasion of the North, Vicksburg fell to General Grant. These two events have seriously hurt our cause. To compound these two setbacks, our Vice-President, Mr. Stephens, was turned back by the Union garrison at Norfolk. He had a letter from me seeking a truce and an offer of a negotiated settlement. Lincoln refused to accept the communiqué, and Stephens returned home. I have in the past two hours received a note from General Lee taking full responsibility for Gettysburg and offering to resign. What say ye?" Davis said.

"I for one will not accept that we were defeated at Gettysburg." Stephens was quite articulate in his response. "Although our losses were significant, the Army of Northern Virginia is intact, and so is General Lee. Perhaps we can't go on the offensive as we contemplated, but we haven't lost significant parts of our country. I say we fight on."

Normally, John wouldn't speak up in the cabinet meetings, but somehow he felt empowered today. "If I may speak, sir? It would seem to me that our offensive strategy requires a full complement of men, materials, supplies and armament. A defensive posture requires a lot less of either category. The further we stray away from our base, the more men, ammunition and supplies are needed; logistics becomes the driving force. But we have to do something, or they'll continue to attack our defensive strategy and eventually find a soft spot in our armor. I would suggest that we do a series of raids that wouldn't *cripple* the North, but would cause them to constantly move men around the country to counteract our initiatives.

"Here's my plan. What if we were to start a campaign of robbing their banks? We use our spy network to find out when gold shipments are being made and attack vulnerable targets where they least expect. We've had great success with some of our guerrilla groups, though it seems that they attack without a military objective in mind. Why don't we form a group of guerrilla bands, patterned after John Mosby, and play havoc up north? My spies tell me that the northern people are tiring of the prolonged war. So if we can employ hit-and-run tactics, forcing them to expend too many assets at a time, then perhaps Lincoln won't be so rigid and we can get a negotiated peace. Unless we hit them up north, they won't feel any pain from this war."

"Wouldn't we have to set up a training site to teach men how to forage off the land and use hit-and-run tactics?" the Secretary of war asked.

"Yes, sir, perhaps we could train at the Citadel or one of our other military academies."

"Whom do you have in mind to run this school and direct the missions? Would it be you?"

"Although I'm a West Point graduate and have some field experience in the Mexican-American war, there are others who're more skilled than I in guerrilla tactics. What about Mosby or Generals Longstreet or P.G.T. Beauregard?"

"Mr. Beauregard, I'll take it under advisement and have it staffed by the army. If the recommendation is positive, we'll move to implement it quickly," Davis said.

Less than a week later, John was called into Jefferson Davis' office and told that he was in charge of the "Quick Strike" program. "I believe we're in dire need of money. I like the idea of robbing banks to supplement our funds. How long will it take you to submit a plan to my staff?"

"Let me have a few days and I'll have a draft for you. Who will be in charge of this activity?"

"The signal corps is in complete charge of the operational plan once approved by me. However, General Young will lead the men in the field."

A few days later, John completed an analysis and determined what the parameters of such an operation would be. The first priority was to find a Union town that had several banks with adequate funds. The second priority would be the ease of access, and the third priority would be a realistic escape plan. John remembered his foray into Canada to rescue prisoners. He looked at a map of the northeast part of the Union, the towns close to the Canadian border, their population, the size of their industry, and their accessibility.

The town that seemed to meet most of his criteria was the city of St. Albans, Vermont, only fifteen miles from the Canadian border. It had three banks and was also a major railroad hub. The population was in excess of two thousand people; their main industry was a foundry that employed hundreds of workers. John knew he could count on his contacts in Canada to go to St. Albans and furnish him the tactical information he required. Within a month he was ready to brief Davis and General Young, who had been part of the Morgan Group that attacked southern Indiana.

Davis was anxious, and he set up the meeting for the three the following morning. John presented a plan that called for twenty guerrillas, plus General Young.

"The group will travel via a Confederate ship to Quebec, where we'll offload, make our way to Montreal and then down to Phillipsburg. We'll stage there before going to St. Albans. Our men will enter the town three at a time, dressed in civilian clothes, carrying their uniforms in travelling bags; they'll stay in the local hotels. Prior to robbing the banks, our men will change into their uniforms. They'll enter each of the three banks in groups of four and demand all their cash, but no coin. The remaining eight must be prepared to disarm and keep under control the population who are not working in the foundry. Initially, those eight will be responsible to steal twenty-one horses and have them in the center of town ready for everyone to make their escape.

"We may run into a lot more trouble on the way back to Canada than we did robbing the banks. I believe the St. Albans townspeople will be irate and will come after us with every able-bodied man that can ride. They'll also petition the Canadian authorities to arrest our people and confiscate the funds."

"What do you suggest?" Davis asked.

John had pinned a map of their ingress and egress routed to and from the town of St. Albans on the wall in front of the three men. "Anyone chasing our men will be after Confederate soldiers. I suggest they offload the money to me as they enter Canada. I'll have a wagon waiting for them at Phillipsburg, and then I'll go back to Montreal and make my way through to Quebec, pick up our ship, and hopefully make it back with the funds."

"That's a long way with all that money, and with only one man guarding it. I want two others with you who can handle themselves—you pick them."

"I have two men in mind."

"I think it's a good plan," said General Young. "I've taken the liberty of selecting twenty men who have considerable guerilla experience. I'll work with the guerrillas during training. It should work."

Three weeks later, after an intensive training course in tactics, including stealth incursion and controlling the enemy, which John attended, twenty-four men boarded the Confederate ship, the *Rosemont*. Leaving from Wilmington, it slipped through the blockade at night, and everyone was on their way to Quebec. Delac, the Canadian who helped John with the Johnson Island rescue, was on hand to greet them at the Quebec harbor. He furnished food and housing for the night and then transportation to Montreal the next morning. They were staying in an old warehouse near the harbor. When they were all present, General Young went over the plan with those assembled, and before releasing the first group of three to St. Albans, he gave a final speech. "While we're in this northern town, I want everyone to remain as inconspicuous as possible; there will be no drinking and no fraternization with the local populace. If asked what you are doing in St. Albans, just say you're from Canada and looking for work at the foundry. Some of you have distinct Southern accents; I strongly suggest you remain silent. Let others do the talking. There could be nothing more suspicious in a Union town than someone with a Southern drawl."

Delac took the first group of three in a carriage to St. Albans. Subsequently, Delac's friends transported the rest of the men, three at a time; they were staying at two of the hotels in town. General Young was in the last group. He told John they would strike at ten in the morning, two days hence. "I think you should be waiting at Phillipsburg around noon of that day."

John had been feeling constant pressure to try to make something happen that would have positive results for the South. He and Delac had dinner in the old town of Montreal that evening, and though it was relaxing, he went back to his hotel early. This had to work. He reviewed his plan again, and on the morning of the raid, he, his two men and Delac made their way to Phillipsburg. They arrived at ten in the morning, checked their horses, and waited in the shade.

The guerrillas had rehearsed their roles for two days in their hotel rooms. The one issue that could have a major impact on their success was the horses they'd need in order to escape. For two days, they looked at all the farms in the area and found two that had enough saddle-broken horses to satisfy their needs. Four of the Confederate soldiers left around six in the morning, on the day of the robbery, and walked to the two farms; they carried their uniforms with them. Both farms were close to town. They took the owners and two workers on each of the farms by surprise and tied them up. They found enough saddles for the horses and drove them to town so they'd be in the city square at ten o'clock in the morning.

The remaining guerrillas led by General Young moved quickly. Four each to the three banks; three went inside the bank, leaving one soldier positioned outside to act as a lookout. When the populace saw the Confederate soldiers, some ran for the sheriff; others screamed. Initially, four Confederates held the village square, but were soon reinforced by the other four with the horses. They tethered the horses to the trees on the common and set up positions to guard against anyone helping those in the bank; General Young was with them. The sheriff and two of his deputies walked to the common and asked what was going on—he thought the villagers were putting on some sort of pageant. When he and his deputies were disarmed and tied up, they couldn't believe it.

The robbery was handled with precision. Two soldiers approached the cashiers and demanded all the cash they had in the till. The third soldier tied up the guard and told all the customers to lie down on the bank floor. There were no attempts to interfere with the Confederates. Simultaneously, all twelve robbers moved to the city square, carrying the cash they'd taken. As the soldiers mounted their animals, a shot rang out. It appeared to come from the hardware store next to one of the banks. Instinctively, one of the Confederates fired back and seriously wounded the shooter. Women were screaming and men were shouting as the Rebels made their way to the road to Canada; they suffered no casualties.

Around twelve-thirty, a group of men on horseback came galloping up to John's wagon, with General Young in the lead. He and his men dropped the cash into the back of his wagon. "You'd better get out of here—they're on our tail, and I'm not sure we didn't lose some of our men who were carrying bags of money. One of our soldiers shot a civilian. If they catch us, they'll hang us! Get out of here quick. We plan to meet you in Quebec. If we're not there by the time you're ready to leave, go without us. That money is too important to the South." With that, Young and his men rode off toward Phillipsburg.

John made an immediate decision. "We're going to take the road to Quebec. If we follow Young, we'll be caught. Cover up the money and let's go!"

No sooner had they gotten underway when they heard the sound of many horses going past where they'd stopped. The St. Albans group was ignoring John and his small group and going after the raiders. John kept to the road until dusk, stopping every half hour to rest the horses. He didn't want to count the money until they were aboard the *Rosemont*. Four days later, they arrived at the dock in Quebec and boarded their ship. John immediately spoke to the captain. "Have our soldiers arrived yet?"

"No, but this newspaper article may shed some light on their location."

The captain had a copy of the *Quebec Journal* from two days ago. He gave it to John, who quickly read the headlines and the accompanying article. General Young and his group had been captured by the Canadians, who refused to turn them over to the irate citizens from St. Albans. Eighty-eight thousand dollars had been recovered and returned to the three banks. The authorities had no idea what happened to the remaining cash. A citizen had been killed by one of the raiders, and St. Albans wanted the Confederates returned to them to stand trial for murder; however, the Canadians refused. They planned to return the Confederates to the South sometime in the future.

"As soon as you get up enough steam, I want to leave," John told the captain.

His friend Delac left with the wagon and said goodbye; John and his two men took the money to his cabin and counted it. There was one hundred twenty thousand dollars in greenbacks. "This ought to help the cause! I'm sorry that Young and the men aren't here to share our excitement," John said as they got underway.

However, the Canadian editorials were explicit in their condemnation of the Confederacy for using Canadian soil to attack the North; sentiment was changing. John had used Canada twice to strike a blow for the South. He might get away with another adventure here; then again, he might have staged his last attack from here.

Davis was delighted with the results of the raid, and he wondered what new plan John had in mind. "Sir, I haven't been home in over six months. I must see what's happened to my wife and family. I need a week, if that's okay with you." Davis seemed disappointed but granted the request.

Louisa was driving with Jerome to Charleston to buy some more material at the lumberyard. She had a second reason for coming this day: she hadn't seen the Fredericks in years, and she wondered if they were okay. Her main reason for the visit was to learn if they were in contact with Jimmy, their grandson. Although mail between both sides had ceased, letters could be delivered by smugglers.

The Fredericks were at home, and were delighted to see Louisa. They welcomed her and Jerome to their home. The two guests sat on the front porch with Mr. Frederick while his wife made sandwiches and lemonade. The shade and a light breeze made the warm day palatable. Just as Mrs. Fredericks poured lemonade for everyone, there was a loud crash and an explosion, followed by a series of crashes and further explosions. They could see billows of smoke and fires erupting in several homes and businesses several blocks from where they sat. None of them spoke; they were stunned and didn't know what to do. "Are we under attack?" Mrs. Fredericks asked.

"I don't know, but I think those are artillery shells exploding in the town," her husband responded. "Let's go inside. It isn't safe out here."

They could see trees cut in half and buildings with their sides caved in. People were screaming, and the frenzied clanging of a fire wagon's bells echoed throughout the town. "My God, Jerome, we're in a war zone, and we're being fired on!"

"Miss Louisa, let's go home," Jerome said with some alarm. "This is no place for us!"

She knew he was right, but that didn't alleviate her concern for the Fredericks. Utter mayhem was being dropped on this large southern town. She didn't want to leave just yet; she wanted to ask them another question. Soon the explosions stopped, people were out in the street again, and she felt comfortable with the idea of leaving them alone. She turned to Mr. Fredericks. "Have you been able to correspond with James?"

"As you know, the regular mail has ceased. But there are ways. A couple of young men from Charleston deliver mail between both sides. It's expensive, so we don't write often. What do you have in mind?"

"I have a letter for Jimmy. It's very important that it reaches him and that he sends a response."

"If you leave it with me, I'll see that the young men deliver it and wait for a response," Fredericks responded. "It takes about eight days to get a return message." She handed him her letter, with enough gold coins to pay for the delivery.

Renard and his two associates had been back twice more, and each time Louisa refused to back off from her offer. She was surprised this morning to see Renard coming up the drive in his carriage. It stopped out front, his servant helped him down, and he staggered up the front stairs. Louisa came out the front door to meet her nemesis. "You're not welcome here! Get back in your carriage, and don't stop until you're off my property!"

"Oh, come off it. I want to buy your property, and you want to sell. There's no reason for me to sit in my carriage while they negotiate for me. I can do it myself!"

"The answer is still the same. Get off my property and don't come back."

"Look, bitch! I'm going to have this property, and I'm going to have *you*, either voluntarily or involuntarily—it's only a matter of time. I've a good mind to teach you some manners before I leave. My slave has a gun, so you'd better be careful."

John had ridden through the night, and he didn't see the carriage parked out front as he came into the back of the house and entered his kitchen. Taking off his coat, he reached for the coffee pot on the stove and was pouring a cup when he heard angry voices coming front the front of the house. When he heard the word *bitch,* he moved down the hall and hurried out through the front door. There he stood looking down at Renard, who was telling Louisa what he was going to do to her. John charged headlong down the stairs and punched Renard hard in the mouth. The man fell backward and landed on his side.

As Renard was rising, with the help of his slave, he turned to John and growled, "I'm going to demand satisfaction for this insult, and I'm going to kill you and fuck this bitch the same day!"

John hit him in the face again, and when the man fell, John jumped up and landed on Renard's right hand with his heel. He could hear the bones snap. As Renard lay on the ground, writhing in pain, John moved forward and stomped on his hand again. "We'll find out whether you'll ever fire a gun with that hand. I accept your challenge; let me know when you have the guts to go through with it!"

His slave pulled Renard to his feet, lifted him into the carriage, and drove off as fast as he could. Before they left, Renard cried out in pain, "I'm going to get you for this!"

"Well, Prince Charming, what do I owe you for your timely presence? I thought I was going to have to shoot him." Louisa produced a small revolver hidden under her skirt. "I suppose you want me to show you some gratitude in my bed."

"I thought you'd never ask!"

CHAPTER THIRTY-FOUR

John and Louisa sat down for a late breakfast the next morning, just like they used to do before the war permeated every aspect of southern society. The day was bright, and predicted to be warm with a slight breeze. They sat at the kitchen table overlooking their flower garden, and they felt content.

"How about bringing me up to date on Magnolia's finances?"

"I have a few dollars left from the amount Jimmy gave us, but I'm going to need much more, or we're in trouble. I wrote him a letter asking for more. Mr. Fredericks is sending it for me. We should hear back in about a week."

"Have you considered cutting back on your staff and workers?"

"I'm down to a bare minimum. We're below the number needed to plant, harvest, run the cotton through the gin, bale and transport. I'm doing some of the work; Susannah does more than her share, and so does Jerome. It isn't an option to let people go. The question is where would they go and who would feed them, if I let them go. I have fewer slaves per capita than the other plantations. But the South wanted slaves, and doesn't seem to realize that there's a cost that no one wants to face, until you don't have any work for them. They rely on us to feed and house them, so it isn't easy to tell them to go some place else."

"I didn't mean to get you upset, Louisa." He put his hand over hers.

"I *am* upset with you, and I'm frustrated. People like you are in charge of the South and what it does. How the hell did we get into this mess? I'll bet that the majority of our citizens didn't want to secede from the Union. It was you power guys that put it in motion, and now you don't know what to do."

"That's not fair. We wanted our way of life, and they wouldn't let us have it."

"What do you mean, you wanted your way of life? That's very self-serving! What about the rest of us, who were happy with our lot? I guess we don't count! Unless you've had your head in the sand, it must be obvious that the world is against slavery."

"It wasn't just slavery."

"Sure it was!"

"Okay, we're not getting anyplace with this issue. Tell me what Renard wanted."

"He and his lackeys want to buy Magnolia. I made them a proposition. It called for them loaning me twenty thousand dollars for four years, with interest accruing until the end of the term. If I was unable to repay the balance owed at the end of four years, they would take Magnolia."

"Was that a reasonable approach on your part?"

"We owe twenty thousand dollars to Jimmy; he won't foreclose, unless I don't know him very well. Another loan would give us enough time to get through this mess. Most people believe the war will be over, one way or another, in two years, so I think it's a good proposal."

"Are they willing to accept a contract that way?"

"Well, they're interested, but they want different terms. The last counter-proposal they delivered was for fifteen thousand for two years."

"What does Renard want?"

"He wants *me.*"

"Has he made an overture?"

"Do you really want to know?"

"I do."

"He came here about two months ago on the pretext that I wasn't getting out to see our friends. He suggested that he escort me to a party at the Evans' plantation on a Saturday night. I told him I didn't go to parties without my husband. As he was leaving, he grabbed me and told me how much he's always wanted me. That progressed to the point where he ripped off all my clothes and dragged me into the sitting room. He was about to penetrate me on our couch when Jerome came into the room with a revolver pointed at Renard.

"Renard tried to intimidate Jerome and walked toward him with the idea of taking the gun away from him. Jerome backed up and started turning to his left. Renard was concentrating so hard on the gun that he didn't see me come up behind him and take the gun from Jerome. There I was, naked as a jaybird, in front of two men with a gun in my hand aimed at Renard. Before I could shoot the son-of-bitch, he ran out the back way."

"I heard some of what he said before I hit him."

"He means to kill you, John, even if he can't hold a gun any more. He's a rattlesnake!"

"I never did like him."

"There's probably more Renards in this country than you think! They don't care about your precious South as much as they care about making a dollar and taking what they want, because fools like you are leaving their families unprotected. I'm never going to forgive you for what you haven't done for your family!"

Feeing guilty, John didn't want to continue the subject. "I heard that Charleston was under attack."

"John, I was in Charleston last week, and Jerome and I came under fire. I don't know whether it was bombs or artillery that was being fired on the town. There was devastation everywhere; buildings and trees were hit. I wanted to talk to Pierre, who I believe is the commander of the town's defenses, but we were too scared and came right home. There must have been at least twenty loud explosions."

"The Yankee commander has a new piece of artillery. They've been building a base to hold it. He gave Pierre twenty-four hours to evacuate the city, and my cousin refused. The Union guy fired a bunch of shells to show what the gun could do. I talked to a couple of soldiers as I got off the train from Richmond. They said Charleston was shelled, but the big gun blew up."

"Have you heard anything from our son James? He's a lot like his father—he doesn't know how to write."

"He stopped by my office last month before I went to Canada. He looked good and was happy so far."

"This is such a nice day that I propose that we go on a picnic. We can take Susannah with us—it would be nice if she saw her father once in a while."

They spent the next four days with Susannah, going horseback riding, picnicking, and just sitting around talking. When it was time for John to leave, his daughter cried, and Louisa made him promise to come back safe. The trains were running at midnight, so he was going to leave at about eight that evening, stop at the Charleston station to talk to his cousin, and take the train back to Richmond.

He arrived back at his office the next day and found a note in the middle of his desk from Jefferson Davis. "It's urgent that I see you as soon as possible."

He went to Davis' office at around ten, and after a fifteen-minute wait, he was escorted in. The Secretaries of State and War were already there. "Please sit down, gentlemen, and I'll tell you what's on my mind," Davis said.

The same day, Richard Lucerne, the Charleston county sheriff, rode up the drive and tied his horse to the rail. Louisa was sitting in the kitchen, having a late lunch, when Jerome told her she had a visitor. She was careful these days, carrying a the revolver in her skirts as she made her way to the front door.

"Why, Richard, how nice to see you! You don't come out here often—is this business or pleasure?"

Lucerne had worked as an overseer when John's family owned Rosebud plantation. Although not close friends, he and John occasionally had a beer together. Lucerne had chosen not to remain when François sold the plantation, and had gone looking for work. Soon he was elected sheriff, and then reëlected twice, because he was well-liked in the community. "Well, I wish it was pleasure, but I must say it's business that has brought me here."

"It's cooler in the kitchen, and I just made a large pitcher of lemonade. Why don't we go in there? It'll be more comfortable." They sat at the kitchen table and she poured both of them a glass. "Okay, tell me what's on your mind."

"Is John at home?"

"No, he left for Richmond last evening. What does John have to do with your visit?"

"I just came from Armand Renard's home. I was told by his servant, Alexander, that John struck Mr. Renard three times outside your home yesterday. He also reported that John stomped on Renard's hand, resulting in multiple breaks."

"Did he tell you why?"

"No, that didn't come up."

"Well, I don't mind sharing that with you. Two months ago, Renard tried to rape me in my home. He tore off all my clothes and dragged me into the sitting room. Luckily, my supervisor came into the room with a gun just in time, and Renard ran. Just as John came home from Richmond earlier this week, Renard arrived, and John overheard him making suggestive remarks to me. John acted just as any husband would and struck Renard. His servant helped him up and Renard challenged John to a duel. He said that after he killed John, he was going to come here and do what he wanted with me. John hit him again and stomped on his hand.

Renard has a reputation of being a great shot with a handgun, so John took steps to protect himself.

"If you're here to arrest John for hitting Renard, you'll have to take it up with Jefferson Davis—and lots of luck with that!"

Lucerne leaned on the table. "Someone went to Renard's home last night and slit his throat. He's dead. I wanted to talk to John to see if had he happened to go by there on his way to Charleston."

Louisa was irate. "Why didn't you tell that when you came here? I thought this was about an assault! And how dare you accuse my husband of such a villainous act! Do you know *anything* about my husband? He's one of this nation's heroes, and an honorable man!"

"I know him well—I grew up with him! And I didn't accuse John of anything. I was going to take his word."

"It would take someone with guerrilla-like skills to enter a property where there are dogs, creep up to the master bedroom without any of the servants seeing or hearing him, commit the crime, and escape undetected. I'd say that it would be *damned* hard! Sheriff Lucerne, I'm not a detective, but it seems to me the most likely candidate for the killing lives in Renard's home."

"You may be right. That was my first impression, but I had to follow up on the account that Alexander gave, to see what you would say."

After Lucerne left and Louisa went to bed, she lay awake for at least three hours wondering. John could kill, and since he was the South's chief spy, she assumed that he could penetrate a compound of sorts without being detected. No, she knew he couldn't kill in cold blood. Or could he?

• • •

While the sheriff was interrogating Louisa on the first of September, 1863, Jefferson Davis was telling those assembled what Napoleon III was up to.

"I have three main issues to discuss. The first is that General Lee has again taken full responsibility for our loss at Gettysburg and again has offered his resignation. I have not accepted it, and I will not. The second issue is: Napoleon has decided to invade and take over Mexico. It seems that the Emancipation Proclamation issued by Lincoln has restrained the English, but not the French. They wanted to intercede on our behalf, but they can't do it alone. The lead has to come from Britain. So what's he up to?"

"Well, France has always regretted the sale of Louisiana to America, and I think he wants it back," said the Secretary of State, Judah P. Benjamin. "With that in mind, it wouldn't surprise me that when he places Maximilian on the throne in Mexico, then that new country, whatever they name it, will want Texas back, and then the New Mexico territory, and then California. I wouldn't trust him to walk my dog across the road!"

"Our sources in France say his plan calls for a recognition of the Confederacy so that there will be four entities: Mexico, the North, us, and the West. What do you make of that?"

"Well, I can guess why he wants to recognize the Confederacy," said the Secretary of War, James Seddon. "Lincoln has told him that if he comes to the Americas, he'll be removed as soon as the North beats us. He's using us as a buffer against Lincoln; therefore, he wants us to succeed."

"What are your thoughts, Mr. Beauregard?"

"It's strictly a power play. He's aggressive and quite the speculator. He's hoping that the silver-rich Sonora mines will regenerate the Mexican economy and draw laborers from Europe, the North, and probably us. He wants to restore Mexico as it was prior to the Texas independence. I think he'll pretend to be our friend as long as it suits his purpose; in the interim, he'll withhold recognition of the Confederacy, waiting to see how we succeed. I agree with Secretary Benjamin—he's no friend of ours!"

"The third issue has to do with our contract for the Laird Rams. Where do we stand?"

"Commander Hudson has been pushing the contractor to complete the two ships as soon as possible," responded Mallory, the Secretary of the Navy. "Union spies are all over the Laird Contracting Company. The Union's ambassador, Mr. Adams, has threatened Lord Russell, in writing, with war if the ships are released. The Union doesn't know the ships are for us; they're just guessing. Hudson has come up with an ingenious way to circumvent the English neutrality laws. He's gotten the French to say they are purchasing the Rams for an Egyptian client. Right now, we don't have the ships, but we're hopeful. With that said, I worry that we really don't have a navy that can challenge the North on the high seas. If we can bring those rams across the Atlantic, they will absolutely disrupt the blockade to a point that we'll probably get about eighty percent of our cotton to Europe."

"Why can't we seem to get recognition from either France or England?" Davis asked the four men. None of the three secretaries said anything.

"I originally thought they would jump in fast, especially with their need of cotton, but it doesn't seem so," John offered. "My guess is that we didn't give them a good reason to enter, and Lincoln gave them a reason not to. Early on, England didn't know who would win, and therefore didn't want to alienate either us or the North. Seward threatened them with war if they intervened; we had nothing to threaten them with, other than the loss of cotton, which they lost anyway."

"We need a major victory to gain recognition, and it looks like we need foreign intervention to gain that victory," Davis observed. "Gettysburg was the ideal situation; it looked like it would happen there, but it didn't. We can't sustain a defensive posture because we're running out of material, men and supplies. The industrialized North seems to be getting stronger; we're not. Anyone want to add anything to that?"

When there was no answer, he turned to Secretary Seddon. "Tell me about the Swamp Angel gun."

"The North brought engineers to Charleston to build a base that would support this large artillery cannon. They demanded that General Beauregard surrender Charleston, or they'd shell the city with the Swamp Angel. When Beauregard didn't evacuate, they shelled the town. They lobbed about fifteen shells into the center of town and General Beauregard, who's responsible for defending that city, called out the Union Commander. He told him in no uncertain terms that it was a form of terrorism to fire the guns on unprotected women and children."

"When I came through town I could see them working on the base, but the gun was set up a long distance from the city. They couldn't possibly tell where they were aiming, though I know they made rubble out of Fort Sumter. Later I was told by General Beauregard that the Swamp Angel blew up after firing another twenty rounds."

When it seemed they had covered everything they wanted to discuss, Davis turned to John. "I'd like you to go to Mexico City and see what the situation is. Find out if there is any commitment from the French, or whether it is just posturing on their part. Our envoy in France suggests exactly that; I'd like a second opinion."

"How soon would you want me to leave?"

"The day after tomorrow would be soon enough for me. See what your schedule is like and let me know. I want you to take two men. You're too valuable and too knowledgeable to fall into the enemy's hands."

It was too hazardous to travel down the Mississippi, so John and his companions left at night aboard a blockade runner from Wilmington, North Carolina, and once out of the range of the Union warships, they headed south to the Gulf and then on to Mexico. Landing on the east coast, they made their way to Mexico City, where they presented a letter from President Davis to the French military chief. Their initial problem was to find someone who spoke English!

They were treated with courtesy, but learned nothing from the French. The Mexicans offered little resistance, and the French day-to-day operations reflected that. The military commander had orders to maintain the area and nothing else; they were waiting for the arrival of Maximilian. John felt that there was nothing he and his assistants could accomplish, so they decided to return overland via Texas.

"Davis is grasping at any straw flying in the breeze," John thought. He sensed that their cause was already lost. The bombardment of Charleston had really brought the war home to him. He had sensed the same feeling from his cousin Pierre when he visited him in Charleston. He hated to admit it, but his wife had been correct—this whole episode for the South was folly.

CHAPTER THIRTY-FIVE

Jimmy Harris missed his children, so he decided to go to England over Christmas and see them. Knowing that he was going abroad, Lincoln asked James to look into another aspect of the South's attempts to purchase ships. It was obvious to Lincoln that if the Confederate navy could break the blockade and ship cotton to Europe, they would never surrender. From past history, it was clear that it would be impossible to stop someone from contracting with the Confederacy to build their ships. What was possible, though, was to stop them from being delivered. They finally applied enough pressure on the British government to stop delivery of the Laird Rams. Subsequently, Britain bought the rams for their own navy.

The Union was dogged in their objective to prevent ships being sent to the Confederacy. One of the most successful operations was by the United States consuls. They were in an ideal position because of their function of assisting trade, collecting fees, and monitoring the shipbuilding operation in England. They did this by using spies, unsavory characters, dockhands, dock masters, etc. They intercepted letters between the shipbuilders and their clients, gathered gossip, and paid informers to provide information, which they summarized and sent to Secretary Seward.

The consuls provided vessel description, sightings, and sailing dates. If a ship left Europe to be subsequently commissioned by the rebels, Secretary Seward knew all about the ship before it reached our shores. Lincoln discussed the problem with James before he left.

"Mr. Harris, I believe that we're finally getting British cooperation, enabling us to stop most of their shipbuilding efforts from being delivered to the South. However, there's another nation to be heard from. We've known for some time about Napoleon's ambition to have a foothold in Central America. His troops have arrived in Mexico with the goal of setting up a puppet government with Maximilian on the throne. We'll take care of that problem as soon as we finish with the South. But our sources in Europe have reported some alarming news. They tell us that some French shipbuilding yards are contracting with the C.S.A. to build Rams, torpedo boats and ironclad warships. We must stop them before anything is launched. I want you to go to France and see what the magnitude of the problem is. I assume you can take care of this mission after you've seen your children."

"I can accommodate that. I was planning to leave by the end of November, if that is satisfactory?" Lincoln rose and shook his hand.

James had written to his law firm in London and told them about his plans, asking them to arrange for some time with his children. When he arrived, he was shocked to learn that Claire had refused to give him parental visitations over the Christmas holidays. "You can't be serious! She's refused to let me see the children?"

"She says it's inconvenient at this time. She had plans for the children; if you had given her advance notice, she would've complied."

"That's utter nonsense! Is there anything we can do?"

"We could go back to court. The agreement is fairly clear that you may visit the children at other times if you give timely notice. The vague part is, what constitutes sufficient notice? Perhaps we can have a reasonable magistrate hear our petition."

They were able to schedule a hearing on December 20th. Claire had her solicitor present. The hearing lasted one hour, and the magistrate ruled that James could see the children five times during the holidays. The judge turned to Claire's representative. "I'm sure you will carry out the court's order."

"I'll try, my lord, but my client has taken the children to Sweden for the entire holidays. She informed me that those had been her plans, and she saw no reason why she should have to change them to suit her ex-husband."

"Then why didn't you notify the court of your client's actions before we scheduled a hearing? I've a good mind to issue a warrant for her arrest!"

James wondered what he'd done to cause so much animosity from his ex-wife. He realized now that this was going to be the norm as long as the children were living in England. He sent a message to Emily Temple, asking for a meeting. He received a response the next day, suggesting that they meet for lunch the day after tomorrow.

Over lunch, he learned that Claire had not been feeling at all well the last few months, and her doctor had suggested that she take a vacation—that's the reason she had left with the children. "Please, Emily, we know each other too well for you to pass on such rubbish as this. We both know that Claire will try to obstruct as much as she can get away with. It seems that I must go to court every time I come to visit or take the children to America."

"James, she's petrified that you'll take them one day and not bring them back. I know she has no reason to think that, but her mental state is not that good these days. She's losing weight, and she sleeps a lot.

"Not to change the subject, but what are your plans for the holidays? The Viscount and I would be delighted if you'd stay with us. It may be a little uncomfortable for you, but John and I like you very much. We look upon you as our son, and are very unhappy that Claire is so obstinate."

"I've plans to go to Paris to meet a friend, but that's not for a couple of days. I would be delighted to accept your invitation. I've not seen the children's rooms. Are you sure?"

The Viscount was at home those two days, and he and Jimmy got along famously. His cabinet assured him that it would be only a matter of time before the South would capitulate.

"Do you hunt, James?"

"I did as a young man. What do you have in mind?"

"I thought we could go to my friend's home and shoot some birds. What say ye?"

"Let's go! I don't have gun or suitable clothing, but I'm game."

"We'll find something for you to wear, and as for the gun, I'll show you what I have, and you can choose."

They bagged three birds each, drank some wine, told each other a few jokes, and came home contented and full of good cheer. "I miss our talks. I hope you'll favor us with a visit whenever you come across the pond to see the children."

"You're very kind, sir. It's been a pleasure to know you. I'll definitely see you on my next visit."

He'd written to Michelle Grande to see whether she'd be amenable to a visit from him. Her response was that she'd be happy to see him. She had plenty of room, and she invited him to stay with her and her daughter.

Accordingly, James took the ferry to Calais and then a carriage to Paris. When he arrived, he introduced himself to Paulette Grande, the daughter, who said her mother would be returning home in an hour.

The American embassy in Paris had been keeping an eye on Commander Hudson, the Confederate liaison for shipbuilding. The American consul was especially helpful to James. Through him, he learned that Commander Hudson was working with a Bordeaux shipbuilder named Arman. Hudson was contracting for two more ironclads and four other ships. Emperor Napoleon had denied that the ships were being built for the Confederacy.

The problem with that assertion was that the consul in Paris, John Bigelow, had an intelligence windfall. A disenchanted shipyard worker provided incriminating documents that proved that the ships were being built for the Confederacy, approved by the French government.

The consul acted quickly, informing both the American ambassador and Secretary Seward. A threat was directed toward the Mexican adventure, and Napoleon was forced to withdraw his approval and have his government purchase the ships for the French navy.

James had developed a special fund to repay the consuls for all the information they had to pay for, in order to keep the ships out of the Rebels' hands. It wasn't just funds for consuls in England and France but for those consuls in Cuba and other countries as well. By early 1864, if any ships were being built for the Confederacy, the U.S. consuls knew immediately where they were being built, who was buying them, and who was providing the funds.

During his two weeks in Paris, James had dinner with Michelle every night in the finest French restaurants. During the days, he was working at the embassy, trying to thwart Napoleon's blatant attempts to assist the South, but in the evenings, he and Michelle partied. Although they weren't lovers, they'd been intimate on several occasions. James enjoyed the woman, and he wished there could be more to their relationship, but both of them realized they'd be good friends and nothing more.

He returned home without ever seeing his children, reported to Lincoln about the French failed attempt, and with that, he decided that he had had enough of government service. He felt that he'd given Lincoln his best, but with the war ending—even though the South wouldn't admit it—he wanted to go back to his three banks. Lincoln was disappointed, but he understood, and he gave James his blessing.

Within two weeks, James was out of the government and had met with his board of directors, notifying them of his intent to reassume management. Since he was the majority stockholder, the vote was unanimous. James moved back to New York and into the home he and Claire had shared during their marriage.

He wondered if it had all been worth it. His marriage had turned out a failure, and he wondered if he had made any impact at all in the grand scheme of things. He thought long and hard and realized he had made no impact. That was disturbing.

James also thought about Claire, and wondered if he had ever really loved her. He knew what he had felt for Sarah; he never wanted to be apart from her. As for Claire, he admired her, her talent, her grace, and the way she interacted with others. If he didn't want a divorce, then he shouldn't have been so firm when she balked at living in Washington. What he had failed to realize until now was that Sarah had been able to travel with him and spend every moment catering to him because she didn't have the additional responsibility of children, as Claire did. He knew he should've been more sensitive to Claire's concerns for the welfare of the children, rather than looking at her actions as pure defiance of her husband.

But as he thought more deeply about their relationship, he realized that he had taken such a strong stance because he didn't really care that much for her. He wouldn't have been afraid to lose her; it would've been okay if he did. That wasn't fair—to her or to him. Maybe that's why she was being so difficult now. She must realize that he didn't love her and never wanted her—she was just something he had wanted at the moment. "My God, there must be many people who marry just for the sense of marrying and nothing else!"

He poured a cup of coffee, wandered into his massive living room, and sat in one of the chairs she had bought. He couldn't remember whether he had ever sat in it before. It was a thing that meant nothing to him. He assumed that he could make peace with Claire if he made the effort, but he didn't want to. It just wasn't in him. That chapter of his life was over.

He looked around the large room filled with paintings on the wall and bronze statues on pedestals. He liked it here; it was comfortable and he could think. He knew what he wanted to do, and it wasn't going to be something that would just fill the void until he'd move on. He thought of John and Louisa. They were still the best friends he had ever had—or would ever have. He wondered whether John felt that his time in the Confederate government had been worthwhile, or was he also disillusioned? John was a practical man, but he had a feeling of destiny. James knew that John would finally see through the façade of the secession, and he'd be angry that he had been caught up in it. James knew that they were so much alike. Could they go back to being friends, or was this war between brothers something like a wedge that couldn't be removed?

He'd been corresponding with Louisa and sending her funds. Initially, he had balked at the amount she wanted all at once, so he had sent several envelopes of cash in smaller amounts until he was assured that she had received them all. He knew how much her place meant to her, but he didn't know how she'd be able to retain it once those idiots in the South finally came to their senses.

His finances were sound; in fact, those running his banks had doubled his assets. He was forty-four years old now, and he still wanted to do so much more with his life and his money. He had had a few affairs, but nothing serious; there was a possibility that he wouldn't find anyone else, and his would be a solitary life other than with his children. Well, if that's what it has to be, so be it.

When this war is over, the South will be devastated. The plantation life as they knew it would be finished. Businessmen would invade the South looking for bargains. The unscrupulous would be like wolves at the gate. The South would be raped for a few years and would probably bear a grudge for quite some time. The blacks would try to find a life amongst the ruins and the rebuilding. James wanted to be part of that rebuilding. Though he lived in the North, and though he accepted what Lincoln believed, he was at heart a Southerner.

•   •   •

James Beauregard also had some thinking to do. His dream of following in his father's footsteps and attending West Point had gone up in smoke that afternoon when his Cousin P.G.T. Beauregard ordered Major Anderson to surrender Fort Sumter in the Charleston harbor. His father had been his idol and constant companion while he was growing up; both were excellent riders and both loved to hunt and fish. His father had learned about the outdoors from his special friend, James Harris, whom he was named after.

Virginia Military Institute was a fine college with an honored past, but it wasn't West Point. He pursued his studies and military training as though he were at the Academy, and by the end of his first year, he was an honors student. But he was restless, and he wanted action. He applied for a commission as a second lieutenant, and it was granted. The young officer corps of the Confederacy had been decimated, and they were happy to have him. When John heard what his son had done, he tried to have his commission revoked. He went to Davis, but the President didn't have time to see him, and when he did, it was too late. James Beauregard was assigned to an infantry battalion at New Market, Virginia in the Shenandoah Valley. The Confederate army totaled forty-one hundred men and were opposed by a Union army totaling ten thousand. Significantly, there were over three hundred students from V.M.I., making up a cadet battalion there.

CHAPTER THIRTY-SIX

During most of 1864, those in the South were hopeful that Lincoln wouldn't win reëlection. The Democratic National Convention adopted a negotiated peace platform and selected George McClelland, the former Union general, as their candidate. Their party was split between the War Democrats and the Peace Democrats.

The Republicans changed their party name to the National Union Party and appealed to the War Democrats; many came on board. Lincoln, according to his close friends, felt that he couldn't be reëlected. Not only was the country sick of the conflict, but many hardliners felt that his program hadn't gone far enough to eradicate slavery.

John was disillusioned with the South's chances of victory. They were undermanned, undersupplied, and underfinanced, and it didn't look as though those problems could be solved. There was only an outside chance that the North would negotiate peace with the South and allow them to keep their slaves.

He was feeling guilty about leaving Louisa to make her way by herself. He felt that he had been to blame for the Renard assault because of having abandoned his wife and his responsibility. He knew that he could never make up for his failure, but he was determined to return to Magnolia as soon as Davis would release him from his assignment. The Confederate president was unwilling to accept his resignation as head of the Signal Corps. The last time John approached Davis about the subject, he was ignored.

In spite of Davis' insensitivity about the subject, John made sure he was at Magnolia each month, and that Jimmy was sending enough funds to keep Magnolia afloat. Louisa had abandoned the idea of another loan, and was encouraged by a letter from James indicating that he would be willing to provide sufficient funds to restore the plantation to pre-war status.

Most of the slaves at Magnolia had been freed. Louisa's instincts were that the Emancipation Proclamation would be strongly enforced. With her slaves free, she'd have a supply of labor when and if the war ceased. Scars definitely lingered, due to their separation, but John assured her that he was committed to do everything to save their marriage and restore her faith in him.

With most of the able-bodied men off fighting for the South, there was a rise in crime. Many marauding bands would show up at the plantations and demand food, money and other personal items that they could sell. Although she hadn't armed her free slaves, their desire to protect their livelihood was apparent. One day, five armed men rode up to the main residence and demanded to see the owner. Louisa wasn't naïve, and she knew that sooner or later she'd be visited by one or more of these gangs. She and Jerome were armed as they went out the front door to confront the men. "You're not welcome here, so state your business and be on your way," Louisa said.

"We want money and food," the leader sneered at her. "If you don't give it to us, we'll take it and anything else we want."

She and Jerome quickly took out their revolvers and pointed them at the shaggy-haired ruffian. "It's time for you to leave. Get out of here," she said, with some emotion in her voice.

The leader laughed. "Two guns against us five. Put the guns down, or we'll kill you where you stand, and then we'll go through your house and take everything we can carry."

No sooner had the bandit uttered those words when thirty of her free slaves appeared and surrounded the armed men. They didn't have any guns, but they did have clubs, axes and rakes. The five intruders looked at the menacing group.

"You think we're scared?"

He and his men took out their guns and were immediately overwhelmed and thrown to the ground. Their guns were confiscated and they were searched for more weapons. "This doesn't mean anything. We'll come back at night with more men."

"I have over sixty free workers here who will protect this property. We now have eight guns. I'll have sentries out at night to watch for you. I'm letting you go this time; if you come back, we'll bury you in one of the fields. No one will ever know where you went. So if you have more men to bring back here, I'll bury all of them."

The leader just couldn't let a woman have the last word. "You think you're pretty smart, but we'll see." With that, they rode off, shaking their fists at Louisa and her workers.

Louisa was standing on the steps leading up to the front door. She turned to her workers who looked at her. "I want to thank every one of you. Together we'll get through this and be able to put Magnolia back to where it was. You all have a place here as long as I own this plantation."

John knew that he was violating some laws when he confiscated about fifty weapons and ammunition that had been captured from Union soldiers. He had them delivered to the plantation, and when he visited, he gave all the free slaves who were amenable a lesson in firing a weapon and how to clean and load it. Now he was comfortable that Magnolia was ready if any of the guerillas came calling. Louisa was starting to feel that her husband was beginning to appreciate what she was doing.

As the months passed, Lincoln's reëlection campaign was gaining momentum. General John C. Fremont, who was running on a radical Republican ticket, decided to drop out of the presidential race, practically ensuring that Lincoln would win reëlection—which he did. He carried the popular vote and most of the states.

Although he was no longer a part of the Lincoln administration, James had many meetings with the president during calendar year 1864. He was convinced that the country would return the man from Illinois to the White House. When he crossed the Atlantic to pick up the children, Claire had taken them on vacation again and he had to wait two weeks before she returned. He still didn't see her, but her mother asked him to be patient. "How patient do you want me to be? I only have the children during the summer, and it seems that Claire wants to make that even more difficult than it needs to be."

"Jimmy, you wouldn't recognize her these days. She's lost a lot of weight and she's under a doctor's care. I take care of the children most of the time. This was the first time in a year that she felt well enough to be with the children, and she wanted to spend some time with them before they went to America. My daughter is not well, Jim."

"Should I petition the court to gain custody?"

"It would kill her, Jim. I don't think you want that on your conscience."

"I have to take everything you say as the truth. Claire won't see me, so I can't confirm what you say. I'm not saying you're lying; I just don't like what's happening. I'll be patient for a little longer, but Emily, I'm relying on you to keep me informed."

"Thank you, Jim."

Over the next year, Jimmy consolidated his business enterprises and set in motion a plan to invest in the South. His orientation wasn't on agriculture, but on construction in the South, along the eastern seaboard and the gulf. He wasn't ignoring the North, because the railroads would be the next growth industry. He kept his word to Claire, returning the children on time in August 1864, and wondered what his reception would be the next summer. To him and to most in the Lincoln administration, it was clear that sooner or later the South would have to capitulate.

Joy and sorrow would come in the spring of 1865. Lee surrendered at Appomattox; Lincoln was inaugurated, but then was assassinated at the Ford Theater by John Wilkes Booth. James remembered Lincoln's resolve to maintain the Union. Here was a man whose every waking thought was to preserve this great nation, and yet someone else, who really didn't mean anything to anyone, decided that he shouldn't live. Jimmy attended the funeral and felt that he had lost a close friend. It took him a month to recover. He couldn't help but think of the time he had spent with the great man—how they shared lunch and a laugh occasionally. They weren't that close, but they were friends. He also wondered about Andrew Johnson, and whether he had the moral fiber to continue reconstruction in the South, as Lincoln had envisioned.

Jimmy sent a wire to tell his law firm when he'd arrive and to be sure there weren't any problems from Claire again. Emily Temple met him at the harbor as he walked down the gangplank.

"I've come to take you to the children. There's been a tragedy—Claire passed away two months ago from tuberculosis. It broke my heart to see her wither away. She was very clear that she didn't want you notified, and she wanted the children to finish the school year, because she knew you'd take the children to America permanently. I have a letter for you from Claire. I don't know the contents; you can read it on the way or after you see the children."

He was stunned at the news, yet curious to know what she'd say as she was dying. He decided to see the children first and then read the letter that evening.

The children were up and waiting for him. "Mommy's dead, daddy. What are we going to do without mommy?" Mary cried.

Cameron was quiet as he clung to James, who read them a story after putting them to bed. "Are we going to America, daddy?" Cameron asked as James tucked him in.

"We'll all talk in the morning after breakfast—you, Mary, grandmother and I."

Emily was downstairs when he finished with the children and poured him a glass of sherry. "Were you with Lincoln when he was killed?" she asked.

"No. I'd left the government a year earlier. I saw him about a month before his death, and he was delighted that the war would soon be over; he was a great man."

"That's exactly what the Viscount said," she replied.

He poured another glass of sherry, and after Emily went to bed, he sat back in their parlor and opened the letter. He was apprehensive.

"My dearest James:

"I'll probably be dead before you return. Lying here, I've had plenty of time to look back on my life and our marriage. I sincerely apologize for the actions I took that caused our family to split. I wish it had been otherwise.

"What you don't know is how much I loved you and how much I wanted you to love me. Early on, I realized that it was Sarah that you still loved, so I took some actions, hoping that you would come to see me and not Sarah. Later, I realized that there was someone else you also loved.

"I was angry when you gave me the ultimatum that I could either stay in New York or come with you and the children. Had I not been so angry, I would've seen the problem from your viewpoint. From that point on, my anger got out of control, and I made poor choices. My mother begged me to talk to you, but I felt I'd gone too far and couldn't humble myself by talking to you. What a fool I was!

"I guess I was waiting for you to come here, tell me that you loved me and beg me to come back home with you. What a waste—you without your family and me without the only man I ever truly loved.

"Please don't think badly of me, and remember me to the children. They love you as I did.

"Your wife,

"Claire."

The tears flowed down his cheeks. He didn't know what to say. She was correct; it had been a waste of their lives. How could two people who were intimate not communicate with each other? He wondered if he was a jinx. He'd lost two wives to prolonged illness—one he loved deeply and the other not enough.

With the war over, his first action was to take his children to Charleston to visit his grandparents. They'd seen them once, but the Hendrickses were aging, and Jim hoped that they'd survived the war zone. He'd been sending them money, and from their letters he knew that they'd not suffered, but they felt isolated. Train travel had been restored between the North and South, though there were still some delays. He and the children left New York two days after they arrived. Cameron was shocked to learn the news, and Abigail cried; Claire had been her good friend and would be missed.

The grandparents were so happy to see the children. Frederick was walking without assistance, but Hilda was confined to a wheelchair. That didn't stop her from fussing over Mary and Cameron. The older woman was suffering from a mild form of dementia. She said Mary looked like her mother, Sarah. They had escaped the war physically unscathed but their home was damaged. Jimmy contracted with some locals to make the needed repairs. He asked if they would come with him to New York; they said no. "This is our home and here we'll stay," Frederick answered for both.

He stayed with them for two days. His grandfather was still alert and as astute as ever. James shared with him his view of the future and his investment goals.

"The South is an utter mess, and it will take at least a decade before they recover," Frederick said. "Land values have plummeted and the freed slaves are in need of some direction. The blacks are without education and haven't been trained for anything other than agriculture. There are programs to help them, but most are not inclusive enough to bear any fruit. They now must support themselves. The plantations as we remembered them are gone, because they've either been confiscated by the Federal government or have been destroyed by the war. I know you've been helping the Beauregards. They're good people, but they're one inch away from foreclosure or bankruptcy. I'd be careful in any investment you contemplate here. If I were you, I'd only invest in the North."

"I know you're correct, grandfather, but deep down I'm a Southerner and I want to help. Eventually, I want to move back to Charleston. This is where I grew up, and this is where I want to be. My focus right now is on my children and how they'll transition to living in America. I want to show them the America that I knew as a youth, and let them decide where they want to live when they're old enough to choose."

"I want you to be careful while you're here. This isn't the South you knew in your youth. There are many guerrilla bands roaming throughout the state. They're made up mostly of young men who came back from the war. They were trained to kill and have continued that in civilian life. Law enforcement is absent, and these thugs are taking advantage of everyone. I have a suggestion for you. The people next door died recently, and we took in their German shepherd. He's a sweet dog, but he was trained by his former owner to attack on command. Why don't you take him with you? I know you'll bond with him, and he's friendly with children; his name is Prince. Let's go outside—he's in the back yard. I want to show you the commands."

Jimmy was intrigued by his grandfather's suggestion and went out back to see the dog. He especially wanted to see how Cameron and Mary would react with the animal. His grandfather was correct. The children had never had a dog, and they seemed to adore Prince. "Daddy, can we keep him?" Mary begged. "Great-grandfather says he wants us to have him. Please, daddy?"

The command was simple. Frederick Hendricks called the dog to him. He placed an empty wooden crate covered by a cloth in the center of the rear yard. He held the dog and shouted, *"Barrel!"* The dog leaped from his grasp and attacked the crate, tearing the cloth into shreds. When he said the word *"Peace!"*, the dog immediately stopped attacking and trotted back to him. Jimmy tried the commands several times to determine what the dog's reaction would be with him. In each case he attacked and then stopped when the second command was uttered.

"We'll take him with us, grandfather; we're on our way to the Catawba village. We'll stop here on our way back."

CHAPTER THIRTY-SEVEN

This was the first time he'd seen Louisa and John since the end of the war. It was as though the three had never been apart. His children had been to Magnolia once before, but didn't remember the experience. John and Louisa still owed his bank a considerable sum of money, but their investments in the North exceeded their debt. Life in the South was difficult, even for them. They didn't have the resources to turn Magnolia into the money-making asset it'd been prior to the war. "I see that the place is active; there are workmen over the entire property."

"Most of our slaves have left," Louisa said. "Those that remain were freed by me during the war. We've divided up Magnolia into forty-acre parcels and do sharecropping. About twenty of our former freed slaves work the land. Our function in this cooperative is to provide seed, tools and expertise. We take one-third of the sharecropper harvest for two years and then our share goes up to fifty percent. That's better terms than anyone else in the area is giving; it's our way of ensuring that our workers get a solid start and prosper. We want this cooperative to work, so we're taking less in the beginning. John and I work one of the forty-acre parcels. Our main effort is scheduling our time, the tools and supplies so it's fair to everyone. After the cotton is baled, we take it to market to sell, and then we divide up the proceeds, less costs, among the sharecroppers. Our expenses have been higher than we expected because we've had to repair their former living quarters and advance the sharecroppers funds so they could buy food and clothing. In spite of all that, I'm optimistic that we'll succeed."

"I was sorry to hear about young James. Where did he fall?"

"He was killed at the Battle of New Market in 1864. He and many of his V.M.I. cadets held off the superior Union Army of the Shenandoah. James led his squad directly into the heart of the Union defenses. When other squads saw what he was doing, they followed his lead and pushed the

Union back. However, James was severely wounded, and he died on the battlefield. His commendation is in a frame on the wall over there. He was truly a hero.

"John and I visited his grave last month. He had so much promise, as did all the young men who gave their lives for their side. I heard that the number of deaths exceeded five hundred thousand between North and South. I don't know how we'll ever recover from the death of nearly an entire generation." Louisa started to cry, and John put his arm around her shoulders.

"We're sorry to hear about Claire," she went on. "She must have suffered greatly during her last months. I'm sorry that it didn't work out for you. You know that John and I love you and will do anything we can to help you through these times."

"I've recently been in communication with Aaron, who is now the chief of the Catawba. I'm taking the children there. I want them to see how those people live and how happy they are. I know most of them supported the Confederacy, but Aaron tells me that the tribe is smaller but still happy. Maybe I'm grasping at straws, but I remember how important my vacations were with the tribe."

"Jimmy, how much money is in our investment account?" John asked.

"There's twenty thousand out of the thirty you asked me to invest. Your investment up North was doing well, but I was sending money consistently to Louisa so she wouldn't have to borrow any more than needed. I think I can make more for you with some railroad stock. Do you need the funds?"

"That money was supposed to be for our children. With James gone, and Susannah married and living in New Orleans, we may have to use it to keep this place."

"I'll do what you ask—just let me know. We're leaving tomorrow for the Catawba village; Aaron is expecting us. I'll stop on the way back and get your answer."

The children had never camped out before, but they seemed to enjoy the adventure along the road on their way to the Indian village. Jimmy knew that times were perilous for travelers, but he was sure he could protect the children; no one had bothered them on their way to Magnolia. When they stopped for the night, he lit a fire and warmed up some of the chicken that Louisa had prepared for them. They sat around the fire eating and drinking some of the lemonade she had provided. Prince lay at his feet. The children were talking about their two grandfathers. It took them a while to understand that the Hendrickses were their father's grandparents. They wanted to know about his mother, and he told them. "Did she die like our mommy?" Mary said.

"Yes."

They were making small talk when they suddenly heard a voice. "You, by the fire, can we come in and get warm?" Jimmy put his revolver under his hat by his side and placed his hand on Prince.

"Come in slowly and don't make any sudden moves," James said.

There were three of them; they walked into the camp and asked if they could have something to eat. "You can have some of the chicken that the children didn't eat."

They consumed the food as though they hadn't eaten in days. When they were finished, one of the three asked, "Is that dog friendly?"

"Yes, he's very docile. The children play with him all the time."

Just then all three stood up, drew their guns and pointed them at the children. "We want all your money, and if you don't give us any trouble, we'll let you go. We're also taking the carriage."

"But these are small children! Leaving them out here with no food and no transportation would be heartless. Take my money, but leave us the horse."

"Mister, if you don't shut up, we'll kill you anyway!"

"Barrel!" Jimmy shouted, and Prince leapt at the three men, who were diverted long enough for Jimmy to reach his gun, rise and hit the leader as hard as he could alongside the head. The other two were trying to fight off the dog. Jimmy hit the nearest man in the head with the butt of his gun and may have cracked his skull. The other man was on the ground, and Prince was tearing at the arm that held the gun.

"Call him off! For God's sake, call him off!"

When he was sure all three were disabled, he gave the command, "Peace," and Prince came back to him and sat down. Jimmy recovered all the weapons on the ground and searched all three men. He found a couple of knives, but nothing of any significance. The children hadn't uttered a sound during the entire event—they were stunned. Only when Jim had bound the three to some trees did they ask him, "Did you kill them?"

"No, son, I didn't. They were bad men and meant to harm us. We'll leave them here, and I'll tell the Chief at the Catawba village to send some of his braves to turn them over to the sheriff."

"Was Prince a good dog?" Mary asked.

"Yes, honey, he saved us."

"Will they come after us?" Cameron asked.

"No, son, I tied them so they can't get away until the Indian braves come here."

"Why did they point their guns at us?" Cameron asked.

"They were hungry, had no job and no place to live."

Cameron and Mary tossed and turned all night; they couldn't sleep. James and Prince kept watch until daylight. James was very critical of himself for not taking his grandfather's advice more seriously; he wouldn't make that mistake again. He called the children at dawn and told them to put everything into the carriage. He could tell by their movements that they were still feeling stunned from the night before. As they were leaving, he made sure all three intruders were alert. "I'm going to send someone back to untie you, but it may take a day. Don't ever let me see you again, because I'll kill all of you."

Aaron greeted them and the village children came up to meet the two new youngsters. James and the children were dressed in their finest, while the villagers wore little more than loincloths. He remembered how shocked he had been when his father brought him here the first time. "Mary, you and Cameron, take Prince and go with the children. They'll take you to their teepees, where you'll stay while were here. We'll eat with the chief tonight."

"But daddy, they don't have any clothes on!" Mary said.

"It's warm here; that's how people dress in the village. You'll be okay. I'll see you at dinner."

He told Aaron about the attempted robbery and where he had left the would-be robbers. "I'll send a runner to the sheriff in the town about ten miles from here and let him decide what to do. You can forget about them going to jail. There's a lot of lawlessness in this area and not much justice. I'll send some of our people with you when you leave."

The village was half the size it had been when he was here last after Sarah died. "What happened to your people?" he asked Aaron.

"I don't know whether you knew this, but we were slave holders. Therefore, our views were similar to those in the South. Most of our young men fought on the side of the Confederacy, and ten were killed. Others didn't come home from the war; a few died of illness. To compound the problem, we haven't had many births."

"Are there any repercussions against the village for your stance in the war?"

"Not necessarily from the war, but the hatred the whites have for the blacks has transitioned to anyone who is not white. We're now lumped with the blacks. Many of the blacks left the plantations after the war, but they've returned because that's all they knew. Sharecropping is nothing but the old feudal system under a new name. The white plantation owner has them fiscally strapped and they have no place to turn."

"You're far enough away from the urban areas that you shouldn't have too many problems."

"There're a lot of unemployed ex-soldiers who are roaming the countryside in bands. They think that the rural areas are fair pickings because the law is thin out here. We have sentries out night and day."

"Will the children be in jeopardy down at the river?"

"We all take turns as sentries; right now, we have four in the trees overlooking the river. They're armed and good shots. So far the gangs have left us alone. They've been raiding family-type farms in the area; a few farmers who put up a fight were killed."

Within two days, the children had lost their inhibitions and were running around like a bunch of wild Indians. Cameron was dressed in a loincloth and Mary had an Indian dress on. The Indian boys were teaching his son to throw a javelin and shoot a bow and arrow. Mary was learning to make pottery, which the Catawba were famous for.

The night before they left, Aaron and the villagers had a big feast in their honor. There were all kinds of competitions. The young boys competed in Indian wrestling and shooting their bows. Jim was surprised when he was invited to compete against the adult men in axe throwing. A target was set up at twenty paces. Each man was given two chances to hit the target. To his surprise, Jimmy hadn't lost his skill with the axe that he learned in this village. He tied with two other villagers and the target was moved to forty paces. He was the only one to hit the target from that distance, and he hit it twice. His children ran up to him and threw their arms around him. "I didn't know you could throw the axe!" Cameron said.

"I learned that skill in this village when I played with the Chief when we were boys."

Three of the men from the village escorted James and the children back to Charleston. But sadness awaited him when he arrived. Both of his grandparents had passed away within four days of each other. The doctor who attended Hilda and Frederick said both had died of natural causes. There was a will; everything was left to James. He and the children visited the gravesite and then visited Magnolia. John and Louisa asked if they could have the remainder of their funds that he had invested up North. "I'll have them sent to you by a secure source as soon as I return to New York."

Jim decided to keep his grandparents' home, in the event that he might return here some day. He didn't want to leave anything vacant in this lawless environment, so he asked several of the neighbors whether they knew anyone who'd want to lease the home for a year. Coincidentally, the doctor attending his grandparents had a daughter who was recently married; she and her new husband needed a home. Jim talked to the couple and rented it to them.

Cameron and Abigail met them at the station when they returned and drove them to their home. They wanted to stay and spend some time with Mary and young Cameron. Jimmy spent the next two days, with Abigail's help, hiring a combination nanny and housekeeper. He wanted the children to have a normal life in the States, and he wanted someone to be in the home whenever he had to leave town for a few days.

Her name was Kathleen O'Rourke, a native of Belfast, Ireland. She was twenty-nine years old, had been married, and had a five-year-old child. Her late husband had worked as a longshoreman, but he had drowned off the harbor in New York. She and the child—named Sean, after his father—couldn't afford the home they were renting and had moved in temporarily with a cousin in Brooklyn. Jim wasn't sure about hiring someone with a family, but her energy permeated the room during the interview, and besides, Abigail liked her. She was a petite woman with bright red hair and an engaging smile. Anyone meeting her for the first time couldn't help but like her.

"You'll have your hands full caring for three children. Do you think you can handle it?" he asked her.

"Oh, it will be nothing for me, sir. I took care of my six sisters when I was thirteen, living in Belfast."

"Can we try it for a few months to see how it works?"

"Certainly, sir, you won't be disappointed."

"Your boy should be treated equal to my two children. We have plenty, and he doesn't need to feel inferior to either of them."

"Thank you, sir."

The New York house had six bedrooms and was adequate to accept two more living there. On the first day of school, Mrs. O'Rourke was up early, had the children's breakfast ready, and packed their lunches. She was small, but to James she seemed like an army sergeant. She made sure the children went to bed on time, wore clean clothes, brushed their teeth and combed their hair. Jim knew within a week that Kathleen O'Rourke could handle the job.

CHAPTER THIRTY-EIGHT

John was restless. Farming forty acres wasn't something he had ever done or had ever wanted to do. The defeat of the South and the forced freedom of the slaves turned his world upside down. The whites were in the minority in South Carolina, and it wasn't even close. The new state legislature had a majority of blacks sitting in seats previously held by the white elite. He could have run for the state senate, but a majority of the whites in the area joined together and boycotted the elections. John didn't know what *that* proved, other than that the former slaves continued to be the majority in the state legislature.

He'd spend part of his leisure time at a local gentlemen's club, where others drank too much and gambled with money they couldn't afford to lose. He went fishing on the Carolina Banks, but he was unhappy, and he knew that he'd have to find something to do, or he and Louisa were going to have difficulties. She'd been supportive, but he knew she'd put up with his failure to contribute only so long.

On his way home from a week's fishing, he stopped in Charleston to have a drink and to see who was at the club. François Boltair was sitting at a table by himself, and when he saw John come in, he signaled him to come join him. John ordered a drink and told Boltair about his fishing trip.

"I've been sitting here for an hour trying to solve a problem, and then I saw you walk in here and I knew that my problem was solved."

"Well, I'm flattered, but I don't have a clue what you're talking about."

"Richard Lucerne was elected sheriff for this county prior to the end of the war. He's coming up for reelection in '68, and most of us who supported him don't think he's got a chance of being reëlected. We're going to have a black sheriff unless we can get lucky and find someone who'll appeal to some of the blacks. We only need about twenty percent of them to sway the next election."

"What does that have to do with me?"

"I've talked to Lucerne and explained to him the facts of life. Here's what I suggest. Lucerne appoints you as his deputy and then resigns six months later due to ill health. He names you as his replacement, and after you accept the position, you bring in that black, who works for you as a deputy. My guess is that you'll be elected for many terms."

"You're assuming that I want the job—and that and Lucerne will go along with it."

"He's already agreed. Why wouldn't you take it? You have nothing going at the moment. Sharecropping isn't the answer. Let your wife run the plantation, and you can run the county."

"What happens to Lucerne?"

"I'll let him run one of my saloons. He's already moved to a room behind the Lucky Lady Saloon. He can't wait until his six months are up."

"Don't the supervisors for the county have something to say about this?"

"Yes, they do. I'm a supervisor and the chairman of the board."

"How large is the area, and how many people are in the county?"

"Here's a map showing the entire county parameters. To the best of my knowledge, there are 65,000 people in the county. You'll need a few offices throughout the area. Lucerne has twelve deputies that roam the district."

"If I take the position as deputy and become sheriff, don't expect any special favors. I'll uphold the law for everyone—there will be no favorites."

"I wouldn't expect less of you. What do you say? Do we have a deal?"

"Let me know when I can start."

Louisa was shocked when he came home and told her what he was going to do. "You have no law enforcement experience! Why would they want you, unless they want to use you for their personal gain?"

"I told Boltair that I wouldn't be used, and that I'd enforce the law for everyone. I have to do that, or the blacks will elect their own sheriff. Boltair suggested that Jerome become my deputy."

"Do you think he'll take the position?"

"I'll never know unless I ask."

Six months later, Boltair made good on his promise, and John was appointed sheriff to fill out the remaining term of Sheriff Lucerne's. During the six months, he'd been evaluating the other deputies to determine their qualifications and whether he wanted to retain them. After Boltair informed him that he had the job, he asked for a meeting with his sponsor.

"How much authority do I have in personnel matters?"

"You want to replace some of the deputies?"

"As a matter of fact, I want to replace three immediately. They're anti-black, and they're drunks. I don't trust them. The others I'm still evaluating."

"John, let me explain the facts of life to you. You can't replace white deputies with black ones."

"Well, we have to do something, because over sixty percent of the population is black, and if I don't at least give them some slots, they'll vote me out of office."

"Of the three slots, how many do you want to replace with blacks?"

"I want two more black deputies. The other can be white, and that person should be an ex-Confederate soldier."

"Do you have people in mind?"

"I do, and I want to make the change immediately."

"The deputies you're going to replace could be a problem for you down the road. If that's what you want, I'll grease the planks for you; just don't do anything controversial until you talk it over with me."

Boltair was correct. The three men he fired threatened to make his life miserable over the next three years. One made the mistake of swinging at John, and really paid the price. He was knocked down, and when he got up, John knocked him down again. The first of the three slots he filled was by a twenty-five-year-old veteran. John knew his father and the boy's relatives. Although, like most whites, he was suspicious of blacks, he assured John that he'd be fair.

Hiring the two blacks was tricky. Jerome checked in the community and found two young men he thought would do the job. John interviewed them at length. He accepted one of the two. Jerome found two other candidates, and after a lengthy interview process, John hired one of them, a black man in his late thirties. He now had twelve deputies, of whom nine were white and three were black. His goal was to have six of each, but he realized that he wouldn't remain in office long if he went too fast.

He relied on Jerome, but realized that he'd need to find one or two of the white deputies whom he could trust, who would help keep the others in line. His first goal was to determine how he was going to deploy his men throughout the county. The major crimes were murder, robbery, gang violence, rape, and slayings in the predominantly black districts. None of his deputies had any investigative experience; their role in the past had been simply to break up fights and haul people off to jail. John knew that the marauding gangs needed to be stopped. The problem was that many of these groups outnumbered his entire force. To counter this discrepancy, he got Boltair's permission to have auxiliary deputies he could call upon when needed to stop these gangs; they'd be paid on a time-served basis.

He set out to recruit twenty men who would serve as auxiliary deputies. He signed up ten whites and ten blacks. All were experienced in the use of firearms, and the whites were ex-soldiers. He spent two weeks with them, going over basic police procedures. He also spent two days on the ethics of the position. They would meet each month for training, and whenever they were needed. Boltair and the board of supervisors were happy with the auxiliary concept. They felt that the gangs were a threat to everyone and were hampering business. The supervisors also agreed to pay for their service, which was important to John if he was going to succeed.

Five of the white deputies needed to be replaced in the future, but John had to play the game with Boltair in order to keep his support. The five were absolute bigots and expressed their views readily. John received word that a gang of eight ex-soldiers were raiding small farms and sharecroppers. With his background in espionage, John was able to receive reports of their raids, plot their attacks on a map, and set up an ambush where he expected them to hit next. To keep the white deputies from being insubordinate when they worked alongside black deputies, he appointed one of his deputies, by the name of Clint Marsh, to be his chief deputy.

When he was sure where he wanted to stage his people, he called Marsh into his one-room office. "Clint, here's where I want us to set up. If you look at the map on the wall, the pins depict where the group has raided; the red marks are potential targets. We'd be about a mile from the most likely ones. I want to split up into two groups. You're leading one group of three men and I'm leading the other of three. Each of us will send out a scout. When the bandits are close, the scouts will come back and we'll regroup. I want to wait until we surrounded these rascals and try to get then to surrender. If not, then we'll shoot them. Do you have any questions?"

Marsh had been a corporal in the Army of Northern Virginia under Robert E. Lee. He definitely understood military tactics. "No, sir, we can handle this. When do you want us to leave?"

"We'll travel by night and leave at about five tomorrow evening."

"Are any of the blacks going to be in my squad?"

"No, I'll take two with me."

The raids usually took place in the morning, so he and his deputies arrived at their planned ambush site before dawn. After he made sure that all their weapons were ready, he set out two guards and sent out the scouts. He and Marsh waited to see what would develop. Around eleven in the morning, one scout reported a raid by twelve men on a farmhouse about a mile away. They reassembled into the two groups and followed the scout to the farm. John could see that the raiders had a man tied up at a hitching post; other raiders had bottles in their hands and were shooting at the farm animals. "Clint, you take your men and circle around back of the farm. I'll wait until you're set, then I'll come up in front of the property and call out to them to surrender. If they don't surrender or if they fire on us, shoot them."

Fifteen minutes later, when John was sure that Clint and his men were in place, he called out. "You men in there! You're surrounded. Drop your weapons and walk to the front gate. If you don't, we'll fire on you. You have thirty seconds to make up your mind."

No sooner did he utter the demand than the raiders scattered and opened up on them with their rifles and handguns. Clint's men were crack shots, and soon two of the marauders fell. The others, now realizing that they were getting fire from two sides, split up, and half of them returned fire on John and the other half on Clint and his men.

John had them boxed in. He knew that it was just a matter of time before they'd surrender or be dead. "Stay down and wait them out," he said to his men. "They're not going anyplace."

Two more intruders fell, and soon the remaining eight tied a white cloth to one of their rifles and hoisted it in the air.

"I want to see the weapons on the ground first," John shouted, "and then I want you to walk toward the front gate with your hands over your heads. Move, or we'll start shooting again."

They watched as the men dropped their guns and walked to the front gate. John counted them; there were only seven. He yelled to Clint, "I think one of them is hiding or playing possum. Check out the farm carefully and look for the one who didn't surrender."

They searched the seven and tied their hands behind their backs. John left the scout to guard them, and he and the two black deputies advanced cautiously toward the farmhouse. Clint's men were coming around the house from the rear. Just then a shot rang out, and one of Clint's men fell. It seemed like the shot was coming from a oneroom hut. John signaled Clint and his other deputy to approach the building from the rear while he and a deputy went toward the front of the house, watching to see if there was any movement. John was shoved to the ground as two shots were fired. One was directed at him; it was Jerome who pushed him out of the way and shot the raider in the chest.

When John fell to the ground, he was dazed when he hit his head on a rock. Within five minutes, though, he had recovered sufficiently to take stock. Seven raiders had been captured, five had been killed, and one of his deputies had died at the scene. He had the seven marauders dig graves for the five, while he had the dead deputy wrapped in a cloth. They were going to take him back and either turn him over to his family or bury him in Charleston. They untied the farmer and helped him clean up the mess the intruders had made; the farmer was grateful, to say the least. He offered all of them some homemade liquor, which they accepted and then rode on.

John knew that there were many other gangs roaming the countryside, but when he reported to Boltair, the man was positively ecstatic. The next two days John spent at home. His married life and his relationship with Louisa were slowly improving. It wasn't that she didn't love him; she was still angry that he had left her to fend for herself during the war.

CHAPTER THIRTY-NINE

The understanding among the elite South Carolinians was that Buford Robert Belanger's family had come to America on the *Mayflower*. Perhaps that myth was helped along by Buford. The reality was that his great-great-great-grandfather had been a privateer who entered the country through Mexico. The family originally settled in Virginia, but as their wealth increased, they moved to South Carolina and bought one hundred thousand acres, five miles from Charleston. As the town grew, its expansion was fueled by land purchased from the Belangers.

No one could argue that Buford wasn't a southern patriot. He had personally loaned a small fortune to the South and had lost it all. What most people in his circle didn't know was that he had also invested a huge sum in Spain before the war. When the hostilities ended, he still had his plantation, along with sufficient funds to continue the lifestyle of a southern plantation owner. Buford didn't mind telling his closest friends of the Spanish investment, but what he didn't—and *wouldn't*—tell anyone was the huge fortune he had made as one of the premier blockade runners during the Civil War.

He'd had two fast ships anchored in the Florida Keys. Although the area between Cuba and the Keys was heavily patrolled by Union warships, Buford had a Union captain on his payroll and knew the times and locations of those patrols. The amount of money he made off the South was obscene. Only his accountant knew some of the details, and he was living in Cuba. Buford made a trip to that island nation every quarter to go over his accounts and savor the local social life.

Buford liked women of all colors and sizes, but he especially like them young. He owned a large house in Cuba and had kept servants living there throughout the war. Not sure whether he'd be caught in the act of blockade running, he'd figured it would be wise to have a place to go if an arrest was imminent.

His wife was from his circle of friends. She'd been schooled in France, and she made sure everyone knew that she spoke five languages and that her clothes were the latest fashion in that country. The couple had two children. Their son, Buford, lost his life at Shiloh; the daughter married a son of one of their closest associates.

The Belangers were among the elite's elite. To be invited to a party at their estate was something to be cherished. They only sent out fifty invitations to their annual fox hunting ball. Those who were lucky to receive such an invitation made sure that their friends, acquaintances and neighbors knew that they'd made the top fifty.

Mavis Belanger had her own little secrets that few even suspected. She liked an occasional roll in the hay with one of the strapping young black men working the plantation. When Buford went to Cuba on his trips, Mavis would take her lover of the moment to a second home they owned on the South Carolina Banks and party for two to three weeks.

The annual hunt ball at the Buford estate was preceded by a vigorous hunt by the attendees, lunch on the grounds soon thereafter, and then skeet shooting or cards for the men and a nap for the female attendees. At seven, they'd meet in Belanger's large drawing room, have cocktails, and then be called to dinner. There was always entertainment during meals. The next morning the event would come to a conclusion with breakfast for all out on the lawns of the plantation. Anyone who attended went away with memories of a significant episode in their life.

There were sufficient bedrooms for all, but occasionally guests would be four to a room. But that wasn't the only thing that was shared at these annual events. Frequently, someone's wife or female companion was exchanged after she'd become completely inebriated. Sometimes the female guest wasn't intoxicated, but the result was the same. On occasion, a gentleman lost a substantial sum in the card game that sometimes lasted throughout the night. In some occasions, he had no other way to pay the debt other than surrender his escort for the night. The lady was kept through the night, and as was the custom, thanked her benefactor when he was finished. It was interesting that more than eighty percent of the time, Buford was the benefactor.

Young Richard LaCroix had cut a dashing figure at the Battle of Shiloh. He won a commendation medal for his exploits, as well as the heart of a very beautiful young woman named Samantha Bureau, who came from a good but not affluent family. This was her first visit to the Belanger plantation, and to say she was overwhelmed by its beauty and sheer splendor would be an understatement.

Whether he got coerced into a poker game or was a willing participant is a matter of conjecture. What Richard lost is clear, though: he lost more than he could ever afford. As he realized what had happened, he sat with his head in his hands and sobbed, heartbroken. The winner was Buford.

After everyone had left the game room, Buford sat down across from young LaCroix. "How do you intend to make good on your losses, young man?" Buford asked.

"I don't know," LaCroix responded. "I made a mistake. My father doesn't have any money. I'm at your mercy, sir."

"I'll offer you a solution. I don't know whether you'll take it—that's up to you. Miss Bureau has caught my fancy, and I'd like to bed her tonight and tomorrow morning."

"Sir, your suggestion is outrageous and insulting! I demand that you withdraw that request."

"I can do that; however, if you find that distasteful, you can pay me now, or I'll let everyone know that you're not an honorable man. You'll never get an invitation from any respected family again, and it's possible the only employment you'll ever find is as a bartender."

"Why are you doing this to me?"

"I'm not doing anything other than trying to collect on your debt. Why don't you ask the woman to see how she feels about this? Perhaps she'd be willing."

"She'd consider it an insult of the highest order!"

"It's your choice."

LaCroix stood up, his demeanor increasingly somber. He walked around the table as though leaving the room, but suddenly he turned and struck Buford in the face as hard as he could with his right fist. The older man fell over, landing on his back. His hands went to his face; his nose appeared to be broken. Grabbing the leg of the table, he slowly raised himself up and tried to sit on his chair, but he fell again. Through broken teeth and a nose that was starting to swell, he spoke softly. "My seconds will call upon you this evening. I demand satisfaction at six o'clock tomorrow morning in the field near the gin mill."

Dueling had been outlawed years ago, but the rage both men felt would ignore any facet of the law at this point. LaCroix went to his room and was met by Miss Bureau. "Tell me what happened, Richard!"

"I can't. It's too embarrassing. I'm a good shot— perhaps I'll have a chance. He's lost some teeth and I think his nose is broken."

"Was this about me?"

"Nonsense. Why would you think that?"

"Someone was listening at the door and heard Belanger agree to discount your debt if he could have me."

"Well, that's not going to happen. I'll figure out a way to repay him, if I live through this."

"If I give myself to him, he'll cancel your debt, and he won't go through with the duel."

"I may be a lot of things, but I have a good name. I can't have him disgrace you and me. I'll prevail!" He wore a determined look as she put her arms around his neck and kissed him passionately.

Most of the guests hadn't heard about the duel and were still sleeping as the two men and their seconds walked to an area near the gin mill. The air was crisp, with a slight touch of dew, as the two men selected their weapons and listened to the judge's reading of the rules of the duel. First, he gave each a chance to make amends and apologize before he issued the count. When that didn't occur, he instructed the combatants to stand with their backs to each other and walk ten paces, turn to face their adversary, cock their weapons, aim, and wait for the order to fire.

LaCroix was tense as he paced off the ten steps and turned. Belanger was grinning at him, and LaCroix felt the rage within himself to be overwhelming. He wanted to kill the older man.

"Fire!"

Both men discharged their weapons, and LaCroix fell to the ground, mortally wounded. Buford didn't escape unscathed, though; LaCroix's bullet had hit him in the right shoulder. He was attended by his second. With LaCroix dead, there was nothing more that could be done for him.

At breakfast the next morning, the rumor of the duel and fatality was on everyone's tongue. Miss Bureau had departed with LaCroix' body, presumably to be taken to his parents. As the group dispersed and went home, Buford looked out the window from his second-story bedroom. His wife was present while a doctor attended to his wound.

"Did you have to kill the boy? We have enough money. You could have given him terms—or was the debt not the real reason he was shot? Miss Bureau is a beauty to fight over." Mavis smiled. She was well aware of her husband's reputation.

Two weeks later, Mr. and Mrs. Raymond LaCroix came to John's office in Charleston. Much had changed in the county sheriff's office during the past two years. Many of the malcontents had been replaced, mostly with blacks. All the white peace officers were former Confederate soldiers; most had been at least sergeants or higher.

It was the first that John had heard of their son's death, and especially that it had been at the hands of Buford Belanger. They told him the bloody details and then told him what Samantha Bureau had said.

"How would she know that Belanger had used the debt to defile her?"

"Richard told her the night before the duel. We believe the card game is rigged. There are things that happen there that are not talked about, but eventually the word gets out. There have been many losers at Belanger's card games. In most instances, the victims are able to pay up, but in some cases they can't. If the man has an attractive wife or companion, the debt is resolved by trading the losses for her favors. Don't be shocked, sheriff! This is a powerful man with a lot of friends and money."

"Those are serious charges to make against a man like Buford Belanger. Do you have any proof?"

"No one will speak of this in public, but what we've told you is true. What are you going to do about it? Richard was a hero to the South, and he didn't deserve to be killed in a duel by the South's most notorious blockade runner!"

"All I can promise is that I will look into it."

He knew that wasn't satisfying to the older couple, but what else could he say? As Mr. LaCroix had said, Belanger was a mighty powerful man. Before John took any action, he wanted to talk to his two most trusted deputies, Marsh and Jerome. He told them what the LaCroix' had said and asked them if they'd ever heard rumors about the card game and what happened there. Marsh said he hadn't heard of anything like that, but Jerome didn't respond right away. John waited.

"There has been some talk about the wild parties that go on at the Belanger place. The owner has a reputation as a great shot and as one who covets pretty things—especially if they wear dresses."

"If we wanted to get some information about the LaCroix killing and the card games, how would we start?"

Marsh said nothing, but Jerome looked at John and asked, "Do you really want to pursue this?"

John was stunned that his deputy thought he'd look the other way on any death, especially a murder. "Absolutely!"

"Then I would ask the help. They know what's going on. They knew it when they were slaves and they know it now as free blacks."

"Here's what I think we should do. Marsh, I want you to go with me to the Belanger plantation to inquire about the death of Richard LaCroix and see what Belanger has to say. Jerome, you take another deputy and talk to the household help and see what they have to say. There may have been other incidents that they remember. Even if it happened as the LaCroix' say it did, we haven't got anything. I also want to look at the dueling pistols. Gentlemen, we need proof. If we can find some shred of evidence against the man, I'll get a warrant for his arrest."

"Good luck with that!" Marsh said.

Three days later the four men rode out to the Belanger plantation. Belanger was busy when they arrived— or at least he passed word to them that he was busy. He made them wait an hour before he came into the drawing room and greeted them. "I haven't seen you since you were a young man, John. I knew your father well and counted him as a close friend."

John introduced his three deputies. "We're here to investigate the death of Richard LaCroix at a party at your home on October 15th of this year. I'm asking that you and your employees cooperate with us, and we'll try not to disrupt you any longer than we need to. Will you instruct your household employees to gather in the kitchen? My deputies will ask them a few questions. At the same time, I want to get your position on what happened."

"I'm sorry about young LaCroix. He seemed like a fine young man, and I sympathize with his family, but I don't intend to round up my help for a couple of your black deputies to question them. Additionally, I don't intend to answer your questions. You came here unannounced and rudely imply that I acted other than as a gentleman. Who do you think you are?"

"I'm the duly appointed sheriff of this county, and I have a warrant to investigate whether a crime has been committed. Now, you and your employees can answer my questions here, or we'll handcuff all of you and take you to our jail in Charleston. It's your choice, Mr. Belanger." John handed him the warrant which he had begged the judge to give him.

The color drained noticeably from Belanger's face but he slowly recovered. One of his servants was within hearing distance. "Henry, gather the help and have them meet in the kitchen to answer some questions these deputies will pose."

He turned to John. "You're going to regret this imposition, and that idiot judge who signed the warrant will feel my wrath. Go ahead and ask your questions."

John had expected something like this from Buford Belanger, so he was prepared. "Tell me in your own words what happened that night."

"He lost considerable funds in a private card game, and he thought the options I presented to him for repayment were ludicrous."

"Could you tell me what those terms were?"

"I offered to allow him to repay the debt over five years at ten percent interest. He thought those terms were outrageous, and when I tried to placate him, he struck me."

"His parents said that the only terms offered were to let you have a Miss Bureau for the night and the debt would be ignored."

"That is a bald-faced lie, and an insult to me personally! I told you what the terms were. You'll just have to take my word on that as a gentleman."

"Who were the others in the game?"

"I don't think it's appropriate that I divulge their names. They are honorable men and wish to keep their identity discreet."

"I'm afraid I must insist."

"I'll tell you what. I'll send a memo to each and ask them if I can divulge their names. That's the best I can do for you; I'm sure you understand." John knew he was being played; it was clear that Belanger wasn't going to cooperate.

"Let me see the dueling pistols that were used."

"Why?"

"Because I want to see them, and I'm the law investigating a death caused by those weapons."

"Oh, all right." Belanger walked to a gun cabinet and took out a box, which he brought over and placed on a table near them. "Open the box, please," John asked.

Buford opened the box, revealing two matched dueling pistols. "They were a present from my father. I treasure them."

"I'll give you a receipt for them," John said. "I won't have them long, but I want to examine them."

"These weapons will not leave this house!" Belanger was red in the face.

"They're going with me."

"I can see why you brought so many men. I could kill you for this insult!"

"Your problem may be greater than me by the time I finish the investigation."

"Count your days—you won't be in office long, and then you and I will settle this accordingly." Belanger didn't want John to have the last word.

Time was not on John's side. He knew that Belanger would use every ounce of his influence to quash the investigation. What John had going was that he knew most of the fifty that had been invited that weekend; some were friends from his youth. Most were interviewed by himself and Marsh, but there were two other white deputies whom he trusted, and he sent them to get statements from about twenty of the invitees.

Though he still didn't have any hard evidence that the killing of Richard LaCroix was murder, what was coming out of all the interviews was that many men had lost at the card game. Each was suspicious that the game was rigged, but they didn't have the courage to challenge Buford, so they paid up. There were two incidences of a duel. In both cases, the men had been wounded but didn't die. Each said that Buford had suggested that the debt could be erased if their wives would surrender to Buford that night.

John had examined the weapons himself, and then he asked a gunsmith to look at them to see whether there was any flaw that made one superior to the other. The gunsmith reported that the guns were equally balanced and flawless, though one of the sights was off somewhat. Depending on which weapon you selected, the aim would be slightly off. John had noticed that although the weapons were identical, there was a notch on the handle of one—the one where the sight was off by a few degrees.

Initially, Jerome didn't get any information from Belanger's employees, but as he continued to investigate, some of the employees' relatives became more candid. There was talk of marked cards hidden in the card room and of women being beaten in the master bedroom. When Jerome asked how they knew that, they said that everyone knew—everyone could hear the women crying. He knew that none of the women who had been forced into Buford's bedroom would give testimony.

As the evidence was assembled, John knew that it was circumstantial, but it painted Buford as a bully and a monster; he was sure he had a case. Whether they'd win was anybody's guess. He knew that it was only a matter of time before Mr. Boltair would visit him and ask him to drop the case, or delay it long enough that it would drop through the seams. Today was the day.

When John arrived at the office, a smiling Boltair was sitting in his chair behind his desk. The symbolism wasn't lost on John. How Boltair got into his locked office was a mystery. John suspected that at least two of his deputies kept Boltair informed of his every move; he'd have to correct that.

"Why, Mr. Boltair, how nice of you to visit me! Is there anything in particular that brings you here?"

"Sheriff, I think you know why I'm here. What the hell are you doing to Mr. Belanger?"

"We're investigating a dueling death, which is not only against the law, but the reasons for the duel are highly suspect."

"Mr. Belanger is a hero to the South and a respected individual of the highest order! You have overstepped your authority. I'm telling you to stop this nonsense here and now."

"Is this a personal request or an official request?"

"It's personal right now, but I can certainly *make* it official."

"Well, Mr. Boltair, you'd better make it official, because your personal request has no merit with this office."

"I can get it in writing, and if I do, I'll have your badge!"

"I thought it might eventually come to this. For the record, I'm prepared to leave this office. I've been thinking long-term, and your seat is coming up for election in three months. I believe I can beat you in the election. It's also noteworthy that your friend Jacques Bascome is also up for election. I think Jerome would also make a good supervisor. It would be interesting to see what the voters would think of our candidacy. I've eliminated the roving gangs, fired the malcontents in the sheriff's office, and given some dignity to it. People feel that they've been treated fairly since I took over. So let me know when my last day is—I'll be ready. In the interim, I intend to investigate this death for the LaCroix family and all people who didn't get a fair shake with the last group that held this office. It's your call."

"Now, let's not be so hasty, John. I'm not trying to interfere. I have great faith that you'll do the right thing. We need not be competitors; I have your back." Boltair was smiling all the time he was talking, and he tipped his hat to John as he left.

Jerome had come in the back door and sat in the other room listening to the dialog. When Boltair left, he came into John's office and sat down. "Do we have enough evidence to arrest?"

"We have a few things. The first is the dueling pistols. I know one of the weapons is sighted slightly off. Significantly, it's also marked on the grip. If you select first, you may get the weapon that has a true sight. If you pick second and get the skewed sight, you can compensate for it, if you know about it. I don't believe the duels were fair. I think Belanger set them up so that he was at less risk than his opponent. I want you to talk to the two men who fought duels with Belanger and survived. Ask them if they were surprised that they missed."

"I can do that, but I have something important for you to look at." Jerome handed John a pack of cards. "It cost me twenty dollars and a fifth of Southern Comfort— I hope I get reimbursed!

"These were hidden behind some books in the card room in Belanger's house. I'm not telling you who gave them to me, but they're dynamite. It took me a while to understand how to read them, but here's how you do it."

Jerome laid the cards out on John's desk face down and pointed to several marks on the back of the cards. "This mark means it's a face card; this identifies it as a six; this is a five, etc. Since most players hold their cards up, anyone sitting across from the individual can see what he has, and of course what he doesn't have. Man, I could make money using these cards!"

"Will the person who found the cards come forward?"

"Not in a month of Sundays. I won't even tell you who it was—they're scared for their safety. From what I could find out, Belanger is ruthless."

The information Jerome was able to get from the two surviving duelists fit a pattern. "The men lost at the card table, and when they were alone with Belanger, he suggested he would set the debt aside if their wife spent the night with him. Both men declined and challenged Belanger. They were both good shots, and were both surprised when they missed Belanger. Neither could remember which weapon they selected; they think it was the one closest to them."

While Marsh and Jerome were interviewing the two duelists, John was visited by two old acquaintances. One was a friend; the other had been a thorn in his side when he was at West Point. James Longstreet had been his roommate at the academy; he not only stood up for him at his wedding to Louisa, but he also married Maria Garland, whom Jimmy Harris had courted. After the war, he'd changed political affiliations and had gone to work for his best friend, President U.S. Grant. The other visitor was General William Sherman, who'd been an upperclassman when John was at West Point. He seemed to have singled out John for his wrath whenever the mood suited him. Sherman had taken over command of the United States Army from Grant when he became President.

The two men were in the area reviewing reconstruction and the effects it was having on the South. "We heard that you were sheriff and that crime in your county was down nearly eighty percent. How do you account for your success?" Sherman asked.

"I could tell you that my charm has everything to do with it, but the reality is, I used what I was taught at West Point to set up my group. I wanted good people, so I gradually weeded out the malcontents and slowly added black deputies. I have five black and five white deputies. The white population was apprehensive at first, but as they saw how fair we were in upholding the law, they gave me a bill of confidence. The black deputies tell the majority black population that we will look at both sides before we act. It may sound naïve, but I've tried to have people who like or at least respect each other in my group. I spent some of the initial months teaching law enforcement procedures and ethics. I think that helped.

"With that being said, we can enforce the law and keep perpetrators out of circulation, but it's still up to the courts to decide whether they're guilty. I don't think the courts have changed much from the antebellum period. Those who served on the court before the Civil War are still on the court in the post-war era. The elite in the South ran this state before the war, and they still do. We're going to find out very shortly how much has changed. We have a high-profile killing, which I think is murder, coming up for trial in the next week. The case involves a very powerful and rich plantation owner, who some feel is a hero to the South. I'll arrest him, but I have doubts as to whether he'll be prosecuted. If I can bring him to trial, I doubt he'll be convicted."

John was glad to see that Longstreet had prospered, though he didn't like his switch in political parties. Sherman was his gruff old self, but he made a lot of sense on reconstruction going on in the South, which he was monitoring.

He wasn't looking forward to arresting Belanger, but he wasn't going out there without being prepared. He called in his white deputies and briefed them on the situation. "You can expect that there'll be some resistance. I want you to have handguns and rifles. We'll set up as though we are storming an outpost. Smith and I will go to the front door and Marsh and a deputy will come up the rear. I want you two to split; one come in from the east side and the other the west. If we're fired on, you have permission to fire and take out anyone that's in our way. I don't want any bloodshed, but you never can tell what'll happen once we get there. I want Belanger in cuffs as well as anyone else who's there trying to prevent this arrest."

When they arrived at the Belanger plantation, they took up their positions, and John and Smith walked up to the front door. They were greeted by Belanger and his attorney.

"What's the purpose of your visit, Sheriff?" the attorney asked.

"I have a warrant for the arrest of Buford Robert Belanger on suspicion of murder."

"That is a preposterous indictment," the attorney scoffed. "You have no cause for this warrant. Mr. Belanger didn't murder anyone."

John could see deputies on either side of house and assumed that Marsh was in position. "Mr. Belanger, you're under arrest for the murder of Richard LaCroix on October 15th of this year. Please turn around—I'm going to put restraints on you."

"I'm not doing any such thing, and if you don't leave immediately, I'm personally going to kick your ass right here in front of your men!"

Before anything could happen, Deputy Smith had entered from the rear and put his revolver in Belanger's back. "Either put the cuffs on," he said calmly, "or I'm going to bend this gun over your head—your choice."

Belanger turned and faced Smith. "I'll get you for this!"

John placed the cuffs on Belanger's hands and led him out to the carriage as the household help and field hands looked on.

"I insist upon accompanying my client to the jail," protested the attorney.

"It's your right, counselor."

The trial was to be held in one week. The prosecutor didn't want to go to trial; his feeling was that they would lose. It was John who insisted that they *had* to try the man; the public needed to know what he had been doing. The two men who were wounded in duels with Belanger agreed to testify, but the household helper who had told Jerome about the cards refused.

The trial was well-nigh the biggest event of the year. Everyone tried to get there early to get a seat in the old courthouse in downtown Charleston. John and the witnesses sat in the front row; Louisa was in the middle of the gallery. Three blacks were able to get seats in the second row. When Belanger was led into the courthouse in handcuffs, there was a large murmur in the crowd. The prosecutor, William Stewart, was an experienced trial attorney, but it was obvious from the start that he didn't have his heart in the trial. After the jury was selected, he called his first two witnesses. The two men who lost the duels to the accused told their stories, and many of the women in the audience gasped when they heard both say that Belanger would forgo their debt if he could have their wives for the night.

The most compelling witness was Miss Samantha Bureau. She told how her fiancé had told her of Belanger's offer to resolve his debt if she would spend the night with Belanger. She told the jury that her fiancé was insulted and hit Belanger and broke his nose. She broke down on the stand when she told them how she waited for him to return from the duel, and when he didn't, her heart was broken. You could hear a pin drop as she told her story, part of which matched the testimony of the two previous witnesses. What was surprising to John was the fact that Belanger's attorney never cross-examined the three witnesses.

John was called as the final witness for the prosecution. He was asked about the weapon and the anomaly that he found when they were examined.

"I had them examined by Herman Geiger, a gunsmith with a store in Charleston. Mr. Geiger is in court today, if needed. One of the weapons has a sight that is slightly skewed, such that when it is fired, it will track five degrees to the left. The other weapon is true. What makes this significant is that there is a slight mark on the handle of the skewed weapon."

"What are you suggesting, Sheriff?"

"I think Mr. Belanger knew which weapon had a sight that was off five degrees. My guess is that since he was the one who was challenged, he'd have first choice of weapons; he'd select the one without the small notch in the handle and therefore have a distinct advantage. That's why he always won."

No sooner were the words out when Belanger's attorney screamed, "I object! This is preposterous! Let me look at the weapon."

The attorney examined the weapon for five minutes and then said to the court, "That so-called notch is infinitesimal. I doubt that anyone could pick it out from the other."

"I found it immediately," John declared, though no one had asked.

"I object, your honor! Please instruct the sheriff not to speak unless he's been asked a question."

But John wasn't finished on the stand. The prosecutor asked the judge's indulgence while they set up a demonstration inside the courtroom. The gunsmith set the dueling pistols on a table and marked off ten paces on the floor. He had an elaborate vise that held one pistol aimed at a large board ten paces away, to which a target was pinned. John narrated what the gunsmith was going to do. When he fired the first pistol, the bullet hit the target dead center. The gunsmith then set up the other pistol similarly and fired from the vise. The bullet hit four inches to the right of the center of the target.

John explained that the pistol with the notch was the one that was off line. To demonstrate it further, they marked off twenty paces on the floor and moved the target to that distance. "This is the same distance at which the two duelists stood when they fired."

Again, the first pistol hit the target dead center, but this time the second pistol's mark on the target was twelve inches to the right. "As everyone can see, anyone selecting the second pistol was at a disadvantage, and that's why Belanger always won."

The defense attorney leaped out of his seat. He said the demonstration was flawed, and the court should throw out this feeble attempt by the prosecution to smear a hero of the Confederacy. The judge said he would rule on it later.

Some murmuring was heard throughout the courtroom when the prosecutor introduced the marked cards. He handed them to John, who was back on the witness stand. "Tell me about these cards found in Mr. Belanger's home."

"This deck of cards is marked on the back, so that someone familiar with the marks can readily see what cards the other players have and bet accordingly." The crowd in the courtroom couldn't see the marks, but they listened intently to everything he had to say. When the prosecutor was finished, Belanger's attorney cross-examined John, as was expected.

"Tell me, Sheriff Beauregard, how did you find these cards?"

"They were given to us by someone who knew where there were kept."

"Again I ask you, sheriff—who?"

"I don't know."

"You don't know, or won't tell?"

"They were given to us anonymously. That's all I can tell you."

"Your honor, I ask that the cards not be entered into evidence. Since the sheriff doesn't know who gave him the cards, this court cannot verify that the cards came from Mr. Belanger's home. They could have come from anyplace. Without anyone to cross-examine, your honor, my client is at a disadvantage, because he cannot confront his accuser."

The judge instructed the jury to disregard the cards. Then Defense Attorney Boileau called his only witness: Buford Robert Belanger.

He walked Belanger through the night of the killing. Belanger explained that the young man had lost at cards and was given fair terms for repayment, but wanted a longer term. When Belanger refused, he was struck in the face and his nose was broken. Richard LaCroix challenged him to a duel. "I tried to talk him out of it, but he said that if I didn't agree to the duel, he was going to beat me to within an inch of my life, so I agreed. I don't know anything about a notch on the handle. Those guns are perfectly matched. If the sights are off, then the sheriff is responsible. They were okay when he confiscated them from me."

When asked about the cards, Belanger denied any knowledge of them or their use. The defense rested, and the jury retired to reach a verdict.

The jury was out for two hours and returned a verdict of not guilty. John was disappointed, but not surprised— Belanger had many friends. Perhaps some members of the jury were going to receive invitations to the plantation. John was outside with three of his deputies and Louisa when a belligerent Belanger came down the front steps and walked to a carriage waiting at the curb. When he saw John, he swaggered over and the two men stared at each other.

"You're going to regret this insult, Beauregard."

"You mean you're going to get me in a card game and then ask for my wife."

Belanger was enraged. He walked right up to John and told him he was going to kill him and then fuck his wife. John struck out as hard as he could and struck Belanger in the face. The man fell to the ground, his nose starting to bleed. He was on all fours and swearing when John walked over and stomped on the man's right hand. When Belanger landed on his side, holding his hand, John jumped on his right arm; he could hear the bones break. "Well, if you're going to kill me, you'll have to do it without your right arm. I think you're fair game for everyone you took advantage of. I'd move on if I were you."

"You certainly don't turn the other cheek, do you?" Louisa laughed.

"He happened to say the magic words that triggered my response. Normally, I'm just a soft-hearted sheriff, young woman!"

Two of Belanger's associates picked him up and took him to the doctor. John learned later that Belanger had sustained multiple breaks in his arm and his hand was almost beyond repair. To no one's surprise, the Board of Supervisors relieved John of his duties; he decided to run for supervisor.

When Boltair called on John to tell him of his dismissal, he remarked, "You're lucky that you're not in jail. He may still file charges against you."

"Good luck with those charges! He threatened to kill me and fuck my wife, and he did it in front of my wife and several witnesses. What was I supposed to do, turn the other cheek?"

Although the vote was close, John came out on top and replaced Boltair. Surprisingly, Jerome also won a seat on the board. Marsh was named interim sheriff.

CHAPTER FORTY

Jimmy's children were his highest priority since returning from England. He wanted them to have a stable life and to gain an appreciation for their native country. He'd gone a long way toward that goal by bringing them to the Catawba village to learn about native culture. He had been lucky to hire a woman named Kathleen O'Rourke as combination housekeeper and nanny. Her energy permeated throughout the household and it was contagious.

As soon as they were settled in New York City, Jimmy gradually took over the management of his three bank branches. The economy was starting to boom. Post-war spending was up and fortunes were waiting to be made. He went public with his bank and his fortune increased considerably. He was elected Chairman of the Board of Harris National Bank and directed his three branches to start investing in the expanding railroad lines. In addition, he started to invest in some industries in the South, primarily shipping. He established bank branches in the cities in the South where he had previously had factoring offices. His personal fortune was growing. He started to invest in other areas besides railroads as well as other countries.

Many of his investments in the South were personal. He was a transplanted Southerner, and he had always wanted to reestablish his roots there some day. Each time he visited his offices in the South, he'd stop in on Louisa and John. He was pleased that they had recovered from the war; John was now the sheriff and had a great deal of civic pride in his native state.

As the years passed, Jimmy was concerned that the boom in railroads would stop, and perhaps even decelerate. Although he was still the major stockholder in the Harris National Banks, he didn't have complete control; he had a board of directors. Their vision was clouded by the enormous profits the bank was making, enriching themselves personally.

In early 1870, James called an emergency meeting of his board at the New York City branch. He was concerned that the three banks had loaned too much to several railroad companies, but the board he had appointed seemed to turn a deaf ear. His vice-chairman, William Sampson, who had been interim manager of the Harris National Banks while James worked for Lincoln, was the most vocal.

"I don't think you can visualize what's happening in America," Sampson said. "We've built over thirty-three thousand miles of track, and a transcontinental railroad has been completed uniting east and west. This is not the end of the railroad boom—it's the beginning! We can't afford to miss out on these investments."

"Gentlemen, I appreciate your thoughts, but I studied economics at Oxford," James responded. "If there's one thing I've learned about businesses, it is that they reach a point of maturation, then level off before they decline. The railroad industry is in the midst of a bubble. We have saturated these companies with unspecified funds and huge debts. There is bound to be a reckoning."

"Mr. Chairman, I think you fail to recognize that railroads are the largest employers in the country," another board member said, "and with their continued expansion, they're going to hire more people, which is good for America. I for one would like to be riding on that train that has many years of growth ahead."

Subsequently, another board member voiced similar concerns. "I agree with Bill—I don't believe your analogy about a bubble is realistic. All I can see on the horizon is more growth. James, I think you're being a worry-wart! I vote that we continue our investments in the railroad sector. I would be glad to address this issue in a year, but I think you're being premature. If you still feel so strongly in a year, I'll vote with you."

James felt they were wrong, but he could live with a year's delay. He hadn't been prepared to fall on his sword, so to speak, but when the next year rolled around, he planned to offer his resignation and sell his stock if the board didn't support him. Looking at the amount of investment the bank had in six railroad companies, he found it disturbing. Their balance sheets were poorly maintained; their earnings versus the price of their stock was too low, and their debt could sink a warship. He was worried for the bank, and he was concerned about his personal portfolio. He saw the three banks as his children. Giving them up would be a personal blow, but he had no choice. The board was on a collision course with bad investments.

When it was time for the annual board meeting, James called it to order. After the preliminary approval of past minutes and the agenda, he brought the first issue up for discussion. "I raised a warning last year at our annual meeting about the significantly high investment our banks have in railroad companies. Before this meeting, I reviewed the current balance sheets of the ten biggest railroad companies. Instead of improving, I believe they're ten percent worse than last year. I firmly believe we should divest ourselves of these investments as soon as possible."

"Are they making quarterly interest payments?" one board member asked.

"They are, but they haven't paid down any portion of the principal since our last meeting," the treasurer said.

"Have you asked their boards about that?" another member asked.

"Yes, we've asked them each quarter since our last meeting, and on each occasion, they said they'd bring the principal up to date the next quarter—but they haven't."

"I know some of these people personally, and they say they're reinvesting the principal into further expansion," said vice-chairman Sampson. "I think we should give all of them more time; interest only should be sufficient at the present time."

"My reading of this scenario is that they can't repay the loans. This is just a delaying tactic on their part. I call for a vote on this issue!" James was firm.

The vote was five to three against James' proposal. "Gentlemen, I feel so strongly about this issue that I'm prepared to resign from the board and put all my stock up for sale."

"James, you can't be serious!" the vice-chairman objected. "You founded these banks and brought all of us onto the board. I can't envision this bank going forward without you."

"I've prepared my letter of resignation in the event you voted against me on this issue. My stock goes on the market tomorrow morning, though I could reserve some for the members of this board. You have been friends of mine for some time. It's unfortunate that we disagree so strongly on this issue."

He handed his signed resignation to the vice-chairman and walked out of the meeting. The three banks had been his babies since infancy, and it mattered to him that the board couldn't see that the direction they were choosing was fraught with peril. He walked back to his office and told his attorney to start selling off all his bank holdings. He estimated that it would take thirty days to liquidate.

He had known that this day would eventually come, because his desire to reëstablish his southern roots was in direct conflict with the fact that he resided in the North. He knew that the South had changed since the war, but some of its grace was still present, and he wanted his son and daughter to experience that feeling. It took forty-five days before all his shares were purchased. The next step was to see about rebuilding his grandfather's home and moving to Charleston.

When he told his household the news, the children were excited. Kathleen O'Rourke was not. "Sir, I've been seeing William Flynn for a year and he's asked me to marry him. I didn't tell you because we weren't sure when we would make the announcement, but I can't move to the South with you."

He was surprised, but he was also happy for her. She was a young, vivacious woman, and she deserved a good marriage. "I don't think we'll move for three months. You can stay in my employ until then and then leave, or you can depart sooner if you wish. You've been a great help, and I wish you every happiness."

"Three months would be fine, sir."

As soon as school was out, they closed up the New York house and sailed to Charleston. Jim had travelled there three months before and hired an architect and contractor to refurbish the home for him and his two children; he was pleased with their progress. They estimated that their home would be ready in another three months, or just when the school term began. After talking it over with the children, they decided to go to the Catawba village for the summer. The kids loved the outdoors, and Jimmy need to kick back after his last six years with the bank; he needed some time to think about his future investments. He was worried that the country could go into a depression if the government didn't stop their foolish spending.

Mary had turned eighteen, and she wanted to do something with her life before she married. James was always sensitive to his daughter's inquisitive nature and supportive of her desire to accomplish something in life. They'd known about Vassar College for Women and visited the campus twice; they found a place for her to live while she was enrolled there. Five other women were at the same location. James gave his consent, and in the fall she went on an adventure.

Although he and the children made their home in Charleston, Cameron and Abigail were still living in New York. They'd sold their own home and moved into Jimmy's. They were close enough to Poughkeepsie, New York, to visit Mary often. Cameron, named after his grandfather, had already made up his mind to attend his father's alma mater, the University of South Carolina, which he did the following year.

Prior to Mary's departure for college, they were visited by two members of the board of directors from Jimmy's former banks. They asked if they could speak with him privately.

"We want you to come back to the bank. You were right, and we need your leadership to navigate through these troubled times."

He was well aware of their concerns. Jay Cooke and Company had gone under, due to their financing of the Northern Pacific Railroad. Following that company's collapse, the New York Stock Exchange closed for ten days and many banks failed. Harris National had closed the Boston and Chicago branches, and the New York branch was overextended.

"Let me see the balance sheets."

They produced a ledger that took him two hours to review. They sat there the entire time he was reading the financial figures. When he was finished, he looked up at them. "There's nothing I can do to help you. You've made some poor choices, and you're either going to have to ride them out or sell off stock to pay off the debt. I tried to tell you this might happen, but you failed to heed my advice."

"James, if you don't help us, many of us will lose our fortunes and be destitute!"

"I'd help if I could, but you've leveraged the bank's assets too far. I can't help and I can't offer any good advice."

His old bank wasn't the only one hit by the recession starting in 1873; businesses were closing and many banks were failing. The unemployment rate reached nearly ten percent.

Jim estimated that he had lost nearly thirty percent of his fortune during this period. He shut down the Mobile and Savannah offices of his shipping company, laid off all the employees at those harbors, and moved his main office to Charleston. He still maintained the New Orleans branch. He was in that city when he heard that John had had a heart attack and died two days later at the hospital in Charleston.

He rushed back for the funeral, but he was too late to see his oldest and dearest friend one more time.

•   •   •

Life had been good to Louisa; she still looked like a southern belle. They buried John in the family plot on the northeast part of the plantation. It was the one fortyacre parcel that he and Louisa still retained. The others were leased out to sharecroppers. Jerome had aged and was walking with a cane. He, his wife and three children stood beside Louisa, Samantha, her daughter and new husband at the cemetery. There were many dignitaries who attended the service in the rural church; all of his fellow supervisors were present. Almost all of their old acquaintances had either died or moved on after losing their properties.

Jim felt that a part of him died that day too. He and John had been friends from the moment they met, and they had survived a war that had made them adversaries. The eulogy given by the local minister was uplifting. It brought a tear to Jimmy's eye when the preacher recounted how John had taken the sheriff 's position and made its office into something that people could be proud of. John had followed that up with a run for the supervisor's position, which he won on a close vote over Boltair, who had fired him from the sheriff 's position three months earlier.

Louisa told him that they had been having a picnic down by the old swimming hole when John complained of chest pains as well as an ache in his left arm. She took him by carriage to the hospital and stayed with him overnight, but he died the following morning with Louisa holding his hand. The doctor said he had complete heart failure. It probably ran in the family, for his father François had died at nearly the same age. John was fifty-five years old.

Cameron was in college, and he lived at home the first year, but the commute was too much, and he asked his father if he could room with two other classmates on campus. James agreed. He spent most of his time commuting to and from New Orleans and doing some charity in the area. He would see Louisa occasionally in town, and they had lunch one day; each time he hated to part from her. There was something unsaid between them, but that was life, he thought.

He was asked to chair a large charity event to raise money for ex-Confederate soldiers. There was no pension for them; they seemed to fall into a category of forgotten people. Jim, always sympathetic to the South, readily agreed. There was a bake sale, a dinner, some entertainment, and an auction. He hoped those attending would be generous.

Money was tight, but at least three hundred people attended, and overall they raised about three thousand dollars. Jim was surprised to see Louisa there, and he sat with her at one of the picnic tables. When the music started he asked her to dance. It was a lively number, and he wasn't sure he could keep up. Whenever they touched, a spark went through his body and his energy level peaked. He was aroused and embarrassed that it would be so obvious. Louisa smiled at him, and when they were near, she whispered in his ear. "Is that bulge I see meant for me?"

Without thinking, he responded. "Yes—are you angry?"

"On the contrary, I'm flattered! Why don't we do something about it?"

"I thought you'd never ask!"

"Can you leave early? You're the chairman, aren't you?"

"I'll tell the co-chairman that you're not feeling well and that I'm going to escort you home. Whether they believe me or not is superfluous! Let's go."

He had walked to the hall in Charleston, so they took her carriage and drove out to Magnolia. They weren't quiet on the ride to her home, both using their hands to explore each other. They handed the carriage off to Jerome, who was the only one still working at the old plantation, and went into the house.

They made their way up the stairs, strewn with each other's clothes, and entered the guest bedroom. It was the one he and Claire used to share when they visited. "I can't stay in the room where I made love to John—I hope you understand?"

Whether he did or didn't wasn't on his mind at the moment. They were both naked, and as he held her to him and kissed her passionately, he realized that he loved this woman very much, and probably had loved her all his life. He lifted her up, placed her on the bed, and crawled in beside her. He explored the two mounds on her chest and spread her legs. He kissed her thighs and ran his tongue inside her. She gasped with pleasure, and soon he penetrated her; they peaked together.

He began kissing and sucking her nipples; she grabbed his manhood and slowly brought him erect; he entered her again, but she rolled him over. "I want to be on top—do you mind?"

"Not at all. I can watch your breasts bounce, so have at it."

They fell asleep in each other's arms and woke up at about eight o'clock the next morning. He rolled over on top of her and she spread her legs. They made love again, but this time more slowly than last evening. "I love you, Louisa—I guess I've always loved you."

"I loved John with all my heart, and I was glad I married him. Sometime in my life—and I don't know exactly when—I realized that I had a great deal of affection for you, and I anticipated that we would spend some part of our lives together. I hope it's from here on."

"I feel the same way. I'll do everything I can do to make you happy, and I hope you will love me as I love you. It's interesting, but Claire once suggested that I actually loved someone else. I assume she must have been talking about you."

"Jimmy, I do love you and want you very much. There's one thing, however, I'd like to do now. Will you follow me?"

"I don't have a robe. Let me put my pants on."

"I don't want you to put anything on! I want you to follow me. Can you do that?"

He followed her down the steps, out the front door and into the yard. "My God, are we going to do what I'm thinking?"

"You owe me a skinny-dipping!"

Jerome laughed as he saw two white people, stark naked and holding hands, running to the pond. He wondered what Jimmy and Louisa would think if people frowned on their behavior. He knew the answer to his question—they couldn't care in the least!

www.ingramcontent.com/pod-product-compliance
Lightning Source LLC
Chambersburg PA
CBHW061335310726
48974CB00001B/53